IS *this* FOR REAL?

KATHY STROBOS

Cover Design: Cover Ever After

ISBN: 9781737713944 (Paperback)

ISBN: 9781737713937 (ebook)

www.kathystrobos.com

Published by Strawbundle Publishing

New York, New York

To the unpublished writers.
Keep writing. Finish a draft.
Once I have a rough draft, and I reread what I've written,
that draft sparks new ideas.

And to my children.

CONTENTS

CHAPTER ONE

ON ANY TOP-TEN LIST of best Sunday plans, today's brunch with my former crush and his new girlfriend would rank number eleven . . . hundred. Times five. But I couldn't say no. We're still friends.

And I'm over him.

Just keep telling yourself that.

Still, there is no chance I will ever say "I love you" to Jamie again.

The subway is oddly crowded for this time of day. I squeeze on, snagging the prime real estate spot leaning against the metal doors, right up against the "Do Not Lean on Door" warning, and hold on to a small sliver of a handrail. As the train approaches Times Square–42nd Street, the conductor announces that this local train is now going express, and groans erupt. Works for me. At 42nd Street, half the train empties out, but it quickly fills back up, as if we've all just exchanged dance partners.

Three stops later, the train car shudders to a stop, spitting me out, along with a stream of passengers jostling each other for a place in the ant line marching up the stairs. The last brush-by, without even a "'Scuze me," skews my hat, my favorite 1920s-style cloche. So much for all the time I spent positioning it just right so I'd look more poised—less cute little buddy—when Jamie sees me again. He's back in New York for a brief visit. I haven't seen him in over a year since he's been living in Singapore. Now if only I can live up to the hat's "superpower sophistication." I adjust it and push through the turnstile.

Even before I reach the top of the steps to the street, the smell of honey-roasted nuts from the Nuts4Nuts vendor cart at the top is making me hungry.

At least my close friend Rory agreed to join me at this brunch with Jamie and his new girlfriend, so I'm not the rejected third wheel sitting across from the happy couple.

Chambers Street is crowded with vendor tables but not many people yet. The phone store and clothing store with back-to-school sale signs soldier on, not yet joining the other boarded-up stores on this block. And then Michaels craft store. The lure is strong. Not that I need any more crafting supplies, but it seems a waste to be in the neighborhood and not check out its sale selection. But I resist. I want to be first to the brunch battlefield, able to plan my strategy as advised in *The Art of War*. Not that I've read it, just *The Art of War for Writers*.

My email pings. I'm taking a hodge-podge of online writing courses while I write my second novel as I query my first novel, *Midnight Masquerade*, and it's a comment from my teacher on my latest online assignment: "You're still holding back, playing it safe. You need to scrape your emotions raw in your writing."

I don't think so. I felt naked enough writing that scene. And I'm not sure how much of me I want to expose for public consumption.

Up ahead, Rory is leaning against a streetlight, reading a book. One lock of his wavy, brown hair has fallen onto his face, and he pushes it away to join the rest of his unruly mop of hair. He could be modeling menswear, except that the cover of the book he's holding is bright pink and yellow. A romcom book I recommended. He wanted to read other books in my genre so he could compare my draft manuscript to the competition, so I gave him a list of my favorites. He looks up, and our glances catch.

"Like your hat, Penelope. Suits you." Rory kisses me on the cheek.

We push open the door to The Barn. Bells jingle, and the buttery smell of pancakes welcomes us. The whitewashed wood gives the restaurant an old farmhouse vibe. Vintage signs with pictures of black-and-white cows and bushels of peaches decorate the walls. We stand in line in the small foyer, waiting to be seated.

I've been seeing more of Rory lately. We're friends from college. I briefly had a crush on him then, but he started dating someone else. When he has a girlfriend, we see each other about once every other month. But he broke up with his last girlfriend about two months ago, and now he calls me to get together for brunch nearly every Sunday. My best friend and roommate, Zelda, who also knows Rory from college, was like, "Well, he obviously enjoys hanging out with you, but you're solidly in the friend lane with this Sunday brunch thing." Trust Zelda for the straight talk. It's not that I thought I was changing lanes and moving to the speeding girlfriend lane. I'm good driving at a controlled sixty miles an hour—and not hazardously heading for a heartbreak on some highway of love.

"How do you like the book?" I ask.

"It's good. Deeper than I expected. Funny. Affirms all my love-lasts-forever bull. Isn't that what you called it?" His tone is mild, but an undercurrent of frustration pulses there.

"I was drunk when I said that." I'm surprised he remembers. It was at a dinner party several years ago. About six of us were drunkenly arguing over the merits of prenups. I don't even remember how the topic came up, except that we have two friends who are on polar opposites of the issue. As were Rory and I. I was for prenups, he was against. I argued prenups define expectations so there's less chance of angry fights when it ends.

"In vino veritas," Rory says.

"I'd say more like, when drunk, debate points are exaggerated. I shouldn't have called it bull."

"I don't think that works as well. In vino debatus pointus exaggeratos."

I laugh. "Anyway, your belief gives me hope." I hope that Rory finds his true love and that she doesn't break his heart.

He gives me a quizzical look. "So, what's with this fake boyfriend trope? This is the second one with it."

"I like that trope." I tilt my head.

"Do you?"

Something in the way he asks makes me look at him more closely. "Yes. I'm writing a fake dating plot in my new book, *Fake Dating Folly*."

"Why do you like it?"

"I like the getting-to-know-each-other-slowly." I shrug. "I don't know. So, what happened on Thursday? Did your pitch win?" Rory works in advertising.

"Yes, but . . ."

"They want you to change it? You don't look that happy."

"No. They like the pitch," Rory says. He flushes. "But his wife groped my butt during our celebratory drinks."

"She didn't," I say, shocked.

"She did. I got this weird vibe from her, but I thought no—she's got to be about fifty, and my client is right there talking about color schemes—and then, she copped a feel of my butt."

"While he was there?"

"Yeah, like what the . . . I was afraid I'd lose the pitch right there." Rory shakes his head in disbelief. "I jumped, which threw her, too. But still, it's freaking awkward."

"That's crazy," I say. Rory still looks upset. "Did she pinch anybody else's butt?"

"I didn't take a poll." He laughs but then looks serious again. "And we've got another client function this Thursday."

I point at the book. “I know what you need. You need a fake girlfriend to protect you at client functions, like a buffer.”

He stills, staring at me. “That’s not a bad idea.”

“I was joking.” But I feel a little thrill of satisfaction that he likes my idea. He takes off his blue jacket, and he’s wearing a worn T-shirt that does little to hide his washboard stomach.

“Aren’t there any women currently in the running to be a real girlfriend?” I ask.

“No.”

“How is that possible?” This brunch line is not moving. The smell of bacon frying is making me even hungrier.

He just gives me his look of annoyance, which is one eyebrow cocked and a slight shake of his head. “It’s not like you date a lot. Did I miss the memo where you’re dating someone?”

“There wouldn’t be a memo.”

“Your sister would definitely issue a memo.”

I laugh. “A legal memo. To whom it may concern. But seriously, Rory, you’re not usually at a lack for dance partners.”

“I am now. Marie was always asking me, ‘So where do you see this going?’ Which really kills any . . . uh . . . magic." He pauses. "It reminded me of my Dad when he asks 'and how did that make you feel?'"

Rory's dad is a psychologist who does couples counseling.

"Did you tell her that?"

"I did. That did not go over well." He smiles wryly. "But to be fair to her, I couldn't say 'forever,' so that was that. And Callie . . .” He presses his lips together.

Another couple enters the foyer behind us. Rory and I move closer together to make space for them.

The man kisses the woman on the forehead and looks deep into her eyes. What if Jamie looks like that at his new girlfriend? I feel nauseous. *No, that would be good.* It would be good if his new girlfriend is his soul mate. Better than watching him with a parade of different women I didn’t merit joining. He wasn't even willing to try dating me. I probably should have asked him out on a date instead—something less dramatic than saying, "I love you." But since we've known each other since childhood, a "date" didn't seem necessary. Not when I've been in love with him since high school. And somehow, I always thought, at some point, he'd love me back.

"Although I recognize that you don't believe in magic," Rory says.

"I never said that," I say.

"You don't have to. It's the way you never discuss it."

I look up at Rory. "That magical connection can be dangerous."

"Is that bad?" He gives me a lopsided grin.

"Dangerously devastating if he doesn't 'feel the same way.'" *Or you lose that person.* "Or if it leads to too high expectations."

"So, you're just looking for humdrum as opposed to magical connection? That explains . . . never mind."

I don't deign to respond.

He flips through the book and reads out a line. "No 'every part of her burned with fire' for you?"

"I'm not particularly looking." I cross my arms.

"But you're writing a romantic comedy."

"But it's focused more on the comedy than the romance—more focused on the midnight caper." Some people are leaving. One bumps me, and I put out my hand to avoid falling into Rory, grabbing his bicep. Rory holds my hand as if we're about to do the jitterbug.

"Hence the title, *Midnight Masquerade*," he says.

"If only the title alone could sell it." I release him.

"You just need one agent and one publisher to love it. And it's funny, especially the scenes with the motley team trying to steal back her painting." He chuckles.

In *Midnight Masquerade*, my artist protagonist has that night to find her stolen painting or lose her chance to participate in a career-defining art exhibit. And if she doesn't learn to trust her feelings for her sleuthing partner, she's going to lose a lot more.

The hostess greets us by name and starts to seat us at our usual table for two, but we tell her we need a table for four. As we settle into the blue booth, I can't decide whether I should take off my hat or leave it on. Jamie is supposed to see me in the hat. All I want is one twinge of regret—one second glance, one "maybe I made a mistake." At least while he has a girlfriend. But eating with my hat on seems awkward. Like I've got an appendage coming out of my head. The hat partially obstructs my side view. I don't envy horses with blinders.

The waitress is new. She reminds me of a collie. She's tall, with a narrow face, and friendly. She asks if we want to order now. As Rory explains that we are waiting for friends, I smile at her. Waitressing is tough. I tried it, as the typical side job for a writer, but I'd jot down impressions of my customers while waiting for them to make up their minds, and I'd inevitably miss part of their order. And my boss was not sympathetic to my using his order pads for my notes.

Now, I'm supporting myself by making miniatures to sell on Etsy, staging doll soap operas for my blog and Instagram to increase my sales, and dog-sitting temporary canine roomies who pay my rent.

"So, what about you? Would you act as my fake girlfriend at some client gigs coming up?" he asks.

I stare at him. He lightly presses my open mouth closed. His eyebrow quirks upward.

"You could consider it research for your next book," he adds.

"Why me?"

"Because you're my best female friend and you won't believe it's for real."

Yes, I definitely won't believe it's for real. I flag down the waitress and ask for a cup of tea. More caffeine is needed.

"Neither will anyone else," I say.

"What? Why not?" He seems genuinely confused. *Cute.*

"Rory, you usually date gorgeous, six-foot-tall women. I am *so* not your type."

"I don't have a type."

I snort. "Oh, really? Let's look at the evidence." I scroll through the photos on my phone. I'm sure I have pictures of Rory with his last few girlfriends at various events. All of whom have been gorgeous and tall. Rory and Marie, five foot eleven inches and blonde. She was so sweet and together. Here's a picture of Ayanna, his college girlfriend, from Rory's Halloween party last year. She's five foot eight, stunning, funny, smart, always up for midnight snacks after dancing. She was my favorite, but now she's engaged. We still chat sometimes on Instagram.

"Okay, okay." He holds up his hands in mock surrender. "No pictures of Callie, huh? Didn't you like Callie?"

"I didn't like Callie."

"Hmm." He looks down at the table.

"Are you sure you don't have commitment issues? These women seemed pretty magical to me." Sometimes I can't decide if Rory has commitment issues, or he's such a romantic that if the relationship is not absolutely perfect, he moves on.

He winces. "I don't think so. But it's important that the relationship feels right." He runs his hand through his hair, which makes his wavy, brown hair look even more tousled. "I feel like I'm parroting my dad." He faces me. "So, you're saying no one will believe I'm dating you because you're five foot five?" He pulls one of my curls and it snaps back. He loves to do this.

I roll my eyes at him. "Whatever. I'll pretend to be your girlfriend if it will help. It will be great research for my next book."

He smiles, and that dimple in his right cheek appears. "Great, then we're on for Thursday. We're having an event with the client that night." A roguish glint comes into his eyes.

I look over at the hostess stand, where Jamie now stands with his new girlfriend. He's wearing this blue shirt that's my favorite on him. I can't see his girlfriend Willow's face, but Jamie is helping her take off her coat to give it to the hostess. An empty pit forms in my stomach. He wasn't even willing to meet me alone. And I had to be the one to suggest we meet. And then I got the lunch slot.

I ask, "Should we start now and see if we can fool Jamie? That will certainly persuade Jamie I'm over him."

"It may even make him jealous."

I laugh. "I don't think so. And anyway, I'm over him." If I repeat it enough, it will come true.

Rory nods, but it's that "you're a poor, deluded soul" nod. "He may see you in a new light. As opposed to a completely self-sufficient sister type."

My tea finally arrives. I add sugar and take a sip. "You're right. Why am I writing romantic comedies? I should be writing cozy mysteries with self-sufficient spinsters investigating crimes."

"I didn't say spinster. I'm just saying that Jamie's protective instincts might be raised if he thinks you're dating a big bad wolf like me."

"You're so not a big bad wolf." And I knew that from firsthand experience. I would've spent college as "the girl whose parents died in a plane crash in Peru on their wedding anniversary," which was pretty much how I was known for a while there until Rory took me under his wing. Instead, I spent college as part of Rory's crowd, trading quips around a round table in our dining hall.

"Okay," Rory says. "So, starting now, we're pretending to date?"

Jamie leans down to kiss his girlfriend as the hostess turns to lead them here.

Jamie will definitely think that I'm over him.

"Yes," I say. *Can't hurt.*

Chapter Two

JAMIE LOOKS THE SAME, those bright-blue eyes, his curly, blond hair slightly darker, and athletic—no weight gain in the year since I last saw him. I ease out from our booth seat to give him a hug. He steps back, almost into his girlfriend behind him.

I stop, standing there, my arms outstretched. Heat warms my cheeks. I drop my arms. The clatter of dishes punctuates my confusion as the waitress clears the table behind me. We used to hug hello. Before I blurted out my feelings for him. The smell of hazelnut coffee fills the air as a waitress passes by with a fresh pot. *Retreat.* Then Jamie steps forward and hugs me. He smells of the same aftershave he's been using since high school. He once lent me his sweatshirt, and I slept with it until he asked for it back. But that's high school crush stuff. I pull away first. *I'm over you.*

"This is Willow," Jamie says, his arm around her.

We both say hi.

I sit back in the booth next to Rory. Willow is muscular, with pale skin, sleek, brown hair, and big, brown eyes that remind me of an English springer spaniel. *I've got to stop comparing people to dogs.* She's wearing a sleeveless shirt that shows off her sculpted arms. I'm relieved I'm wearing sleeves. Not that there's anything wrong with my arms.

She's totally Jamie's type. She scoots closer to him.

The waitress returns to take our order.

"I'll have a coffee and the market salad, dressing on the side," Willow says.

Jamie asks for scrambled egg whites and black coffee, while Rory and I order our usual, less-refined brunch of whole wheat bagels, waffles with bananas and strawberries, and eggs to split. This is our perfect breakfast—some protein, some whole wheat fiber, and a little sweetness. I catch an exchanged glance between Willow and Jamie.

"Still the same type of food here?" Jamie asks me. Jamie and I used to come to this place in high school with our crowd of friends. It had been the neighborhood hangout, kindly tolerant of having groups of students who ordered little but sat there for two hours at a time, talking and doing homework until it was time to go home for dinner. Jamie joined us after soccer or baseball practice. It was more of a casual diner back then.

"It's better now. Organic." I frown. I should've suggested someplace different, especially for Jamie, Mr. Let's-Live-in-Singapore-for-Five-Years. I thought he'd want to come back here, for a feeling of home, of connection.

"How are you?" Jamie studies me.

"Good." I straighten.

Willow smiles at me. I smile back. I lean back against the rubber booth seating, as if I am relaxed. The waitress pours coffee for the rest of the table. The savory smell fills the air.

Has Jamie even noticed my hat? I don't think so; I should wear it a little longer.

Jamie turns to Rory. "Haven't seen you in a few years—since I moved to Singapore. Still in advertising?"

"He just got promoted," I say.

Rory nods. "Forever, until I get kicked out. Still in IT?"

"It's called tech now." Jamie covers Willow's hand with his own.

Willow says, "So, Jamie tells me you're a writer? How cool. What have you published?"

"Nothing yet," I say. "I'm in the rejection stage."

Rory's hand is on the table. I reach out and hold it, curling my fingers over his. I glance at him to make sure he's okay with my touch. His hand is warm. His skin is still tan from the summer, though mine is already fading. He smiles mischievously at me. *Uh-oh. Trouble.*

"Is there an acceptance stage?" Jamie asks. Willow sips her coffee with both hands, as if warming them up.

"I hope so," I say. "After the rewrite stage."

Rory looks down, smiling; he's got this half-smile when he's amused. It's like he's trying to hide the smile, but he can't.

"Well, you seem to be taking it very well," Jamie says.

"Oh, I'm used to rejection." And then, realizing what I've said, I flush.

Jamie looks down. Willow shifts closer to Jamie. I can feel my blush extending to my neck. I drink some water in the hope that it will bring the heat down.

"Aren't we all?" Rory says.

I raise my eyebrow at Rory. *Please.* Who would reject Rory? He gives his innocent look back at me.

"I guess Stephen King was initially rejected," Jamie says.

"It must be tough," Willow says. "Is there a point where you stop trying?"

"No," I say, firmly. I've had this conversation so many times. And some famous author who was rejected over thirty times is always mentioned.

"She only gets better with the feedback. Penelope's taking the marathon viewpoint," Rory says, pulling his hand back to add sugar and milk to his coffee.

"Yeah, Rory convinced me to take the long view." I had wanted to be published by thirty, so I had decided at twenty-eight to give myself two years to write full time. Now I'm almost at the end of my second year, with no agent in sight, but I could wallpaper my bathroom with rejections.

Willow asks, "But how do you support yourself?"

"I'm making some money with my Etsy store. My dollhouse blog was just ranked in the top twenty of dollhouse blogs."

"The posts are really good. You should check it out and sign up for them," Rory says. "Just google Penelope's dollhouses."

No, they shouldn't. In my blog storyline, Piper, a doll with curly, brown hair like mine, was dating Julian, a doll with blond curls like Jamie. But then Julian abruptly broke up with her. Followers are still upset. Many of them took that breakup quite personally and shared their own personal stories of how they've been dumped. I definitely tapped into something; I think, in part, because the breakup was so unexpected. But once Jamie told me he wasn't interested in me, I lost all desire to play with his doll avatar. And I used those feelings to write the opening chapter of *Fake Dating Folly,* where the protagonist, Piper, learns that her boyfriend, who dumped her a year ago, is now engaged.

"Can you monetize the blog?" Jamie drums his fingers.

"My blog increases sales on my Etsy and eBay stores." But that's not why I blog. Or at least, that's not why I began blogging. I just liked making scenes of perfect lives in miniature. Initially. Until Piper was dumped. Which is when my followers suddenly increased.

I continue, "In four months, I'll get a job with a paycheck."

I fold my arms over my chest. We don't need to discuss my finances over brunch. I inherited some money when my parents died. The trick is not to spend. *Too much.*

"Two years is too short. Two years into advertising and I still didn't know anything." Rory puts his hand back over mine on the table. "Penelope's writing is solid, funny."

Stop looking at Rory like a mooing cow just because he believes in you. Maybe I feel like this because I've met him after I've just written a really funny scene and I am euphoric from the experience. Like I've fallen in love. He teases me that no man can live up to my book heroes.

I jerk my gaze away.

"My mom would love for you to help her out with the store." Jamie leans in as if he's closing a sale. "And I really appreciate that you've been having dinner with her once a month. She always sounds so upbeat after your dinners."

"That's definitely a possibility." Not that working at Theresa's Sports Store would give me a lot of time for writing. It's like death by a thousand sneakers. I'd be running home to write every night, like I had with my last job. But it's a backup plan. If I don't find a publisher for my book, which would give me just enough income—with my odd jobs—to allow me to continue writing full time.

Willow unbuttons Jamie's cuff at the wrist and sticks her hand *and* arm up Jamie's cotton shirt sleeve. My glance meets Rory's. *Is she for real? She needs to be inside his sleeve? At a brunch? With the girl he rejected?* She could tone it down a bit, have a little sympathy for my bruised feelings. *Just unbutton his shirt, why don't you? Why bother with just his arm?*

Rory puts his arm around me, although I feel like he has to make an extra effort to get around The Hat. Should I relax into him? That seems too intimate. But otherwise, I am sitting very stiffly between The Arm and The Hat. I lean against Rory.

Jamie's brow furrows. A feeling of glee makes me snuggle even closer to Rory.

"I didn't realize you knew anything about writing or publishing," Jamie says to Rory.

"I don't particularly. I'm learning along with Penelope. But I do know about marketing a product. And Penelope's book is good, although the male lead needs to be a bit more human."

"Not with my poor male lead again." I narrow my eyes at Rory. Rory thinks I've based my male lead on Jamie. Because he has curly, blond hair. Just to pay him back, I'll model the romantic lead in my current novel on Rory's looks—tall, lean, wavy, dark hair, blue eyes, a strong jaw with a cleft. How to describe his smoldering sexuality that makes him irresistible to so many women? It's like an invitation to see if one can light that candle, or at least have fun trying, if the mischievous twinkle in his eyes is any indicator. I'm immune now, but that was definitely my first impression. I will note that Zelda says he's attractive, but he's not "all that."

"What's wrong with your male lead?" Willow asks as she turns her head to look at me. Her body is facing Jamie, her arm is still up Jamie's shirt sleeve, and her other hand is rubbing Jamie's back. It looks uncomfortable—for Willow.

Rory rubs my back. I feel like a cat that wants to purr. Did I just "mmm"? Rory gives me an amused glance. Warmth flushes my cheeks. I shouldn't be having this reaction to Rory.

Now Willow's hand is in Jamie's hair. Not to worry, though. Her other hand is still up his sleeve. Rory's hand moves to massage the back of my neck. I arch my head back and my eyes close.

"He's an arrogant investment banker," Rory says.

My eyes open. Jamie shoots me a look.

"Based on Jamie?" Willow laughs.

Am I so obvious?

"Hey, I'm in tech now," Jamie says.

"Based on New York men encountered in the dating scene." *By Zelda.* Rory's right that I don't date that much. But admitting that will only make Jamie think I'm still pining for him. "And he's not that arrogant. He just comes off as arrogant initially. But agents keep telling me that the arrogant hero is no longer appealing to modern women."

"Is that true?" Willow asks.

Yeah, I don't believe it, either. A lot of women still seem to be seeking Mr. Darcy. There's all the joy in the comeuppance. Rory is snorting next to me. I don't know if it's because of the discussion or because Willow is so entwined with Jamie. One writer friend uses Barbie dolls to check her descriptions of physical contact, but Barbie dolls aren't flexible enough for this. I wouldn't have believed it possible. How are they going to eat? Rory stops massaging my neck and is typing on his phone next to me.

> Rory: *I was treating it like a drinking game where every time Willow touched Jamie, I touched you. But CAN'T keep up.*

Willow pulls her hand out of Jamie's shirt sleeve. She rubs Jamie's back.

"Apparently, in fiction now it's the sweet, sensitive man that's hot. I gave my male lead a cat." I shrug. "In my most recent rewrite. He's secure with his masculinity."

"Yes, and now he's so amazing that no man can compete with him," Rory says.

"He's a book boyfriend. He's not real," I say.

I unpin my hat, and Rory places it carefully on top of his book next to him.

"I didn't realize you got out much in the New York dating scene," Jamie says. *Is that a hint of interest?*

"Book research. Before Rory," I say.

"Before Rory what?" Jamie asks, sipping his coffee.

"Before Rory and I started dating." I look down at the table.

"You and Rory are dating?" Jamie deposits his coffee cup with a clatter and sits back, almost squishing Willow's arm. Willow pulls her arm back. "When did this happen?"

Rory and I glance at each other. *We don't have a cover story.* The waitress arrives and sets down our plates. We move dishes around to make space for all our choices. *Think, think. I make up stories.* I take my half of our breakfast.

"Recently." Like an hour ago. "You're the first to know. I was crying over an agent rejection and Rory was comforting me, and one thing just led to another." Which is a phrase I sometimes use in my plot outlines when I don't know what is going to happen, other than it all has to go wrong. I pause. The thing is, I don't cry over agent rejections. I'm not much of a crier anymore. So, Jamie might see the hole.

Rory kisses my cheek, lingering. It doesn't feel like the casual brush against my cheek of a hello kiss. His nose nuzzles my neck. My insides do a little dance of butterflies. *Unexpected.* When he pulls away, I lean my head on his shoulder, hoping that looks lovey-dovey. Also, that just leaves the top of my head to kiss. *Safer.*

"It's the best friends-become-lovers thing. My personal favorite of the romcom tropes," Rory says. Our glances meet, as if he's trying to tell me something. I can't recall which book I gave him with that trope. He says, "My favorite romcom movie is *When Harry Met Sally.*"

Jamie leans back, apparently recovered from his shock. "It's great that you guys got together."

He believes it.

He continues, "Mom will be thrilled, especially because she always tells me that you're not dating anyone."

I sit back up. My shoulders tense. Rory shifts to put his arm around me.

Obviously, Jamie hasn't told his mom that I declared my love for him. But then he wouldn't—because his mom and my mom, who were best friends, always joked about our dating.

"Some things are worth the wait," Rory says. His hand rubs my neck, under my curls, the pressure of his hand easing the tension. I had no idea Rory was so good at massages. We've always kept a certain physical distance between us—as friends. I stretch my neck and glance at him. Our gazes catch. *Zap.* Like a current of electricity between us. *We're better at this than I thought possible.*

Jamie looks transfixed. Probably because he's never seen me being physically affectionate with a man before, only cats and dogs. His eyes have narrowed. *Unless he's onto us? Maybe we're going overboard?*

"How do you like living in Singapore?" Rory asks Willow. I give him a "thank you" look, as I'm quite desperate to move away from my dating life—and to eat. The eggs are fluffy with just a hint of butter.

"I love it, but that's also because Jamie's there." Willow dips a piece of lettuce in the dressing.

Rory guides the conversation into less personal waters—for me—asking them more about life in Singapore. Jamie tells a funny story about some over-the-top party they went to. Willow pipes in with additional details. Her brown eyes are fringed with long, black eyelashes. I can definitely see her appeal.

"Where are you from?" I ask.

"I'm from Seattle," she says.

"How do you like New York so far?" I ask.

"New York is nice, but a bit dirty," Willow says.

Rory puts his hand on mine. I get very defensive when people criticize New York. He asks quickly, "What made you move to Singapore?"

"I got this amazing job in hotel hospitality."

I hope she doesn't hospitably tell visiting New Yorkers that their city is a bit dirty.

Rory asks what she does. I listen carefully to her response because I'm always looking for careers for my characters. It does sound like a great career for a character, if not an entire novel, based on the hotel staff and visitors.

We discuss what they're planning to do in New York. Jamie has almost finished his food.

"So, are you going to catch up with Lex?" I ask. Lex is Jamie's best friend from high school.

"No."

"Why not? Is he traveling?"

"No, we had a falling out. He lied to me. He started dating Sally and lied to my face that he wasn't."

I shiver. I hope he doesn't feel the same way about my pretending to date Rory, even if he did react strongly to the announcement.

Jamie's phone beeps. As he reads the message, he strokes Willow's hair. "I have to run. The counter-offer has come in, and we're meeting to discuss it back at the office." He kisses Willow on the lips, then says to her, "Sorry about this. Maybe we can arrange to meet your friends for drinks another time."

I shoot Rory a "don't you dare" look. I am not doing fake kissing on the lips.

"That's okay." Willow gives Jamie an adoring look.

"You're welcome to come to The Met with us." Rory hands the check back to our waitress with the two credit cards sticking out of the fake-leather check presenter.

Willow declines, saying she made backup plans with girlfriends in the city.

Picking up our coats, we follow them out of the restaurant. I don't move to hug Jamie goodbye. He has his arm around Willow. I have a sudden flashback to my parents' memorial service and Jamie putting his arm around me as we stood in the line greeting people and accepting their comfort. Jamie carried an extra box of tissues in case I needed more.

They hail a taxi as Jamie says, "My mom would love for you to work in her store."

"I know," I say.

"It was good to see you. I probably won't be back again until Christmas."

So, that's it. We used to spend days together when he came back. I thought our friendship was stronger than one romantic declaration.

They get in the taxi, and it pulls away.

"Let's take Citi Bikes to The Met," Rory says. Citi Bikes are my usual mode of transportation, given my budget. We walk over to his apartment a few blocks away to pick up helmets. "Jamie believed us."

"He did." I smile. "But I told you he wouldn't get jealous."

"I don't know. I think he was definitely thrown."

I smile wryly. *It was worth it not to be taken for granted.*

I give Rory my hat to leave at his apartment. *The hat didn't really work.* I sit on his stoop while he runs upstairs. I shouldn't have thought the hat would work. It reminds me of *The Unbearable Lightness of Being* when the hat works with one lover but has no meaning to a different lover. Not that I was Jamie's lover. But we had grown up together and been friends forever. The first time he visited from Singapore, we spent the whole week hanging out—to the extent that I lost the guy I'd been dating. And the last time he visited, I declared my love.

Rory lives in a brownstone in Tribeca across from a playground and park with basketball courts. One basketball court is right across the street, which he considered a plus when he picked the apartment. He plays basketball most weekend mornings, if he's not out surfing with his best friend, Jake. My phone beeps. It's my sister, Olivia.

Olivia: *Can you babysit Sunday night?*

Me: *Sure.*

Olivia: *Crafting emergency. Some Frida Kahlo-inspired diorama. Just opened his school folder.*

I call her. "Just have him draw some self-portraits, glue them to the walls of the shoebox, and then put plants around it. Use tea for dirt. I left some stuff in your craft drawer the last time I was babysitting. Remind Thomas how we made the plants. Cut the wire for him, he dips it into glue and flock, and voila, you've got a plant." I explain how to create a few other plants.

"Thanks. This is like homework for me, not Thomas," Olivia says.

"It's fun, Olivia."

She scoffs. Her attitude is that crafting and serious, professional Wall Street lawyer don't mix. She says "hobbies" like it's a bad word.

The front door slams shut behind me, and Rory bounds down the stairs. I say goodbye to Olivia. He pulls me up off the stoop and hands me a helmet as there's a shout from the basketball court. A young woman is high-fiving one of her teammates.

He snaps his helmet on. "Do you really cry over agent rejections?"

"No. I mean, they hurt, but not enough to induce tears. It's just part of the process."

"Success will come. I'm sure of it. Anyway, let's go see how many artists we can find in The Met who were unappreciated at first—mocked, even."

I laugh. I do love Rory, even if it's just in the close friend sense, so I'm not really lying. At least not about my feelings. That zap of electricity was just a loose wire connection that needs to be sheathed.

Chapter Three

WE CLICK OUR BICYCLES into the bike rack and, passing by the hot dog carts, amble up the stone steps to The Metropolitan Museum of Art. A line of tourists follows a bright-red umbrella hoisted high by a tour leader explaining how The Met was founded in 1870 to be a museum and a library of art. I like that phrase.

Rory suggests we make a wish in the fountain and hands me a penny. I squeeze my eyes tightly and toss my penny into the pool. *Please let me get an agent.* But it's not luck that will get me an agent. Only hard work. Improving my writing craft through classes. Coming up with that pitch that sells. Same for Rory and developing ad campaigns. He understands the ups and downs of creative life. I'm happy that his ad campaign was chosen this time.

We walk up the rest of the steps to The Met entrance.

"First stop has to be Van Gogh," he says. "Only one painting sold during his lifetime."

"Ouch. That's not a good prognosis. But I'd take one book sold."

"Would you?"

I stop short. "No."

He pulls on my hand.

We walk into the marble hallways of The Met, clearing the security inspection. As we pass the round information desk in the center of the great hallway, I grab some brochures so I can cut out the pictures to make miniature paintings for my dollhouse.

The Beaux-Arts Hall is already bustling with visitors and conversations.

“How was seeing him with Willow?” he asks.

“Okay.” I look down, then glance at him.

He gazes at me as if he’s about to ask another question, but he doesn’t.

So many different languages are being spoken in the line for tickets. We flash our library cards for the NYC resident free admission, show our stickers to the guard, and walk through the columns up the stairs, weaving our way through the crowds. We reach Gallery 825 with Van Gogh’s painting, *The Irises*. We stand in front of it and absorb it. I like being able to see the layers of paint, the heavier application adding depth. The text next to it explains that Van Gogh used pink as the background, but that has since faded.

“This is one of my favorites,” I say. “The blue with the green.”

“Have you considered taking another year to write full time?” he asks. “I feel like you’re so close. And you work all the time, between your writing and your writing classes.”

I step back to look at the Van Gogh self-portrait in the middle of the room. “Most writers have full-time jobs. I have to accept that. And I feel like I'm hemorrhaging money, what with paying for editing and classes.” I don’t tell him that I’m losing faith. Maybe my writing doesn’t have what it takes.

“How’s your class coming along?”

“Good. Our first task was word-intensity exercises.” The explanatory text on the plastic-plated card accompanying the Van Gogh self-portrait notes that he often used himself as a subject because he didn't had the funds to pay for models.

“What’s that?”

I bite my nail to think of what I did. “Take a word like ‘sad.’ And then a word-intensity line is ‘downcast, sad, glum, melancholy, distressed, despairing, weepy, bawling, wretched.’ The emotion gets stronger as we progress.”

“Oh yes, we find the sizzle words, too, for ads. Like sizzle.”

“And slither,” I say.

We finish viewing the paintings in this room, and Rory leads us to another room with more Van Goghs. My rubber-soled boots squeak on the polished floors, disturbing the contemplative silence.

“You know exactly where the Van Goghs are?” I ask. I visit periodically, but I don’t know where all the paintings are.

“I spent a lot of time in The Met with my parents when I was growing up. At least once a month, we’d come here and wander around.” Rory looks closely at one painting. “Okay, next artist, Cezanne. He was rejected for years by the Paris Salon but ultimately successful while alive. So, there you go. He’s a better example.”

If only it said what had inspired him. Was it the desire to see his painting in a gallery? It was probably more fundamental—like needing to breathe. I wrote my way out of my grief over my parents’ death as if it were a maze, and with my pencil, I could find the exit. I take in the blue, ocher, and green of Cezanne’s landscapes as I compose myself.

Rory steps closer to the painting to study it. His head is bent.

I say, “I can’t believe I didn’t realize how much you know about art. You have The Met memorized.”

He snorts. “I don’t.”

While we wait for the people in front of us to move from the next Cezanne, I quiz him on artists in The Met collection. Mr. I-don’t-have-The-Met-memorized is able to answer all of my questions.

We exit the Early 20th Century European paintings exhibit and pass by the gift shop. Rory suggests we check out the Surrealism Exhibition Gallery.

"Don't you remember that I took a lot of art classes during college?" he asks.

"No." Parts of college, immediately after my parents died, are a blur, but I should remember Rory taking art classes. Especially because I met him several months after my parents' death. "Did you want to be an artist? Or do you? Is that why you're always after me to pursue my dreams?" *How do I not know this about Rory? I am a terrible friend.*

"No, definitely not." Rory put his hands up, palms facing me, as if to say stop. "I'm good in advertising. It's still the creative process, but with an income and with other people. Painting or writing would be too solitary for me. I like seeing the different ideas firing off each other. But my mom wanted to be an artist, and I feel like she's frustrated she didn't pursue her dream. Maybe that's why I want you to pursue yours."

"I can't believe I'm just learning this." His parents have an amazing art collection, and his mom's an art dealer, but I didn't realize she'd wanted to be an artist. I should be more observant as a writer, but I wouldn't assume someone with an amazing book collection wants to be a writer.

"I'm not sure my mom would appreciate my sharing her frustration," he says. "It's not like you share that much. I feel like you keep your cards pretty close to your chest."

Sometimes. I stare at the Miro painting titled *Constellation* and the one bright-blue star in the midst of the more somber red and black colors. The text next to it explains that it represents Miro's escape from the terrors of World War II by his closing down within himself. *Apt.* "Don't we all?" I ask.

"Not with friends. You share with Zelda."

"Zelda has seen me at my worst, and she's stuck with me, so I know I'll never lose her." I blush when I realize what I've said and hurriedly say, "Plus, Zelda will straight up ask me what's going on, so I can't keep secrets from her." I shift from foot to foot. "I don't think most people really want to hear it. I mean, when people ask how you are, they don't want a real answer."

"No, but I do. You're not going to lose my friendship, either. We're best friends."

I nod. "I know." And I need that security. I have a small inner circle of family and found-family, and I rely on them, like a circular life preserver holding me up in turbulent waves.

We pass by the guard, nodding at him, and enter another room. A woman and a man are huddled together on the bench in the middle, the man gesturing and the woman inclining her head.

He says, "I like when your dollhouse blog captures the messy moments of life, not the picture-perfect ones."

I laugh. "You liked the recent post when she tacked the rejection to her bulletin board."

Rory nods. "I want my next advertising campaign to be more realistic and emotionally raw. It needs to really connect with viewers."

"He gets lost because of a detour in your current pitch. That's realistic."

"Yes." Rory had successfully pitched a "romcom" ad to sell an eco-friendly car. The company's brief was that they wanted to sell more cars to women.

"Your mom could still try. Does she?" I ask.

"Not really. She finds failure frustrating."

Don't we all.

We walk down a hallway and into another gallery with Miro's paintings.

"I remember we took that surrealism art class together," I say. We are alone in the gallery, with just the guard at the door. I step closer to the Miro painting. "I love Miro's work. I love how playful he is. It makes me feel happy. The best part of that surrealism class was when she showed us that movie out of order, only figuring it out halfway through, and none of us realized that because it was a surrealist film." And that I sat next to Rory every class, securely part of his inner circle.

He laughs. "That movie didn't make any more sense when we viewed it in its proper order."

"The film felt like a dream. Dreams seem logical when you're dreaming, but when you wake up and try to explain what happened, they make no sense." *Our brunch date as a couple just felt like a dream.*

He nods. "And the emotion that you feel in a dream is real, too. That's why you wake up just before something bad is about to happen."

And the emotions—being together—felt real.

He moves to the next Miro painting. "And I found advertising because of that class. I wrote my paper on surrealism in advertising."

I remember. Sitting in Rory's dorm room on his bed, typing up my paper as he wrote his, U2 playing in the background. When I first met Rory, I thought he might be the one who would get me over my unrequited Jamie crush. I still had feelings for Jamie, but they always seemed to fade into the background when Rory was around. But nothing ever happened. It left me wondering why we were just friends when we connected so profoundly—almost instinctively understanding the other—one creative person finding another. Or if we were just friends because we were too similar and got along so well.

The text on the plastic-plated card on the wall explains the criticism levied at Miro's painting when it was first seen. I wish it explained what made him keep pushing on despite the criticism. Is there a time when I should give up?

"We should change the story of how we met. Especially since I don't usually cry when I get rejections," I say as I read the text next to a Miro painting that he painted when he had a nervous breakdown.

"I agree. So, how did we start dating?"

How would we have started dating? Rory seems so familiar, and yet not. But I can't think of how we would start dating. I shiver. I can't imagine telling him I like him the way I told Jamie. Especially when that went so poorly. Rory seems more unattainable. Jamie was my boy next door. But Rory is *not* the boy next door. He looks like the one your parents warn you against because he's going to break your heart. Then when you get to know him, you realize he *is* going to break your heart—not because he's a bad guy, but because he's just such a good guy and yet not romantically interested.

"It has to be something close to that so that we have some consistency in the story."

"How does the couple in *Fake Dating Folly* start fake dating?" he asks.

"They're casual friends, and they both need dates for weddings where their exes are getting married, although not to each other. It's not the most original, but I think I'm giving it a fresh twist. And I wanted to deal with the whole ex thing."

"Because of Jamie?"

"Everything doesn't come back to Jamie. But yes. Those emotions. But also, just rejection in general. I mean, one of my favorite novels is *The Sun Also Rises*, and especially the ending when she says if only they had been able to be together, and he suggests that the reality may not have lived up to the dream."

"Definitely in my top-ten list of books to take to a desert island. She wouldn't be faithful to Jake even if they could have sex."

"No, she wouldn't be," I say. "She's the type of person who is always looking for that drama and a new conquest."

"Is that a type of person?" Rory asks. We stop in front of Miro's bronze sculpture of a crate with an egg on top entitled *Femme*. An egg seems vulnerable to me, easily cracked and broken.

"Yes, totally." Rory's former girlfriend, Callie, is that type of person, but I restrain myself from saying that. Rory was torn after she broke up with him. For months, he'd reminisce with stories about how good Callie had been to him, as if kicking himself that he hadn't fought harder for their relationship. "But maybe the fact that she and Jake can't have sex and the illusion that they love each other allows them to keep their friendship, which wouldn't have lasted if they could have had sex. So, his infertility saves that."

"Is their friendship worth it?" Rory asks quietly.

"I think so."

We glance at each other. I look away at another Miro.

"Rory!" a woman's voice calls from across the room. We turn around.

"Callie," Rory says.

I can't believe I conjured up Callie. She's looking as fashionable as always, wearing brown, leather, high-heeled boots and a leather mini skirt with a black sweater. I wish I was wearing my hat.

"No surprise to find you here," Callie says.

Really? Even Callie knows he spends hours at The Met?

She gives him a hug and stays holding him. "It's so good to see you." She leans back to look into his eyes.

Hello? As long as Callie doesn't start using my head as a coaster table, I am good. I'd like to pretend to be Rory's girlfriend, but he hasn't given any indication that he wants me to. We need some kind of code.

"I was just about to head to your favorite place. The Shōin Room." The Shōin Room is a Japanese room that is bare, except for grass mats on the floor with gold-leafed sliding doors decorated with a twisty-tree. It inspires contemplation and reverence. Meditation seems appropriate. That's the opposite of Rory—not that Rory isn't thoughtful, but he's definitely more social than me. Sometimes I feel he collects people, like his parents collect art, like he found me in college. This Metropolitan-Museum-Shōin-Room Rory is the opposite of my Rory.

Rory steps out of her arms. "You remember Penelope."

Callie doesn't. She doesn't say it out loud, but she wrinkles her forehead when she looks at me. "Of course."

"We're about to head to my favorite place, the roof garden," I say. The Cantor Roof Garden is in the opposite direction from the Shōin Room. I don't want to hang out with Callie.

"I'll come with you," Callie says.

We stroll out of this exhibit, past the lobster telephone, while the Ted Joans jazz music plays, and Callie keeps talking a mile a minute but in whispered tones. I can barely hear her on the other side of Rory. Rory suddenly moves so that I am in between them.

We take the elevator up to the fifth floor and walk out onto the terrace. It's a beautiful, crisp day in New York. The sky is all blue, with no clouds, and Central Park is spread before us. Some of the trees are starting to turn red, and auburn spots, like little fires, dot the lawn of green treetops. I like fall with its comfy sweaters, crisp breezes, chai tea, and lots of excuses to stay inside and write. I like all the seasons, but spring and fall are my favorites in New York. We order drinks from the bar and stand off to the side, a sculpture by Alicja Kwade in front of us.

Ten-foot, rectangular, metal frames intersect each other, with swirly-colored stone spheres, looking like planets, interspersed throughout the structure. Some hover on top of a frame, some hang suspended between two frames, and some rest on the floor.

Should I disappear as I usually do, leaving Rory to flirt? Ugh. Not Callie. I'll never see him again. When they dated, she moved into his apartment, and I barely saw him for brunch.

Callie has picked up the card describing the artwork and is using words like "post-modern," "spiritual," and "apocalyptic." She says, "I think it is almost post-conceptual, evoking the fragility and randomness of life vs our suppressed emotional memories represented by the stones."

I have no idea what that all means, but I do think that some emotional memories are better off suppressed.

"Curls, what do you think of this piece of art?" Rory asks.

Callie's eyes narrow as if she realizes that my nickname implies an intimacy beyond casual acquaintance. I don't want her to feel threatened. She eviscerated Marie once when Rory wasn't around. But I'm also not conceding the field.

"I like it. I like Callie's interpretation. And taking Callie's interpretation, some stones are up in the air, some are held up by the framework, and some stones or memories have dropped. To me, the metal frames look like a revolving door, and so it's like a series of doors to walk through. Or it's like frameworks to conform to."

Rory glances at me and nods.

"The revolving door?" Callie looks slyly at Rory. She takes his hand. "C'mon, Rory, we're supposed to walk under it. Do you dare?" She pulls him through, giggling.

I walk through the other metal frame and stand in the middle, studying the spheres against the bright-blue sky. It doesn't feel that secure. This is what Theresa, Jamie's mom, thinks of my striving to become a published author. The plaque says that the artist was conceptualizing the stones, which took years to form, as compressed time. Even though I can feel that my writing has gotten stronger these past two years, I don't have the budget to take another year off.

I rub the red stone. Rory comes over to me as Callie takes a phone call. He rubs it, too.

"Sorry Callie interrupted our time together. She's kind of like a force of nature," he says.

"The Shōin Room is your favorite?"

"No, she must be confusing me with someone else. This roof deck is one of my favorites. That and the modern art gallery with the slanted glass window ceiling. Some of my favorite art is there."

"What's your interpretation of the sculpture?" I ask. Callie walks back over.

Callie interrupts us again. "It's like Rory's shiny new ball syndrome writ large."

I step back. Rory laughs easily. "All ad execs have shiny new ball syndrome. We need to be able to understand how to create that same excitement in individuals. It's not necessarily a bad thing. It means I come up with a lot of ideas."

Callie's phone pings. Some of her business school friends are in the neighborhood, and she suggests we meet up with them for a drink. Rory looks tempted. I need to go home to walk the dogs and write, or, in reality, stare out my window at the birds instead of the blank screen in front of me. I get cranky otherwise. And I need to clean up my mess from making miniature Etsy orders before Zelda comes home. I made a dozen miniature waffles with strawberries early this morning.

"Are you sure you don't want to come?" His blue eyes are so vivid and entreating. "All that partying gave those artists material."

I smile but shake my head. Maybe if Callie wasn't there. And it wasn't a bunch of successful B-school friends asking me if I'm published yet.

"Well, come with us to 91st," Rory says.

We walk up to the café/bar between Fifth Avenue and Madison. Tables have been set outside, fenced in by a red banner that cheerfully proclaims the café name of La Belle Vie. Some women wave from a table, laughter breaks out; there's the murmur of conversations, a shout of excitement. I say goodbye, and he goes off with Callie. Callie puts her arm through his.

I walk back to Fifth Avenue alone. Maybe I should have gone with them—especially since Rory wanted me to come. I check my email. An agent has replied to one of my queries:

> To: Penelope
>
> From: Agent Assistant
>
> Thank you for sending us *Midnight Masquerade*. We don't feel the emotional engagement to take it to the next level. We think it needs more

> backstory. This process is subjective, so we are sure another agent will feel differently. We wish you the best.

That about sums up today. I can't seem to get my novel to the next level. Jamie didn't feel the emotional engagement to take it to the next level. And instead of being in a real relationship, I'm faking one and lying to Jamie. Just as long as I don't lose my real friendship with Rory. My backstory doesn't need any more loss.

CHAPTER FOUR

I STRIDE DOWN THE dirt pathway next to the Jackie Onassis Reservoir in Central Park against the flow of the joggers, hoping not to get yelled at that I am going the wrong way. *I shouldn't have agreed to fake date Rory.* I don't want to lose my friendship with him. He and Zelda are my closest friends.

Maybe I should've walked on the parallel path through the trees, but there's no view of the deep-blue waters of the reservoir there or of the skyline. I stay far to the side as a jogger runs by. And then I exit the pathway to walk across the bridge and down the steps. The air is chilly out of the sun.

But the research component for *Fake Dating Folly* is gold. Perched on a park bench, I make a list in my always-handy, little, black notebook of what we should explore:

(1) What are the rules?

(2) How did we start dating?

a. Why is that question always asked, as if it holds the clues to the relationship?

b. Can it predict whether we will last?

(3) Given my book plot, we need to fake date in front of exes. But Jamie made it clear that I wouldn't see him again. Maybe Callie?

I close my notebook and walk again. Rory didn't suggest fake dating in front of Callie. If he gets back together with Callie, he won't need me as a fake date for client functions. I need to work fast. I will have to read some fake dating books to find out all the tropes.

My favorite kind of research.

I skirt along the bottom edge of the Great Lawn, which is filled with teams playing baseball. I used to watch Jamie play baseball here in high school, off on the sidelines. Today at brunch, I was in the game—with Rory as my teammate. I smile as I recall Willow sticking her hand up Jamie's sleeve. I check to see if I feel any pangs of jealousy. No. Hmm.

I pass by the boarded-up Shakespeare in the Park theatre. Posters for this summer's performance of *Twelfth Night* are still up. I turn left and walk down the narrow sidewalk next to the joggers and bicyclists speeding by.

I might be over Jamie. Brunch felt more like ripping off a Band-Aid than creating a new wound.

And finally, I arrive home to a furry-dog welcome with some wet kisses thrown in for good measure. I have two dogs boarding with me at the moment. Benson is a German shepherd, and Gilda, named after Gilda Radner, is a golden border collie mix. My other regular client, Cleo, a Labrador mix, usually just hangs out with me during the weekdays. Cleo is the beloved pet of my friend Miranda's uncle. He works in theatre so he's gone most nights. All three of them get along with my orange tabby cat, Goldie.

Benson and Gilda bark as soon as I grab their leashes to take them to the dog run.

At the dog run in Riverside Park, I let them off their leashes and hang out off to the side, throwing their balls when they want to play fetch. I chat with a few other dog owners I recognize. It's a perfect lazy Sunday afternoon. I'm about to call the dogs and head home when my phone rings. It's my sister, Olivia.

"I can't believe you didn't tell me you're *dating* Rory," she says. "Rory. That's amazing."

Another person who finds it amazing. Don't hold back now.

She continues, "You never tell me anything, but still, I thought you would have called me to tell me this. I can't believe I had to hear it from Jamie."

I shake my head. "I can't believe Jamie blabbed it to everyone. I thought he was in the middle of working on some time-intensive deal."

"I called him to make sure I saw him before he left," she says. Our families grew up together, even spending vacations together. "And why shouldn't he be telling everyone? You should be blabbing it to everyone. Why didn't you want to tell me?"

I don't know what to say.

"We're the only family we have. Why wouldn't you tell me something like this? I mean, this is significant. Rory is like your best guy friend, other than Jamie. I don't understand why you don't open up. I worry about it."

"You don't have to worry about me." We should have never pretended to be dating in front of Jamie. But I can't tell Olivia the truth. She can't keep a secret. Corporate secrets, yes. My secrets, no. And Theresa is also going to want details. Jamie's definitely told his mom if he's told Olivia.

Olivia says, "And I even talked to you after the brunch. So, you'd just told Jamie, but you didn't tell me."

"I didn't mean to tell Jamie."

"I always thought it would be you and Jamie when we were growing up," she says.

I've never told her that I told Jamie I liked him.

A couple with a dog enters the dog park and lets their terrier off the leash. The man hugs his partner, and they seem to be talking intently, their heads close together, while their terrier runs over to meet Gilda.

"But Rory's a much better match for you. He gets you."

I should tell her the truth. I throw Benson's ball. He lopes over to get it, then brings it back, but he doesn't want to drop it. He lies down a few feet away, his paws out, slobbering over his ball.

She says, "And Rory supports your writing. I was telling Theresa about that rejection you got—where the person told you to put the book in the drawer and work on the next one. I don't know how you keep going."

I rub my forehead. "I don't actually need everyone to know about that piece of advice." Much as I love Olivia, it annoys me that she views my life as fair game for discussion.

"It's just Theresa. She's worried about you; it seems impossible to get published nowadays. She's as impressed with your perseverance as I am," Olivia says. "Anyway, we should double date."

"Except that I'm your babysitter."

"We'll get Theresa to babysit. Wow. Rory. So, I want all the details. How did it happen?"

Uh-oh. Rory and I never did finish discussing details of how we started dating as we were walking around The Met. I am *so* not prepared to withstand Olivia's third-degree examination. She's a corporate lawyer. Rory and I need to map out our "fake" relationship like plotting out the arc in a book.

"Hold on," I say, "someone is texting."

I sit on a bench under a tree and text Rory: *Jamie told Olivia and now she wants DETAILS.*

Olivia is waiting. A family with two little curly-haired girls who look like mini versions of Olivia and me pass by the dog run. They are probably heading to the playgrounds by the Hudson River. The smaller one runs to catch up to her older sister, but the older sister doesn't see her.

"It just happened," I say to Olivia. We need to keep to what we told Jamie, anyway. "He was over here, comforting me about an agent rejection, and I don't know, suddenly there was like electricity zipping back and forth, and I kissed him." Luckily, I do write romantic comedy, so zipping electricity is standard fare. *And maybe it even exists. I felt it today with Rory.* But I'm sure only I felt it. Clearly, I need to bolster my immunity. Watching him with Callie at the café could have been a booster shot.

Rory: *Would you give her all the details if it was real?*

No, although I would have told her.

"And it's just so new and magical that I don't want to spoil it by talking about it," I say. "I can't quite believe it's happening, either."

Olivia sighs happily. Unlike me, she's a true romantic. She was always singing "One day my prince will come" when we were kids, whereas I had little interest in boys and was usually writing or playing in my dollhouse. And because I had no boy dolls, most of my dollhouse dolls were single. The mom was divorced. I have now bought all the Topper boy dolls I didn't have as a child. And some male and female action doll figures. Now all my female dolls have partners or potential partners.

Rory: *Or you could just tell her we were just fake dating for book research.*

Wait, are we done already? A sinking feeling fills my chest. I need to concentrate on what Olivia is saying.

"You guys should come for brunch next weekend," she says. "I'm so happy for you. I really thought you were just going to be a single aunty. Not that there's anything wrong with that. In fact, it's great for me and the kids. Oooh, this means that there might be cousins. Amber has been asking for a little sister or brother, but I'm done. Now I can tell her she might get a little cousin."

"Hold on there. We just started dating. I'm not bringing Rory over for brunch if you're going to talk about our having babies. You'll scare him off."

"I won't. But Rory will be a great dad. Anyway, you should date for a long time before you have kids. Establish a solid foundation. Have lots of sex. Travel." My niece, Amber, says something in the background. Olivia tells her she's on the phone. Amber keeps talking. My sister shushes her again. "It's like they have no idea what a phone call is. So how come you're not together now? John and I couldn't be separated when we first started dating."

Good question. I shift uncomfortably on the metal bench. "He had plans, and I have work to do. I need to finish some Etsy miniature orders, and I haven't eked out my thousand words for today. And I'm taking care of Benson and Gilda, so I need to be with them. He might come over after, but it just seemed easier if we separated for the night and actually got some sleep." *That should satisfy her.* I need to get off the phone so I can address Rory's last comment. "Rory just texted. I have to go."

"Give him my best." Olivia hangs up.

I want to keep dating Rory. I wrap my arms around myself, rubbing my elbows.

Me: *I thought you needed a fake date for your work engagements.*

Rory: *Yes. Still do. Definitely. But I don't want you to have to lie to your sister. We can still be fake dating for my work.*

I let out a huge breath I didn't realize I'd been holding. But now I have lied to Olivia. And I definitely don't want Jamie to find out I lied to him. I bite my nail. I hunch over. This is a mess.

I whistle to the dogs. It's time to go home. They come over, tails wagging. I clip on their leashes and we walk home along 72nd Street.

I call Rory. He tells me to hold on while he walks a few feet away from their table.

"Damage is already done. I kept to the Jamie storyline. Olivia can't keep a secret," I say.

"She might have been able to keep this secret."

"I doubt it. And if she told Jamie, maybe he'd completely cut me off, like Lex," I say.

The silence at the other end of the phone feels accusatory.

"So, you're still interested in Jamie?" he asks.

"No, but he seemed really mad at Lex. I'm trying to stay friends. Obviously."

"Don't you think your sister and Theresa will be able to tell that we're not really together?"

Perfect segue for my plan: lots of research for my book.

"Hello?" he asks.

"That's a good point. We need to practice, especially before your work parties. At least we're close friends, but I don't think we give off the 'passionately in love' vibe."

"Is that the vibe we're going for?"

"If I'm going to be some possessive girlfriend at your work party, we're not going for the 'we've been dating for a million years' vibe. And Olivia wants us to come for brunch this weekend so she can see this in person. We need to up our game." I let the dogs off their leashes as we enter my brownstone building. They precede me up the stairs to the third floor and into our apartment.

Benson immediately runs to his food bowl. He has to check that it's still there. Benson was a stray from the pound, and he had a few owners before Dave. That's one of the reasons Dave pays for me to take care of him when he travels for work. He doesn't want Benson to think he's going back to the pound or anything near it. Just Aunty Penelope.

"All right, how about dinner tomorrow night?" he asks. "I can cook and then we can go out to dessert at this little French bakery around the corner."

"Is that your usual approach?" I hang up my coat on the hook near the door.

He laughs. "It's the opposite of my usual approach."

That's not good. "Really? Why?"

"If it's a first date and we're already at my house eating dinner, I'm not going to suggest leaving to go outside to eat dessert."

I laugh. That makes sense. Then another thought occurs to me. "Your girlfriends don't eat dessert, do they?"

"Not many, so I'm glad you do."

"Smooth talking, pretty boy," I say.

He laughs. I love making him laugh. "So, it's a date?"

"Yes," I say. A fake date.

CHAPTER FIVE

I CROSS OUT THE last item on my to-do list for today:

Sunday

~~*Create mini hot chocolates*~~.

~~*Package up Etsy orders.*~~

~~*Write 1000 words.*~~

~~*Submit writing class homework describing character's inner conflict.*~~

~~*Sign up for class on First Five Pages.*~~

~~*Create dollhouse blog post.*~~

~~*Take Benson and Gilda to the dog run twice.*~~

Gilda is sprawled out on my floor right now, recovering from a frolic in the dog run. A happy golden border collie mix. Who needs more? I take a picture of Gilda for her mom, who's shooting a commercial in LA, and send it to her.

I check to see if anyone has commented on my blog post. I created a scene where Piper was at an art museum with a dark-haired guy. The doll, which just arrived in the mail yesterday, has dark, tousled hair like Rory. Several followers want to know if Piper has a new love interest. Posting at least once a week maintains my blog rankings and my Etsy store business, which then pays for my writing classes.

Olivia smiles at me from the photos on the wall behind my writing desk, moments captured with us and our parents. I shouldn't have lied to her.

In the center of the wall above my bulletin board is my first rejection letter, from when I was ten. I mailed in a short story about Calico the Caterpillar. I glued my rejection onto construction paper and taped it to my wall for motivation. My dad framed it to encourage me to keep going. My bulletin board is filled with ideas scribbled on Post-its, writing advice, and my typed-up to-do list for this year:

- *Query* Midnight Masquerade*/Revise per feedback*
- *Write second book,* Fake Dating Folly
- *Post to dollhouse blog*
- *Build writer website and blog*
- *Build Etsy store business*

Nothing on that list is crossed out. My back tenses. So much still to do and only four more months of full-time attention. Then it's back to writing in fleeting snippets of time, dreams delayed.

Zelda's footsteps reverberate in the living room.

"You won't believe what happened today," Zelda says. Benson follows her into my bedroom. He lies on the floor at my feet and rolls over. I give him a tummy rub.

I don't know how she manages to still look so crisp after working a full day at the law office. She's brightened up her white blouse and navy slacks with this jade necklace that glows against her brown skin. She fluffs out her shoulder-length, curly, black hair.

"What happened?" I swivel my chair to face her.

Zelda smiles and pushes her bangs out of her eyes. "The junior associates nominated me for the firm's Values Award." Zelda unfolds a typewritten letter on fancy paper and hands it to me. She pushes some clothes aside on the bed and sits down. Clothes are strewn all over because I was figuring out what to wear for my dinner date with Rory. Benson shifts to his feet and promptly puts his snout on her knee. She pets him.

"That's amazing." I read the letter. "Aww. They called you inspiring, a team leader, caring, legally brilliant. I'm so happy for you."

"I'm so grateful to the associate who nominated me. To go through all the effort of putting together that application to help me." Zelda's eyes tear.

I give her a big hug. "Because you're worth it."

Zelda smiles. "Shouldn't you be getting dressed already for your date?"

"I am dressed."

Zelda grabs a pillow off my bed and throws it at me. I duck.

"You're *so* not wearing that," she says, hands on her hips.

"My hat is at Rory's. I'm adding that." Otherwise, my outfit is my usual going-out ensemble of jeans, black top, and black boots, but I added this cool, blue necklace I inherited from my mom, copying Zelda's style from this morning.

"That's your hot date outfit? You're wearing combat boots." Zelda talks to Benson in a baby voice. "Do you think Aunty Penelope should be wearing that?"

"They don't suggest the possibility of hand-to-hand combat?" I smile.

"No, they say 'stay the frick away.'"

I untie the laces of my boots. "I thought the jeans gave the message of 'casual, but still sexy.' As opposed to my usual yoga pants. Wearing jeans is a compliment."

"Welcome to the real world." Zelda shakes her head like she despairs of me. Zelda and I were freshman roommates in college, which was odd because we're both from New York, although different boroughs. We immediately decided to room together because, hello, New Yorkers. But we became best friends with our roommates from Alabama and Colorado as well. I often give thanks to the anonymous admissions person who put us all together. Zelda and I moved back to New York after college. We were going to rent an apartment in Brooklyn, with its cheaper rent and more diverse neighborhoods, but then Zelda's aunt offered Zelda this apartment when she moved out of the city.

"I tried on my little, black dress, but I worried I looked like I was dressing up. And it's still a fake date, after all," I say.

"But you want it to be a real date."

"I don't want it to be a real date," I say.

"Oh please."

"It's not going to work."

"Okay, so humor me," she says. "You're attracted to him, right?"

Oh no. Zelda is going into full prosecution mode.

"Not anymore," I say.

Zelda gives me her "don't even try it" look. I once watched one of her trials and saw that look visibly reduce a grown CEO. She asks, "No?"

"Maybe a little."

Zelda snorts. She points to our framed collage of photos from college. "Look at the way you're looking at him in this photo." I'm laughing in the photo and gazing at Rory with my heart in my eyes.

She continues, "You're attracted to him, so it's just a matter of whether he's into you."

"Just."

"Go get 'em, tiger." Zelda winks at me. "Did you ask him whether he liked the ending in those fake dating trope books?"

"I'll add it to my research questions."

"So, here's the plan: dress as if it's a date, and see if he shows any flicker of physical interest. Dressing the part is one of the easiest ways to make that change."

Zelda should know. She's a corporate lawyer, and she always dresses the part at work, even though she wears sweats and yoga pants around our apartment. She looks hot in either outfit.

Zelda is rifling through my closet, muttering. All my clothes look pretty similar to this outfit, so it's a mystery what she's hoping to find. She pushes aside a bunch of clothing and pulls out this blue-gray sheath dress I wore to one of her work functions. We found it at a vintage clothing shop in Brooklyn.

"This one. It looks great on you, but it's still low-key enough that it doesn't look like you're trying too hard."

"I hope it still fits." Way too many cookies have been consumed lately as a reward for finishing a chapter. Occupational hazard.

Zelda nods. "And wear your blue heels." Zelda swears by heels, whereas I am firmly in the camp that it's better to be able to wear sneakers and run fast if need be. Then again, Zelda could outrun me in her heels.

I try the dress on and twirl. It does make me feel feminine and flirtatious. "I should've worn this to the brunch with Jamie."

"Ugh. Jamie. Jamie should be dead to you. Dead. But Rory—Rory is still very much a live possibility." She puts her hands on her hips. Zelda thinks I like Jamie because he's safe and I won't get hurt. Not too hurt, anyway.

"Not really. He said I can be his fake date because I won't think it's for real." I fold up the clothes on my bed.

"Hmm . . . that's not good," she says. "But this means it's even more important that you see if there's that flicker of interest. So you know whether you should keep your guard up. Because I worry that you're already in love with him and you'll fall hard for him in a fake dating situation and be really heartbroken."

"I'm not in love with him, and it's not like the books."

"You don't think?"

"I don't know," I say, thinking about it. "I do think that fake dating creates an intimacy, which helps."

"See?"

I take a deep breath. "I don't want to get hurt."

"I get it. I'm not out there looking for lo-o-ove. I've come to terms with the fact that I may be on my own." Zelda sits back on my bed. “But there’s something there with Rory, given the fact that he keeps calling and hanging out with you.”

“Do you think it could mean he’s interested?”

Zelda shakes her head. “I wouldn’t get your hopes up. Rory seems like a big enough boy that he could just ask you out, but you *are* close friends, and you’ve been obsessed with Jamie. I can see that being an obstacle to his just asking you out.”

“He said I didn’t share much.”

“A real relationship requires opening up and trusting each other with your secrets.” Zelda smiles. “Do you share secrets with him?”

“Like what secrets?” I ask, almost afraid of Zelda’s answer. “He follows my blog.”

“Your blog is just the tip of the iceberg, although as you yourself have said, you got more followers when you revealed real emotion about rejection.”

“I think he’s pretty familiar already with the messy side of me,” I say. “He just sees me as a friend.”

“Let’s just see if there’s that flare of attraction when his eyes check out your legs or your . . .”

“Okay, okay. I got it. Mission accepted,” I say. “But I know we’ve already moved past any possibility of dating. I think there’s a window at the beginning when you first become friends with a guy, and one of you then makes the decision whether this will be friends or more.” I should have remembered that before I told Jamie I loved him.

“Ah, but you defined it as a window. And windows can be opened.”

Sometimes I hate that my best friend is a lawyer.

“Pretend you’re a character in one of your books who wants to seduce the guy. It’s great research for your book.” Zelda grabs her iPhone and plays “You and Me” by Cassie. “Let’s dance!”

Zelda is a big believer in the pre-party dance session—and the pick-me-up dance boogie, and the I’m-over-you groove. The music fills my veins and I shimmy.

"He's not going to know what hit him," she says, a wicked grin on her face. "If you need any on-the-spot advice, text me. Miranda and I are going to a dance party in Brooklyn." Miranda is our upstairs neighbor.

I pat Gilda and Benson on their heads before I leave. Some dog hair sprinkles on my outfit as a good luck charm. I grab my bike helmet from its hook and step out the door.

I unlock a Citi Bike and ride down the Columbus Avenue bike lane toward Tribeca. I'm flashing a lot of leg. No one seems to notice. That's not exactly a boost of confidence before my date.

I slow down because I don't want to arrive all sweaty. I park in my usual Citi Bike rack, then I stand with my arms outstretched, trying to air out my arms. I forgot about sweat stains. I should've taken the subway. And that's another reason why I don't date. I've biked here a million times before and just bounced right up to Rory's apartment, not caring about whether I'm a sweaty mess.

"Penelope?"

It can't be. I rotate my arms in slow circles. I turn around. "Rory."

He looks perplexed. As he should. He's carrying flowers. Bright-yellow tulips.

"What are you doing?"

"Arm circles." I look away at my outstretched hand. "I like to work my back and arms after biking so that it's not all legs."

He smiles. "Aren't you supposed to be moving your arms in circles when doing arm circles?" He's onto me. It's a problem when you're trying to fool one of your best friends.

"I like to warm up to it first by just extending my arms."

He nods seriously, but he half-smiles.

Then he crosses over and hands me bright-yellow tulips. "For you."

I say thanks and kiss him on the cheek. I wonder if he knows that yellow tulips used to mean "hopeless love."

We stand there. I sniff the flowers. He pulls me close to him, his arm around me, his hand curling around my waist.

"So, I'm all for practice," he says. As my body fits against his and we amble toward his brownstone, I realize I'm committed to this charade now.

We walk up the stairs to his apartment on the top floor. He's dressed up as well. He's wearing an ironed, white, button-down shirt, untucked, and jeans. Sexy.

I smell smoke. "Something's burning."

The smell is getting stronger the closer we get to his apartment. "Fire. Fire," a robotic voice intones. And a fire alarm is beeping.

"Aargh. I hope I didn't forget to turn it off." Rory bounds up the stairs ahead of me. I follow closely behind.

We burst into the apartment. Smoke is rolling out from the kitchen. Flames leap from the pot on the stove. He grabs the fire extinguisher from the wall and sprays it at the pot, putting out the fire. White spray gook covers the kitchen.

Rory puts down the fire extinguisher. He looks upset.

I give him a hug. The table is set for two, with candles even. Rory is really taking this "dating" business seriously. He gives me a squeeze back.

"Takeout is good, too." I move out of his embrace and walk toward his windows. "We should open the windows and air this out before your neighbors call the fire department."

The sirens of a fire department truck wail outside. Rory and I open the windows. As the firefighters emerge from the truck, Rory yells down that the fire is out. They confer, and the second truck pulls away. The first says that they will send a team up. He runs down the stairs to let them in.

I hurry to the back of his apartment and open up the rest of the windows. There's no acrid smoke smell in the back.

Rory has a spacious, loft-like apartment in Tribeca, which could look like a magazine spread, but not in its usual condition of rumpled disorder: stacks of books and magazines piled around the room, a sweatshirt draped over a dining chair, a basketball and high-tops by the door, his jacket hanging off the back of a chair as if he rushed inside and didn't have time to hang it up. I prefer that very relaxed and casual vibe, though. Very Rory. But today, no clothes are strewn around, there are no piles of sports equipment in the corner, and the books are neatly stacked in almost artistic piles.

I'm reading more into this than I should. I look around his bedroom. I haven't spent a lot of time in Rory's bedroom. His bookcase reveals the most: classics, art books, Hemingway, Fitzgerald, detective stories and thrillers, three romcoms I recommended, books on marketing and advertising, a framed picture of Rory with his parents on holiday in Italy, another photo of Rory holding up a fish with his dad. Several modern paintings decorate the walls. A Nerf basketball hoop hangs over the door. The painting over his desk is a portrait of Rory laughing. It really captures him. I step closer to see the artist. His mom.

Deep voices echo from the living room. I walk out to join them.

Rory is explaining to the two firemen that he thought he turned off the burner before he went to buy flowers. Two firemen are looking at the remains of the pot on the stove—and the white spray gook. The kitchen seems really small with these tall, heroic men in it. They turn around as I enter the kitchen. Firemen just radiate heat.

"Penelope?" one fireman asks.

It's Anthony, a fireman I dated briefly two years ago. I popped by our local fire department to ask some research questions. (Seriously, they were real research questions. I was writing a short story with a fireman as the romantic lead and their "meet-cute" happened when she started a fire in her kitchen making French fries. It wasn't particularly original, but I still liked that story. I used it as a free giveaway to build up an email list.) Anyway, I met Anthony, and he asked me out. I don't think he believed that I was really doing research. We had a few dates, but then it faded. He was a very good cook, however.

"Anthony," I say. "You've switched stations." Rory looks surprised, as does the other fireman.

"Yeah, I moved down here a couple of months ago." He looks at me and at Rory. "Hi, you must be Jamie. Nice to meet you."

"No, Rory." Rory shakes his hand. Rory and Anthony exchange a look.

"Well, good luck here. I'd stay away from lighting those candles for now," he says. Ah, he noticed the candles, too. "You might want to eat out until you get a chance to clean this up and the smoke smell clears out. Penelope is particularly sensitive to that smoke smell."

I flush. He's remembering how when he came over to my apartment straight from work, I always tried to air the smoke out of his coat out by hanging it up outside on our small balcony. Or is he just being possessive with an "I know Penelope" comment aimed at Rory? Rory looks skinny compared to these two, who are seriously muscular.

The firemen leave. I busy myself by trimming the flower stems and putting them in water. Rory throws the pot into the garbage and cinches the bag up.

"I'm really sorry. I had a romantic dinner planned." Rory looks sheepish. I find it endearing. He runs his hand through his hair. "So that's Anthony the fireman. Why did he think I was Jamie?"

I squirm. "We were dating when Jamie first visited from Singapore, and I hung out with Jamie that whole week."

"He didn't meet Jamie?"

I look away. "I didn't tell Jamie I was dating someone. It was not my finest moment. And we broke up after I was 'busy' seeing Jamie for that whole week."

Rory nods. I can't tell what he's thinking.

He asks, "Shall we go out?"

"Yes." The table even has wine glasses and placemats.

My hat from yesterday's brunch is on one of the hooks by the door. I grab it and position it just right. I walk out the door. Rory follows, carrying the garbage bag.

As we leave the warmth of his building, he reaches for my hand and pulls me close. I squeeze his hand. Okay, this isn't that bad. But what are the chances that Anthony would show up on our first date?

"A new Tex-Mex opened in the neighborhood. Should we try it?" he asks.

"Let's." We turn the corner. The last employee of the candle store in the middle of the block is pulling down the iron grate with a screech and locking up. The restaurant on the corner looks cozy and inviting in the dusk.

"We need to discuss the rules of our fake dating," I say.

Chapter Six

"RULES?" RORY ASKS. HIS hand is warm and solid, holding mine in the crisp night air as we amble along Chambers Street.

"Yes, like no kissing." I stare straight ahead. The couple holding hands ahead of us turns into a French restaurant, opening the blue, wooden door and disappearing quickly inside. Glowing globes of warm, white light hang from the ceiling, visible through its glass storefront. Almost every fake dating romance sets a "no kissing" rule.

"No kissing, huh?" he asks.

I sneak a glance at him. Just a quick one. I can't tell from his voice if he is upset. And he angles his head to look at me at just that moment. Our glances collide. A jolt of anticipation courses through me.

His gaze is intense. "So, I shouldn't have kissed you on the cheek yesterday?"

That wasn't just a kiss on the cheek. *You lingered, nuzzled my neck.* I look away. Heat steeps my cheeks. Thankfully, the light is dim on the street. I straighten my shoulders. Clear my mind of that buzzing, intoxicating feeling. "No, that was okay. No kissing on the lips." Keep walking. The blinking, neon light of Diego's TexMex Café beckons.

"Only okay?"

I stop and turn to him under the streetlight. His hair is tousled. His thumb strokes my palm. I swallow. My stomach flip-flops. *I'm in control.* "No, that was . . ." I pause. *Let him suffer.* "Sensual, intoxicating, overwhelming."

He blushes faintly. "Is this from your word-intensity exercise?"

"Yes." I walk again, pulling Rory along by the hand. "So, I'm not sure I can take the real thing."

Rory snorts. "I can understand that. But we can hold hands, right?"

"Yes. Hugging, holding hands, affectionate touches . . . I think we need all that." I can take that, I hope. I'm all for finding out if Rory is interested, but if we kiss, I'm afraid I'd be the only one revealing I want more. I stop. "Are you okay with that?"

"Yes."

He doesn't even pause to think about it. He must be sure that he won't be affected.

I glance at him. "You won't get carried away if I caress your cheek with my fingers?"

Rory's jaw tightens. "Getting hotter."

The Tex-Mex restaurant has a yellow front and an orange awning. A cactus is painted on the door. We push open the door, joining the line to talk to the guy behind the counter. He's seating people while also answering the phone and packing up take-out orders. Mariachi music is playing. The walls are this bright and happy orange, yellow, and green, with an orange, stone floor. It smells delicious—cilantro, lime, cumin, and garlic.

I smile at Rory. "I like the vibe."

"Anthony believed we were dating."

"He believed we were on a date."

"The difference?"

"Candles and flowers," I say wryly. "That can stop when you're dating." A delivery guy in a bright-orange reflective vest, his bicycle helmet still on, squeezes by us to pick up the next delivery order.

"Candles and flowers are not just for dating. My dad still buys my mom flowers every Friday," Rory says.

The counter guy tapes the receipt to the brown bag, hands it to the delivery courier, and says, "Thirty-minute wait. Should I put your name down? Or would you be interested in our couples cooking class? It starts right now, and we have a spot available for one more couple. You'll make puffy tacos from scratch, shredded chicken, and the sides—queso, guac . . ."

"That sounds fun," I say.

"Normally, I'd be all for it, but I'm not sure I should be let back in a kitchen." Rory dips his head.

"It's discounted because of a cancellation," the counter guy says, putting the next call on hold.

I tut. "Back on the horse, as they say. I mean, c'mon, puffy tacos from scratch. Let's do it."

Rory nods and pays for us. He puts his hand on the small of my back. We are ushered through the busy kitchen to a partitioned section off to the side where we won't interrupt the kitchen staff. Three other couples are working around a long table, in silence or whispered conversation, each with an electric burner and cutting station with several bowls lined up in front of cutting boards.

We hang up our coats on a coat rack while the hostess offers us white aprons and chef hats or hair nets. It's a hard choice when both are incredibly sexy. I reluctantly remove my cloche hat and replace it with an oversize chef's hat. The apron completes my transformation. So much for my seductive outfit.

We take our spot. Another chef comes over and explains what to do. First, we're making the shredded chicken. While that cooks, we'll make the toppings and the tacos. It feels very serious.

Rory introduces us to the other couples and asks them each a little about themselves. The atmosphere changes to a more festive feeling of camaraderie.

I dice the peppers and the garlic while Rory cuts up the chicken.

"So, you're not looking for magic. I'm still intrigued by that statement," he says.

I push my chef's hat back. It keeps falling into my eyes.

Okay, I should be more open. "Did you think I was looking for magic?" I ask and then frown. *That's asking him, not revealing myself.*

"I thought . . . you thought that you'd already found the right person with Jamie. But I didn't realize you weren't expecting magic with Jamie." He side-eyes me as he drops the chicken pieces into the boiling water, and then he leaves to wash the cutting board. I think about my response.

Returning with the clean cutting board, knife in hand, he plops the garlic into the water.

"It's not that I didn't expect any magic with Jamie." I cut the onion.

He says, "So, Jamie's like your perfect partner if you had an arranged marriage?" He scoops up the cut-up celery and adds it to the pot.

My eyes tear—from the onion. "Well, he would be, wouldn't he? Our parents would have totally set us up. They often joked about it. And I mean, similar life experiences growing up." I wipe my eyes with my sleeve. I can share what I really think with Rory. "I just think the magic is overrated. The magic disappears in the mundane."

"It's not overrated. It's the whole thing. You need the magic to survive the mundane," Rory says.

"I saw it with my parents," I say. "I mean, why do you think they arranged a second honeymoon? They were trying to get the magic back."

Next to us, a couple is squabbling in whispers about how to cut the onion. The wife says, "I just think you should dice it in smaller pieces."

"Okay, then you cut it," the husband says, thrusting the cutting board toward her.

The chef compliments us on our teamwork. He then explains how to make the tomato sauce, the guacamole, and the queso. Together, we cut up the tomatoes and the peppers. The oil sizzles in the pan.

"The magic is like the heat applied to this dish. It makes everything come together," Rory says. "You need that heat and that sizzle to get through it all."

"That sizzle needs the heat, which you can't maintain when you're tired because you've been up all night with the kids. Why do you think Olivia keeps scheduling date nights?" I roll my neck. It's stiff from staring at the computer screen all day.

Rory adds the tomatoes to the pan. Small pops sound as the tomato juices meet the oil. A yummy smell fills the air. "I think you can keep up the heat. It just takes some effort. My dad always counsels patients to make the effort to keep the romance alive."

He kneads my neck. I feel like the tomato, which is currently melting in the pan. This is dangerous territory because I'm supposed to be an immutable-iceberg-friend, not a puddle of conflicting feelings. I focus on grating cheese for the queso.

I say, "Well, as long as you recognize some work is required. If you only expect magic, then your higher expectations are going to be disappointed when you're arguing over making the bed."

"What's your position on making the bed?"

"I don't feel strongly either way."

"Same." He smiles. "We won't fight over that."

I roll my eyes.

He removes the chicken from the pot and puts it out to cool. Next up is shredding the chicken to add to the sauce, and then we're going to make the tacos. I quickly make the guac while he shreds the chicken. The chef is setting up a station in the corner with boiling oil to deep-fry the puffed tacos. We finish our dough balls, but other couples have queued up. As we wait, my phone beeps.

"I bet it's Zelda," I say. "She's going out to a party tonight, and she wants me to provide feedback." I hand Rory the plate of dough balls.

Zelda: *Status report!*

Me: *Wearing HUMONGOUS apron and chef hat. Doing couples cooking course.*

Zelda: *You've still got legs. Think Claudette Colbert in* It Happened One Night *or Irene Dunne in* The Awful Truth *when her skirt rides up and she catches Cary Grant looking. Show some leg.*

Zelda and I have spent many a happy Sunday watching romantic comedies. I text back a dancing flamenco girl emoji.

"What'd she ask?" Rory is leaning against the white-tiled wall. We're next in line.

"Whether I've seen the movies *It Happened One Night* and *The Awful Truth.*"

He looks perplexed. "Is she having a movie night instead?"

"Movie reference questions."

He nods. We bring over our dough balls to drop them into the oil. The chef is standing by, supervising. The heat radiates off the professional, stainless-steel range.

"Looks like something we shouldn't try at home," I say.

"Not until I replenish my fire extinguisher anyway."

I laugh. "At least at this point, we'd have some food to serve the firemen when they show up."

We drop the dough balls into the oil, listening carefully to the chef's instructions. I breathe in that smell of corn oil frying. The oil crackles, and our doughballs transform into puffed tacos—like a magic trick.

The waitstaff clear away the cooking gear and set the long table for four couples. We scoop out our puffed tacos when they're done and wait by the wall until there's a place set for us. Across the partition, cooks are yelling that orders are ready, and waitstaff keep coming in and out of the swinging door. The food smells delicious.

We set our plates down next to a new couple, away from the fighting couple. They're older—in their fifties. We hang up our aprons and chef hats on the hooks on the side wall. I sit on the stool at the table, and my dress slides up. Rory's gaze lowers to my leg.

I can't believe it. Zelda is right. I'm channeling the power of Claudette Colbert as she lifts her skirt to hitch a ride in *It Happened One Night*. A spark is there to kindle. I swing my foot and let my heel dangle. My stomach flutters, but I focus on compiling my taco, not daring to meet Rory's gaze if he looks up.

The new couple asks us if we just started dating. I say yes. Rory gives me a smug "see, people believe we're dating" look.

"How could you tell we just started dating?" I ask. I'll add this type of detail to my novel.

"It's the way you two look at each other."

I change the subject quickly. "So how do you keep the magic alive in your relationship?"

"Oh, we do something like this once a week. Or at least, we try."

Olivia needs to up her game. The conversation turns to general topics. Rory periodically touches me as he leans across to take more dip or fillings or when he picks up my dropped napkin. I wonder if he's doing this on purpose or if that's just what he's used to doing with a girlfriend. We've never been so touchy before—other than at our bizarre brunch yesterday, which was a crazy touchfest. Or else my awareness of his touch has just gone into hyperdrive.

The couple next to us is getting drunk on the wine, and they're really being touchy-feely. They could give Willow a run for her money. The wife is now feeding the husband a taco.

I look at Rory.

"We should try that when we next eat with Willow and Jamie," I say.

He laughs. "Are we meeting them again?"

"If Jamie would agree to it. For research purposes, given that my book is about fake dating in front of exes."

"That brunch didn't give you enough material?" he asks.

"Yeah, I don't think we need to see them again."

The dinner is delicious. We all thank the chefs and leave.

"I really enjoyed that." His hands are in his pockets as we walk along the street. "It's too nice a night to end. Nightcap back at my place?"

A nightcap. Interesting choice of words. In college, a nightcap was code for "let's fool around." But Rory and I often end up back at his place just to hang out, chatting.

"Sure, we still need to discuss how we met."

He takes my hand as we walk up the stairs. Butterflies are cavorting in my stomach. I don't know why I'm so nervous. There's no smell of smoke when we open the door.

He turns on the warm, white light in the corner of his living room as we enter his apartment. It's cold. He closes the windows. I take off my jacket, putting it on the back of a dining room chair, but leave my hat on. I stand there, uncertain for a moment. As he closes the shades, the room feels more intimate, smaller. His wavy hair is a bit disheveled. *I want to dishevel it more.*

My phone rings.

I answer the phone. "Jamie, what's up?"

"Mom had a heart attack," he says.

I stop breathing. "What? When? Where is she?"

"She's at Weill Cornell. She was closing up the store and didn't feel well, so she got herself in a cab and directed it to the hospital. She called me on the way."

Tears well up. I couldn't take it if Jamie's mom died, too. She's like a second mom to me. "Is she okay? Can I come see her?" I sink into the couch.

Rory is looking at me, concerned. I whisper that Theresa had a heart attack. He comes over, sits next to me, and puts his arm around me.

"She's sleeping now. She wanted me to tell you that she's okay." Jamie's voice catches. "She's a strong character, and she's going to be fine. The doctors said that, too. But she needs to take it easy. They're just keeping her here for observation. We can visit her together tomorrow morning."

"Okay." I take a deep breath. I don't think I will ever get over losing someone I love. It's like a cut with a scab, and the scab can easily be pulled away, the pain felt anew, only slightly dulled.

"Can I come over?" Jamie asks. "I'm on my way back to the apartment, but Willow is there, and I need to talk to someone who knows my mom." My apartment is near Theresa's on the Upper West Side.

"I'm at Rory's, but I can meet you back there."

I hang up the phone. I explain to Rory what happened. I blink back tears. *Don't cry. Don't scare him.* I stare down at the floor and will myself not to think of her dying. *Think of something positive.* I think of those two birds that often alight on my balcony while I'm making minis at my desk in the living room, fluffing out their feathers. Brown doves. *If I cry in front of Rory, I might lose him.* That's what happened with my college boyfriend Michael. My parents died and I couldn't stop crying, huge, wrenching sobs. He couldn't handle it. I can still see him looking away. Backing away. The two birds seem very devoted to each other. First one lands on the balustrade and then the other. I picture them and take deep, calming breaths. He didn't break up with me immediately. Or directly. That would have looked bad. Instead, he just disappeared. Came over less. Was busy. Out with the boys. Until I seemed emotionally ready to handle our publicly breaking up.

Rory pulls me into his arms. “Are you okay?”

His arms around me feel warm, soothing. “Yes.”

“She’ll be okay.”

My legs feel weak. “Yes.” I nod, still staring at the floor, all light, whitewashed wood, the grain peeking through. I need to look up, show him I’m okay.

“Do you want me to come with you?”

I shake my head. “It’s probably better if it’s just me. If he wants to come over to my place and not go straight home to Willow.”

“He doesn’t want to go home to Willow?”

“I don’t know. He said he wants to talk to someone who knows his mom.” I sniffle. I need to pull myself together.

“Theresa’s going to pull through,” he says.

I gaze up into his eyes and nod.

“I’ll come with you in the cab and then come back home. Just so you’re not alone.”

I nod again and pull on my coat.

The taxicab ride is silent. I am afraid that if I talk, I will cry. I rest my head against his shoulder, and he holds my hand. It is solid and comforting around mine. We arrive at my brownstone apartment building. I get out of the cab. I turn to say that I really did have a good time, but the cab has already pulled away.

Chapter Seven

JAMIE IS STANDING IN our vestibule, staring at his phone. He looks pale in the yellow, fluorescent lighting. I pause outside to warn Zelda.

Me: *Bringing Jamie up.*

Zelda: *Jamie? Still at party. BUT date with RORY?*

Zelda: *Don't tell me you're mixing them up.*

Zelda: *You and RORY should come to this party. It's LIT. Dancing. Thinking "You and Me" time.*

Zelda: *Miranda brought Max. He's so funny.*

I love Zelda. I decide not to explain because I don't want to bring down her buzz.

Me: *Enjoy!*

I look back at Jamie and my smile fades. I join him. He hugs me. We cling to each other for a moment. I have to be strong for him like he was for me when my parents died. We walk up the stairs to my apartment on the third floor.

I open the door, and the two dogs bark. Gilda keeps barking at Jamie, so I pick her up and try to calm her down. Benson sniffs Jamie and then retreats back to his dog bed.

Jamie takes off his coat and hangs it over a chair. He doesn't sit, though, pacing instead. He isn't one for sitting still for long. I was the one who'd sit for hours with our moms when we were kids, crafting little dollhouse items.

"She's going to be all right. That call . . . thankfully I was in New York and not in Singapore." He rubs his forehead. "Are both of these dogs guests?"

"Both guests. Benson and Gilda. This month, they're paying more of the rent than I am. Benson's dad has a consulting gig in Ohio for the month. And Gilda's mom is shooting a commercial in LA." I keep talking nervously. "It's lucky Theresa thought to go to the hospital."

"She just read some article about women's heart attack symptoms, and so she got worried when she started having similar symptoms. She needs to take a rest. She wants me to take over Theresa's Sports Store, just for a bit."

I almost laugh. *Jamie? Taking over the sports shop? Mr. Jet-setting-around-the-world in that neighborhood shop?*

"Just for a little while until she can get back on her feet and find someone or sell it," he says.

"Oh no, not sell it!"

"If I don't want it. Or if you don't want it." Jamie fidgets.

"Me?"

"She suggested I reach out to you. You've helped with the store. You built that dollhouse gym for the window. And she said that you've been learning marketing with your dollhouse business. Are you and Rory whispering marketing tips across the pillow?"

"Very funny. He does give me a lot of tips. Not while in bed, though." I smirk. "But marketing is all about creating that emotional connection."

"And you've got that."

I frown at Jamie.

Jamie shrugs. "Couldn't resist. But you are a bit like an old married couple."

I don't think I'll share that feedback with Rory. I can't take any more physical contact than our last brunch. "Except without the digs."

Jamie's gaze is thoughtful and assessing. "You're so contradictory sometimes. I don't understand you. Just because my parents divorced and yours almost divorced doesn't mean marriage is doomed."

Apparently, it's everyone-pile-on-Penelope night about her romantic love cynicism.

"I don't think marriage is doomed," I say. "I just think it's complicated." That if the expectations are too high, it might not live up to them. Or I could lose myself trying. I don't want to lose myself—or my creative drive—in a relationship. I don't think Jamie would understand. Even if I saw it with his mom and how she had so much time to explore everything she wanted after the divorce. Not immediately, of course. At first, she was devastated. Jamie can't see it because his loyalty has always been divided between his two parents.

Jamie gazes at me, as if considering this, and then turns away, surveying the apartment. I look at it through his eyes. We have a two-bedroom, duplex, brownstone apartment facing the backyard. A duplex sounds fancier than it is, but it does have ten-foot ceilings. Zelda and I both think our living room/dining room gives off a happy vibe, with our blue couch and pops of brightly colored pillows. Olivia said the pillows looked like we'd thrown a bag of M&Ms on top of our couch. We took that as a compliment. I've managed not to spread out from my craft desk in the corner to the oak dining table or the coffee table in front of the couch, so it all looks tidy. And Zelda's desk is immaculate, as always.

Our bedrooms are in the nine-by-ten extension. A spiral staircase in the southern corner leads to Zelda's bedroom below mine. We joke to guests that the spiral staircase leads to another floor with a gym and a ping-pong table—like that New York dream where you open the closet doors and find you have another room.

"Are you making these?" Jamie asks, picking up the miniature French bread on my crafting desk. "These are really good. They look real."

"Thanks." Saying a miniature looks real is the highest compliment you can pay a miniaturist.

"And this dollhouse is great here in the living room." My white, Malibu, modern dollhouse, which luckily gives the impression of being a piece of décor, sits on one shelf in the wall unit. He opens its front doors. "Is this your only dollhouse?"

Um, no. Theresa has her own dollhouse, so Jamie is familiar with adults owning dollhouses. Theresa is more disciplined than me, with only one. But Theresa has a friend with a roomful of dollhouses and room boxes. Most of her room boxes are period living rooms or kitchens, like a one-inch-scale replica of Julia Child's kitchen. Luckily, her husband has his own train room. Their kids moved out, and the hobbies took over.

"No, I have one in my room and a few room boxes." But the room boxes are hidden in my closet. I pared down my wardrobe to add space for them. I don't want to reveal my obsession to everyone who comes over.

"Is there a couple having sex in this bed?" Jamie asks.

Oh no, I hope it's not my Jamie/Penelope couple.

"That's Zelda. She likes to tease me by putting the dolls in all sorts of compromising positions." I look over Jamie's shoulder to see who is cavorting and breathe a sigh of relief. The dark, curly-haired female is with the dark-haired guy in the upstairs bedroom.

"And this Jon Snow doll is cooking in the kitchen."

Definitely Zelda's machinations.

"Wouldn't you want Jon Snow cooking for you in the kitchen?" I ask. *Especially if it leads to cooking in the bedroom?* "But he should have taken off his cape first. Bit of a fire hazard."

Jamie laughs. "Maybe Dany." His glance meets mine. It reminds me of when we used to play with his Lego figures in his mom's dollhouse. "Theresa thought you could help out with the shop while she's in the hospital and during her recuperation. Give you a bit of an income. And maybe you'll like it. She thought maybe you could do the window displays."

"What will you be doing? Jetting back to Singapore to complete a big deal?" I ask.

"No. Obviously, I'm coming back if Mom's sick."

"You're getting transferred to New York?"

"No, I'm quitting. But I work for a British company. It's not like an American company where you can quit and leave the next day. I have to give four weeks' notice; Kareem can take over and work more shifts until I'm back." Kareem is his mom's most senior store employee.

"But your job?"

"I can always get another job. I can't get another mom." He pauses—that awkward pause when people remember that both my parents are dead. "I didn't mean it like that."

To ease the awkwardness, I say, "You're right, you can't, as I know. But I did come pretty close with your mom." I couldn't ever repay her. This is a small way to do it, and it isn't like my writing career is sky-rocketing right now. And it isn't going to unless I actually write words on the page—butt in the chair. "I don't know that much about marketing. I'm still writing my book, not yet marketing it." I pause. "But I can do the window displays." *I can't say no.*

"Thank you." His voice is deep and sincere. He sits on the armrest of our couch and pets Benson.

"What about Willow?"

"Well, obviously, we'll break up. I don't do long distance. Her career's doing well there, too," he says. "And it's not like she particularly liked New York."

"But I do think she particularly likes you."

"Yes, well, I like her, too." Jamie glances away.

I study one of Zelda's photographs on the wall, from when she took a photography course in college. It's a picture of a couple kissing outside a bar in the rain. *Wrong photo to look at.* This is the first time we've been alone since I told him I was in love with him last year. My chest tightens. For the rest of that visit, Jamie made sure we were chaperoned anytime we were together. I joked to Zelda that I felt like we were a Regency couple who had to be accompanied at all times. And it wasn't as if I had physically thrown myself at him.

We'd been sitting out in lounge chairs, drinking wine on the rooftop deck of his mom's apartment building. It was this comfortably warm September evening, the night air caressing my skin, and we were reminiscing about old times. A full moon shone above, bathing our chairs in a warm light, reflecting on our wine glasses on the table between us. And it seemed like the perfect moment to say, "I love you, Jamie." I cringe now, thinking about it. I wish I hadn't said it. I wish I hadn't used those exact words. He stilled. An excruciating, long pause followed, and he said, "I don't feel the same way." I nodded. I didn't press the point. I didn't throw myself at him in the lounge chair. I stood, picked up my wine glass, and said, "I'll go see if your mom needs any help with the cleanup from the party." And I had pulled myself together on the elevator ride back down to his mom's apartment. No tears.

Jamie walks to the window and looks out. His back is to me. "It's time for me to come back to New York. Maybe Willow will consider coming back in a year. She could certainly get a job in hospitality here."

Unless she tells people it's dirty. I shouldn't be so catty, even in my thoughts.

"We'll put you on the payroll," he says.

"That seems like a lot of effort." That sounds permanent, too.

"No, she wants you on the payroll. She worries about you, too."

I huff, annoyed. "She doesn't have to. I know what I'm doing. And I'm very careful with my money." Except for some extravagant miniature purchases and the fact that I've never seen a writing course that I didn't think I should take.

Jamie sits on the couch. I stay seated at the table. I don't want to disturb his newfound comfort in being alone with me by joining him there.

"I think this will make her feel better." He looks at me. "I'm telling you, she's stressing out about the store." He runs his hands through his hair. "I don't understand. I mean, she takes care of herself. She works out."

He looks pale, less sure of himself.

"But the doctor said she's going to pull through, right?"

"Yes." He stands. I stand, too, but stay by the table. "Anyway, thanks for letting me come over. Thanks for helping out with the store. I should get home to Willow. I'll pick you up at eight tomorrow morning to go to the hospital."

"Yes. She'll be okay, Jamie," I say, hugging him chastely. "She's a knock-'em-down, get-back-up type for sure and—"

He cuts me off. "I know she'll be fine." His façade is back up, and I don't dare cross behind it. "She will."

I nod and walk him out. Hugging myself, I climb back up the stairs and let myself into our empty-feeling apartment.

I don't have time to work on windows for the store. I've got to revise the first book to add more backstory, send it to the developmental editor, and finish my second book. My chest tightens. I have to create a website. And I've signed up for two writing courses. Plus, I was hoping to build up my mini business and make more stock to sell. My head feels heavy in my hands. My fingers rub my forehead in circular motions.

I pull out my planner from my desk drawer. My gaze catches on my framed first rejection. Next to it is the picture of my mom with Theresa when they were young. When Jamie and I were just babies. They have their arms around each other and huge smiles. Best friends. My mom's smile is so open. Both my parents were open books—or maybe blunt is a better term. I think it was their Dutch background. Olivia inherited that, but somehow it had the opposite effect on me. I closed up. I hated my life being dissected in public. But I still was more open than many—until it cost me Michael and demanded too much emotionally from me.

My mom is glowing with that vitality she had. The tears I've been holding back pour out of me.

Chapter Eight

I LOVE READING HOSPITAL dramas, but I don't want to be in one. Jamie, Willow, and I walk down the sterile, green hall. A nurse pushing an IV bag on a metal roller enters the room in front of us. Jamie and Willow are holding hands. I'm nervous about seeing Theresa weak and not herself. *Game face on.*

Theresa's hospital room smells like Vick's VapoRub. She is sitting up in a narrow bed. The curtains are pulled back, and Theresa is chatting with her roommate. She looks good—a little frail, but cheerful. I breathe a sigh of relief. Jamie's glance meets mine, and he smiles at me as if he can feel the tension leaving my body. He hugs his mom.

Theresa introduces us to her roommate. I give Theresa a hug, a bit gingerly with all the wires attached to her. She hugs me back. I should be conveying strength to her, and instead I'm drawing sustenance from her.

My eyes tear. Apparently, I didn't exhaust all my crying last night.

"Don't cry," she says.

"I can't help it." I wipe away the tears with my sleeve. I can't seem to stop. I gaze at the picture of the sailboat on the wall and focus on happy days sailing.

"Why are you crying? You didn't even cry like this when your parents died. I'm going to be fine," Theresa says. I hug her.

I did cry back then. Huge, wrenching sobs alone in my bed at night. I just didn't do it in front of them.

"I'm just going to check with the doctor about how you're doing," Jamie says. He and Willow leave the room, and Theresa clutches my hand.

"What am I going to tell Jamie? The store isn't doing well," she says.

"I thought things were going okay?" I ask in surprise.

"No, I just can't compete with online shopping and rent going up. Maybe if we did more marketing outreach."

"I'll try to see what I can do with my Instagram marketing and dressing the windows, but I don't have much experience."

"Maybe if Jamie takes it over, it will do better," she says. "Are you sure you don't want to take it over? You're almost up with your two years."

"But maybe two years wasn't enough time," I say.

"Two years is a long time. You should get a paying job. I'm worried about you. You need to have a paying job to support yourself. Then you can do whatever you want on the side. But don't do what I did and not have a job outside, thinking my marriage was going to last, and then be at a loss when it all falls apart."

I'm not even relying on getting married. I wish Theresa understood. She should be my ally, having started her own business.

I say, "You weren't at a complete loss. You opened up the store, and it's done well for many years." It took Theresa time to find the products that would sell in the store's neighborhood. And every time she doubted herself, my mom, Olivia, and I said, *You can do it.*

"It's not that I want you to give up your dream, but be realistic. Get a nine-to-five job and then write at night."

The machine is beeping.

I school my face to look like I agree.

Jamie, Willow, and a nurse rush in. I stand back as the nurse adjusts something and tells Theresa all is okay.

Jamie and Willow take up seats by her bed while I stand in the back. Willow is rubbing Jamie's back as she chats to Theresa. It's not me who needs to be strong for Jamie.

The nurse tells us Theresa should rest and we all leave, me trailing Jamie and Willow.

When we get outside, Jamie hails a cab and then turns around, almost as an afterthought, and asks if they can drop me off. But I'm going Uptown and they're going Downtown. I say thanks, but no.

I bicycle up First Avenue to Theresa's store to update the display windows. I feel guilty that here she is, ill, and she's worrying about my lack of income. My bike wheels splash through the puddles, spraying water. The wind whistles through streets as soon as the shelter of the buildings disappears. It's dark and gray, and not many people are out. The rain pelts my face. I keep pushing my hood up to see the winding road ahead and then pulling it down to protect my face. The truth is, things aren't in great shape. My Etsy store isn't doing that well. The agent rejections keep coming. And my current career choice is apparently creating stress not only for me but also for my substitute mom. And Jamie—I'm not sure if we can restore our former closeness. There was a moment, when we were in my apartment, but it was based on our shared childhood. The wind is against me. I peddle harder.

I should have created a fake job, not a fake boyfriend. I should think more seriously about an alternate career, one that would make Theresa worry less for me. But an alternate career just makes me feel like one of those dark clouds above. My mix of jobs works for me—making minis and miniature scenes feeds the creativity in my writing. They may all end up making money. Like those stones in The Met exhibit, these things take time.

Even though it's mid-September, I still go with a "back to school" theme for the store windows. One mannequin is bench-pressing various books that we sell—workout books, biking books, bike trails in NYC—and another is running with a backpack overloaded with books. The mannequin's running clothes, in sunshine yellow and gray, along with the pops of colors on the book covers, give an inviting impression.

As I am putting the window together, Kareem fits a customer for sneakers. Kareem is a runner and even coaches a high school team. He's getting a master's degree and working here in the meantime. Kareem asks the customer questions about her running style and looks at her foot arch to find her the best-fitting sneaker. He's really a treasure trove of knowledge. And he's so passionate about running that his enthusiasm just shines through.

She tries on several pairs. Kareem suggests she take a walk around the store in them. She's found a pair she likes, but then she checks her phone. She says she'll think about it and leaves. Kareem looks disappointed.

"I can't believe she didn't buy the pair," I say.

"She might come back, but she might get them cheaper on Amazon," Kareem says. "We're not selling enough. I hope your windows lead to an uptick in business."

No pressure.

"We should do an Instagram video with you demonstrating how you fit a shoe to advertise your expertise."

"That will just get us a whole bunch of people trying on shoes and using Kareem's expertise, but then buying elsewhere," Brian says. Brawny Brian is my least favorite employee. He scoffed openly at my little mini gym.

"At least they'll come into the store," Kareem says.

Brian films us as Kareem fits me for a pair of sneakers. Kareem looks at my flat-footed arch and recommends this brand of sneakers that specializes in this, as well as an extra insert. I try them on, and I feel like I'm walking on air. I bounce all over the store.

"I love them." I buy the sneakers with probably my pay for the day. I'll check later to see if they are cheaper on Amazon.

We play back the video. Brian filmed me bouncing all around the store. Brian and Kareem both laugh when they watch it. I thought he had stopped filming.

"It's good." Brian nods. Kareem nods, too.

I don't trust Brian. Yet it seems joyful to me. I think it has the emotional honesty needed to bring in customers. I send it to Jamie for approval. He approves it, and we post it.

I take pictures of the windows and post them on the store's Instagram account.

And then I bike home.

I set my timer for twenty minutes to write five hundred words. And if I write one thousand words, I can watch fifteen minutes of clips of my favorite scenes in *The Proposal*. And call it research. Even if it does make me feel like I'll never measure up to the brilliance of that banter.

In the next scene in my fake dating novel, they practice like Rory and I have practiced. The heroine, Piper, is an artist, and she and the hero, Rob, decide to practice their fake dating at an art opening.

"Piper!"

That voice haunted my dreams, but it couldn't be. Julian. Julian had crushed my heart when he'd broken up with me and moved to England. Where, after a year, he was now engaged to a Miss Charity Heath—a name seared into my mind in flowery script from the wedding invite I'd received.

I turned. Julian.

He looked the same. My wish of a steady diet of scones and sugared tea fattening him up had definitely not come true. If anything, his European-cut jacket made him look sharper, as if I'd put on my glasses and all the blurred edges had become defined. And I still felt that pang of pain that he hadn't wanted me.

He kissed me on the cheek. "You're looking stunning."

I should have her *not* looking gorgeous to be realistic, but dumped girlfriends should always be looking good when running into exes who still make their blood pound. And she would be dressed up for an art opening.

Then he said, "Let me find Charity. This will be a great opportunity for you two to get to know each other before the wedding."

I didn't want to get to know Charity. I wanted to attend the wedding with my new, amorous "boyfriend," looking like I was completely over him and then only exchange Christmas cards for the next thirty years.

Rob returned and slid his arm around me. "Champagne, Piper?"

"Yes, please, darling." "Darling" was our code word to add extra affection.

Ooh, I should suggest that to Rory. But not "darling."

Rob slid his arm around me and pulled me close. I suddenly felt breathless, but it was the contact with Rob that was making my blood pound, not the conversation with Julian.

I could never let Rory read this.
I might have to write another book for him to view.

CHAPTER NINE

RORY SAID HE'D STOP by after work. He had to work late preparing for the client party on Thursday.

I set up a miniature scene where Piper and Rob have a date cooking in the kitchen of my mini town's restaurant and then post it to my blog. My followers are still excited that Piper may be dating someone after being dumped abruptly by Julian. Not that past posts didn't give signs that it wasn't going to work out with Julian: Julian not supporting her artistic career or Julian flirting with another woman at the gym.

I just wrote the same scene in *Fake Dating Folly*, but now I'm stuck. Rob seems romantically interested, but if he is, he is assured enough to say so. And Piper doesn't trust her gut because she thought Julian was the one, but he definitely wasn't. She can see that in hindsight, but she should have been able to see it at the time. Still, it feels like both Rob and Piper wanted to kiss after the cooking date, and now they're frustrated that I blocked them.

I submit my resume for a position teaching writing at a local high school. That will make Theresa happy. Because of the continuing string of agent rejections, I also send *Midnight Masquerade* to yet another developmental editor, but this one writes mysteries.

I work on some miniatures for my Etsy store.

An email from Maya, my dream agent, pops up. When I pitched *Midnight Masquerade* to her at a writing conference, she asked me why I wrote the book. I talked about my love for comic caper movies. I said I was going for the vibe of *The Thin Man* with *Midnight Masquerade*. She asked for my first thirty pages at the end of my pitch.

To: Penelope

From: Maya

I love the premise and your writing is very strong.

Please send me the full manuscript.

Yes! Finally, a request for a full manuscript.

But I've just sent it to the developmental editor, who is not going to get back to me until the end of the month. And then it will take me some time to do revisions. I could wait, but that might look unprofessional. Ugh. The question of "Is the manuscript ready to send?" and the politics of following up with agents cause me more stress than the actual plotting of a novel.

I had thought it was good enough to send out.

I submit the full manuscript via the portal, and then I return to making miniature roses.

My materials are spread out on the table. All the buds are done, and I'm adding the first row of pink petals to each rose. Each petal has to be shaped on an eraser with a ball-pointed tool. The store Instagram account post is doing well enough so far—about eighty likes.

The doorbell rings. Benson and Gilda bark. I buzz Rory in and wait in the hallway for him to come up the stairs. The top of his head finally appears and then a big smile. I smile back.

"All okay with Theresa?"

"Yes, I think so. If all goes well, she'll be home in a few days." I hold the door open for him to enter our apartment. Gilda and Benson come to greet him. He hangs up his coat and bag on the hooks by our front door.

He pulls out a chair by the table. "The Best You've Ever Had" by Andy Powell is playing.

I clear some of my papers off the table. "Did you eat? I can heat up some lasagna."

"Sure, I was going to order something in. Did you make it?" he asks. Gilda puts her head on his foot. She definitely has a doggy crush on him.

"Stress baking." When I came home for my parents' funeral, everyone made Olivia and me lasagna. We had so much in the freezer. Lasagna is still my go-to comfort food.

"I have so much to tell you," I say. I need to put a positive spin on working for Theresa.

"You seem upbeat."

"You look tired."

Rory smiles. "Way to boost a guy's ego." He rolls his head as if to loosen his muscles. "Tough day at the office, but your lasagna will perk me up." He picks up the Styrofoam block holding mini purple roses. Which are on the table. And shouldn't be. The roses are standing in a row in various stages of completion, with tweezers, an eraser, and glue sitting to the side. "I don't know how you do that detailed work."

"It's soothing." I move my Styrofoam square and tools to my craft desk before Zelda comes home and sees that I've expanded beyond my allotted space—which is already a lot in our apartment. "Do you want a massage?"

That just popped out.

"You're offering lasagna and a massage? What, have I stepped into heaven?" he asks.

"If that's your idea of heaven."

"You're hanging out with the wrong people if it's not."

I have to agree.

"It's been a while since I took that massage course, so I may be rusty, but I'm always looking for willing victims." I leer at him.

"When did you take a massage class? Did I know that?"

"When I was writing that novella with the fireman meet-cute, the protagonist was a masseuse, so I took a class. I'm kind of miffed that's not what Anthony remembered about me."

Rory follows me into the kitchen. I put the lasagna in the oven.

"He wasn't going to ask how the massages are going," he says. "And he definitely remembered you."

My cheeks grow warm. It is true that massages can get pretty intimate. I shouldn't have suggested it, but I don't know what I'm doing anymore. Rory is not for me—I need someone who is more down to earth than all roses and rainbows. I don't know what he's looking for, but none of his other girlfriends have captured whatever it is.

"It's probably easiest on my bed," I say.

We walk toward the back, Benson trailing behind us. My cat, Goldie, is on the corner of the bed.

Rory takes off his shirt. He's lean and muscular. *Okay, not the best idea.*

Depends on what the idea was, my evil inner voice says. I haven't seen Rory without a shirt in a while. And I've never massaged Rory without a shirt. He lies down on my bed. *He's in my bed.* He raises himself on his elbows and looks back at me. The air seems heavier.

I stop, afraid I'll shock myself if I touch him.

In a funny Swedish accent, I ask, "So, vhere do you hurt?"

"Shoulders and lower back." Rory lies down flat.

I get on my knees on the bed, warm up my hands and place them on his back, and rub up and down, feeling first for tight muscles. *Keep it professional. Professional thoughts only. It's just a man's back. The perfect man's back, professionally speaking*. I dig deeper with my hands into his shoulder muscles where they're tight.

Rory groans. "Yes, that feels good."

I feel that groan deep in my stomach.

As I work my way down his back, Goldie gets up, stretches, and comes over to sniff Rory. She massages Rory's arm, purring.

I should be purring, too.

"Oh, a little added Goldie action," Rory says, his face in the pillow.

"No extra charge," I say, almost in a whisper, as if I've lost the ability to speak aloud.

The front door closes.

"Penelope! Something's burning in the kitchen," Zelda shouts.

I turn around and Rory raises his head. "I put the timer on."

Zelda pops her head into the bedroom. "Oh, sorry. Dudes, you got to keep the door closed."

"Not my lasagna." Rory puts his shirt back on and buttons it.

I get out of the bed and run quickly to our kitchenette. It's a small, narrow room off our living room. "It's okay. It's just a little crispy on the edges." I take a minute to catch myself. I feel a little raw around the edges.

It was just a massage.

Rory comes into the kitchen and takes three plates and a pitcher of water. I keep my head down and carry the lasagna back to the table. We both sit at the table, next to each other. I steal a glance at him, and he catches my look. His face is more relaxed already, and his shirt isn't fully buttoned up.

I roll my neck and shoulders, which are stiff from sitting and writing all day.

He smiles, his dimple in his cheek appearing, and then he leans slightly over to knead the back of my neck. I let my head fall forward to give him access.

Zelda sets down a carton of cut-up pineapple and some bowls and joins us at the table. She pours the water while I serve the lasagna to the three of us.

“Hello, you two lovebirds.” Zelda takes a bite of lasagna.

“I told Zelda,” I say to Rory.

“How’s Theresa?” Zelda asks.

“She seems like she’ll make a full recovery,” I say. “But she wants me to create window displays for the store and help with marketing. I agreed to do that.”

“Really? Are you sure that’s a good idea?” Rory asks. “I mean, you’re going to be giving up valuable writing time, and maybe this is all part of Theresa’s plot to get you to take over the store permanently and to give up on writing.”

“I don’t think that’s Theresa’s goal anymore.”

“Yes, it is.” He puts down his fork. “She always asks you if you have a deadline for how long you’re going to try this and whether you’re making enough money with miniatures. I’ve been there when she’s given you the lecture on being realistic about pursuing your dreams.”

“Yes, but now she says the store is in trouble and she can’t compete. This is a last-ditch effort. But she did ask me again if I want to take it over. Mostly she wants me to get a ‘real job’ and write on the side.”

“I just think Jamie should be the one stepping up and giving up his time to help the store,” he says. “Not you.”

Zelda harrumphs in agreement. *Okay, I agree, too. But then, I’m the one who needs the store job as a backup plan. Jamie doesn’t.*

I reach over and squeeze his hand. “I appreciate so much that you believe in me and you don’t think I’m crazy for pursuing this writing career.”

“You’re good. And I’m not even speaking from my admitted bias. Your story in our college literary magazine just blew me away,” he says. “And I’m not the only one who was impressed by that piece.”

“That piece” was about my parents’ death in a plane crash on a wedding anniversary second honeymoon in Peru. But now

I'm not writing about those dark moments. I'm trying to write light comedy, not dwell in the dark.

"Anyway, Jamie is quitting his job and coming home, so he *is* going to take over. So, he's taking the pressure off of me to step up for Theresa," I say.

"Jamie is quitting his job and coming back to New York?" Rory asks sharply.

"So he says. I'll believe it when I see it." I don't tell him that Jamie also said he'd break up with Willow. "I have this great idea for the October window display. I want to create a ghost and skeleton and keep the running mannequin that's already there but add a sign saying, 'Outrun the Halloween ghouls and ghosts.'"

Zelda chuckles and Rory laughs. I love making Rory laugh. Sometimes I feel I write scenes, and I judge whether they are funny or not by whether Rory will laugh. Which is a difficult standard given that I'm writing for women and he's a man—who reads thrillers.

"And then after Halloween, we can create a window display that says, 'Work off those treats,'" I say. "And before Thanksgiving, 'Make space for your turkey dinner.'"

"Those sound great," Zelda says.

"So how are you going to balance it all? Do you think it will take a lot of time? I still find it suspicious." Rory serves himself another piece of lasagna. He can really eat.

"It's good for you to get out. It will give you more fodder for your stories," Zelda says.

That is the benefit of getting out and about, unless there are really no customers in the store, in which case the only new material will be the sportswear. "I'll get paid for it, so I'll cut back on making miniatures at night and write then."

"But you were just gaining momentum with your Etsy store, and you need to keep that going for a steady income," he says.

He's right. But I'm getting discouraged by the rejections, and maybe I can help the store and give back to Theresa. But I can't share my doubts with Rory. He'll be disappointed if he thinks I'm giving up. Not that I am—even if I did just send out my resume for a "more normal" job.

"I just have to be more efficient."

Rory raises an eyebrow at me skeptically.

"And I owe Theresa a lot," I say.

"You don't owe Theresa anything." Zelda shakes her head. "She took you guys in after your parents died because she loves you and she was best friends with your mom. Your mom would've done the same. Theresa is thrilled she has more family—female family. I mean, it's not like Jamie is going to have kids anytime soon, and your sister already has two babies she's 'Grandma' to."

That's true. Sometimes it even makes me feel worse when Olivia's kids call Theresa "Grandma." She's not supposed to be their grandma.

"And I don't understand why Theresa doesn't understand that your miniatures business is like her sports store business, only your store is online," Zelda says.

"That frustrates me, too," I say.

"Maybe you need to show her your sales/expenses statements so she can see that you have your own business, too," Zelda says.

"I'm not making a huge profit," I say. "Although this month has been my best month yet because I sold so many magically pouring pitchers for dollhouse Halloween scenes."

"Just show her this month, then," Zelda says.

She asks if we want to try a new wine she just bought. Rory says that he will just have one glass because of work. Rory washes the dishes while Zelda pours us each a glass. We sit around the table and chat. Then Zelda finishes her wine and says, "See you later. Have fun." And she winks at me, not even hiding it from Rory, who is sitting right next to me.

I smile as Zelda sashays out of the room.

"We need a password for when we should act more affectionate," I say.

"Is there a guide to this?"

"All the fake dating trope romances. No, but seriously, when I was writing today, that's what my characters did."

"What was their password?"

"Darling. But we should think of something more creative. I was just doing a writing sprint, so I should fix it."

Rory studies me. "Carissima," he finally says, looking at me.

My heart melts. Then again, he could say a street name in Italian, and I'd swoon.

"Dearest in Italian," he says. "What would you use in Dutch?"

I think of two, "liefje" or "schatje." "Liefje" means my love. I don't want to use it for fake dating. My dad used to call my mom "liefje." "Schatje" means little treasure. I say, "schatje."

"Those sound good to me. Do we need a word for when not to be affectionate?"

"In English or another language?" I pour us some more water from our Brita pitcher.

He smiles. "I can't think of what that would be in Italian."

"Yes, and someone might understand it. We need an unknowable code word."

"Darling?"

I nod. I push out my chair so I'm facing him.

"Do we need any other code words?" he asks.

"I don't know. I'll have to read up on it."

"Okay, I don't want my client's wife, Myrtle, to sneak up on me from behind, like last time, so once you've met her, if you see her approaching, point your index finger in that direction. Either overtly or more subtly, depending on what seems appropriate." He demonstrates by placing his hand against his cheek with the index finger pointing out.

"That's not subtle," I say.

"Subtlety is not what I am seeking here," Rory says. "This is full-on defense."

"What do you think her endgame is?"

Rory shakes his head. "I don't know, but I don't want my client thinking I'm flirting with his wife."

"We need our dating history down pat, like how we met and how we got together."

His eyes crinkle at the corners. "We met in college when you were holding your own against all those drunk guys and I finally had an excuse to talk to you."

So, he does remember. I was coming home late from the art studio when some drunk guys from a frat party spilled out onto the street in front of me, harassing me. I gave them what-for, and I was handling it, but then Rory appeared and said, "Hey Curls, sorry I missed you at the library. Can I walk you home?" The boys melted back.

I recognized him immediately from my dorm. He had this brown mop of hair, unshaven, square jaw, a ready smile, and the physique of a basketball player. And I had seen him at some of our dorm dance parties. When he and his roommates announced a party, people would start quietly lining up outside their dorm room hours before it even started. I'd never mustered the courage to approach him at one of his packed parties. Our eyes had met once when I'd been cheering him on at a basketball game, but I still didn't think he knew who I was. And as much as I'd fantasized about our midnight walk blossoming into a romance that night, I also knew, deep down, that I wasn't in any emotional shape for a new relationship. I was mired in grief for the loss of my parents, and my free time was spent sleeping. My main memory from that time is my single bed in my darkened dorm room, the afternoon light peeking through closed curtains—interrupted by Zelda making me get up and go out socially.

"And then how did we start dating? But let's not say I was crying over an agent rejection." My agent rejection sob story is a little too close to reality.

"A few weeks ago, I was walking you home after dinner and a movie out. When we got to your door, I just went for it and asked you if I could kiss you."

Our glances meet—and hold. My heart melts just a little bit. Rory's warm, blue-green eyes slayed many a woman in college. I cross my legs. It sounds so simple.

He gives me that half-smile. "Just make sure you stick close tomorrow when Myrtle is around. Maybe we can hold hands or something."

"But isn't this a professional function? Won't handholding be weird?"

"Handholding is not weird. It's a celebratory party, so I think handholding is fine. Do we need to practice?" He holds my hand.

I pull my hand back. "I know how to hold hands."

"But do you?" He gently takes my hand and laces his fingers with mine. With his thumb, he makes circles in my palm. My pulse quickens. Deliciously.

Our hands look good together. Like a partnership. A promise.

CHAPTER TEN

RORY HOLDS MY HAND as we walk into his office party celebrating the new ad accounts that he and Disha landed. He's doing the commercial campaign for the eco-friendly Adventurer car, and she won an ad campaign for premium gas. The two teams are going to work together, so this party is kicking off their collaboration.

The murmur of music and conversation greets us. Fashionably dressed people are chatting in groups, tropical drinks in hand, all part of the adventure theme. I feel like I should have dressed up more. I'm wearing my blue dress again. New clothes are not in the budget.

The playlist is all songs referencing adventure or gas in the lyrics: "Gas, Gas, Gas," "Life's a Gas," "Adventure," "Keep Your Eyes Open," and "Drive All Night." They're still working on licensing the actual music for the ads. I've been to Rory's office before, but never for this type of party or in this spacious room with floor-to-ceiling windows giving views of the Hudson River. The lights of New Jersey glint in the distance. One bar is in the middle of the room, and another bar is against the north wall. Against the east side wall is an elaborate food spread, including iced shrimp and a charcuterie board.

Rory points out the actual physical storyboards for the campaigns on easels in the east corner of the room, the slogans above them on banners hanging from the ceiling.

Rory and I spent one Sunday afternoon in his apartment after a brunch trying to think of ad slogans for this campaign pitch. We put up all sorts of different combinations on his whiteboard: Go on an adventure, be good, hit the road, roll down the windows, seize the day, joie de vivre, all in, live your life, broaden your horizons, grow your world, road less traveled, make lifetime memories. Anything we could think of that was related to cars, travel, adventures, and being good for the environment. The process was similar to the way we brainstormed the title for *Midnight Masquerade*.

Rory thought of "All in, all good." I like it. Catchy. Even if maybe it's the opposite of my life slogan. That would be more like "Not in, all difficult." These thoughts are not particularly helpful. I need to convey confidence. For this party, I need to be "all in."

Rory drops my hand to greet his boss and introduce me.

My hands are sweaty. I resist wiping them on my blue dress. I've been giving myself pep talks. *I am a possessive girlfriend. Let no woman or man touch MY man.* No fading into the background like a good wingman when someone flirts with Rory. Now I am under strict instructions not to leave his side. I feel a desperate need to go to the bathroom.

We part from his boss, and Rory pulls me over to see the final storyboards on the easels.

It's cool to see the actual drawings in physical form. The first storyboard shows the "meet-cute" when the guy mistakes her Adventurer car for his because it's the same color. She says, "You have good taste in cars" and drives off. In the next storyboard, the guy observes her with a James Bond-type guy in a car that looks like an Aston Martin. Cue comparative advertising soft sell. Or so Rory tells me. Car makes are not my forte as a New Yorker. But show me an IND subway car vs an IRT subway car and I will tell you which one is which.

In the next storyboard, she is walking home in the rain, and the guy gives her a lift. In the following scene, he is lost and refusing to ask for directions. She stops because he has an Adventurer car and figures out how to get to his destination. The original thought was she gives his car a jump-start. (Rory wanted to play with "jump-start"—jump-start a relationship or an adventure, "jump-start your life.") But Adventurer didn't want to imply that their car might need to be jump-started, so Rory came up with this idea. And then the final scene where they go off for a road trip a la *Bridget Jones*. And yes, I repeatedly made Rory watch that *Bridget Jones* scene where she arrives at the hotel with her frizzed-out hair. A classic.

The food spread looks amazing. I suggest we go eat before we have to hold hands. I pile up strawberries, cheese, and crackers on plates as Rory and his colleagues discuss office gossip. I hand Rory a plate of his favorite food.

"Ah, Rory," a gravelly voice says from behind us. Rory grabs my hand, so this must be his client with the overly friendly wife. We turn. Now we're holding hands, but our other hand holds a plate of food, so we can't eat our food without letting go of each other.

The man is smiling broadly at us, but that doesn't seem like his usual expression. The wife is very muscular, thin, tight face, high cheekbones, very attractive, but she doesn't look like she laughs a lot. Her sleeveless dress shows off enviable arm muscles. She looks pointedly at our clasped hands and frowns.

"I love the new campaign," she says. "And who's this?"

"Penelope, my girlfriend." Rory sounds proud. "This is Bernie and Myrtle."

"Nice to meet you." I put my plate on a nearby high, round table and hold out my hand to shake. This is his career, so I don't want to mess that up.

"I didn't realize you were dating anyone," Myrtle says. She squeezes my hand. She has scary, long, red fingernails. I have no fingernails because I bite them, especially when I am writing a particularly tricky scene.

Bernie also has a practiced power grip handshake.

"We just started dating, but we've been friends forever." Rory looks at me like he's devoted. I try to give him the same moony look back, but then I stop because I don't think I can do that convincingly. Who knew that Rory was such an actor? I've never even seen him look at his girlfriends with that type of look.

"Ah, true love, Myrtle. Do you remember those early days?" Bernie grabs her hand.

If they had "true love," then they could be the poster couple for my "love doesn't last" campaign.

"How'd you start dating?" Myrtle withdraws her hand to take an appetizer off a tray being circulated by the waitstaff.

"I asked her if I could kiss her." Rory pulls me closer, and I lean into him.

"As I recall, I kissed you first." I wink at Rory. I can't help revising our agreed story.

"But you missed. And hit my cheek."

"Because you moved your head. And then I thought you didn't want to be kissed," I say.

"But, when I realized, I asked her if I could kiss her. And she said yes."

Our glances meet. *If only the story was true.*

Myrtle's lips are pursed. It looks like she believes us.

"Should we get drinks?" she asks.

If we get drinks, we can't hold hands.

Rory says yes. We walk over to the bar with them. Rory puts down his plate of food. Rory's boss comes over and pulls Bernie aside. Rory joins them, releasing my hand, but gives me a "look" as he does. But a look meaning what? We should've developed a more expansive non-verbal code, like I have with my girlfriends when we go out dancing. Pulling on your earlobe means "not interested." Twirling hair means "interested." We need a code for "stay near me."

There's a commotion over by the storyboards in the center of the room, but I can't see what's happening. I'm left with Myrtle, by the bar, as the men retreat to a corner table. She examines me up and down.

"And you and Rory were friends before?" Myrtle removes the umbrella from her cocktail and puts it on the tray of a passing server.

"Yes, since college."

"And no sparks back then?" Myrtle is like a dog with a bone.

"Well, there were sparks on my side. How could there not be?" "Adventure of a Lifetime" by Coldplay is playing. I can't help but sway to the rhythm of it.

"Indeed." She gazes appreciatively at Rory.

The discussion among the men looks intense. Rory's brow is furrowed, but he's nodding.

"What do you do?" Myrtle takes a sip of her cocktail.

"I'm a writer. What do you do?" We move away from the center bar to the corner of the room near Rory and Bernie. Some younger employees are laughing in a circle next to us.

"What do you write?" she asks.

"Romantic comedy."

She looks surprised. A passing waiter offers us Thai chicken skewers. I take one.

Bernie comes up. She says, "Penelope writes romance."

Bernie says, "Myrtle has read me some of those sex scenes. Hubba-hubba."

Lovely.

"What do you do?" I ask.

"I'm a yoga teacher now."

That explains her sinewy body.

"I really should do more yoga," I say. She agrees and raves for several minutes about all the benefits of yoga. Then she suggests that Rory and I come for a couples' yoga session. She just convinced her husband to try it, and it has strengthened their relationship. I don't want to alienate her, but I really don't want to do a couples' yoga session with her supervising. Or even a singles' yoga session under her direction.

Rory joins us.

She hooks her arm into Rory's, saying, "I'm trying to persuade Penelope here that you guys should come do a couples' yoga session with me."

I've been outmaneuvered. Rory looks at me. *That look I understand. Channel Willow.*

I try to unbutton his sleeve so I can stick my hand up his sleeve, but the button refuses to come undone. Also, she's still got his other arm. I am just inexplicably messing around with his shirt sleeve. Or we're having a tug of war over him. *Go "all in."*

I hug him tightly. Which is awkward because she's holding his arm. It also feels very public. I say, "I'm all in for couples' yoga. Is there a hugging pose?"

"No." Myrtle purses her lips and pulls her arm away from Rory. "But you do lean on each other."

"Sounds intriguing." Rory hugs me back. "Maybe we should try it in the privacy of our own home." He winks at me. "At least initially anyway. Especially if you're going to be wearing a yoga leotard."

Myrtle excuses herself to refresh her drink.

I can't imagine wearing a yoga leotard.

"The question is, what are you going to be wearing?" I ask.

Rory whispers in my ear, "A suit of armor, especially if Myrtle is supervising." We separate. A waiter offers us s'mores. We each take one. I manage to eat mine without dropping any on my dress.

Rory's boss and Bernie return with drinks to discuss the logistics of shooting the campaign in the UK. I try to look gripped by the discussion of permits, but I can't help looking over at the party scene. I frown. The ad boards have been moved.

Oh no. The "All In, All Good" slogan is hanging above a board for the petroleum gasoline, which has a picture of the gasoline nozzle stuck into a car. It looks like an ad placement fail. That gives the "all in" a sexual connotation that I hadn't thought of before. I need to move that easel.

Rory is still talking with Bernie. Bernie has his back to the storyboards. Now that I see it, I can't unsee it. I say to Rory, "Darling, I have to fix something."

Rory looks confused.

I widen my eyes to signify "crisis." "I'll be a minute."

I walk away, but then glance back. Rory has a puzzled expression on his face. I use our hand signal to point toward the sign. He shakes his head. He doesn't see it. Bernie starts to turn around. I come back and gently place my hand on Bernie's elbow to steer his vision away from the offending sight. Rory is still looking at the ad boards. He blanches. He talks earnestly to Bernie about the location scout results.

I rush over to the easel, pick it up, and move it closer to the rest of Disha's campaign boards. Disha comes over.

"What are you doing?" Disha asks.

"Someone moved this away from the rest of your campaign."

Disha shakes her head. "I told the waitstaff that these had to be together. They said something about the fire code, but my client interrupted me. Thanks for putting it back." She flags down the head waiter and asks what the issue is. I help her set it up so it's not blocking an emergency exit.

Rory comes over and puts his arm around me. "Thanks, Curls." He frowns. "I need to change that slogan. Back to the drawing board. That's not good. But I have to raise that sexual connotation to my boss." He wrinkles his brow.

At that moment, Rory's boss walks over and congratulates him on the campaign. Rory looks nervous and asks if they can speak in private. They go off to the side. His boss nods, says something, Rory bites his lip. Rory is talking, and the boss looks concerned. I probably look like some crazy, possessive girlfriend staring at them from the corner of the room, nursing my drink with its pink flamingo topper.

They approach Bernie. Rory smiles at me. It seems to be going okay.

Rory comes back to me. Apparently, the British office also commented that "All in" could mean "knackered," so they'll work up some new ad slogans. They still like the campaign itself. Bernie, however, doesn't mind the sexual connotation of "All In, All Good."

Rory is so relieved. "Freaking roller coaster of a night."

I suddenly put my finger to my face to point out that Myrtle is approaching. I nearly poke out my own eye.

Rory stills. "Behind me?"

"Yes, about twenty seconds to touchdown."

"Hopefully not literally." Rory turns and puts his arm around me. He whispers, "Carissima, put your arm around me, and your hand needs to be playing defense."

I put my arm around Rory and slide my hand into his rear pants pocket. Maybe that's too constrained. Then it's not free to swat any other hand away. Maybe my hand should be playing defense like a windshield wiper. I slide my hand across Rory's butt.

Rory jerks his head in my direction. "What are you doing?"

"Windshield wiper defense?"

Rory snorts. "Let's stick to in-the-pocket defense for now."

Bernie joins us and says, "I still like 'All in, all good.'"

"It's always good to explore other options," Myrtle says. "Although what I really love is the ad story. Was it your idea, Penelope?"

"No, definitely not," I say.

"Just her influence," Rory says. He did share his ideas for the campaign with me. Since he'd given it a romcom flavor, he wanted my "expert" opinion.

The lights dim for a few speeches. Rory gives a short one, and I feel like he's looking at me for encouragement. He does well.

As people are gathering coats to leave, Disha comes over to invite us out dancing to celebrate with other colleagues. We pile into cabs and head Downtown to Lola's Bar. It's a casual place with a long, wooden, old-school-style bar and tables upstairs. A flight of carpeted stairs leads to a dance room in the basement, complete with a disco ball. We order drinks at the bar and take them downstairs.

The DJ is in a booth in the corner, and red, velvet banquettes line the walls with little, round tables in front of them. The club is packed with people who just want to dance and have a good time. The music ranges from the seventies to now.

At first, we're dancing with his colleagues, but then we separate off. It's just the two of us in our own groove, copying each other's moves, finding our rhythm together, the music pulsating. His glance holds mine as I shimmy close to him, teasing. I step back. He follows. My shoulder tilts forward, holds it for the beat as his leans back, as if we are connected by a tight string.

A slow song comes on, and he pulls me close. My head rests against his chest, and I feel so protected in his arms.

The song ends.

"Break?" he asks in my ear. I nod.

He sits down at a banquette and pulls me onto his lap where I fit well. His arms enfold me, and I lean against his chest. Rory whispers to me, "Curls, you know you're my girl, right?"

I look up. He lowers his head. His lips are inches from mine.

My heart skitters. And I panic. I'm afraid. I'm afraid to jump into this with Rory. I duck my head. I nuzzle into his neck and don't respond. Or maybe I *mmm*. His arms are around me, stroking my back. Now I know what that romance book was talking about—my whole body is on fire. I keep my head buried into his neck. He smells of laundry and Rory. I don't want it to stop. My heart is pounding, but I also feel a pit in my stomach. I can't lose Rory, too.

Rory's hand stills.

"Are you going to keep hiding in my neck?" he asks. His voice sounds deep, but less tipsy; he doesn't sound angry, though, more amused.

I nod, keeping my head down.

"Why?"

"Shy," I say into his neck.

He nods. He kisses the top of my head. "Shall I put you in a cab to go home?"

I nod. I peek up at him. He smiles at me. "C'mon." I stand, and he takes my hand. We say goodbye to those colleagues still in the club.

It's brisk outside, and I zipper up my coat. The wind hits my legs, and it's freezing. I should say something. He hails a cab.

Rory looks at my legs as my dress whips around. "You need a longer coat if you're going to keep wearing those short skirts."

Another point for Zelda. He noticed.

He kisses me on the cheek and opens the cab door for me.

As I slide into the cab, I look back. Our glances meet, but there are no answers to be had. Fake dating is a dangerous game. I am so confused. I don't know what I want. I don't want to get hurt again. And I don't want to lose my friendship with Rory like I lost my friendship with Jamie. We're too different to last in a long-term relationship. He's more emotionally open than me. For it to work, I would really have to reveal all my emotions. That's the thing with Rory—he would ask that of me. He wouldn't be content with a façade or keeping it on the surface. Jamie might be, but not Rory.

And why is he suddenly interested in me? When we were with Callie, he didn't want to pretend that I was his girlfriend.

The cab drops me off at my door. I tiptoe into the apartment. Benson shuffles up to sniff me. Zelda is asleep, so I won't get the third degree about our date. And if I told her that I turned Rory down, she'd never understand. I don't even understand. I hope I didn't hurt him. I feel slightly nauseous at that thought.

CHAPTER ELEVEN

I'M WALKING CLEO, A black Lab mix, along Central Park West. Cleo stops short as she spots another dog down the block. She is now lying in wait to meet the other dog; she's low on the ground, alert, tail wagging. She's submissive, as if she's one of those females who needs to be pursued. All demure. *But no.*

"She's going to lunge," I call out to the approaching dog owner, who looks confused.

And indeed, as soon as the other dog nears, Cleo lunges, scaring the hell out of the other dog and its owner. It's not the most successful approach.

As I am trying to hold Cleo back, my phone rings. It's Rory. I pick up.

"I'm sorry," I say to the other dog owner. "She's friendly, just enthusiastic."

"Look, I'm sorry about last night. I forgot the rules." Rory's voice is low in my ear.

"No, no, I'm sorry," I say.

The other dog owner starts to pull her dog away. "Not friendly?" she asks.

"No, no, very friendly. My dog is friendly." My leash tangles with hers. Cleo is back down, wanting to play. "Maybe if I go under you."

"I think that was definitely against the rules." A slight laugh lifts his voice.

"No," I say to him. "Our lines, I mean leashes, are crossed."

"I'll go." He hangs up.

No. Don't go! I shouldn't have picked up the call. But now it's done. The rules are re-established. We're still friends. I should feel happier, but I don't.

I quickly create another miniature blog scene before I leave for my writers' group meeting. This time, Piper runs into her ex, Julian, at the supermarket, and he asks her to meet him for dinner on Thursday—to stay friends. I post the picture on Instagram, asking my followers if she should go.

I bundle up and grab one of the last Citi Bikes from the dock near my apartment. My writers' critique group meets in a Starbucks just below 14th Street on Eighth Avenue. I stop short when the cop car in front of me flashes red, pulling over a taxi. I wait for the light to change, my foot resting on the cement partition between the cars and the bike lane. Running a red light on a bicycle is a two-hundred-dollar ticket. My budget can't afford it.

Starbucks only has a few people inside, nobody from my group. Light jazz is playing. Most of the customers are sitting at the front tables for two. I order a soup from the barista wiping down the counter in the middle of the shop and grab our usual table for four in the back. I pull over another chair because we have a new member joining us.

The four of us have been meeting here for a year, every two to three weeks, on Friday evenings. We each submit a chapter to the group a week in advance, then we read each other's chapters and give our comments over coffee. Tabitha found us all at a writers' conference and formed this critique group. Even though we're writing in different genres, it works. I'm writing a romantic comedy, Tabitha and Esther are writing women's fiction, and Aarav is writing a dark thriller. Tabitha is pitching her book as a modern-day *Joy Luck Club* meets *Where'd You Go, Bernadette* as two sisters try to reconstruct the past of their mother and aunts through letters and other documents while the family travels back and forth between Taiwan and the U.S. Aarav's book is a bit dark for my taste, but he's a huge help to the group as "the male perspective." I hand-made T-shirts of our most frequent comments, and his was: "A guy would never say that."

Tabitha has just invited a fifth person, Maria, to join us. She met her at an agent-pitching round robin. Maria's chapter was solid. She's writing a cozy mystery, although it is more edgy than is usual for the genre. The female protagonist seems more bitter, less tea and cats. But maybe that's a unique selling point. Or she could just label it a hard-boiled detective series instead.

I check my email for the first time since lunch. It feels good to just sit and savor my hot soup. I click on the email from *Mini Mania*, a miniatures magazine I subscribe to, expecting it to be an announcement that the latest issue is available. I usually devour this magazine for inspiration as they showcase projects and give tips on creating miniatures.

Dear Ms. Anker,

We would like to feature your dollhouse and storyline about Piper and Rob (and Julian) in our December issue. Our staff writer Jeannie will interview you and discuss photo requirements.

As you may know, APT-TV is also collaborating with us, creating a special TV show event called "Meet the Miniaturists." The featured miniaturists will each create a miniature room box to be auctioned off to benefit the Fresh Air Fund and the Boys and Girls Club at an event on December 19. We hope that you will consider participating in this exciting opportunity as well.

Best,
Maryann Hughes
Editor-in-Chief, *Mini Mania*

I stare in shock at the text. My dollhouse is going to be featured. I can't quite believe it. I've finally joined the stars of dollhouse land. But that's not even the whole of it. I reread the second paragraph. I've rocketed to the very top; my work is even going to be featured on TV. Participating in the room box charity event will be great for my Etsy store. I need to make more merchandise now, although first I'll have to make the room box which, admittedly, takes me forever to build. I'm always envious of those people on Instagram who are like, "Here's my fully decorated dollhouse. I just whipped it up this week." Either they don't sleep or they've got magical, miniature elves working with them. I'm still working on my Malibu dollhouse, and it's been seven years. Maybe I need to put a miniature door on the bedroom wall with some offerings before it and hope an elf appears to help me.

Esther arrives next. She's a lawyer, but her firm allows associates to work remotely on Fridays. We meet on Friday to accommodate her schedule. She puts down her bag and hangs her coat on the back of the chair next to mine. I show her the email. Pushing back her curly, brown hair, she reads it. "Are you going to do it?"

"Definitely. This will be a huge boost to my miniatures business." A little voice nags, *"But how can you do this, too?"*

"What's the miniature storyline in your blog?"

"Similar to the book, basically. In both storylines, Piper was dating this guy named Julian and they abruptly broke up. In *Fake Dating Folly*, Julian announces that he's engaged, and she asks a friend to go as her fake date to the wedding. Meanwhile, now on the blog, it looks like she's dating someone new. I haven't said whether they're dating, yet, but the mini scenes look like dates. I'm about to announce that they're friends who are practicing fake dating, and he's going as her fake date to her ex's wedding. Where they will turn into a real dating couple."

Esther claps her hands. "Okay, you need to pitch this book to my publisher. This is a brilliant opportunity. You can ask APT-TV and *Mini Mania* to include your book in the publicity. That's a big hook."

"But it's in less than three months. A publisher can't turn it around like that."

"My digital publisher can. It's just a few months from submission to publication." Esther pushes her glasses up on her nose.

"But it's not done yet. I've only written half of it."

"But we've read the first few chapters, and they're good. I'll talk to my editor. They might be interested, depending on the final version. If you can get it written in a month. And if not her, then you have to self-publish your book and tie into this publicity."

"I don't think I can finish it in time. Given that I'm still rewriting *Midnight Masquerade,* although it is getting better." I hate that I sound like I'm making excuses. But I have to be realistic. At least once in a while.

Esther waves her hand dismissively. "You can't pass this up. APT-TV. This could be your big break."

"I can't pass this up," I say, a little flicker of hope igniting inside. Maybe this is it. Maybe Maya, my dream agent, will love *Midnight Masquerade,* and I can tell her about *Fake Dating Folly* and APT-TV—if they agree to include it in the publicity.

"Ask them on Monday if they can bundle the book into this charity auction. Even if you can't buy the miniature room box, you can buy the book. You have to do this. I'll talk to my editor first thing on Monday. Send me your first three chapters and your pitch."

"I don't even have a pitch yet," I say wryly. "But I'll write one this weekend."

Tabitha and Aarav, each carrying a coffee, join us at the table; they say hello and shed their coats. Tabitha puts down her bag and pulls out a pile of clipped papers. Aarav is carrying a folder with our chapters under his arm. He puts it down on the table.

"I'll call you later," I say to Esther.

As if by mutual agreement, we don't discuss it in front of Tabitha. Tabitha and Esther often argue about the merits of self-publishing vs traditional publishing, while Aarav and I sit on the sidelines. Tabitha is committed to holding out for a traditional publishing deal, while Esther self-published one book with modest success and then found a home at a digital publisher.

Aarav is wearing a dark-blue, buttoned-up peacoat; he looks rather spy-like in keeping with the characters in his books. It's the perfect look for his author's photo on the back cover of a book jacket. I tell him that and he laughs.

Maria arrives last in a flurry of scarves and a long, swirling coat. She's attractive, probably late thirties, polished, wavy, brown hair. She snaps her fingers and says she'll just go order a coffee.

Five minutes later, Maria is back with her order. Tabitha introduces us all and asks Maria to tell us a little bit about herself. Maria explains that she's always wanted to write her own novel. She even worked as an editor's assistant in her twenties. Everyone leans forward. It's like she has the secret wisdom to explain why we've been getting rejected by agents (even if that job was ten years ago).

"Can I start first with my critiques?" Maria asks, rubbing her hands together. She pulls out a clipboard from her Louis Vuitton briefcase.

Tabitha nods.

Maria starts with mine. "Yours was so light and frothy, easy to read. I don't usually read romantic comedies—a little too superficial for my tastes—but I enjoyed it."

I am aiming for light and frothy, but my romantic comedy has some substance.

She continues, "But I just don't see the need/desire in this at all. It's just funny banter. It doesn't seem to be moving the plot along. You need to remember goal and motivation. I don't see it. And I don't find your protagonist emotionally engaging enough." She hands the chapter to me.

Ouch. Everyone else leans back, too, as if they have ventured closer to a fire to feel its warmth and the flames have suddenly leapt out.

Okay, the customer is always right, so this is good. This will make my novel stronger. "So, in that chapter, her goal is to spend time with him to persuade him that they should date because she likes him, without asking him out directly—in case he doesn't like her back. Doesn't that qualify as the need/desire and the goal/motivation?" I ask. I don't want to appear defensive, but I also want to understand her comments. And as a single woman sporadically out in the dating world, I think this scenario has substance, even if it's not about to create world peace.

Maria takes a sip of her water. "That's the whole issue. Why doesn't she just ask him outright? Remember, it's not a real conflict if you can just talk about it and resolve it. And that's probably why I don't find the protagonist compelling. She's weak." Maria taps her pen against her clipboard with the other chapters. "Shall we move on?"

I sit back. Well, there's that. My protagonist could just ask him straight out, but the whole point is that she doesn't want to be vulnerable first. Maria's point about finding her weak is valid.

"We usually all give comments on one piece at a time," Tabitha says. The others give their comments, which are more positive. Aarav tells me he laughed out loud at several points. That's the gold I'm seeking. I feel better, but I can't help dwelling on Maria's point, even though Esther says the goal and motivation are clear and I should keep the chapter. Maria's eyes narrow.

We discuss Aarav's novel next. Maria's commentary is light, and I agree with it. So maybe that means she's onto something with my novel. And me. Maybe I should be more forthright with Rory. I should ask him if his desire to kiss me was a momentary buzzed blip or if it signified something more.

We turn to Tabitha's submission. Maria is quite complimentary. In fact, I feel like I am being too critical. Maria disagrees with my comments and says that it's fine the way it is. Tabitha smiles at me and says she will think about it. Tabitha has gotten the most nibbles from agents. She has one agent right now who has asked for a rewrite but seems keen to sign her.

We all discuss Maria's work and give our usual constructive criticism. I don't tell her I think it's too edgy for a cozy mystery because I don't actually read that genre—yet.

Next up is Esther. Her book is about female friendship. This time, Maria waits to comment until everyone has given their feedback.

"I think you need another antagonist to propel the book along. The dynamic between the two sisters and their best friends is good, but it's not compelling enough. We've seen this trope done before, so it calls for an added twist. And I like the way you were experimenting with developing different voices in your dialogue."

Experimenting? Esther has been writing this for years. It's past the experimental stage. Esther's eyes widen. Two pink spots of color dot her cheeks.

"Another antagonist is something to consider," she replies. "Did you find the voices different?"

"Yes," Maria says.

I want Esther to say, in attorney mode, "No further questions, then." But she just nods.

I chime in, "Your dialogue is so realistic, and the voices are very different. I know who's talking without the dialogue tags." I sound fawning. I'm not helping the situation. But it's true. Esther smiles at me, saying thanks.

We schedule our next meeting and disperse.

The air is cold outside. I zip up my jacket and stick my hands in my pockets to keep them warm. I'll have to find my gloves when I get home.

Suddenly, Maria is next to me. "I didn't want to say this in front of the others, but I feel like you're skating on the surface of emotions in your writing. I mean, what does she feel? She clearly likes him. Isn't she freaking frustrated that he doesn't see that she's perfect—like he should be on his knees, begging her to date him? Not playing patty-cake with some fake dating scheme?"

I look at her in surprise. "Yes, she's frustrated. But he isn't throwing himself at her feet, so there's a good chance she's going to get her heart crushed if she tells him her feelings."

"Hmm . . . there is that," Maria says. "There's my Lyft. See you at the next meeting."

I'm not sure I want to explore all my feelings about being rejected—at least not publicly.

It's too cold to bike without gloves, so I hurry down the subway stairs.

As I wait on the crowded subway platform for the 2 train to head back Uptown, I feel like I've just been through the wringer. Usually, I walk out of our critique meetings all inspired, and I can’t wait to get home to write another scene or revise the one we just discussed. I pull out my little, black notebook and write down what I’m feeling. Maybe Maria does have that secret publishing insight, and our novels will all be the stronger for it. But I miss our lost supportive dynamic.

Chapter Twelve

EVEN THOUGH THE PLATFORM is crowded, it's another five minutes until the express subway will arrive. I text Rory that Maria criticized my chapter as being just banter and not moving the plot along.

Rory: *Consider her advice, but don't follow it if you don't agree with it.*

Me: *Can I come over?*

I should talk to him about us. But I need to do it in person.

Rory: *I'm out with Callie.*

I stare at the text. Aargh. I messed up last night. Rory is a serial serious dater. Our fake dating arrangement is just a temporary stop gap. Maybe I missed my chance. But being Rory's girlfriend for a year and then being his friend wouldn't work, either. I'd be heartbroken. And I don't want to watch him with another girlfriend. It was hard seeing Jamie with another woman, and I'm not as close to him as Rory. I bite my lip as I realize what I'm admitting. I really do like Rory.

I hesitate over what to write back. My usual response would be "have fun." But I don't want him to have fun with Callie. And I definitely don't want him to get back together with her.

The subway pulls into the station, and I board. I don't have to reply, and I can't now anyway because my phone has no connection.

I take the romcom I'm reading out of my backpack, but I don't open it. What I want to write back is "Darling Callie." In other words, keep your hands off her.

It's just as well he can't meet up. I should revise this chapter while the critique is still fresh in my mind.

I get off at my subway stop and walk home to our apartment. Zelda is hanging out on our big, blue couch reading a book, with Gilda next to her, her head in Zelda's lap. Zelda puts down her book.

"How was the meeting? How was the new woman?" Zelda asks.

First, I tell her about the *Mini Mania* letter and Esther's offer to pitch her publisher, and then I tell her what Maria said about my chapter.

Zelda says, "Well, you can add more emotion into that chapter, then. Explain why she doesn't want to just tell him that she likes him."

I stare at our framed poster of Robert Doisneau's photograph, "Le Baiser de l'Hôtel de Ville," left over from our college dorm days. The couple kissing look like Rory and me. "Because she doesn't want to mess up their fake dating relationship. She still needs him as a date for her ex's wedding. And if she tells him and he doesn't like her, that makes it awkward between them."

"Anything more you could add to increase the stakes?"

I squirm. Next to the kiss poster is another framed poster—this one is a Faith Ringgold painting of a woman singing, giving it her all, in front of a jazz band. "I could change it so that they are best friends before this, and she doesn't want to lose their friendship."

Zelda's eyes narrow. "Yes, add that. And then I think you should ignore the rest, which just sounds like a bit of critique gobbledygook that has no meaning."

"This is why I worry I can't meet this deadline to pitch the book to Esther's publisher. I'm still in the middle of figuring it out. I could easily spend two months revising and polishing a finished draft. I don't even *have* a finished draft."

"You can do it," Zelda says.

"Rory is out with Callie tonight." I can't tell her that Rory asked to kiss me last night, and I turned him down. My stomach clenches.

"Oh no, not Callie. She's so awful," Zelda says.

"She's not awful. She's bright and very with it," I say.

"Yes, but she chooses friends as if she's padding her resume. She was nice to me when she found out I was a lawyer, and she was dismissive to you, an unpublished writer."

I laugh. "That's true. The best was when she asked how I made money and I said I was a dog walker."

"I think she physically recoiled."

"I don't like her. And if he gets back with her forever, I'll never see him again."

It was true. If he married Callie, our friendship would be over. I wasn't really risking our friendship if I told him I liked him because I'd lose it anyway if he got back together with Callie. But then I remember how I felt when Jamie rejected me. That gut-twisting, sinking feeling. But Rory is not going to say no, if last night was an indicator. So, I should tell him I like him.

"I just don't see Rory going for Callie again. I mean, I can see her appeal initially, but he's got to see her for who she is." Zelda stacks our magazines on the coffee table in a pile. "And

I didn't get the chance to hear what happened yesterday. How did that go? Did everyone believe that you were dating?"

Yes. Including Rory. Until I shot that down.

"Yes." And then I proceed to tell her about the "All in" averted ad catastrophe. She laughs.

My phone rings.

Rory says, "Sorry I couldn't talk earlier. I was with Callie, but I'm on my way home now. I'm just approaching my building." I can hear the sounds of cars honking in the background.

Hurray, he's on his own. I give a thumbs-up sign to Zelda and mouth *Rory alone*. Zelda nods knowingly.

I go into my room and shut the door. "Oh, I just talked it over with Zelda and she made me feel a lot better."

"Did she criticize anyone else?" His voice sounds the same, a little distant maybe, but not like he's cutting me off after I said no to kissing.

"Esther. I think because Esther defended me." I prop the pillows up on my bed and lean against them, turning on the reading light over my bed. It's dark outside.

"You should reach out to Esther and see what she thinks."

"I've never talked to Esther outside of the group meetings, but . . ."

"Well, if you like her, you should," Rory says easily.

The doors to my Waterside Way dollhouse are open across from my bed. "Across" is a euphemism. There's no space between the bed and the shelf holding up my dollhouse. I have to kneel on the bed to stage scenes in it.

"I'm going to be talking to her a lot now. Because *Mini Mania* magazine wants to do an article on my latest blog storyline."

"The one with the doll that looks like me?" he asks wryly.

"Yes, but he's named Rob. Your secret is safe. And I haven't said they're fake dating online. I've left it ambiguous so far."

"Your followers think they're dating."

"They hope they're dating. And they've also invited me to participate in a 'Meet the Miniaturists' APT-TV charity event where they will auction off a room box of my creation. This should boost my Etsy store business."

"That's huge." It sounds like he's walking up the stairs now to his apartment. I feel like I am babbling because I am nervous as I consider broaching our "real" dating. I can't do it over the phone. I need to see his reaction—be able to gauge it so I don't reveal too much if it seems unwanted.

"And Esther suggests that I either pitch her editor with *Fake Dating Folly* or self-publish it in time to include it with the room box for publicity." I bite my nail.

"That's a really smart idea. That will give you press and a huge push to your marketing."

My stomach tightens at the thought, both with excitement and trepidation. "I'm calling her tonight to see what the deadlines are."

"You can do it." He continues, "Brunch tomorrow at your sister's?"

"Yes, we should go over together. Otherwise, Olivia will be suspicious that we didn't sleep together."

"Okay, I'll pick you up at your place. Around ten. I'm beat, so I'm going to go."

We hang up. That conversation felt flat, like something had changed. I look out my dark window at the lit-up windows of the apartments across the way, TV screens flickering in some. He could just be tired. At least we're meeting in person tomorrow so I can see if I'm just imagining this change and if I can restore "us."

I pull down my shades and call Esther, who is still enthusiastic.

"You have three weeks to write forty thousand words, then a week to self-edit, so that's October 9," Esther says. "Then I'll read it for a week, looking for gaps, plot holes, etc. You'll give it to Strawbundle Publishing on October 16. That gives them almost two months, which may be enough time. And if they're not interested, then you self-publish. If you decide to go the self-publishing route, we need to line up an editor starting October 16. While she has it, you'll work on the book cover and peripherals."

I write the deadlines down on my wall calendar—with its cheery pet pictures—and then put them in my phone calendar and planner. I'm tempted to write them on my arm as well.

"This seems very tight. If I publish a crap book, that will end my writing career. And I prefer to have a developmental editor look at it before I give it to your publisher." I pace in my room, staring at the rejection framed on my wall.

"It's not crap. You've shared the first five chapters with us, and they're good."

"Maria didn't think so."

"Maria is not your reader. Thick skin and all that. Maria clearly likes slightly depressed, bitter characters. That's not your character at all. Don't let her criticism get to you."

"Are you going to add another antagonist?" I ask, powering up my laptop.

"No. At this point, I'm almost done with this book, and I haven't heard that feedback from my editor, whom I trust more than Maria. But I'll keep her comment in mind for my next book. Anyway, I'm your developmental editor for this one." Esther sounds so confident.

"Okay, I'll do it."

We hang up. Two thousand words a day. While keeping my blog going—because that is the driver. And don't forget making a mini room box. It's not possible. I give myself a stern talking-to. It's my dream ticket. I can write and blog at night. Many authors write two thousand words a day. I've been coddling myself. If I want to join the big leagues, I have to step it up. *Right now.*

I write back to *Mini Mania*, telling them I am thrilled to accept this offer and asking if I could include *Fake Dating Folly*, some of which parallels the blog scenes, as part of the charity donation. I revise my chapter, raising the stakes and addressing the other criticisms. I write the next chapter. I reread it quickly, and it's good.

I get ready for bed, but I'm too wired from writing and the possibility of publishing. I pull out my miniatures to create another scene for a blog post. This time, Piper and Rob are at a costume party. All my different mini dolls—witches, wizards, my seventies Topper dolls, Cleopatra—are hanging out, and the scene really looks like a fun party. Rory loves costume parties and has a Halloween party every year. Piper and Rob stand in a corner, Piper looking up at him—like she's about to tell him a secret.

I bite my nails as I think about telling Rory tomorrow that I like him. It feels completely different from telling Jamie. But that wasn't pre-planned. I just blurted it out. And in this case, Rory seems to be having second thoughts, but that's not what really scares me. What scares me is that if he says yes and then we date, and it doesn't work out. Because it won't live up to Rory's magical expectations. He never says exactly why he breaks up with a girlfriend, but he does seem to shy away from conflict. I wonder if it also has something to do with his parents—that he doesn't want to disappoint them, or even worse, become a case study for his father.

And if we date and then break up, I'm not sure we can then return to our comfortable friendship, and I need that. I have a three-legged chair of emotional support and he's one of the legs. My chair will fall over without one of those legs. And I've chipped one leg already by lying to Olivia.

Chapter Thirteen

RORY ARRIVES EARLY. I'M rereading yesterday's chapter, which is total crap. I don't know why I thought it was good yesterday.

My brain hasn't yet clicked into top gear when he bounds into the living room. He's looking good—jeans and a worn, olive T-shirt that brings out the green in his eyes. He kisses me on the cheek and sits on the couch, one arm outstretched along the back. I'm on tenterhooks, but he seems totally normal. That strikes me as a bad sign, implying it was just a momentary glimmer of interest because he was tipsy.

"You're wide awake. Zelda is still sleeping." I stretch. Rory glances at my stomach, and I pull down my T-shirt. I pick up my mug to make another cup of tea. I'm hoping it will jolt my synapses awake.

"I've already played two pick-up games of basketball this morning. Thought I'd better get my mind going before we face your sister." He pets Gilda. I woke up early to walk her and then went back to bed.

I sit next to him on the couch, clutching my tea. "Did you win? I probably shouldn't have stayed up so late writing, but I hit my two thousand words. That's my daily goal now."

"Tied. You're going to do it?"

"I'll talk to the *Mini Mania* editor on Monday and see if they'll include the book in the donation for the APT-TV auction." I definitely feel daunted as I look at the schedule.

"Is Zelda joining us for brunch, or is it just us?"

Our couch is one of those comfortable, overstuffed ones, made for lounging. But right now, it feels like there's a sinkhole in the middle, pulling us together.

"Jamie is coming, too," I say.

Rory narrows his eyes. "And Willow?"

"Willow went back to Singapore. They broke up. Jamie said he doesn't do long distance."

"Nice." Rory raises an eyebrow. "Poor Willow."

"Yeah."

"Are we going to continue fake dating now that Jamie is back?" he asks.

"Yes, I mean . . ." I am not awake enough, and I can't get the words out to say we should date for real. I shiver just thinking it. I am not functioning well enough to be treading in these dangerous waters. He is just staring at me. I feel a prickle of unease. I can't tell what he's thinking now. I take the coward's route out. "What do you think?"

He shrugs and looks down. I shouldn't have said no when he asked to kiss me. Or something happened with Callie last night and fake dating me isn't necessary.

"We don't have to decide it now," he says.

"Yes, I can't think of a breakup story right now. I mean, I can't think of a reason why we'd break up," I say. The heat of his thigh touching mine makes me check if there's smoke.

"Too comfortable with each other? Boring? Not enough sizzle?" Rory looks at me. Actually, I'm feeling way too much sizzle right now. Rory is sitting too close. My heartbeat is accelerating. It doesn't feel comfortable at all. Definitely not boring.

"I hope you don't find me boring," I say.

"Never."

"We haven't done nearly enough research for my book. We need to go on more dates. You don't have any weddings of exes coming up, do you?" *Is it too much to hope that Callie is about to marry herself off?*

"No."

"Too bad."

Rory laughs wryly. "I'm rather relieved about that."

"This brunch is enough of a substitute."

"Especially if Jamie is there, unattached." He leans back against the couch.

I should go for it, or at least hint at it. I should have prepared something. "It's not that I'm not . . ."

The clanging of the spiral, iron stairs announces Zelda's arrival. *Yeah, so that was an awkward start.* Too many double negatives as I tried to say "it's not that I'm not interested in you."

Zelda yawns as she arrives at the top of the stairs. "You guys need to look a little more rumpled, like you just rolled out of bed, although the unshaven look is good, Rory."

He smiles. "That's what I thought." He puts his arm around me and rubs his unshaven cheek against mine. "How's that feel?"

I squeal. "Rough."

"It's not that you're not . . . what?" he asks.

Goldie jumps up on the couch, but when I pet her, she flicks her tail, annoyed.

Aargh, I just can't. Baby steps. "It's not that I'm not over Jamie. I am."

"Hallelujah." Zelda perches on the couch arm rest. "What's your game plan?"

"Stick to the truth as much as possible," I say. My life of deception is making my stomach queasy. And this is my sister. I should have told her. If she finds out, she might really give up on me, like I'm this lost cause who's afraid to ever share secrets or emotions.

"We were able to pull it off on Thursday, and we're best friends anyway, so it's not that much of a stretch." He pets Goldie, who purrs. Traitor.

"We need some non-verbal signals," I say. "I wasn't sure what you were trying to signal at the cocktail party. I thought your look was stay close, but I wasn't sure."

"You read it correctly," Rory says.

"We need another one for help if the questioning gets too close, although Rory remembered the chin-stroking from college," I say to Zelda.

We all stroke our chins and look intellectually serious. We were forced to develop a "rescue me" sign because of this one incredibly boring professor who cornered students. A student would stroke their chin and nod, and that was the signal for other students to rescue them.

"How could I forget? How about rubbing the back of your neck?" he asks.

"Good. Works for both of us."

We get up from the couch and say goodbye to Zelda.

Olivia's apartment is several blocks away on Riverside Boulevard. The postman is wheeling his blue bag down the nearly empty streets. Contrary to reputation, New York City is a city that sleeps late. A doorman steps out to open the door of a cab stopping in front of his building.

"Is the story that I slept over at your house after your writers' critique group meeting?" Rory asks.

I nod. "What'd you do last night while I was at my writers' meeting?" I ask, so we have our stories straight. Not because I want to know if he went out on a date with Callie.

"I met up with a bunch of friends. And then Callie and I went out for a drink afterward. She hit on me, so I told her we were dating. Handy." He's looking at an ad campaign on a bus shelter for a new movie coming out. Not at me.

Warmth fills me. There's still a chance. He didn't want to date her. "I bet she didn't take that well."

He side-eyes me. “She was very gracious about it. Said she’d always suspected there was something more there.”

Now I feel bad that I was catty. We walk down a brownstone-lined block, passing a mom carrying a mesh bag of balls, heading in the direction of the playground with her children.

“What’s happening with your writer’s website and your blog?” Rory asks. “I thought you were going to start that up.”

We turn onto Riverside Boulevard. The Hudson River is choppy today, and the wind whips my curls around.

“I haven’t had time, what with the store and all the mini orders. Once I finish a solid draft, setting up a website is next on the list. With this wind, I am definitely going to look rumpled.”

Rory snorts. “I thought the word was windswept.”

“You *have* been reading romance novels.”

He laughs.

We arrive at Olivia’s apartment building and say hello to the doorman. The ornate lobby with its fresh flowers feels like we’ve stepped into an entirely different ecosystem from my brownstone apartment. We take the elevator up.

As we walk down the carpeted hallway, we hear children screaming inside Olivia’s apartment.

“It sounds like a children’s party,” Rory says.

“We’re probably the entertainment,” I say.

“Carissima?”

“Schatje.” I look into his eyes.

He holds my hand. Our feet slow almost in unison, as if we’re en route to face a firing squad.

Rory rings the doorbell. Olivia opens the door. Her glance darts to our clasped hands, and her eyes widen. She kisses me and then Rory. “John got called into work—again—so it’s just me holding down the fort. And the kids each have a friend over. Welcome to the family, Rory. I’m thrilled you guys are dating.”

Nothing like added pressure and guilt.

It's kid chaos inside the apartment. Four kids are running around having a pillow fight in the living room. The living room is big and comfortable, its former sharp glass and stainless-steel coffee table replaced by a solid-wood coffee table with drawers for games and art supplies. A rug covers a padded gymnastics mat.

Olivia disappears into the kitchen. I'm expected to follow her and help out. But then my nephew Thomas hits me with a pillow and I say, "Girls against boys." I grab a pillow from the couch and swat my nephew back. If it's play with the kids or get grilled by Olivia, the choice is easy. The kids are also using small, snowball pillows I gave them last Christmas. Olivia was not happy. I thought she'd thrown them out. The kids must have overruled her.

"Hey, you're too big," Thomas says.

"You shouldn't have hit me," I say.

Whoosh. Into my back. Rory has hit me with a pillow. "Ouch," I say, more from the shock.

"This means war." I throw a small, snowball pillow at Rory. He catches it. So much for my powerful throw. I'm better with real snowballs. Rory and I have a tradition that we meet for a walk in Central Park for the first snow of the season. It usually devolves into a snowball fight.

We're now all hitting each other with pillows. No feathers are flying—yet. The two girls and I retreat to hide behind Olivia's blue, leather couch with a stockpile of the pillow snowballs. Rory and the two boys have taken up positions behind the armchairs. Some snowballs are scattered off to the left. I tell the girls to cover me so I can get them. I run out. Rory emerges from behind the chairs, surprisingly undeterred by the hail of soft snowballs from behind the couch. I am trying to scoop up the snowballs, but he keeps knocking them out of my hand. The girls and boys are all screaming for their respective players. I am laughing so hard I can't speak. I hug the snowballs close to my body and curve over them, hip-checking him so he stumbles slightly. Ha.

"Oh, so you want to play dirty," Rory says and grabs me around the waist from behind. I use my self-defense class move and go limp. We both tumble down onto the carpeted, padded floor, Rory taking the brunt of the fall as he shifts so that he is on the bottom. The doorbell rings. Olivia yells that it's open.

Rory's arms are still around me. And the heat of his body envelops me. I shift off him to the side, so that I'm lying alongside him. His hair is messed up and I want to smooth it back. His gaze is warm and intense.

"Are you okay?" he asks.

"I'm fine." I give him a wicked smile. "Are you? I fell on you."

"I'm good." Rory smiles. It's a full smile, not his half-smile.

"I still have my balls," I say.

"And I still have mine," Rory says, his eyes twinkling. "But you won't have yours for long."

He tickles me. I laugh, shrieking, "No, no." I twist so that I cover the balls.

"Get the balls, Thomas," Rory yells.

"Help!" I say to the girls.

Jamie's voice sounds above, "I thought this was a PG-rated brunch with the kids."

We both still.

"This is about as PG as it gets," Rory says.

Rory's hand is on my back. The heat of his hand sears my consciousness. Whereas before it was play, now it feels like more. I sit up, trying to tame my curls, straightening my shirt, which had ridden up in the struggle, but I think all that was showing was my back. Still PG.

Rory takes my hand and pulls me up. But he doesn't let go of my hand. I lean against him.

"Uncle James," Thomas says. "Another boy on our team."

Jamie pats him on the head. "Only if I'm on Penelope's team." His tone sounds almost flirtatious.

Olivia emerges from the kitchen with a platter of omelets. “What’s going on? Brunch is ready. C’mon and eat while it’s hot.”

The kids gather up the snowballs while Rory and I pick up the pillows and arrange them back on the couch.

We join Olivia in the kitchen, offering to help. Jamie sits at the dining table with the four kids. The dining room is an alcove off the living room, next to the kitchen. I carry out the milk and fresh orange juice pitchers from the kitchen, followed by Rory with a quiche. Olivia brings out a tray of sliced bagels and toppings and sets it down on the sideboard, moving her wedding picture off to the corner. A coffeepot and hot water dispenser, tea bags, milk, and sugar for the taking are already set up on one half of the sideboard.

We all sit. Rory serves both of us food. Olivia is a good cook, so silence reigns as we all take our first bites of the quiche.

Jamie gives us an update on Theresa’s health. She’s home but still weak, so that’s why she didn’t come. He has to go out to Fire Island to clean the house, remove the food, bring in all the deck furniture, and generally close up their summer house so the electricity and water can be turned off.

He asks, “Do you know anyone who does that? I’m worried I don’t have time.”

Fire Island in the cold? No way. The icy wind off the ocean seeps into your bones. The one time I made the mistake of accompanying Theresa out there to close up their house in a wintry October, I felt chilled for days.

Both Olivia and I shake our heads.

I announce that *Mini Mania* is going to do a feature on one of my blog storylines and how I am pitching my book to a publisher, but that means I only have a month to finish it. I sound panicked. Rory squeezes my hand under the table.

“But can you do that? You don’t want to publish something that’s not good,” Olivia says.

"I am worried about that." Especially given my writing schedule. I twist my napkin in my lap.

"Strawbundle Publishing will only publish it if they think it's good," Rory says. "And if they reject it, then you still have two months to revise it. It's a good marketing opportunity."

"Is it? Do dollhouse enthusiasts read romantic comedy?" Jamie takes another half of a toasted bagel.

I narrow my eyes at Jamie. What is up with him?

"Probably," I say. "And my storyline, which parallels the book, is getting more followers every week."

"Why won't you let me read it?" Olivia pours some more milk for her son.

Because I can't take your criticism. "You can definitely be a beta reader. I'd love your feedback."

"I'd be happy to read it," Jamie says, "once I'm done with the tech due diligence for this M&A deal. I can give you the guy perspective." He winks at me. *Winks.*

"Rory gives me the guy perspective." I put my hand over Rory's. "And this guy, Aarav, in my writers' group."

"But I'd like to do it. It's the least I can do—the store's Instagram account has really picked up from your posts. Isn't it better to have as many beta readers as possible?"

"No offense, but you're not really my target demographic. And I like to stick to other writers as beta readers because friends can leave you hanging."

"But you give it to Rory."

"The burdens of being my boyfriend."

"The joys of being your boyfriend." Rory puts his arm around me, and I lean into him.

Olivia asks what we're doing tonight. I look guiltily at Rory. We had no plans to spend the evening together. I was planning to write as much as possible today.

Rory says, "We're going to an art show opening, which includes one of my mom's new clients. She's representing this up-and-coming painter." He takes another bite of his omelet.

I nod.

"That sounds exciting," Olivia says.

Jamie gets up to pour himself another cup of coffee and asks, "So if you get the teaching job, does that start in January? That won't interfere with this, right?"

"What teaching job?" Olivia asks.

Rory darts a sharp look at me. I can feel his shock next to me.

"Yes, what teaching job?" Rory asks.

"Mom told me. Was it supposed to be a secret?" Jamie asks.

"No, I . . ." I don't know what to say. I know Rory is disappointed in me. "I applied for a job teaching writing, but it's a long shot. It won't start until January. I told your mom because I thought it would alleviate some of her worry about me. But I'm not giving up writing." I turn to Rory as I say the last bit, willing him to understand.

Rory looks down at his plate.

"Well, you were only planning to take two years to write full time, right? And that's up in January, so that makes sense. I hope you get the job," Olivia says. There's a pause. "What kind of art will be shown at the opening tonight?"

I look at Rory. His eyes seem a colder slate gray than their usual blue and green.

"Paintings. Abstract paintings," Rory says.

Olivia turns to me. "Do you ever still draw? Will you illustrate your own cover?"

"No." My lips press together. "I'm so out of practice."

"Oh, you used to draw all the time. Do you remember?"

This brunch has been enough of a disaster. *She is not about to go there, is she?* I put down my fork. I don't want to have food in my mouth if I need to change the topic quickly.

"Penelope took portrait drawing classes in high school." Olivia points to a portrait I drew of her that I gave her as a gift. It's hanging on the wall above the sideboard. I also did one of our parents and one required self-portrait. Other than those, I drew tons of portraits of Jamie. My jaw clenches.

"I didn't know that." Rory studies the portrait. "It's good."

"My mom framed the portrait you drew of me," Jamie says.

"That's not the only one she drew of you." Olivia sips her coffee.

I shoot Olivia a warning look. "Do you have any coffee filters? We've run out." That's our code for my complaining that she has no filter.

Olivia rolls her eyes. She usually thinks that I'm too sensitive. "I can imagine. Weren't you using coffee filters to make the miniature tulips in your recent blog tutorial?"

"Yes. They worked perfectly." She does follow my blog faithfully.

The conversation moves on. *Crisis averted.*

I finish my omelet. The four children ask to be excused, and they run over to the living room to set up a Lego village.

"I was thinking I could adopt a dog, now that I'm back in New York, if I can take advantage of your dog-sitting services, paid, of course," Jamie says.

"Oh, you've always wanted a dog," I say.

"I have." Jamie nods. "Maybe you want to come with me to pick out a dog at the pound?"

Rory stiffens next to me.

"I'm afraid that if I went with you, I'd end up with my own dog," I say.

"Don't you want your own dog?" Jamie asks.

"Yes, some day, but for now, I'm good being a doggy aunty to the dogs that come live with me," I say.

Rory and Jamie help clear the dishes. Thomas comes over and asks Rory if he can separate two Lego pieces. Rory sits on the couch by the Lego village and works at it. Jamie's phone rings, and he asks if he can take it in Olivia's home office.

I help Olivia with the dishes, even though I want to berate her for bringing up my Jamie crush—as if that wouldn't be a sore topic with a new boyfriend. She brings in the final dishes and says, "You didn't tell Rory about applying for a job, and you didn't look like you knew about the art show tonight."

I face Olivia. I think she suspects. "I didn't. Because we weren't planning on spending tonight together. Because I need to write. Because I have to finish this book in three weeks. We don't spend every night together. You're presuming that I'm living up to the standard set by you and John. We're different. I need my own space to create." I place the last of the dishes in the dishwasher. "And John knew immediately that he wanted to date you, and he courted you like a crazy guy, sending you flowers and meeting you for late-night snacks after you left work. This is a different scenario." Very different. I feel bad for lying to Olivia, even though she does drive me crazy. Maybe I can tell her after this. But she'd be hurt.

Olivia places the remaining condiments in the refrigerator. "Okay, okay. I'm sorry if I'm pressuring you. But it is a Saturday night. Why wouldn't you go to the art opening? Meet other creative artists?"

Because Rory hasn't invited me. "I find Rory's parents a little bit intimidating. It's one thing to meet them as 'the friend.' It's another to meet them as the 'girlfriend' of their only son."

Olivia squeezes my arm. "I'm sure they're delighted Rory is dating you."

"Oh, yes, the orphaned, struggling writer—every parent's dream." I cross my arms.

Olivia shakes her head. "Think positive. And hopefully in three months, you'll be a successful published author. That's so exciting." Olivia hugs me. I hug her back. "And Rory is so great, his parents must be cool."

So, you'd think. But I always feel tongue-tied when I talk to them. Especially because his dad is a psychologist. And I think they wonder what Rory sees in me. And this is when I was just his close friend. Anyway, Rory didn't invite me, and we're not actually dating, so it's not like I'm going as his girlfriend.

Rory enters the kitchen. "Do you need help with any washing up?" He puts his hands on my shoulders and massages them. That's good. That's very couple-y. Maybe he's recovered from his disappointment. Olivia smiles.

"No, we're all done."

"Suspicious timing," I say to Rory.

He laughs.

We join the others in the living room, say our thanks for brunch, and leave. Jamie rushes to join us. We all enter the elevator together. Nobody says anything. Rory's arms encircle me. Jamie stands straight next to us. The awkward silence is so loud that I hope some other people join us in the elevator. But instead, the elevator goes straight down to the lobby.

"Do you want to come over to visit my mom tomorrow?" Jamie asks as we exit the elevator. "She'd love to see you."

"Sure," I say.

We say goodbye outside and turn to go Uptown while Jamie goes Downtown. As soon as we're out of earshot, I say, "I'm sorry that I didn't tell you about applying for the teaching job."

"I won't say I'm not disappointed." Rory's face looks stern.

"I'm sorry."

"It's just something I thought you would tell me—as a good friend."

"I should have told you," I say. "I just really did it more to placate Theresa than with any real hope of getting it." And I was afraid to tell him because he'd be disappointed. But now he is disappointed that I didn't tell him.

"But you'd do it if you got it."

"Yes." I nod. "Teaching might be a good career path for me."

"You've got to do what you want to do and not worry about Theresa."

"She was giving me her usual lecture in the hospital, and the machines started beeping," I say. "The nurse directed us to leave."

Rory rubs my back. "I'm sorry."

"I'm also sorry Jamie was weird."

"I think he just saw you as more than a friend," Rory says.

I snort. "Too late now." But is it? I wanted this for so long, but I just don't feel any desire for Jamie. I feel annoyance. That he felt he could act like that when I had a boyfriend. As far as he knew, anyway. Jamie has changed. He's become more corporate and less the best friend that I played with. The sun glints off the Hudson River. "Anyway, I don't think he's really interested. I think he did it to annoy you." And as I say that, I know it's true. Jamie is never going to like me romantically. Jamie did it because he's still annoyed that Rory was the one who ended up dating Marie, Zelda's work colleague. Both Jamie and Rory pursued her when they met her at one of our parties two years ago. *That* was a fun party for me.

Rory asks, "Would you like to come to the art show tonight? As friends?"

"It's okay. I don't have to come. Olivia knew I didn't know about it, and I told her we hadn't had plans. And she was putting too much pressure on us."

Rory entwines his fingers with mine. I was expecting him to drop my hand now that we've turned the corner. "Well, I'd still appreciate the company. It's my parents' thing, so I didn't think to invite you. I'm going as more of an obligation to them. It will be more fun with you there."

The wind dies down now that we're away from the water.

"I'd love to," I say. "And ironically, I am writing this scene at an art show, so this will be perfect."

"I'm having dinner with my parents first. Do you want to join?"

I bite my lip. "I should probably write. I'm worried about meeting the deadline." I squeeze his hand, willing him to understand.

Rory nods. "I'll meet you at the art gallery, then."

He kisses me on the cheek and says goodbye as he jogs down the steps of the Broadway subway station. I should have tried to tell him again that I like him, but I was too thrown by repairing the damage done by my revelation about applying for a teaching job and Jamie's behavior. Tonight.

Chapter Fourteen

THE ART GALLERY IN DUMBO, Brooklyn is an open, white space with eleven-foot-high ceilings, gothic columns, and a tin metal ceiling. A bar is by the windows. Lots of people mill around, their dark clothing standing out against the white backdrop. No Rory is in sight. At least I accomplished my writing goal for the day, even if I just eked out those last words. I've also decided to do a miniature art gallery for the charity project. I considered making another gym, but an art gallery is easier. It can showcase my food and my flowers, the things I'm best at making in miniature.

I sip my drink and study the paintings. At least at art shows, it's okay to be alone admiring the art. The artist's palette is mixed—some very vibrant pink, yellow, and some more pale green blue—very much like a romcom book cover. The pale green blue evokes a misty feel. One orange-and-black painting gives off an angry vibe. The painting in front of me has hieroglyphics and stick figures over a very pale lavender and green color. Two stick figures look like they are dancing. Hearing Rory's voice, I search the crowd for him. More tall, attractive men are here than I expected. I should have brought Zelda.

I wander through groups of chatting, well-dressed people. Rory is leaning against a white column. He sees me, and a big smile breaks out on his face. I love the way he smiles when he sees me. He leaves whomever he is talking to and joins me.

"What do you think? I really like the work," he says.

"Yes, it looks like the artist has developed this whole language, kind of like Miro."

He nods. "Exactly."

I smile. "Do you know what the hieroglyphics mean?"

"No, but he's about to talk."

Ting. Ting. Ting. A spoon strikes a glass, asking for silence, and the conversations die down. Rory's mom, Ciara, introduces the artist, Rafael; he takes the microphone from her. He's tall, with his hair in a ponytail. He speaks passionately and explains the meanings behind the symbols: one means giving, another means to reveal the truth, and another means façade.

Rory and I are standing next to each other. It feels weird that he doesn't have his arm around me or isn't holding my hand. I shake my head. What is happening to me? It's like I crave his touch, this closeness, this intimacy. I have to remember it's fake, but it's no longer fake for me. I'm pretending it's real for others and not real for him. *Conflicted much? Nope, not me.*

Rafael walks to a large, lavender-and-blue painting dominating the far end of the gallery. He explains that he painted this work after he and his girlfriend had a fight. That's why the stick figures have their backs to each other. And then she came back into his studio and said, "I'm sorry." He wrote "I'm sorry, too" in the middle of the painting. The paintings are a record of his life.

A chill goes through me. A happy chill, though. An "I get it" kind of chill. The artist looks away from the audience, at the painting. The stick figures are so actively posed that they look like they could jump off the canvas. How can he part with it? And how can he be so open and vulnerable? Doesn't he worry that he will be exposed and dissected, both positively and negatively, and then lose his creative drive? Or even lose a part of himself as others speak for him as they interpret his work? When I published a piece in college, I took the criticism so personally, and I had to learn to step back and separate myself from my work. It made me think of a carcass picked over by vultures until just the bones were left. Not that that was why Georgia O'Keeffe painted all those bones, but I sometimes wondered.

But if I am not going to write about what I feel and stay skating on the surface, how can I ask anyone to read me? I stare at the "I'm sorry, too."

Everyone claps. I clap, too, a little bit late.

"Are you okay?" Rory asks.

I nod. "That was so powerful."

"Wasn't it?" Ciara, Rory's mom, says. She hugs me hello. "I'm so glad I've found him."

"He's so emotionally open," I say.

"Are you still writing?" she asks.

"Yes."

"Good for you. Stay committed to your dream," she says.

Behind them, a familiar voice compliments Rory's mom on the show.

Callie. Rory invited Callie. *I wasn't the one who was supposed to be here with him.* My stomach sinks. *I should leave.*

Except Rory has that little wrinkle in his forehead he gets when he's trying to puzzle something out. That's the way he looks at me sometimes—like I'm a mystery he can't quite figure out.

"Hey, you two!" Callie's high-pitched voice has a clear note of forced friendliness. "Rory and Penny, together at last." She lifts her chin as if pondering some great thought.

I hate it when people call me Penny and not Penelope. Penelope is a weaver of stories, someone who managed to outwit many suitors, whereas Penny is a coin that gets dropped to the bottom of the drawer. I'm sure she did it on purpose. I should shorten her name to Cal or Lie. Actually, better stay far away from "lie."

Ciara looks at me and Rory. She has the same bemused expression Rory makes. We're standing close to each other, as if united against Callie. Together at last. That could mean something other than dating. Or not.

Callie is still peering down at me. "Rory always said you were just friends."

Uh-oh. Rory tenses next to me. I don't think either of us envisioned having to fake date in front of his parents.

I take her arm. "You missed the artist talk. Come on, let me explain the hieroglyphics to you. It's so cool." I pull her away from Rory and his mom. She doesn't want to go, but my grip on her arm is ironclad.

I march her over to one of my favorite paintings, where the stick figures dance across the canvas. "These represent joy."

Callie's mouth is set in a tight line. She looks back to find Rory and his mom, but they have been swallowed by the crowd.

I give Callie's arm a little shake in a not-so-subtle attempt to redirect her attention. "Joy," I repeated. "Do you know why they represent joy?"

Callie finally turns back to the painting. "Probably because they're dancing." Her tone is condescending, like she thinks I'm wasting her time.

Guess you're not here for the art appreciation.

"And this one?" I ask. The stick figures have their arms up in the air, like they are stretching or reaching for the sky. The artist said this was dreaming, striving. The colors of the painting are bright pink, yellow, and blue, happy, with some slashes of gray and black. Because there are setbacks. And the figures go up and down, the path is not linear. Maybe this is my favorite painting of the show. No, my favorite is the gut punch of the "I'm sorry" painting.

Callie focuses on me. Like I'm an ant under a magnifying glass. "You guys just started dating a few weeks ago?"

"Yes."

Her eyes narrow. "How did that happen?"

As if it's impossible. Thank you for that reassuring vote of confidence. I hope Rory stuck to our story. "Didn't Rory tell you?"

"He didn't give me any details. You know how guys are. And especially Rory. Guys don't kiss and tell, honor code crap." Callie flips her hair.

As if he'd be giving his *ex-girlfriends details. And who asks the new girlfriend for details?*

Rory's dad, Lucio, joins us. "Great to see you both." We move away from the painting, as another guest peers closely at it. *Shouldn't Rory's parents be schmoozing people to buy art instead of talking to Rory's friends?* I smile. *Callie can probably afford to buy art.*

Callie kisses Lucio on the cheek. "I never miss your wife's art shows. I was just asking Penelope here how she and Rory started dating."

Lucio glances at me, but he doesn't look horrified. I probably look more dismayed. He looks contemplative. Like he's about to start stroking his chin.

I massage the back of my neck. *Don't lie to Rory's parents. What's Callie up to?*

"You're his ex-girlfriend. It's up to Rory what he wants to tell you." I stop rubbing the back of my neck. If Rory came over, he'd be put on the spot. We need a signal for "stay away." While we're at it, we also need a code for "meet by the bathroom so we can debrief and plan our next moves." Like we're undercover. And I don't even like spy movies. Too tense. "Will you excuse me? I'm going to ask the artist a question." *And text Rory.*

I walk into the crowd, determined to find the artist. Hurray for tall people and for DUMBO converted warehouse lofts with columns. I dart behind one. Leaning against it, I whip out my phone and text Rory: *Callie just told your dad we're dating.*

"Are you hiding or spying?" Rory asks. I jump.

"You scared me," I say.

His blue eyes are laughing. "I didn't mean to." Rory leans against the column next to me. Our shoulders touch.

"Callie told your dad we're dating."

He stills. "It's okay. I'll explain it later." He frowns. "I don't even understand how she knew about this opening. I didn't tell her. Maybe she's on my mom's mailing list."

I look around the room for Callie. The crowd is thinning out. I don't see her. We may be safe.

"Can I ask your mom if any of her artists would be willing to make mini art for my mini art gallery for the charity project?"

"Yes, she'll think that's cool."

The cheese and crackers are beckoning. We retreat back to a corner after I grab a plate of food.

Rory takes some grapes off my plate. "I don't even know why Callie is doing this. She broke up with me."

My stomach sinks. I'm not sure Rory is over her. She certainly still has the power to wind him up.

"Said I was too idealistic; said that maybe my advertising career cycle of a month per idea made me cycle through girlfriends, that I was trying all the different types—she was a hard-hitting career girl, Ayanna was the artistic visionary; she called Marie the girl next door."

Callie isn't too far off with her descriptions. I am probably "introverted bookworm." That sounds like the worst option.

He shakes his head. "Anyway, is there anything we need to practice for your book scene?"

"I think I've got enough material."

Ciara waves us over.

"We usually go out for drinks with the artist and his entourage after an opening. Do you want to come?" Rory asks.

"Yes, that sounds like fun."

We walk over to where Ciara is standing.

"We're about to go to the restaurant," she says.

Rory excuses himself to run to the bathroom.

"I was just invited to make a miniature room box for an APT-TV charity event," I say. "I was thinking of making an art gallery. I was wondering if you thought any of your artists would be interested in making one-twelfth-size paintings? The proceeds benefit the Fresh Air Fund and The Boys and Girls Club. And I'd ask APT-TV to include the artists in the publicity."

"I should think so." Ciara nods. "That's a great opportunity for you, too."

"I know," I say.

"Rory told me about your blog. I've been following it. Your scenes are really like art. I love those first dating scenes of you and Rory."

Ah, so that's why she didn't look surprised at Callie's announcement. "It's not actually me and Rory."

Ciara raises her eyebrow skeptically. "Yes, I'm impressed that Rory doesn't mind that it's so public," Ciara says. "Lucio sometimes minded when my paintings were too revealing—and I never went as far as Rafael."

"I'm not . . ."

"You don't have to defend yourself to me. I just like the way you pose the dolls, like the way Piper looks at Rob when he's not looking, and Rob looks at her when she's not looking. You really capture that feeling of desire and insecurity. But I do hope you're not actually considering that ex-boyfriend?"

I feel like a deer caught in the headlights, even though I'm not considering Jamie. "No. I'm definitely over him. But every storyline needs an antagonist."

Ciara smiles. "Good point." She glances over at the corner where Rafael is holding court. "Well, I should scoop up my guests, and we should head over to the restaurant. I'll ask Rafael if he wants to donate a miniature painting."

"That would be amazing. Thank you!"

Rory joins me. We walk toward the door. Many of the paintings have green stickers, so the show did well.

My gaze meets his. “What did you tell your mom?”

He rubs his forehead. “I said it’s complicated. And then someone interrupted us.”

“We should sit apart during these drinks so we don’t have to be lovey-dovey.”

Rory shakes his head. “Lovey-dovey. Is that from second grade?” He gives his half-smile.

“I wouldn’t put it past Callie to start singing, ‘Rory and Penny sitting in a tree, K-I-S-S-I-N-G.’”

His gaze meets mine, then drops to my lips; he looks like he is contemplating kissing me. My pulse skitters. I lean toward him, like I am being pulled; I hold myself upright.

His jaw tightens, and he says, “Well, she doesn’t know our rules, so she may be afraid of the consequences of that.”

“Maybe.” I step back.

His mom is shaking hands and saying goodbye to the remaining patrons. Then she raises her hand and gestures for us all to join her. Callie comes back in through the front door and meets us. Ciara shepherds her little group down the tree-lined street to the café at the corner.

“Your parents didn’t seem to know that you guys are dating,” Callie says.

“I don’t tell my parents everything,” Rory says.

“Yes, you do,” Callie says.

Rory is very tight with his parents. Sometimes it hurts to see how close they are because it reminds me of the big, gaping hole in my life.

I shiver. It’s cold outside, and I button my coat all the way up.

Ciara has reserved a table for twelve. I sit across from Rory. Callie looks surprised—but pleased—and sits next to him. I turn to the woman on my right. She introduces herself as Rafael’s girlfriend.

“Who are you?”

I whisper, “A friend of Rory’s.” I don’t want Callie to hear.

“What?”

"Family friend." And I jerk my head over to indicate Rory. I feel my face flush. Callie is now fully turned toward him and has her arm around him. Their conversation looks intense, like they're arguing. Callie puts her hand on his arm, and he moves it away. I focus on my dinner companion. I don't want Callie to think I'm worried.

"Oh." She nods knowingly. *About what? What have I revealed?* "He's very attractive."

"Yes." I glance at him again. I probably look like I like him. That's good for the deception.

I turn back to her. Since it's just the two of us, I ask, "Rafael is so emotionally open. But that also involves you. Are you okay with that? How do you do that?"

She shrugs. "It's an emotion. Emotions are universal. And it's still only the surface. The surface of what we said. The painting should evoke the emotion of what we felt, but I think, maybe, you have to have felt that, too, to feel it again. I'm not sure it can evoke a feeling you've never felt. What do you think?"

I nod. "I don't know. I mean, when I read certain writers, I can feel the pain or the terror or the tension, so I have felt that emotion before, obviously, but not at that level. I think artists can make you feel something even if you haven't felt it before." *But she hasn't really answered my question. And I am prying.* "I'm a writer, and the latest feedback from agents is that they're not emotionally engaged enough. I need to expose more of myself. But I'm having a hard time with expressing so much publicly." If I express what I feel, and if Rory says no tonight, he will see *all* that I felt if this book is published.

She nods. "I don't know how he does it. It used to bother me, that our relationship was part of his art, but"—her eyes soften as she glances at him—"most artists seem to have a muse. And it's just the way he is."

I need a muse.

Ciara clinks her glass and toasts Rafael. Rafael gives another little speech, thanking Ciara—and his girlfriend. Lucio has his arm around Ciara, and he kisses her lightly on the cheek. Rory's parents seem very much in love still. I can see why Rory is looking for magic.

Lucio says, "Penelope, you had a question for Rafael. Did you get to ask him?"

Absolute silence. Everyone turns to look at me. I feel a heated flush spreading from my cheeks down to my shoulders and chest. *Just ask.* I shake my head. "It's okay."

His girlfriend says, "No, no, you have such interesting questions. Was it about how he is so emotionally open?"

I swallow. "Yes, you expose so much of your life in your work. How do you do that?" My voice wavers. I focus on Rafael, ignoring the rest of the table.

Rafael says, "At first I didn't. But I react to the emotion in other works, so exploring feelings and going deeper was what I wanted to do. For me, it was worth it to do that deeper excavation."

I nod. I have to decide if it is worth it. The conversation erupts again.

"I didn't mean to embarrass you," his girlfriend says.

So much for hoping that my embarrassment wasn't obvious.

"No, no, I'm glad I could ask him. Gave me a lot to think about."

Rory is suddenly there. He pulls over a free chair from the empty table next to us and sits. He introduces himself to Rafael's girlfriend. He puts his arm around me, and I lean against him. It feels right.

"Shall we go home soon?" he asks.

"Yes. Let me just run to the bathroom." After I say goodbye and thank his parents, I make my way around the tables in the restaurant to the back of the room where a chalk sign says *Toilette.*

One woman is fixing her makeup in the little foyer lined with mirrors. I pass her and squeeze into one of the stalls. The outer, wooden door to the bathroom clangs shut. The click-clack of heels approaching the mirrors announces that another person has entered the bathroom. *I hope it's not his mom. I don't want to be the one to field questions about our fake dating situation.*

As I exit the stall, Callie is standing there by the mirrors, her back to them. Waiting.

"I didn't think Rory would dare date you."

I push the dispenser for soap. I'm not sure how to respond to that. I don't want to encourage her attack.

"'She's one of my best friends.'" She imitates Rory's voice.

"Doesn't it make sense to date your best friend?" I ask.

"Not if you're Rory and you can't commit. Mr. 'Nothing is going to be as perfect as my parents' marriage.' Now he's going to lose you, too."

My breath hitches. I keep my eyes down so she can't see she's affected me. Just keep lathering that soap and rinsing my hands under the warm water. I steal a look at her and she's twisting her ring. I ask, "Why did you break up with him?"

"I didn't break up with him because I wanted to. I gave him an ultimatum—either we get engaged or we break up. He said he wasn't ready. I broke up with him. I am not wasting my time if he's not sure." She rubs her eyes. "But now I miss him. Maybe I was too . . . I don't know. It was really good in the beginning." She shrugs. "Take that for what it's worth. I shouldn't be giving advice to you."

"I'm sorry." I feel like I should hug her, but that would be weird.

She straightens. "Well, we'll see how you guys work out. Rory wasn't afraid to tell his dad about us." She walks past me and into the stall.

I leave the dark room quickly. Rory never said she wanted to get engaged. I joked that he had commitment issues, but I didn't really think that he did. Why would Rory be afraid to tell his dad about us? I shake my head. *We're not even dating. I keep forgetting it's not real.*

Rory is waiting by the front door of the restaurant, leaning against the wall, talking to his mom. I walk over to him, and he takes my hand. We say goodbye. His mom regards our clasped hands but doesn't say anything.

We walk out.

I glance at Rory. "Why are we holding hands?"

"I wanted to." Rory smiles at me. "I missed holding your hand."

Rory's hand around mine feels solid and comforting. We walk to the subway station. Rory would take a cab home, but he knows that I bike or take the subway, given my finances. He used to offer to pay for my cab the rest of the way, but I'd never accept, and so now he takes the subway with me.

Only a few people are standing on the platform as the train pulls in. We sit in a nearly empty subway car. I lean against Rory, and he puts his arm around me. This feels more like old times, coming home after a night of dancing.

"I'm sorry my dad put you on the spot."

"I'm actually pleased he did. I'm glad I asked the question." I nod. "Did you get a chance to tell your parents we weren't dating?"

"I was planning to tell them I told Callie we were dating to deter her, but then I could just hear my father saying in his psychologist voice, 'Why did you feel the need to do that? Why can't you tell the truth to Callie?' Now I don't know what to do. I almost told my mom at the end there, but we were talking about the show anyway." Rory rubs his face. He glances at me. "I did tell Callie I wasn't in love with her anymore. But she said that once you're in love with someone, you don't get over them. Do you think that's true?"

"I think there's always a little piece of your heart that loves them, but it's not your whole heart. I definitely think you can fall out of love." *I may not have entirely succeeded yet, but I don't want to be in love with Jamie anymore. I want to be in love with someone who's in love with me.*

"I'm not feeling that piece right now. I don't know why she wanted to go tell everybody we were dating."

I don't know, either. It does seem counter to her strategy to win him back. "She said you broke up with her. Because you wouldn't commit."

"It wasn't working at the end. It was too much about her and this 'perfect' life we had to lead. Which wasn't my idea of a perfect life. I don't need to be out at every function. I can't even do that. I work late hours. And I definitely have no desire to be in the society pages, whereas Callie would love that. I wasn't going to commit to something that wasn't working. And you probably heard the dig about 'revolving doors' when we were at The Met. It was like that constantly at the end."

He's not getting back together with Callie. I take a breath. "So, about Thursday night—"

He cuts me off. "I'm sorry. You were right. I certainly don't want to risk our friendship. Man, Callie was all over me today about my 'commitment' issues and how surprised she was that I was dating you. But maybe she's right and I'm not good at forever. She's right about my track record. A year or two and I'm out. Thanks for keeping a clear head."

My stomach sinks. I've missed my chance. But I don't want a fling.

The subway pulls into the Chambers Street station. He jumps up to make his stop, saying goodbye.

Rory isn't interested in anything more than friendship with me. We've been friends for years with nothing happening. Except that I feel flickers flaming when we're dancing or competing against each other in minigolf or billiards. I sigh. But then I remember his glance when my skirt hiked up. And when our lips almost touched in a kiss. And his smoldering glance when we were lying next to each other in our snowball tussle. I'm not the only person feeling that electric charge. But he's not willing to try dating me. He's the one who suggested we fake date. Not me.

The train is still sitting in the station. Stuck.

The conductor says, "We're being held momentarily by the train dispatcher. We should be moving shortly."

The passengers all look at one another, annoyed. I check my email once I realize that I have reception. An email from Maya pops up. What if this is an offer? My body warms as if I'm standing on a precipice. I'd be so happy with even some feedback and a request for a revised version.

> To: Penelope
>
> From: Maya
>
> Thank you for sending me *Midnight Masquerade.* I'm afraid that I didn't connect with your writing the way I had hoped to. More tension is needed. It's too easy for your protagonist. More needs to go wrong. But this is a very subjective business, so another agent might feel differently. I wish you the best with your writing career.

My stomach sinks. I take a deep breath. I had really hoped she was the one. She was so easy to talk to, and we just clicked. I should have waited to send it to her. It wasn't ready —even after all the revising. How can *Fake Dating Folly* be ready in three weeks?

Maybe I should just give up on *Midnight Masquerade.* But she did give me constructive criticism. I can create more disasters. It's fixable. It's not ready for the drawer where manuscripts go to gather dust.

If *I* don't know when my work is good, that doesn't bode well for *Fake Dating Folly.*

An older couple is sitting across from me. He reads her a quote from his book. She laughs and grasps his hand. I wanted to be that couple once.

And if I'm honest with myself, I thought Rory and I could be that couple. But I also thought agents would love *Midnight Masquerade*.

I need to get rid of these "feelings" for Rory and focus on writing *Fake Dating Folly*. I look down at Maya's email saying more should go wrong.

A few disasters or excursions dealing with mundane practicalities—not remotely romantic—should do the trick. I can't count the number of fights my parents had over who was doing what housework, even with a weekly cleaning service.

Closing up Theresa's Fire Island cottage should be a routine, tedious—definitely not magical—activity. There is a reason Jamie wanted to outsource it. I can't go next weekend because I really have to concentrate on writing. I check the two-week weather forecast, and it says cold and rainy for the last weekend in September. A storm is moving up the coast. Perfect. Usually, it's still warm in September in Fire Island so I wasn't sure that the weather would be cold enough.

If I'm cold and cleaning a house, I should be grumpy enough to repel Rory and to stop myself from seeing him in this glowing light. Theresa certainly said she would never bring me again to help close up because I was so miserable.

Me to Rory: *Weekend in Fire Island might be fun, even if we are closing up house. Should we volunteer for last September weekend? Will be work.*

I feel like I have to give fair warning.

Rory: *By ourselves?*

Me: *Yes. Only us. If Jamie has time, then he can do it.*

Rory: *Then, yes. Love the beach in the fall.*

I frown. If he likes cold, windy beach days, he's in for a treat. And my plan may not work. But it's still worth a shot.

Me to Jamie: *Rory and I can close up cottage for you if you want.*

Jamie: *Are you sure? You hate being cold. Freezing out there. Heaters not working. And lot of work to clean.*

Me: *Romantic weekend for us.*

Jamie: *If you like camping in late September. There is a fireplace.*

Cleaning and "camping" in the cold should smite these flickers of attraction. We'll see the worst of each other, and I'll get over this crush I have.

CHAPTER FIFTEEN

ON SUNDAY AFTERNOON, *Mini Mania* editor Maryann Hughes calls me and says they will include *Fake Dating Folly* in *all* the publicity. They need my art gallery project in mid-November. I can't believe my writing career is launching at the same time as my mini career. Even though I've always maintained that my two passions support each other, particularly to Theresa and Olivia, I certainly never contemplated that I'd be able to launch my book as part of a miniature project. I meant that they fueled each other creatively. And I've never argued that they work well together in terms of time commitment.

As I put my phone down, it rings again. It's Esther.

"Vera is interested!" she shouts into my ear.

I scream, "Yes!"

"She can't commit until she sees it in full, but she says Strawbundle Publishing would be willing to work with you to get it ready for the APT-TV auction if they commit to *Fake Dating Folly*."

"Oh my God." My legs feel weak. I collapse into the chair by our dining room table. "My book could be published."

"Get writing, my friend. She also loved the miniatures blog angle, so keep that up, too. Okay, I have to go. I have to finish drafting this contract, but I'm so excited for you."

"Thank you so much. This would not be happening without you. Thank you."

I text Rory.

Me: *Publisher interested!*

Rory: *Yes!*

I turn back to my manuscript. Two thousand words and then I'll do a blog post. I can't believe a publisher is finally interested. I can barely sit still. I'm buzzing with joy. My body feels like one of those sparklers on the Fourth of July.

But it's not a done deal yet.

I add more details to the art opening scene based on Saturday night, and then I write a scene where Rob and Piper are sharing a room as fake dates while attending Rob's ex-girlfriend's wedding. Piper decides to wear sweatpants to bed, along with her sports bra, and Rob is also wearing sweatpants. He jokes that they're ready to work out in the morning. As Piper lies there, listening to Rob's breathing, she is frustrated by their fake dating situation. All the other guests have commented on how happy they look together and how glad they are that Rob has found "his perfect match." Even his ex said it. She had thought fake dating would create an intimacy that would lead to dating, but maybe it is also creating this "perfect relationship" that hinders actual communication.

When I finally stop to go to the bathroom, I realize I've written three thousand words.

My blog and miniature Instagram posts have garnered lots of likes and comments. This new storyline of Piper hanging out with Rob is really taking off. I've left it ambiguous as to whether they are actually dating; much speculation abounds in the comments. After the post where Julian asked Piper to meet for dinner, the feedback in the comments was mixed as to whether she should meet him. Most suggested drinks, not dinner, so she could exit quickly if need be.

I created a mini scene where Piper had drinks with Julian. Julian announced that he was engaged, but they committed to remaining friends. It was all exceedingly proper. I kept the bartender nearby so they never looked like they were alone. And I left the lighting very bright. I can't believe Rory's mother follows my blog. Piper was about to ask Rob to come as her fake date to the wedding, so I could finally conform the plotline of my blog to *Fake Dating Folly,* but maybe that's too revealing of reality for Rory's mom. Unless Rory tells her we're fake dating.

Later that afternoon, I arrive at my sister's apartment to babysit, and she pulls me into the kitchen because she's started cooking dinner for me and the kids. Luckily, it's spaghetti night; the sauce smells of basil and green peppers.

I put down my backpack with my laptop. I'll continue writing once the kids go to bed.

Olivia puts a pot of water on the stove to boil. Then she turns and gives me a look. It's not a good look. It's a lecture-is-coming look. "You know, I thought about it, and it didn't seem to me that you and Rory are dating."

I can feel my eyes widen. I step back. "Why?"

"Are you dating or not?"

"Why don't you think we're dating?"

Olivia rolls her eyes. "You want to play this game?"

"No, you're right. We're not dating. We're fake dating for book research. And for Rory's work."

"Why did you tell me you were dating, then?"

"Because I thought you wouldn't be able to keep it a secret otherwise. And you would tell Jamie and Theresa. Please don't tell them that we're not dating."

"I can't believe you lied to me. We're sisters. We're family. Family should come first."

"I agree. Then why don't you keep my secrets? Why did you tell Theresa about that agent's rejection, the one where she told me to forget about this book and write my next one? You know Theresa thinks I should just give up on this 'writing hobby.' Why give her any material to feed that?"

"She supports your ambitions; she just worries. I was using that advice as an example of how you're committed," Olivia says. "You take these things too seriously."

"You know I do," I say. "And why did you bring up that I drew a million pictures of Jamie when I'm with Rory, who you thought was my new boyfriend? How is that at all helpful?"

"I stopped talking about the drawing when you told me to," Olivia says. "And at that point, I knew you and Rory were not dating. And Jamie was flirting with you, so I thought I was helping fan the flames. What about Jamie? Maybe you should go pick out a dog with him."

"No, I think I've truly gotten over him. And you know if I went to the pound, I'd come home with a dog, if not two." The water is now boiling. As am I. I need to calm down before I say something I regret. I add the pasta. "So, why didn't you think we were dating? We needed to persuade his work colleagues last week that we were together. Someone keeps hitting on him, and he wants to deter her. But it seemed to work."

"I don't know. It's probably just that you didn't look at him like you'd slept together."

"How do you know what I look like then?"

"I know how you used to look at Michael."

I deflate. Michael was my first serious boyfriend. I was on cloud nine when we started dating. He met my parents and Olivia and John on Christmas break. I am sure I looked at him like I adored him. Which I did—until he disappeared when my parents died. "Well, I've changed."

"Yes." Olivia's mouth turns down. "Still, you veered between being on edge with each other and then really relaxed." She leans against the counter.

I nod. "That's perceptive. That about describes it."

"I'm sorry I talked about your drawings; I was also mad because I'd just realized that you probably weren't dating. But I know it's my fault that you don't trust me. I feel guilty that I wasn't there for you when Mom and Dad died."

"You shouldn't feel guilty. The reason I don't trust you is not because you weren't there for me when Mom and Dad died. It's because you don't protect my confidences."

Olivia steps back and looks down. She then gazes at me. "I'm sorry." Olivia hugs me. "I really am."

"Maybe you should think of my secrets as protected by attorney-client privilege," I say.

"I will try," Olivia says. "But I still feel guilty. I shouldn't have believed you when you said you were fine. I was working and I had John, and it was easier for me to believe that. But I shouldn't have. I mean, I knew how upset I was—that Daddy wouldn't walk me down the aisle and Mom wouldn't hold my babies."

I hug Olivia as I tear up. "We have each other, at least. I knew you were working eighty hours a week. I knew you were busy. I don't blame you. And I didn't want you to worry. And I got through it and now I'm fine."

"Except that you're faking a relationship," Olivia said.

"Touché. But my feelings for Rory run deeper than my feelings for Michael. The relationship is not for real, but the feelings are."

"Oh, Penelope, do you think he feels the same way?"

"I was going to ask you, Ms. Perceptive."

"I don't know him as well as you." She scrunches up her face and then nods. "He might. I'd say he was on edge, too." She suddenly hugs me. "I can't believe you told me how much you like Rory."

I can't believe I did, either, and it worries me. I say, "So, I'm trusting you again, but please don't tell anyone else."

Olivia says, "I won't tell anyone else."

John pokes his head in the kitchen. "Ready to go, Olivia?"

She kisses me on the cheek. "Thanks for babysitting. And thanks for forgiving me."

"It's fine. Unless you tell Theresa and Jamie. You promise not to tell them, right?"

"I promise." She tears up.

We hug tightly, and then she leaves.

I bring the plates to the dining table, telling Thomas and Amber that we have about five minutes until dinner. I can't believe we didn't fool Olivia. I thought we were convincing, given that I keep falling for it myself. She is more perceptive regarding me than I give her credit for. Myrtle and Bernie seemed to believe it, but they don't know us as well. Maybe Jamie was so forward because he didn't believe it, either. It's a bit depressing if no one believes it—as if I really am not Rory's type.

Telling Olivia how much I like Rory made me feel better. A little. I was hoping she'd seen some sign that Rory felt the same. But no. Operation Mundane Misery is still a go.

Chapter Sixteen

RORY IS DRIVING OUR rental car out to Fire Island as rain pelts the front window. It's cold. It's definitely an auspicious start for a disastrous time. This should definitely kill my feelings for Rory. We left late, and there is only one last ferry to Saltaire. Rory even suggested we leave tomorrow morning instead, but I said we should go.

Rory is concentrating hard on the road, as visibility is limited. I feel bad now that I'm putting him through this. On the Cross-Island Parkway, it's bumper-to-bumper traffic, and Google Maps suggests alternate routes. We discuss it and decide to try it—even if it does look like it's a bunch of back roads. Normally, my preference would be to stay on the known main route and just sit in the traffic.

My parents often fought while driving; they'd yell at each other for not communicating driving instructions clearly. Once, my dad pulled over and refused to drive farther unless my mom figured it out. Maneuvering through back roads should be a good test, but also, if we sit in traffic, we definitely won't make the last ferry. And although I have a contingency plan, it involves a two-mile walk in the rain from the public beach parking lot. A bridge connects Fire Island to Long Island, but cars are not allowed past that parking lot unless they have a full-time resident permit. As the rain pelts down, even I'm not willing to do that for the sake of Operation Mundane Misery.

The wipers swipe back and forth as we turn off and head down a series of winding roads. I direct Rory, following the directions on my phone. It's hard to see ahead, but Rory is not complaining. I am impressed.

"I'm sorry. We should have waited to go in the morning," I say.

Rory glances at me. "It's supposed to rain tomorrow, too." And then after a beat, "So, did you volunteer for this, or did Jamie talk you into it?"

"It was all my idea."

Rory connects his phone to the car, and the mood changes from dark and depressing to intimate as he plays the "All In, All Good" party playlist. He smiles at me. And I give him a huge, grateful smile back. We're in a snug bubble, and the warmth fills my heart. He makes me so happy.

I look out my side window at the gray, coursing rain.

A tear escapes.

I turn back to deciphering directions. We have to turn right in a hundred meters. If we miss this exit, there's a good chance we won't make the ferry. I really don't want to walk in the rain. But I need to kill these feelings. He says he doesn't want a relationship. I can do it.

I let us pass the exit.

"Ohh, that was the exit," I say. "We need to take the next exit and go back." I lower the music and put on the audio for directions.

The voice says, "Recalculating."

"I'm sorry." And I am. I shouldn't have done that.

Rory says, "Don't worry about it."

We circle back around and get back on the route, but it's time lost. The navigator says we will arrive with five minutes to spare. Now four minutes.

We are not talking, both just willing the car to make it in time, and I don't want to interrupt Rory's concentration.

I'm watching the clock as we're stuck at a stoplight in Bay Shore. The navigator shows us arriving with a minute to spare.

We pull into the ferry terminal just as our ferry pulls out. We both sit there, stunned that we actually missed it.

"I'm sorry," I say again. My stomach twists with guilt.

"It's not your fault. I was late from work, and I took it slow in the rain." Rory shrugs. "Is there a backup plan, or should we head back to New York City?"

He's so reasonable. I'm almost annoyed that he's so laid-back about this. The rain is still coming down.

Hesitantly, reluctantly, I reveal the backup plan. "We can park here and take a taxi to Field 5 and then walk two miles to the house. Over the beach. Or there's a sand path." At least there's no lightning or thunder.

Rory nods slowly and, tilting his head, looks at me. "I once invited you to join me in a MUDder's Day Run, and you said that wasn't your thing."

I laugh. Apt comparison. "Maybe I didn't think that was challenging enough?"

"That must have been it."

"I mean, we weren't going to have to carry two-days' worth of food and clothing," I say. The one supermarket is closed in the off-season.

"And it wasn't at night and in the pouring rain," Rory says. "Well, let's get some dinner at Nicky's Clam Bar so at least we're well fed. I'll park the car."

"Let me make sure we can get an Uber or taxi to Field 5 first." I arrange a taxi and get a table in the front as Rory parks the car. Our luggage—one cooler on wheels, my suitcase on wheels, and Rory's backpack—are stacked next to me. There's no way we're going to be able to wheel them through wet sand. But I'm not going to think about that now. If Rory can stay positive, so can I.

Rory comes in, wiping rain off his face, and hangs his dripping-wet jacket on the hook by the door.

"I hope they have hot soup," he says as he sits.

"We should probably take some to go."

"Nothing says beach vacation like hot soup and cold rain," Rory says.

"I'm sure there's an ad concept in there somewhere."

"It's certainly a new spin on the tried and true."

We eat our clam chowder and fish and chips quickly; I don't think either of us wants to be walking across the dunes at midnight. We take turns using the bathroom, and then we each pull on our still-soaked rain jackets. The taxi is outside, waiting.

"Terrible weather," the driver says as we pile in. "Missed the last ferry?"

"Yes," I say.

"What town are you going to?"

"Saltaire."

"At least it's not Lonelyville." He laughs at his own joke. Lonelyville is the name of a town three towns over from Saltaire.

Rory chats with him about fishing, having noticed the fishing equipment in the trunk when he stowed our luggage. As we cross the Robert Moses Bridge, the lighthouse beams. It's really picturesque, even on this dark, rainy night.

We clamber out of the sedan at the wooden barricade preventing cars without year-round resident permits from proceeding further.

The car lights fade away. It's just us and a sandy road ahead, carving out a path between mounds of dune grass. I've got my roller suitcase and Rory has the cooler-wheeler and his backpack. A cold trickle of water is seeping through at the back of my neck as my raincoat proves to be more fashionable than functional. I shiver. I can't believe I thought that rainy suffering was a good idea.

We both try pulling our roller bags on the road. Oomph. They stop, stuck in sandy water.

I hoist my suitcase up. We trudge forward, the rain sheeting down around us, the sound of the waves crashing off to our right.

I hunch over to push against the wind. The cold air sweeps through my jacket, blowing through the openings in my sleeves and chilling me. My suitcase bangs against my leg. That last bump will leave bruises. I hold it with both arms in front of me. My fingers feel like icicles.

"You should walk behind me so I protect you from the wind," he says.

"We can switch." As I say it, I realize I'm too short to provide protection for him.

"I'm good."

I step behind him. He does provide some protection, and I'm warming up now from the exercise of carrying the suitcase and the backpack. My hands are still icy, though.

Rory splays the flashlight from his phone ahead. The warm beam of the lighthouse off to our left beckons. Rory's light reveals a pathway to the ocean to our right.

"Maybe we should walk along the ocean since we're carrying these anyway," Rory says.

"It will be harder to walk on beach sand." This sand pathway has the benefit of being slightly packed down by the cars of those few year-round island residents. I step in a puddle; water soaks my shoe.

"It's the journey, not the destination."

"I don't think this was the journey they had in mind." I shift the suitcase to carry it with one hand.

Rory takes my hand. "Exactly. So, let's go check out the ocean."

The ocean is tempestuous, with high waves, but it's not that windy, and since my feet are already wet, I remove my shoes. He does, too. We tie them by their shoelaces onto our bags and head toward the surf. My toes curl into the cold sand.

We walk along the surf, running up every now and then to avoid a wave swamping our clothes and, more importantly, our luggage. The water is not that cold compared to the air.

He offers to carry my suitcase, too, but it's okay. He's got the unwieldy, heavy cooler, and even though some of the food is in his backpack, it's no easy feat to carry.

"Are you going to be able to recognize where we need to go inland?" Rory asks.

"I think so. The houses near her walk haven't changed, thankfully," I say. "This one stretch has all new houses, and it's so disorienting. I can't seem to replace the old ones in my head to recognize these."

We've made it to the first town, Kismet. A few houses have lights on, so we're not totally alone.

My legs are soaked. Several waves have caught me, although I did manage to save the suitcase from getting wet by raising it above my head. It was freezing at first, but now I don't feel it. I stop to roll up my pants again.

Rory is setting a brisk pace.

We reach the town of Saltaire. We're in the home stretch. I'm hot now from walking with this suitcase for a mile and a half.

I catch up to him.

"You look too dry," I say.

"You look like you've been swimming. But with clothes. You're not a fan of skinny dipping?"

"Hmm . . . you know what? I'm a fan of the wet pant look on a man." And I kick my foot into a wave, spraying him with water. And then I run up the beach, slowly, because my bag has not gotten lighter.

"Chicken." He chases me.

I dump the suitcase down as I hear him behind me and face him, knees bent, ready to dart in the opposite direction.

He puts down the cooler. I shrug off the backpack. I wipe the rainwater off my face. We're a few feet apart.

"You know how I like my chicken?" he asks.

"Soggy?"

"Breaded and crunchy. You need a little sand on you." He lunges for me. I twist away and run back down to the ocean.

He catches back up as I reach the surf. He's left the backpack up with the other bags. I spray him again, but he's got a handful of sand that he bends down to throw at my legs.

I swipe my wet hair out of my eyes and push back my rain hood. I can't see, and I'm wet anyway. I spray him again, and he returns the favor. We're both laughing. I am tempted to try to get him off-balance so he can fall into the waves, but it's more likely to be me who ends up in the ocean.

"Truce?" he asks.

"Okay."

I reach out to shake his hand. He pulls me against him and wraps his arms around me. I feel warm and protected. He smells of sea air and wet jacket. I hug him back and wish we could stay like this—just for a few more minutes.

"Let's go make some hot chocolate," he says. I release him and step away.

We walk up the beach together toward our bags. My sand-heavy pants are sticking to me, and yet I am grinning.

We pick up our bags and walk the last stretch to the wooden steps off the beach and down the wooden pathway, where we can roll our bags. We turn down the main walk and go a few more blocks until I turn right again, and we squelch up to Theresa's beach house.

The key is in the outdoor shower, hidden in a plastic, soap bar case. Rory unlocks the door while I pull off my sand-covered pants in the shower, so I don't fill the house with sand, even if I am the one who will be cleaning it up. The "no sand in the house" rules from my childhood die hard.

We escape to separate bathrooms to strip off our wet clothes and take hot showers. Brrr. The water takes forever to warm up. The house feels like an icebox. I hate being cold. Frick. This is turning out to be more a test of my character than our relationship. And I definitely don't want to get sick when I've got a book to finish.

I feel better after I'm warmed up by the hot water. I quickly put on several layers of warm clothes. A Pillsbury dough boy theme is emerging here in my clothing choices when I'm with Rory. I walk up the stairs. It's an upside-down house. The living room and kitchen are upstairs, while the bedrooms are downstairs. Rory is making hot chocolate, and it smells delicious. And it's warm.

"You look like a snowman."

That's the look I'm going for. "It's Fire Island fall fashion. Two sweaters. And long underwear." I sit, cupping my mug in both hands.

"Do you think we can make a fire?" Rory asks, pointing to the fireplace with the neatly stacked wood next to it.

"Yes. What's your fishing cabin like?" I ask. Rory and his dad spend time every fall up in a fishing cabin in Maine. I've always thought it must be some sprawling house that they just call "the cottage" given their chic tastes, but now that Rory seems unfazed by shlepping a cooler across two miles of wet sand in the rain, I'm wondering if it is just some lean-to cabin with a fireplace, a potbelly stove in the corner, fishing rods next to hooks by the door for wet rain fishing gear, and hammocks to sleep on.

Rory describes it, and it sounds like the beautiful, wooden house I first imagined. The fire is now roaring away, and I take off a sweater.

He lounges next to me. The rain is still sleeting down outside, but we're in this warm cocoon and it feels lovely. I'm also very much aware that we are alone in front of a roaring fire. I sigh.

"What's wrong?"

"Nothing," I say sadly. "I love the fire." If Rory is interested in me romantically, this scenario couldn't be any more perfect for him to kiss me. And I feel like he's interested, after that playful tussle on the beach, and then I caught him looking at me when he was making hot chocolate, and it was not a playful look.

"Theresa certainly has a lot of pictures of Jamie around. It's like the opposite of subliminal advertising," he says.

It's true. There's Jamie at two, Jamie at five, Jamie at ten, Jamie as a teenager, Jamie in college. It's like a shrine to Jamie. There's also one picture of me and Jamie standing together at the dock at sunset, two peas in a pod, one with brown curls, one with blond.

"Should we make s'mores?" Rory asks. "They have marshmallows and graham crackers in the cabinets. I brought chocolate."

"So did I. Yes, definitely." And there's the final piece of proof that we're just friends: that's more camping buddies than romantic. Because we're closing up the house for the winter, we have to eat up, bring back, or throw out any perishable food so there's nothing for mice or bugs to find during the off-season.

Rory jumps up and gets long skewers and potholders, as well as the food supplies. I move closer to the fire, and we toast our marshmallows over the flames.

"So, did you spend a lot of summers out here?" Rory asks.

"Yes, Olivia and I shared the bedroom with bunkbeds downstairs, and Jamie had the other bedroom. My parents slept up here on a pull-out couch on weekends when they came out, and Theresa and her husband had the main bedroom. And then they spent the winters with us, skiing at our house in the Catskills. It worked out really well, mostly because Theresa wasn't working then and could watch us all for the summer." And because my parents didn't fight in front of Jamie's parents. Maybe it should have been a red flag—that both couples worked better together than alone. I look over at the couch area. Theresa replaced the pull-out couch after they died.

"And nothing ever happened with Jamie? No romantic walks on the beach?" he asks.

"Jamie has always thought of me as a sister. Which makes sense, given the way we grew up. I don't know why it didn't work that way for me." I can smell the shampoo fragrance of

Rory's freshly washed hair. I keep my gaze on the flickering fire.

"Are you sure you're over him? He might be interested now."

Rory is not looking at me as he makes his s'more, smooshing the marshmallow down between the graham crackers and the chocolate. It's oozing out, like emotions.

"I was really nervous before our brunch with him and Willow, but I didn't actually feel any great longing or desire for Jamie," I say. "But then, that's not very reassuring either, is it? I was in love with him and now I am not. See, it proves my point that love doesn't last."

"Not with the wrong person. I don't think there's just one love. I've been in love with past girlfriends, but it didn't work out long term. But that's not to say it wasn't real at the time."

This is exactly why we shouldn't date. I might still be in love even after Rory will have moved on. I shift slightly away and ask, "So, then how do you know what's going to last and what's not going to last?"

"I don't know. My parents say that it's when there's both that attraction and a strong friendship—that you feel you can talk to that person about anything. My mom said she knew when my father helped her set up her first art show. He just came by and did whatever he could to help out."

"That's so sweet."

"Yeah, and then after they tell that story, they look at each other, and I realize I should leave the room." Rory laughs. "Jake also says the clues are there if you look for them." Jake is Rory's best friend.

"Jake and his top-ten question survey?" I ask. Jake swore by it after meeting his partner, Audrey.

Rory laughs. "It's a start. What did your parents say?"

"I never asked them that. Given that I wasn't sure that they would last. Too dangerous a topic." Our glances meet.

He asks, "Should we play a game?" The bookcase under one of the windows is filled with board games.

"Yes." Let's get off this topic. We play Scrabble, the board between us. I win two of our three games.

I run downstairs to use the bathroom, and the first floor is still ice cold.

"Should we move the single mattresses and sleep up here?" I ask when I come back up. "It's warmer up here now, and because of all the windows, the sun usually warms this up in the morning." Not that it's supposed to be sunny tomorrow.

He agrees. We carry the two mattresses up the stairs and set them up in front of the fireplace. It looks like two pals camping out. We get ready for bed. I burrow under my blankets, and he puts out the fire with a mug of cold water. It works well for putting out that blaze; unfortunately, the cold rain has done nothing to dampen my ardor for Rory.

CHAPTER SEVENTEEN

CLEANING HAS TO BE as unromantic an activity as a couple can possibly do together, especially when it's dreary and raining outside.

Rory makes a fire again, and we cook our usual breakfast together—pancakes, eggs, and strawberries. It feels very domestic, like we're starring in a cute-couple-cooking commercial. I tell Rory that he can work, he doesn't have to help me clean, but he says it will be quicker if we both do it. I can't argue with that.

Once pop music is blaring from the speakers in the living room, it feels quite lively. Is this the secret? Should my parents have just played pop music instead of arguing about who was responsible for cleaning what?

And that is before we find the pink cleaning gloves. Rory dons one pair and I wear the other. Then he suggests we might need the aprons, too. So now we each have an apron and pink cleaning gloves. I can't stop laughing at what Rory looks like. He grabs a bucket and a scrub brush and then suggests we take a picture together. We look happy. And the thing is, I am happy.

We separate to each clean a bathroom.

I'm just starting to scrub the tub when Rory sticks his head in and imitates a cleaning commercial. "Leaving any streaks? Grit? I hope you're cleaning to the shine." He holds up a Mr. Clean bottle.

He rubs a finger along the tub and tsks. "I expected better. Especially after last night's Scrabble win with 'ablution.'"

"Do you really want to criticize my cleaning job when I'm holding a paper towel covered in mold?" I ask, showing him the evidence from behind the toilet.

Rory backs away, hands up. "Don't shoot. I come in peace."

"Scary, isn't it?" I ask. I don't understand how he looks so good in pink cleaning gloves and a frilly apron embroidered with "Super Mom." I should continue cleaning the tub and take a cold shower.

"It's good we already ate our breakfast," he says.

He disappears back to his bathroom, and I finish mine. It is quite a satisfying experience to make it sparkle.

We compliment each other on our shiny bathrooms and then head to the bedrooms. They're easier. We strip all the beds, wash the linens, dust, vacuum, and mop. And then close the bedroom doors. Now it's just the top floor with the kitchen, living room, and dining area.

"Let's do the rest tomorrow since we're still using this area and bring in the Sunfish from the bay," I say. We eat a quick lunch. It has stopped raining, but it's still cloudy. Rory checks the weather forecast.

"Why don't we go sailing? It looks clear for the next two hours. No thunder or lightning," Rory says. Rory is an avid sailor. He and his dad sail a J-24 up in Maine at their cabin.

"That will be fun—unless the water is freezing. But I saw wet suits in the closet."

We suit up and bicycle down to the bay with our life jackets, the rudder, and the daggerboard.

The bay water is cold, but not yet unbearable.

We lift the boat off the wooden rack and slide it into the water. As the wind grabs the sail, we jump in. I handle the daggerboard while Rory takes the tiller—the long handle that steers the rudder. The wind is strong, and we tack out to the little islands in the middle of the bay. A Sunfish is small for two adults, so we're tight together.

"Coming about," Rory says. We both duck low, heads bent as the sail passes over our heads, and the boat switches directions. My body is right next to Rory's, our legs scrunched up in the cockpit.

Rory catches my glance; he has a huge grin on his face.

"I love sailing," he says.

"Me, too." A seagull cries out.

The air smells of seawater and fresh wind.

"Does Theresa sail?"

"Yes."

We sail ashore at one of the islands. It's mostly mucky marsh, so we just sit on a slim stretch of sandy beach for a bit, looking out over the bay in front of us, with Fire Island across. Rory leans back, stretching his feet out.

"It's good to get away from it all," he says.

"Yes," I say. "You know, Olivia didn't think we were dating."

"Why did Olivia not believe we were dating?"

"We seemed on edge around each other." I'm not going to say that I didn't look at him like I've slept with him. There's nothing we can do to address that. I let the sand sift through my fingers. It's cool to the touch.

"Maybe I wasn't caveman enough when Jamie was hitting on you," Rory says.

"He wasn't hitting on me. He was just being more flirtatious than usual."

Rory raises an eyebrow at me. "I'm not inviting any random woman to choose a dog with me."

"It could have been in my professional capacity as a dog boarder. But no, you're right."

"And why do you think your sister brought up the pictures?"

"I don't know. Maybe she was trying to encourage Jamie since she didn't think we were dating."

"Or make me jealous. You haven't done any pictures of me," he says. He almost sounds jealous.

"I've taken photographs of you."

"That doesn't count," he says.

If we were dating, I'd give him a frame with the picture Zelda took of us—the one where I'm looking at him with all my heart.

"Well, now I know what to get you for Christmas. I'll draw a picture of you." I stand to go back to the boat.

We get back into the boat and sail around the islands, then head toward shore, with me steering. The tiller suddenly feels looser in my hand, like it's not responding to my shifts in direction.

I push the tiller up. Nothing.

I push the tiller down. Again, the boat doesn't change direction.

The tiller isn't attached to the rudder.

"Luff the sail," I yell. I slide down the stern toward the tiller. The screw connecting the tiller to the rudder is gone. The rudder is locked into place on the boat, but the tiller is not attached, so we can't steer. Rory has luffed the sail, so the boat is facing into the wind and not moving.

There's nothing to fix it with in the Sunfish—no spare parts.

We look at each other in dismay.

"We could paddle," Rory says. He does go surfing with Jake.

That's definitely not going to be fun. We're in the middle of the bay, only halfway to shore. And I'm not even sure it will work.

My arms and back are still sore from carrying my suitcase for two miles. And we're cleaning the whole top floor of the house tomorrow. I look at him bleakly. I did seek to summon a fairy godmother of disasters, but this is going too far.

The boat jerks. Our daggerboard has hit sand. Rory lifts it up quickly, as our rudder pops up.

"Or ask a motorboat for help?" I ask. But no motorboats are around on this gray day.

"Okay, let's paddle." We take down the sail and lay it on the boat in between us. Then we lie down next to each other. We're shoulder to shoulder, and our hands are touching as we each grip the boat handle to hold on while we paddle with the other hand. Rory is stronger than me, so the boat turns to my side.

"This is not working." He sits up. "Let's take turns paddling. I'll go first."

I sit back in the cockpit while he goes out on the bow and paddles with both arms as if the boat was a surfboard. We inch forward.

We need another solution. Think, think. My bathing suit top has wire in it, but I don't think it's flexible enough to use to attach the rudder to the tiller. Plus, I can't actually strip in the middle of the bay. I've got elastic in my bikini bottom and then I have my wetsuit on. That's it. I push back some stray hair that's escaped from my ponytail. "Or I could try to use my ponytail holder as the screw to reattach it. Like a piece of string."

Rory gives me this look—like I've just impressed the heck out of him. I feel this warm burst of pride. I hope it works.

He paddles us several feet to a shallow part of the bay where we can stand. We both jump out. He holds the boat still while I thread my ponytail holder through the holes formerly occupied by the screw. And then tie it into a knot. It just might hold long enough. We raise the sail. He pulls the boat toward deeper water. I pop the rudder back down and clamber back into the cockpit.

He jumps back in. The boat picks up speed, and we are back on our way, sailing toward the sandy shore.

"It's working," I say. "It's responding to me, enough anyway."

I sail us right onto the shore. We hit land hard and jump out. He high-fives me.

"I can't believe you thought of that," he says.

"Desperation. My muscles still hurt from carrying our bags and cleaning. I really didn't want to paddle to shore."

We load the boat into a carrier and wheel it up to the house, then lift it and slide it in its storage space under the house. I take a picture of the rudder and tiller. I'll stop by the marine store in Manhattan—in the spring—and see if they carry the missing screw part.

"Don't you need to write?" he asks.

"I do. Do you mind?"

"No, I've got to answer emails."

We set up our laptops across from each other on the kitchen table. Cue the commercial for cute couple working.

The sky darkens.

I stare out the window at the rain coming down in straight lines. The weekend is not working to quell my feelings for Rory. If anything, the opposite. My feelings are deepening. It's like he sprinkles this fairy dust over our encounters, making them magical. He is right about love.

And I'm at a loss for more disasters I can create. I like eating too much to destroy our food supply. And my body is pretty sore and tired from the activities of the weekend already.

The best way to get over Rory might be to take a break from him. I should suggest we stop fake dating—for self-preservation. I can't cling to another unrequited crush. Even though I don't think it is an unrequited crush. Rory is interested, but apparently not enough. Anyway, I can't get involved now, just when I'm on the brink of success with my novel. I need my head filled with plot twists and deepening emotional connection—not Rory.

The outdoor patio umbrella on the upper deck is rocking back and forth in the wind, trying to stay upright in its cement stand. The umbrella itself keeps fluttering up; it's not tied tightly enough. That would be my feelings—trying to spread out and twirl but getting knocked over by the turbulent air. I grab my coat. I go outside, head bent against the wind and rain, to lay the umbrella down before it falls over and breaks.

“Time to take you out of this battle,” I say to the umbrella.

Chapter Eighteen

To: Penelope

From: Agent

Date: Sunday

Thank you for sending us *Midnight Masquerade*. I am sorry to say that it wasn't the perfect fit for my list. Although I like your voice and your character, there's too much backstory. This process is subjective, so we are sure another agent will feel differently. We hope you soon find a home for it with another agent.

I STARE AT THIS rejection. I only have one more query outstanding.

This confirms my decision not to tell Rory we should date for real, and instead, I should pull away. We finished cleaning the rest of the house this morning, and we were back in the city by midafternoon. He dropped me off at my apartment. It was quick, as if we both had made the decision to retreat and not cross any more lines. I was about to suggest we stop fake dating, but then he brought up that Callie was having a birthday party dinner catered at her house on Thursday. I asked him if he needed me as a barrier. He said that he hadn't wanted to interfere with my writing schedule, but he would love for me to come. I'm far enough ahead in my writing that I felt okay saying yes. Then I mentally kicked myself for not sticking to my resolution to disengage. But I decided that, after dinner, I will end this fake dating arrangement.

The last agent said there wasn't enough backstory in *Midnight Masquerade* and this agent says there's too much. I need to figure it out for myself. If only my own backstory was not holding me back.

Chapter Nineteen

I AM A WRITING machine. Pages are pouring out of me as all the confusion and mixed emotions of fake dating someone I've fallen for are translated into words. But now I close down my laptop. Tomorrow is October 1, so it's time for a Halloween-themed store window, even though I'd much rather stay here and keep writing, especially when the words are flowing. But I've made this commitment. And later, I'm going as Rory's fake date to a dinner party hosted by Callie.

I bike over to the store with a full backpack of props. I hang bats upside down from the window display ceiling. A mannequin is running full-out, with its head looking back to see what's following it.

Brawny Brian surveys my supplies by the windows.

"Well, at least we're saving money by not hiring a window decorator," he says. "Really, a sheet for the ghost?"

"Why did you think sales was a good career for you?" I ask. "Your encouraging vibe? All the positivity emanating from you?" Brian should be the model for my antagonist in *Fake Dating Folly*. "Do you have any more creative ideas for making a ghost?"

The sheet is draped over a wire, ghost-shaped contraption. I take my "ghost" out to the store's small backyard and hang it from a plant hook that used to hold a rhododendron. I drape the sheet in a ghost-like way and liberally spray it with starch. This is the way I'd make a dollhouse curtain—but with a lot less spray starch. I bring the ghost back in and hang it in the window, chasing the fleeing mannequin.

Brian goes outside and then comes back in, and I brace myself for his biting feedback. "It actually looks good," he says. "Especially the sign to get in shape before the ghosts get you. I like it."

I wonder how much window decorators make. Yet another stream of income to add to my motley mix of jobs. But at least it's another creative career and meshes well with my mini-scene skills. I know Theresa thinks I need a "real" job, but these are real jobs, and I am supporting myself.

I pose my two "Penelope and Rory" dolls in my miniature gym that still sits in one corner of the window. Rob is spotting Piper as she lifts weights. I post the photo on Instagram. I'll write up a blog post later tonight, after Callie's birthday dinner.

I'm seated at the opposite end of the table from Rory. Callie has place cards. Rory is next to Callie. But at least I'm next to Jake, and we were both part of Rory's circle in college, so we're friends. The place card for his girlfriend, Audrey, seats her on the other side of Rory. I wasn't expecting Jake to be here, but he is Rory's best friend, so I guess Callie knows him well from when she and Rory dated. Callie's business school friends seem to comprise the rest of the guests.

Audrey is the last to arrive, as she has some big case at work, and when she kisses Jake hello, she whispers to me, "We can always switch later if you want, so you can sit next to Rory. Or Jake and I can switch so I can hear all about your novel. I can't wait to buy it."

"Thank you for supporting my Etsy shop. You don't have to," I say to her.

"I love minis. I give the mini flowers to my friends for their birthdays. It's the perfect New York City gift—it's beautiful, it doesn't take up much space, it doesn't die, and it's unique."

"You should put that on your website," Jake says.

Audrey smiles at Jake. "I put that in all my reviews."

Jake and I catch up. He and Audrey visited Tokyo over the summer, and I never heard all the details, although I saw the pictures on Instagram.

"You have to tell me about your Mario Kart experience. That looked crazy," I say. Jake posted pictures of himself and Audrey, dressed as Mario, driving go-karts through the streets of Tokyo. "I can't believe that's allowed."

Jake laughs. "It was so wild. We did this two-hour Shinagawa course."

"In costume?" I ask.

"Would you expect anything less?" Jake says.

"No," I say.

"I have some video." Jake turns on his phone and searches. "How's the writing coming along?"

"Good. A publisher liked my first three chapters and wants to see the rest, but I'm still writing it." I explain what's going on, but I think I hear my name being mentioned at the other end of the table.

I hear Callie say to Rory, "You expressly said to me that you preferred a private life."

I don't hear his response.

"Penelope, your blog is so cute," Callie calls out. "I love how you've based it on your relationship with Rory."

I look up, shocked.

"You write stories on your blog about you and Rory?" someone asks.

"No, she enacts little miniature doll scenes. They're like Barbies, but smaller," Callie says.

I want to sink into my chair. It sounds awful. And very public.

My face flushes. Rory looks equally upset.

"It's not actually Rory and me," I say. It's true, given that the dolls are actually dating. I made that clear on my blog with an earlier breakfast scene where Piper is in Rob's pajama shirt and he's in his pajama bottoms. The fake dating was short-lived on the blog. Luckily. If Callie is following my blog, too. "One post was inspired by one of our dates—the cooking at the restaurant one—but other than that, it's fiction. Just like what I write."

"It feels like you and Rory," Callie says directly. She has the tone of someone who is asking casually, but she smiles slyly as if she's about to pounce. "Do you write about you and Rory in your book?"

Rory shakes his head.

"Not specifically, but obviously, I try to convey emotions." I pause as I think how best to answer. "I would say that I do try to capture the love underlying our relationship."

"Oh, that's right, you write romances," she says.

"I think Penelope's miniature scenes are art," Rory says. "They combine storytelling and visual imagery, almost like a film, and somehow she manages to invoke emotion with those scenes. Some artists work with paint or clay. She works with miniatures."

Callie sits back. Her lips compress into a thin line.

Audrey switches places with Jake and leans in to chat as the catering staff serves us a dessert.

She shakes her head. "Callie. Is she still interested in Rory?"

I look at her, surprised but also relieved at her bluntness. At least I'm not alone with my suspicions. "Yes."

"Oh Callie," Audrey says. "You're the only couple she separated. Jake texted me that he switched the place cards so he sat next to you. She had put you sitting with the lawyer I sat next to."

"Oh, I'm sorry, he shouldn't have done that," I say.

"He didn't think it was exactly fair that you were seated between strangers while we were all together next to Callie. Anyway, I caught up on law firm gossip." Audrey takes a bite of her cake. "She's not exactly being subtle, is she?"

"I'm not sure you can be subtle when you're hitting on someone else's boyfriend," I say.

Audrey snorts. "It's ironic because she's the one who broke it off. But then again, maybe that's why she can't move on—because she regrets her decision." Audrey's mouth tilts downward as she gazes at Callie.

"Yes, she even said that directly to me," I say. "And I think it's also that she's normally successful at getting what she wants." At least that's the impression she gives me. There are some bounce-back resilience benefits to being used to rejection.

Callie's catering staff clears our dessert plates, and Rory comes over. He says hi to Audrey.

"Are you ready to go?" he asks. I hug Audrey goodbye and face Rory. We look at each other in that moment. Others are also departing, so there's a bustle around us. But between us, there's just silence, as if we're taking stock of each other and this new threshold that we have to cross.

"I have to say thank you to Callie for the dinner," I say.

He takes a deep breath. "I suppose so."

We walk over to Callie, holding hands.

"Thanks for the delicious dinner." The catered dinner was good.

Callie says, "I'm looking forward to your art career taking off, and then I can say I knew you when."

I duck my head. "We'll see."

Rory and I walk out. This time, I don't argue when he suggests a cab.

"Two stops," he says to the cab driver, giving my address and then his.

His workbag is on the cab seat between us.

"I can change the doll, you know," I say.

"And devastate your blog followers? I don't think so." Rory looks out the window.

"Thanks for defending my miniatures in there," I say.

"I said what I believe. And we both know that what's happening on your blog is not what is actually happening in real life."

The cab turns onto Fifth Avenue to head south.

The cab makes a right turn to cross Central Park.

"I maybe haven't fully considered the effect of my work on the real people in my life," I say.

Rory glances at me. Lights from an oncoming car play across his face. "I hadn't considered it, either."

Ah. Callie knows him well.

"I guess that's it now," I say. "We don't need to fake date anymore. Myrtle's no longer pinching your butt, and I don't need to convince Jamie I'm over him."

Rory glances at me sharply. He starts to say something and stops. Suddenly, the cab is at my door.

"First stop," the cab driver says. The hazard triangle light on the dashboard is blinking red.

I reach for my wallet. Rory puts his hand over mine to stop me. I want to lace my fingers through his.

"You know I'm not going to take your money," he says. "I'm sorry about Callie."

"You don't have to apologize for Callie," I say.

"Did you get enough material for your book?" he asks.

"Yes." All the bewildering emotions. Now being deciphered on the page. If I dared showing that much of myself. "I got more than I expected." And now I'm worried it invades Rory's privacy.

I get out of the cab.

"See you soon?" I ask from outside.

Rory leans over across the seats and says, "Penelope?"

A car honks behind us. It can't pass.

"Friday? I know you're on deadline, but maybe we can hang out on Friday?" he asks. "Are there any places you need to research for your book? Unless you have your book club meeting on Friday."

I should say no. I'm already pressed for time. But maybe it's good to keep all these confused emotions going while I'm revising. The car honks again.

"My writers' critique group is on Thursday this week because Esther is going to a wedding this weekend. Friday works. I need something romantic they can do in New York," I say.

It's like we both know we shouldn't date, and yet we can't stop seeing each other.

"I'm on it," Rory says, smiling.

Chapter Twenty

THE DEVELOPMENTAL EDITOR I hired *hates* the opening scene of *Midnight Masquerade. Oof.* I sit back as I read her critique. And I'm thankful that I'm not hearing this in person so she can't see my face falling. She says I can't start out with my protagonist practicing to steal a painting with her friend because she comes across as an unlikable thief. She suggests I demonstrate her work ethic by showing her working to put together an art exhibit in the first scene.

I don't agree. But it has been getting rejected by agents so she could be right.

I stare at my first rejection on the wall. Discouragement is taking hold like a vine creeping up a house. *Midnight Masquerade* is in much better shape than *Fake Dating Folly*. I shake my head, stand, push my chair in under my desk, and decide to play by creating a mini scene. Piper is reading her novel at a local bookstore event, and Rob is in the front row. At least I can make my dreams come true in mini.

I should just put this critique to the side and continue revising *Fake Dating Folly*, but the critique is rolling around in my brain. Maybe I'll learn something if I follow her recommendation. The rest of her advice is good, and I can use it as I edit.

Enough procrastinating. I rewrite the beginning of *Midnight Masquerade*. My protagonist is at the office, running around, helping her boss to get ready for an art exhibit. Will they make the 5 p.m. deadline? When they do, I feel a sense of relief—but it's not a sexy hook. If I started a book where the protagonist was in an office collating and scanning an exhibit catalogue, I'd put it down. My gut feeling is that this does not work. I email my new opening chapter to my writing critique group for feedback Thursday night, and I return to revising *Fake Dating Folly*.

I am the last to arrive at our critique group meeting. My revised chapter is up first.

"It doesn't work for me. It's well written, but I wasn't riveted," Maria says.

I flinch. That's the kiss-of-death criticism. I should have been happy with light and fluffy. Instead of light and fluffy pancakes, I've cooked up hard rocks that should be thrown into the garbage.

"I think it's just this new chapter. I just couldn't get into it. But I liked the original chapter—and the book," Aarav says. Esther agrees that she likes the original version of the chapter better, but I made this new chapter more amusing than she expected.

It's back to my previous first chapter. I'll delete some dialogue and tighten it up. We discuss the rest of the chapter submissions. Esther and I leave the meeting together.

"How's *Fake Dating Folly* coming along?" Esther asks.

"It's complete crap."

"We all think that. Did you finish a draft?"

"I'm on my second draft."

"I find it's only my third draft when it all comes together," she says.

I sigh. "Let's hope."

I bike home.

Zelda and our neighbor Miranda are sitting on the couch, both in sweats, and eating ice cream out of the pint. I drop my bag on the floor. The apartment feels empty without any of our dog guests. Goldie is curled up on the couch, purring.

"Nobody liked my revised chapter," I say.

"I liked the original chapter," Miranda says.

"The original chapter is the right hook," Zelda says. "You have to trust your own judgment."

"Why the ice cream pints?" I ask.

"I was just telling Zelda that Oliver rejected me," Miranda says.

"Oliver rejected you?" I ask. I don't find this reassuring. Miranda is like an Amazon warrior goddess with her long, wavy, red hair and lithe body.

"Yes, I invited him up to my uncle's place for the weekend," Miranda says. "When we were getting ready to go to bed, I asked, 'Should I make up one bed or two?' And he said, 'Two.'"

"Ouch," I say.

"Exactly," Miranda says. "I pretended to be fine the next morning, but I was glad when I was back home and I could lose myself in painting." Miranda is a struggling artist.

"It's his loss," Zelda says.

"At least now I know. And I feel better that I put it out there," Miranda says. "I'm happy with the painting." She shows us a photo on her phone of an abstract painting. "See the two blocks of color? That symbolizes the two beds. And then I added the newspaper text as a collage over it." The newspaper collage bits say "Move On" and "Don't Enter."

"I like the painting," Zelda says.

"Me, too," I say. I can understand Miranda's point that it is better to know, but Oliver is not one of Miranda's best friends.

"I forgot to tell you," Zelda says. "I met Max the other day for lunch. We're both representing defendants in this stock exchange case."

"You guys were really cutting it up on the dance floor at that party," Miranda says.

"He's a good dancer," Zelda says.

"He is," Miranda says. "I love going to parties with him."

"But neither of you are romantically interested?" I ask.

"Definitely not," Miranda says.

"Nope," Zelda says.

"Why not?"

"The chemistry isn't there," Zelda says.

"Same," Miranda says, nodding. "Unfortunately."

Zelda picks up *Four Weddings and a Funeral* from the coffee table. "Did you watch this again last night?"

"Yes. I just don't get why Hugh Grant likes Andie McDowell over Kristin Scott-Thomas." I grab a pillow from the couch, stuff it behind my back, and lean against it.

"I thought you were over Jamie."

"I am over Jamie." *I'm in love with another best friend. Nothing like repeating mistakes.* "But I thought there was something there. So, how do I trust my judgment? What was missing for him? Yet it worked for me?" I know there's something there with Rory. I mean, we are hanging out all the time. It's like he can't let go, even if he's not quite willing to commit. And I'm not willing to take a chance, either.

Zelda sits next to me. "If you look at Andie McDowell's character, she was American, kind of an unknown quantity, kind of free, kind of like a man in her attitude, she sleeps with him on the first date and then tries to slip out of the bedroom. Kristin Scott-Thomas's character even calls her a slut."

"Are you saying Jamie didn't like me because I am not a slut?"

Zelda tilts her head. "No, you're not listening. Kristin Scott-Thomas's character is upper-crust British, constrained. Hugh Grant wants the unknown. You're part of Jamie's family. You're not new. It could be as simple as that."

"But then best friends can't ever turn into lovers?" My shoulders slump.

"Are we still talking about Jamie?" Zelda gives me a knowing look. "I'm saying that was the case for Jamie. Rory is a different story."

He is.

I'd been holding on to this story of Jamie as my soul mate because he connected me to my parents. But that's just a myth. Dating Jamie is not going to bring me any closure on the death of my parents. That's something I have to find on my own. But I feel like I'm getting closer, now that I recognize that Jamie isn't the partner for me.

Rory is the one who appreciates me just as I am. And I don't want to be holding back my emotions, afraid of censure, nor do I want to keep wrestling with these past regrets. I need to open up more to Rory, and, once the book is done, tell him how I feel. I have to trust my judgment.

Chapter Twenty-One

I AM A GLUTTON for punishment. I can't believe I suggested to Rory that we do something romantic. I'm standing at Chelsea Piers by the Hudson River, waiting for him. He suggested we take a city lights night sail on the 105-foot, three-masted, Schooner *America 2.0* with live jazz. The three sails and the jib of the beautiful boat are billowing in the wind. Small waves are lapping against the hull while the onboard jazz band is warming up their instruments.

Rory appears with a backpack. "I brought dessert."

"So did I." I hold up a box of Levain Bakery cookies.

"Great minds think alike." He opens his knapsack to show me a box of beignets. "We'll be okay, then, if we get shipwrecked."

"As long as the other passengers don't see our contraband," I say.

"We can take them," he says. "Just use those skills you showed me during our snowball fight." We walk across the plank to board the boat. We take our seats along the side.

The Boat Band, a jazz trio, is playing "I Thought About You," "No More Blues," "Autumn Leaves," and "Along Came Betty."

There's a breeze. Rory breathes in beside me and says, "That's one of my favorite things about New York City, that we're so close to the water."

"Did you really go surfing this morning?" I ask. Rory had texted me a picture of him surfing this morning.

"Yes, the guys said that the waves were great yesterday and I figured I could still get back to work by 10:00. I didn't have any morning meetings."

"What do you like about surfing?"

"I like being in the water. And when you catch a wave, it's the most exhilarating feeling. It's such a rush of adrenaline. But even when you're just waiting, I don't know. I get some of my best ideas sitting out there on my board. I feel like it gives me balance. I can get really caught up in work, and it gives me perspective. If I miss a wave, I will catch another. And I like the camaraderie."

I nod.

We sip our complimentary glasses of champagne as the boat sets sail down the Hudson River, passing Battery Park, toward Ellis Island. Seagulls swoop, the Staten Island Ferry passes us, and the salt air washes away my stress. I lean back against the wooden ship. The sun begins to set. Rays of pink, orange, and light blue streak across the sky as if exploding in joy, while an egg-yolk sun slips down under the horizon.

As dusk creeps in, the lights of the city shine like fireflies in the night. I lean my head against Rory's shoulder, and he puts his arm around me, warming me. Nobody knows us here, so we're not faking it. This is real. But I don't dare disturb the equilibrium to express my feelings in words to Rory. This is enough for now. Just being together in the moment, not the future. It's more than enough for now.

Chapter Twenty-Two

IT'S SATURDAY, AND JAMIE'S over helping me with my website. He's sitting at my desk. I've pulled up one of the dining room chairs next to him to watch what he does so I can do it myself if it needs fixing. We're chaperoned by Goldie, who is spread out on the bed, sleeping.

"I'm impressed," he says. "I don't think you really needed me to get this done."

"That took me several hours of watching YouTube videos. It was painful and I gave up. You're almost done, and you've been here for an hour."

"You should've asked me earlier."

"Yes," I say. I should have, but I was worried it might stir old feelings. But it just feels like old friends between us. There are no sparks; it's nothing like what I feel with Rory.

I check my email as he works. Trilby, my favorite teacher, posted comments on my opening five pages of *Fake Dating Folly*. I'm taking her online class, "Your First Five Pages." She writes: "*Okay. First two sentences. Gripping. I'm THERE. But then you start explaining in a long, convoluted sentence. Trust the reader.*"

I barely trust myself.

Jamie is peering closely at the computer, typing away. I can't believe I don't feel anything—except fondness. He's muttering to himself about widgets.

He looks up, and I smile affectionately at him.

"You know, I've been thinking about what you said last year," he says.

I freeze. I don't want to rehash this. He runs his hand through his curly hair. That signature move of his used to keep me awake at nights when we were in high school.

"I made a mistake," he says. "I feel more for you than I thought. I keep thinking back to you saying so frankly, 'I love you.' And—"

I put my hand out to stop him. "I'm happy with Rory."

And as I say that, I know it's true, even if, at the moment I said it, I thought I was in a relationship with Rory. It's just a very complicated relationship.

He looks down. "Yes, I didn't mean to imply otherwise."

"It's the big gesture of romance novels," I say. "There's a reason why they work. Because even when they don't work, there's something about the laying it all bare that lasts. And creates a certain fondness." Not that Jamie was even willing to lay it all bare here. "I feel more for you than I thought" isn't much. Lame, really. I shake my head.

He nods. "I spoke out of turn. I'll get back to widgets."

I don't want it to be awkward between us. "Why do they use the term widget?" I ask. "They have to know that that brings back painful memories of math exams. If Penelope buys ten widgets and four plug-ins, and Jamie adds ten plug-ins, how many updates will Penelope have to monitor?"

"I'm thinking that for coders, those memories are not painful." Jamie smiles. "Regardless, I've put it all on automatic updates."

"Brilliant."

"Don't forget to check the Yoast SEO of your content before you post. Here, click it. It's ready."

I hit publish. "A Yoast to me. My website is live."

He laughs. It feels like old times, and I'm happy about that.

The doorbell buzzes.

"That's Rory." I run to buzz him in.

I jog down to meet Rory on the stairs.

"Trilby just sent me comments on *Fake Dating Folly* and it's mind-blowing!" I say.

"She liked it?" He hugs me hello. He smells of cold autumn air.

"No, she wrote that the first two sentences were lovely and then I lost the reader. But she showed me what I'm doing wrong. I finally understand what I need to do to make it right." I do a little dance at the top of the stairs around him. "I get it now."

He laughs and holds up the bag of takeout burritos. "So, we can celebrate tonight, and I can feel less guilty about taking you away from writing to see this ghost tour?"

"Yes, definitely. And my website is done. Jamie just finished it. We just pushed it live."

We enter the living room and cross over to my bedroom.

"Hey, Rory, good to see you." Jamie stands and grabs his bag from the floor. "I'll be going, then. I'm having dinner with my mom. Who, by the way, is super impressed with your miniatures business. How did you accomplish that?"

"I sent her my sales/expenses statement for October," I say. "Zelda suggested that idea."

Jamie nods. "It worked."

"She didn't say anything to me," I say.

Jamie moves back as Rory admires my website sufficiently. I cross off "build website" on the to-do list on my bulletin board. It feels so good.

Jamie leaves the room, and I follow him, Rory behind me.

"Thanks again," I say.

"Anytime," Jamie says, smiling. "Have fun tonight."

I close the door behind Jamie and say to Rory, "You don't have to feel guilty. My characters are going on a ghost tour. I need to be able to describe it—and the house." I go to the kitchen to get drinks and plates.

I place the pitcher on the table. Rory takes off his coat and hangs it on the hook with his messenger bag.

I say, "Plus, it'll give me more ideas for window display decorating. And I can't wait to do a mini blog scene where Rob and Piper visit a haunted house. That will be perfect for my Halloween post."

Rory is fiddling with the dollhouse. Piper and Rob are eating on a miniature patio. The patio lights up. Rory picks up a dog from the dollhouse apartment and adds it to the patio. I sit at the dining room table and unwrap my burrito. Rory is still standing away from the table, his back to me.

"Are you excited about going to London for the shoot on Friday?" I ask.

He turns around to face me. "Yes, but nervous, too. I wondered if you want to come along and use it as a writing retreat. I'll be working late, so I won't see you much, and I know you need to write, but maybe we can squeeze in a few hours of fun. I can pay for your ticket with my frequent flyer miles."

I only have thirteen days until I submit my manuscript to Strawbundle Publishing. I can't say yes.

"I know I shouldn't ask you, but you did say that you had one scene in London and you were worried that you were not capturing it correctly from memory, so this would give you that opportunity," he says. "And I just think it'd be more fun with you. You've been such a part of this campaign, and you should come to the wrap dinner. But not at the cost of your book." Rory looks at me as if he really wants me to go. He walks forward, closer to me.

My book—which could be rejected upon receipt by Strawbundle Publishing—*or London. With Rory.*

I can't say no to Rory. And I love London. I was last in London a few years ago when I attended the Romantic

Novelists' Association Conference. And I'll be writing in a hotel, with no distractions. Couldn't be better.

"Yes," I say.

He smiles, and it's such an unreserved smile of joy that I catch my breath.

"Myrtle is coming, so I was hoping we could fake date one more time in front of her," he says.

I hesitate. *I don't want to fake date anymore. I want to be the real date. I should say that now.*

"Or we can say we broke up and we're just friends," he says. "I don't want to fake date anymore, either."

Why? Is it a hardship to fake date me?

"But why don't you want to fake date?" I ask.

"It's not for real," he says flatly. "I can book a room with two beds."

It was real for me. It doesn't sound like he agrees. He turns away. I stare at his back. It looks stiff and unyielding.

I had really hoped and believed . . . I stare at the Robert Doisneau picture on the wall, swallowing my disappointment, and say, "It's fine. We can fake date one more time. We shouldn't destroy all our hard work to deter her. To paraphrase you, when I suggested I change the Rob doll, and you said we couldn't devastate my blog followers. And I'll pay for my ticket."

"No, really, it's okay. These points are about to expire anyway." He smiles, and it's the warm smile from before. "So, one last time fake dating? It would probably be weird to tell them we broke up and we're still traveling together."

"Yes," I say, smiling back. The important thing is keeping our friendship. "When do we come back?"

"Back the following Sunday."

Luckily, no dogs are booked to stay with me. Benson, Gilda, and Cleo are all at home with their owners. And Zelda can take care of my cat, Goldie. "I'll have to write."

"I'll be working most of the time."

"Yes. Ooh, I can email my writing friend Julia, whom I met at the RNA conference, and see if she's free to meet up for lunch, if I have time. I'm excited."

We eat our burritos quickly while Rory explains his schedule in London. He'll be working most nights as well, so I will really be on my own. But that's perfect. We agree that we will take off the Saturday we arrive and enjoy London. This trip will be my reward for finishing a third draft tomorrow.

We take the subway down to Eighth Street and walk over to East Fourth Street. The Tradesman's House Museum is a three-story, brick house, Federal style. A black-clothed wreath hangs on the door. We walk up the stone stairs to the front entrance and push open the heavy, wooden door.

"Welcome to the haunted mansion of New York," a wavery voice whispers as we enter. The hallway is fairly narrow and dimly lit with an ornate, wooden staircase ahead of us. About eight other people are in the hallway. A door clangs shut. I flinch. Rory puts his arm around me. *More fake dating advice for my protagonist: definitely go on a haunted house tour.*

A person in a long, flowing, black gown holding a candle welcomes us. She directs us to enter the parlor.

A coffin covered with flowers holds center stage there. A fire crackling in the fireplace, and candles on the mantel, provide the only light. The curtains are drawn, and the air smells of camphor. I wouldn't want to work here. I'm going to smell of camphor if we stay in this room for very long.

"Please pay your respects to our patriarch. Then you may sit in the wooden chairs along the wall. The couches are off-limits. The relatives are still sitting there." She chuckles.

I shiver. I don't believe in ghosts, but the dim lighting and the very real-looking mannequin in the coffin are definitely creepy. I hope it's not an actor who is going to pop up and scare us. The wide-planked floor creaks as we solemnly file past the coffin and sit on the wooden chairs. I whisper to Rory that we should make sure we are in the middle of the group—harder to surprise.

An eerie whistle breaks the silence.

Rory whispers, "I need to add that to my Halloween party soundtrack."

A man enters, wearing a black suit that looks like it's from the nineteenth century. He tells us about the ghostly visits that employees and visitors have experienced—mostly from Miss Ingrid, the last resident of the family who owned this house before it became a museum. She died in the 1930s, in her nineties. A log cracks on the fire. Everyone jolts. He speaks in a very low, very deep voice, forcing us all to lean forward to hear him. It has the atmosphere of ghost stories over a campfire, heightened by the coffin with the dead guy in front of us. "See the original plaster. The egg and the dart. Symbolizing life and death. The line between life and death is very close. We may not think that today, but back then, the thought was ever-present."

I know that. One day I had my parents, the next day, I didn't.

"For Miss Ingrid was only twenty-five when her father died. Life and death. Life and death." He breathes the words out. I shiver. Rory takes my hand.

"Are you okay?" he whispers. His nose brushes my hair. I shiver for a different reason.

"This is eerier—more morbid—than I expected," I say.

A door slams ahead of us.

The man says, "It's time for us to depart. They are calling us."

We leave the room and walk up the staircase to the second floor.

The man says, "Not only Ingrid, the final mistress of the house, comes to visit. Other family members also appear from time to time. One employee saw Ingrid's sister leaning over the railing on the landing. Do you feel the concentration of energy at the top of the stairs?" We are now standing at the top of the stairs. The landing is lit by one light and our guide's candlelight.

One woman says she does feel it. She's closed her eyes and is humming.

I whisper to Rory, "Do you think they plant actors among the guests?"

His hand tightens around mine.

"Let's go to Ingrid's bedroom," the man says.

The floor creaks as the ten of us narrowly file down the hallway toward the bedroom. A cobweb hits me in the face, and I shriek. It's fake, but effective.

"I'd also recommend cobwebs in the pitch dark for your party," I whisper to Rory.

The woman at the front screeches. "I didn't see the mannequin until the last minute," she says. Now we're all forewarned. At the end of the landing, next to the door, is a wax figure dressed in black, gesturing for us to go into the bedroom.

A mannequin in a white nightgown is sitting up in a wooden bed, looking very Ebenezer Scrooge.

"Close your eyes. Can you feel the energy in the room?" the man asks. This room has a different, stuffy smell of linen that's been in the closet for too long.

We file through the bedroom into a well-lit room, where photographs of rooms from the house hang on the wall. Our tour leader shows us how each has an unexplained, glowing orb. It's definitely peculiar.

We tour the rest of the house, following the flickering candle. I hold tightly to Rory's hand, but no more cobwebs.

The tour is over, and we leave by the front entrance.

"That was weirdly spooky," I say. The wind is cold off the East River. I button up my coat and wrap my scarf around my neck. Most of the stores on the block are now closed.

"Yeah. Were you okay when they . . . ?" Rory looks at me, concerned.

I squeeze his hand. "Yes. I just thought, it's true. And I felt bad for Ingrid that she lost her father at such a young age, too." I smile. "I wish my parents were still available for chats."

"We could always try a medium." He gives me his half-smile.

"Add that to the list for your Halloween party."

"I don't know how you handled it so well. If my parents died, I would be devastated. They're like my best friends—but the older, PG version."

We turn to walk up Lafayette Street, past the Schermerhorn Building with its huge, arched windows.

"I didn't handle it well. I was a wreck."

"But you're not a wreck anymore. It would be worrisome if you hadn't been a wreck when it happened."

"Michael couldn't handle it," I say. Lafayette Street has beautiful buildings built in the 1880s, with huge, arched windows.

The lights are on in the New York Sports Club on the second floor across the street. Through the arched windows, a woman is running on a treadmill. We pass the more modern, curved-glass façade of Astor Place.

He says, "He probably didn't like feeling helpless and unable to fix it. I can imagine that's how I'd feel."

"Zelda really pulled me through by just being there and listening and letting me express my grief. And writing out my feelings helped, too."

"That's what my dad says about therapy. That talking about it—not leaving it bottled up inside—can help. He also always recommends journaling."

"That's good advice."

"Hey, we're in the neighborhood of Veniero's," Rory says. "Should we go? Are you still off the clock?"

"Can't pass up Veniero's. I always need fuel for writing."

We walk a few more blocks over to Veniero's. It's not too crowded. The front area is a bakery with glass displays of pastries. In the back, the hostess is taking reservations for tables in the seating area. She hands us two menus and takes us around to a table on the other side. We order two hot chocolates, a cannoli for Rory, a strawberry tart for me, a plate of cookies to share, and a box of cannoli and fruit tarts to go as a surprise for Zelda. The waitress takes it all down without batting an eye.

Rory talks about his ad campaign preparation, and I discuss the stumbling blocks I'm running into in my book. We work through some issues, and I scribble notes in my little, black notebook. It is very comfortable, but more than that, it feels so right—like we're some dynamic duo together. I don't discern any frissons of electricity, except for once when our fingers touch as we both reach for the same cookie. That was more like a bolt up my arm. Something flares in Rory's eyes. But it disappears so quickly that I could have imagined it. Rory shifts in his chair.

At 10:30 p.m., I say I should be getting home. Rory nods. He's got a big week ahead, too. We take the subway Uptown. He kisses me good night on the cheek when he gets off, but it's our old "just friends" kiss on the cheek.

I'm going to interpret his "it's not for real" as him saying he would like it to be real. I know this plotline from romance novels. In novels, it causes weeks of confusion as both think the other isn't interested. So, even though I lost my nerve at that moment, what with his "two beds" comment, his back turned to me, I know he is attracted to me. Okay, he doesn't seem to be rip-my-clothes-off attracted, but then he wouldn't be. That's not his style. London is an opportunity to change this friendship dynamic. I can use this fake dating scheme to persuade Rory that we could last long term. This is the last chance for our pretend dating and spending a significant amount of time together. I go home to revise the final scenes of my book when she changes the dynamic, and their fake dating relationship becomes a real relationship.

Chapter Twenty-Three

MY ALARM WAKES ME up at 7 a.m. to write on Monday morning. I add and delete scenes as I tighten it, now that I know what I'm aiming for. Esther was right about the third draft.

I sent my revised first five pages of *Fake Dating Folly* back to Trilby yesterday afternoon. I don't have her skill, but I could feel that I improved it.

She writes back: "You're 90 percent there. Did you feel it? You need to write to that feeling." *Did I feel it?* I knew when my description was good. So, I felt something there. A feeling of yes! *Write to that feeling.* I go back through the manuscript.

Zelda is up and moving about the living room.

"It's coming together, finally," I say as I send the first fifty pages to Esther, ahead of schedule.

She high-fives me. "That's excellent." Zelda stretches on our living room floor, getting ready to go to the gym.

"Rory invited me to London for a writing retreat. I'm leaving Friday."

"You're going to London? I thought you had to write." Zelda looks horrified.

"I'm going to write there. He'll be working, so it will be like a writing retreat."

"Wouldn't it be better to stay here and write? Less distractions?" She rolls her legs on our foam roller.

"Probably. But I'm not going to turn down a trip to London with Rory." I stretch on the floor next to her. I'm tight from sitting in my chair.

"Even when this is your chance to publish your book?" she asks.

"This isn't going to interfere with my chance to publish my book."

"But you're losing two travel days."

"Not really. I'm sending the whole manuscript to Esther on Friday, so I'll be waiting for her comments anyway, and it's good to take a break from it. And then I'll travel back after I submit it."

Zelda shakes her head. "It seems like really bad timing. You need to give up on Rory—and certainly not sacrifice your writing career for him. I'm disappointed in him that he even asked you to consider it."

"That's a bit harsh. I'm my own person, and he trusts me to be able to make my own decisions. If I really thought this would interfere with my writing, I would have said no."

She snorts. "Aren't you still holding out hope that you and Rory will date for real?"

"This is my chance. It's like the fake dating trope setup where they go away together for a week."

"You tried that already, and it didn't work."

"I didn't try it for real. This time, I'm going to go all in."

"Then you should tell him you like him. Because you're stuck there together. That would be going 'all in.'" She gives me a "don't kid yourself" look and curves her arm over her head. "My neck is so tight. But not until your book is finished."

"The only problem will be if he doesn't like me, and we have to travel back together in excruciatingly awkward silence."

"But if he does, you will have a really romantic time in London."

"So, the reward is worth the risk, but . . . imagine if Jamie and I had been stuck together after I told him I loved him and he said he didn't love me. That would have been brutal." I shudder. "And I agree. I need to focus on my writing. That will be my final week to incorporate Esther's suggestions."

"Is it really worth going?"

That was a good question. I wasn't willing to say no to a trip to London with Rory. A different environment might be the key to making this a real relationship. We've never taken a week vacation together, and traveling together can be revealing. It's like a relationship on steroids. A shiver runs through me. My parents vacationed to get back the magic. I shake my head. That was different. That was a small plane, a fluke. We will be flying in a big, commercial plane.

Zelda shakes her head. "I don't think you should go. You need to finish your book before you tell him you like him—just in case he doesn't like you back. That would throw you off your game emotionally. But if you're not going to tell him before London, and you're going to be sharing a room, then you're constrained to cementing this narrative of being friends and fake lovers in a really intimate setting. You'll be afraid to push it further when you should be pushing it to becoming real lovers. It's a mistake."

I thought Zelda would think it was a great idea.

"When we're together, does it seem like he likes me?" I ask.

"He definitely likes you. As more than a friend? I can't tell," she says. "But you have moved to the Saturday night date slot."

"That's because he's not dating anyone else."

"And why is that?" She crosses her arms. "Frankly, I'm surprised he hasn't made a move."

"He did," I whisper.

"What?"

I wince. “It seemed like he was going to kiss me when we were dancing, but I moved my head . . . I was scared.”

Zelda leans over and hugs me. “Oh, honey, you should give Rory a chance. You take so much rejection in your writing. You are stronger than you think.”

I hug Zelda back. “I was about to tell him I liked him, but then he said I had been right to keep it to just friends. But I should try again, shouldn’t I?”

“If you rejected him, yes.”

“Okay, Operation Seduce Rory in London is on. After I’m sure my book is in good shape.”

“Yes, finish the book first.”

And I have friends in London. Not just friends but romance writers. They’re the ideal people to email asking for ideas of romantic things couples can do.

Chapter Twenty-Four

I WAKE UP IN my airplane seat when they put the lights back on to serve us breakfast, only to find spittle on my chin. At least it's not on Rory. I fell asleep on Rory's shoulder right after dinner. So much for starting this on a romantic note. I was just so tired from working fourteen-hour days to pull my book together. Esther is reading the whole manuscript now.

Honestly, I'm not sure I can get both the guy and the book deal, but I'm willing to try.

We pull our rolling carry-ons up to the hotel entrance on Piccadilly. It's only 10 a.m., but Rory was able to get an early check-in because of his hotel point status.

"I love London," I say. "But I need a nap first." I do not look gorgeous after a transatlantic plane flight. I do not hit the ground running. Rather, I look like someone whose face has been mushed against a sweatshirt pillow. As indeed it was. But it's good for Rory to see me as I am.

"Me, too. Nap until one," Rory says. "And then sights."

We check in and get our room keys. We take the elevator up to our floor, push through some glass fire doors, and then open the door to our room. A double bed greets us.

"But I thought you said we'd have separate beds," I say.

He blushes. “I asked for two beds. I can call the front desk and ask them to change our room.”

Aargh. I want to kick myself. I freaking shouldn’t have said anything. Now it looks like I want us to have single beds. I was just so shocked by the double bed. “No, no, it’s okay. We can manage a double bed.”

“No, I should call.”

Why doesn’t he want a double bed? He won’t be able to resist me, or he’s afraid I’ll attack him?

Rory calls the front desk. He nods his head. Then, holding his hand over the receiver, he says, “We can have two separate beds, but it will be this afternoon.”

“No.” I shake my head. “I want to nap now. We can share the bed.”

Rory nods and says into the phone, “It’s okay. We’ll keep the current room.”

“I call the bathroom first.” I unzip my suitcase, take out my toiletries, and disappear into the bathroom. I shower, wiping away the plane grime. I wish I’d brought my regular, cotton T-shirt and pajama pants. I only brought sexy nightgowns that Zelda made me buy for the trip. But they were supposed to entice from afar. I can’t believe I acted all prim and proper about the beds. I’m such an idiot.

I wrap my fluffy, white towel around me. I forgot to bring a change of clothes into the bathroom. *Okay, channel Bridget Bardot in a towel.* I have the chest, at least.

I walk out. “All yours.” I smile.

Rory looks up from his phone and does a double take. *Wait until he sees my nightgowns.*

I sashay past him toward my suitcase. The room is very small. There’s just the double bed, a desk and chair, and two couch chairs with a round table in-between in front of the window looking out over a back courtyard.

Rory grabs his stuff and retreats into the bathroom. I packed three casual T-shirts. I put on one and jump into bed, pulling the covers up. Sexy nightgowns must be saved for nighttime, not now, when we're both desperate for sleep.

"Do you have a preference for which side of the bed?" I yell at the bathroom door.

"Right," he says. I move over to the left side.

"Okay, I set my alarm for 1 p.m." I curl on my side and close my eyes. I'm so jetlagged that Rory could get in the bed naked and I would not notice. And I need my beauty rest because I have a list of activities planned for the time that we have together, all courtesy of my romance writer friends.

Chapter Twenty-Five

ROOSTERS ARE CROWING. IT'S the alarm. I hit snooze. But then I remember I'm in London. With Rory. In the same bed. I turn around to face him. We're so close. Barely a foot separates our faces. And his hair. I just want to run my fingers through it. He's got the most perfect chiseled cheekbones. It's almost unfair that he gets that as a guy. His blue-green eyes open.

"Hey, Curls."

"Hey, you. Ready for lunch?" I sit up in our incredibly luxurious and comfortable bed. The crisp, white sheets are rumpled now.

He covers his eyes with his arm. "I haven't slept enough."

"Too much and you won't adjust." I pull his arm off his eyes. So close now. He's not wearing a shirt. I am definitely awake. "Up and at 'em."

"I thought you weren't a morning person."

"I'm not. It's afternoon, and we're in London. C'mon." I get up, grab my clothes, and get dressed in the bathroom.

When I come out, he has changed into a worn, blue, button-down and jeans. *All mine. For this week, anyway.*

We have a quick sandwich lunch at a place nearby. I look at what plays are available tonight and read the summaries out loud.

"Are you talking in a British accent?" he asks.

"I am, darling, I am. I may talk in a British accent for the whole trip." I lean toward him. "Unless we actually talk to British people, in which case I will not embarrass myself."

"Let's see *The Importance of Being Earnest*," he says. "That's one of my favorite plays."

"Are you serious? That's so old-fashioned. And we know the ending."

"I'm an old soul. And you can't go wrong with Oscar Wilde."

"But there's *Upside Down*, the one about women and relationships."

"You know, that could go either way." He leans back, the chair scraping against the wooden floor.

True. It could be excruciating. Or too revealing. Or both.

"Fine. Oscar Wilde it is." We walk back to Piccadilly Circus and buy tickets for the play.

And then Rory suggested a RIB boat ride in the Thames. I choose the seat by the water. The guide is knowledgeable and gives us a great tour of London from the Thames, from the Tate Museum onward, with lots of witty commentary. And now it's the high-speed part. The boat takes off quickly, and I grab Rory's hand, laughing. The spray hits my face.

"In case I wasn't awake," I say.

Several high-speed turns and it's over. We disembark. We decide to walk around London and just enjoy the city before we have dinner and watch the play. For an early dinner, he picks a rooftop bar overlooking the Thames. The river is all lit up, and it's spectacular.

We take the Tube from Waterloo back to Piccadilly and walk to the theatre, joining the crowd of theatregoers finding their shows. We hand in our tickets and take our plush, red seats.

His phone beeps, and he silences it. He shakes his head. He puts his phone back in his pocket. "It's Callie."

"Didn't you tell her we were going to London?" I ask. I love saying "we."

"Yes."

"Do you think she doesn't believe we're actually dating?" I ask. She'd have that similar insight into Rory that my sister had for me.

"No, she believes it. She just thinks she can get me back."

I raise my eyebrows and nod my head in acknowledgement. That's Callie and confidence—especially if she sees me as an introverted bookworm or, worse, a writer mining and exposing all of Rory's inner thoughts.

"What attracted you to her in the first place?"

He hesitates and glances at me. I have a feeling he's choosing his words carefully. "It started out so well. Callie is driven; she's outgoing, sociable, charming . . ." *The opposite of me. This is brutal. Maybe he's not choosing his words so carefully. Why did I ask this question?* "Ambitious. When we first started going out, it was like this mad energy and we motivated each other." He looks down at the theatre program. "But then it became all about her."

So, he does see that.

"And if I said anything, she'd become distant, emotionally absent. I don't know. I thought we'd work through it. But we didn't. And then she gave me that ultimatum. And that was not the solution. But I was still surprised when she dumped me. I guess I remembered the good, and I wanted that back. And now *she* wants that back."

Definitely don't encourage him to go back. But I can't badmouth her. I nod.

He looks at me. "My dad said she wouldn't change."

"He did?" I knew it. His dad does weigh in on his relationships.

"Well, he was trying to make me feel better that she had rejected me."

"But he's a psychologist. He must believe in the power of people to change. I mean, psychologists say that children who lost their parents young can have commitment issues, but not all do." *I need to address head-on what his father may have said about me.*

"Did you get counseling after your parents died?"

"No. Maybe I should have." I rub my forehead. "But I did express a lot of my feelings in writing."

Rory nods. "You did. I should show that piece to my dad."

As if I've been a topic of conversation. It doesn't have to mean that. It could mean that he thinks my writing might help others coping with death. *I was very emotionally open with that piece. Why did I stop? It may really be the problem with my writing.*

"But after that story, everyone wanted to call me and talk to me about grief and dying and losing someone, and I was this safe person to talk to about it. That definitely helped me initially, but then it got to be too much. I didn't want to talk about it all the time. Strangers called me to talk to me about someone they'd lost, and it would make me so sad. But I felt I couldn't *not* talk about it with them because most people don't want to talk about grief, and they needed an outlet. And I certainly didn't want to add to their pain," I say. "But the pressure of 'you handle this so well' became too much—especially when I didn't feel like I was handling it well. I was falling apart, but Michael's reaction made me afraid to share that with anyone. Except Zelda, who obviously knew since she lived with me. And I didn't want to just be that person who lost her parents. You really rescued me there. Because you treated me like normal." I place my hand over his.

"Not like normal. That's way too boring for you." He squeezes my hand.

"Like quirky in a good way."

"Yes." Rory meets my glance and holds it. "Your reaction makes sense to me." His thumb moves up and down my palm.

The lights dim and the curtain rises. His arm brushes against mine on the seat armrest. Finally, the world of Oscar Wilde quiets my mind and I relax into the play, as much as I can when I am attuned to Rory's every shift.

Chapter Twenty-Six

ON A HAPPY BUZZ from a good story, we walk around the Shaftesbury Memorial Fountain in Piccadilly Circus and down Piccadilly Avenue toward our hotel. Just as we're about to enter the lobby, Rory grabs my hand. Surprised, I look at him, but then I hear Myrtle yoo-hooing.

Myrtle stands way too close to Rory and keeps poking him in the chest as she tells us about the play they saw. She invites us to join them in the hotel bar, but Rory says no because we're jetlagged. He suggests that we have drinks another night.

We escape into the elevator. Rory just shakes his head.

I am gathering up my courage for tonight's nightgown reveal.

He unlocks the door and clicks on the light.

I suggest he take the bathroom first. I'm tempted to wear my T-shirt again. *Stop being silly.* It's no more revealing than a bathing suit. Except it's lacy and red. But not sheer. Zelda and I checked that.

Rory comes out of the bathroom in a T-shirt and boxer shorts. His legs are thin, but muscular—like runners' legs. He clears his throat. "Eyes up here, Curls."

"Just admiring the goods. My fake dating self has very good taste."

He ducks his head and smiles crookedly.

I sashay off to the bathroom.

I slip on the red nightgown. It didn't look this revealing at home. And I do not have the body of a gazelle. I'm more like your friendly cocker spaniel. And who would you rather be in bed with—a gazelle or a cocker spaniel? Clearly a cocker spaniel. So, I'm good.

I walk out of the bathroom and straight into Rory. He steadies me with his hands. I look up and say, "Eyes up here, Rory."

Rory's gaze meets mine, and he blushes. "I didn't picture you as the type to wear red negligees to bed."

I'm not. But now I am. "I'm full of surprises."

We each climb into bed. Sitting each at our respective edges. Gazes ahead.

There is silence. My stomach feels all fluttery with Rory so close.

Rory turns to me. "Should we put that long pillow between us? I don't know. I turn in my sleep, and I can't promise I won't touch you."

I should say we don't need a buffer, it's okay if you touch me, but I can't. I just can't. I must finish my book first. "If it makes you feel more comfortable."

"It does." He leaps out of bed, grabs the long pillow from the armchair, and puts it between us. Good sign or bad? He wants a buffer? Or he needs a buffer so he behaves? I'll ask Zelda in the morning.

I rest my head on the buffer pillow and stare over at him. "This reminds me of Olivia's pregnancy pillow."

He chuckles. "Keep up the sexy talk."

I want to smack my forehead, but okay, he asked for it. "Olivia bought a pregnancy pillow, and John could barely fit in the bed. And Olivia became very attached to the pillow. And didn't want to throw it out even after Amber was born."

He turns on his side to face me. "You tell the best bedtime stories. So, what happened?"

"John challenged the pillow to a duel. Olivia was distraught. She didn't want either to lose. She kept saying, 'It doesn't have to be a choice between the two of you. There's room in my heart for both of you.'" I sit up.

Rory is grinning. I look at him sternly. "This is no laughing matter." I point my nose in the air. "At the crack of dawn, the two suitors for Olivia's bed met in the living room. They chose their weapons, and then they had to shake hands. But Poor Pillow had no hands. Olivia demanded that John hug the pillow. Hug the pillow."

"What?"

"You have to hug the pillow."

He hugs the pillow, and his hand grazes my leg, leaving fiery waves in its wake.

I'm never going to be able to fall asleep while sharing a bed.

"John hugged the pillow. And then he didn't want to stop hugging the pillow. He understood why Olivia loved the pillow so much. They got back into bed, but then John wanted to hug the pillow, too. And then Olivia decided that the pillow was in the way and put the pillow in the closet. But she was still going to hug it when John was traveling. The end."

He turns the lights off, and I snuggle under the covers.

"Good night, Curls." His voice is deep in the dark.

"Good night, Rory." I turn so my back is facing him.

I count sheep.

CHAPTER TWENTY-SEVEN

WE WAKE UP AND have an enormous breakfast in bed, which arrives on wooden trays with folding legs. Our breakfast experience has clearly been lacking prior to this. I'm adding breakfast in bed to my top-ten list of best Sunday plans.

We had planned to spend a few hours in the morning wandering around the Tate because we both agreed that we can't go to London and not visit the Tate, but after the first exhibition, Rory keeps checking his phone. He looks stressed. This campaign is a big deal. I'm also feeling guilty that I am not revising. Esther emailed me a round of edits and suggestions last night.

"You should go into the office now. You'll feel better if you're there. And I need to edit anyway."

Rory kisses me goodbye on the cheek. "Probably won't be able to hang out again until Thursday night. I hope we run on schedule."

"I'm in London. I'm happy. Go get 'em." I wave goodbye.

At my break for lunch, I text Zelda: *Red negligee 1. Rory 0.*

Zelda: *Spill the DETAILS.*

Me: *He suggested we put up a roller pillow between us so that there was no inadvertent touching. Good or bad sign?*

Zelda: *Bad sign.*

I slump.

Zelda: *Take that back. Good sign. Wouldn't need pillow if not attracted. But. You. Guys. You may be a perfect match.*

Me: *:)*

Zelda: *How are you going to bring down the walls of Jericho?*

I should have known she'd find a movie to quote. *It Happened One Night* is one of Zelda's favorite movies.

Me: *Blue negligee tonight.*

Zelda: *Hold your fire until he's done with work and you're in good shape with the book.*

Me: *You're right.*

I keep revising. For distraction, because I'm not perfect, I check my email. I came in second in a romance writers contest! They liked my first three chapters. I am ecstatic. Shocked, because I'd given up. I shouldn't lie to myself. I did keep refreshing the contest page just to check last week when they said they would announce the winners. I still had a forlorn hope. But then they never announced anything on the website, and I made myself stop checking. Their email ends with: "You will be published."

I text Rory: *I came in second in contest!*

Rory: *Yes! Calls for a celebration!*

Me: *Yes! Celebrate Friday when you're done.*

Rory: *Tonight? Done what we can before the shoot. See you back at the hotel around 7 p.m.*

I finish revising the first half of the novel per Esther's suggestions. And now it's time to consult the list of recommendations from my romance writer friends. I book us a slot at the minigolf bar called Swingers in the West End of London and text Rory to meet there.

Rory: *That's how you want to celebrate? Sure? You lost last time.*

Me: *Rematch, baby. You're probably rusty.*

Rory: *Just keep writing that fiction, Curls.*

I change into a scoop-necked sweater, a miniskirt, and boots. I practice swinging a golf club to see if it shows too much cleavage. Fine line. Seems good.

The Tube is crowded, but I still get a seat. Compared to New York City subways, the cushioned seats give the Tube the air of a time when travel was considered something special.

Arriving at Swingers, I wait by the bar for Rory. The bar is elegant with tall, swiveling, leather chairs, dome-shaped lamps, and a tin ceiling. It's in the basement, but it has high ceilings so it doesn't feel claustrophobic. Rustic wood blocks with crawling ivy separate two minigolf courses that have turf-green grass surrounded by leafy, fake trees. I choose the windmill course. Dutch luck had better help me.

A British guy strikes up a conversation as I nurse my drink, then I notice Rory is handing his coat to the woman at the coat check. I say goodbye to the guy and go meet Rory. His smile takes over his whole face.

"Can't leave you alone for a second." Rory hugs me. I breathe in his scent. And I feel like the hug lasts longer than it has in the past. His hard chest against mine feels solid and warm. He says, "That's great news about the contest." We separate slowly.

"I'm so happy." I raise my margarita to him. "Do you feel like you're ready for tomorrow?"

"As ready as we can be." His jaw clenches. We walk back to the bar. The bartender asks him what he wants to drink. He orders a seltzer. "I want to keep a clear head for tomorrow."

I nod. "I appreciate the bubbles."

He laughs. Some lines smooth out in his forehead.

I smile saucily. "Are you prepared to go down in defeat?"

He shakes his head sadly. "Delusions of grandeur. I'm not the one who's going to lose here."

We put in our order for burgers and fries. The hostess alerts us that we're on, and we take our places at the first hole on the golf course. It's two straight shots, and the ball is in the hole for both of us.

The next hole is trickier. Rory hits his ball, and it jumps off the course. I shake my head. "So rusty. Maybe they sell some WD-40 at the bar."

Rory grins. "Let's see what you've got before you start trash-talking."

I need to hit the ball off the side and bank it to get it close to the hill. I narrow my eyes to judge the angle. I swing and yes, it is right in line for the hole. *Take that.*

Two shots. My ball is in the hole. Rory takes four shots to get it in.

He's biting his lip as he analyzes the next course. He rolls up his sleeves. Rory's forearms are sexy. *No time to get distracted.* He catches my glance and winks. This course is curved. Rory gets it in three.

"Just needed to warm up." He swings his golf club nonchalantly.

I also get it in three shots. We catch up to the couple playing in front of us and have to wait. They are on a date. She asks him to show her how to hit a certain shot, and he puts his arm around her to demonstrate. *I should take notes.* Rory is also looking at the couple. Our glances meet and skitter away.

Rory pushes his hair out of his eyes. "I forgot how much fun it is to play minigolf with you."

"We should check out that minigolf course on the Hudson this summer," I say. This summer. *Rory will probably have a new girlfriend by the summer.*

The next one is a loop. I hit it too hard, and the ball flies out into the parallel course. I apologize and pick my ball up. The guys on that course are drunk, and one says, "Thrown for a loop." Ha-ha. I chuckle politely and return to the course. I hit the ball, again too hard, and the ball jumps off the course—again.

Rory gets it in one shot because the ball shoots out of the loop right into the hole. He leans against the wall, holding his club, watching me. I hit it too softly, and it drops out of the loop. The four behind us have now caught up. *Concentrate.*

Rory saunters over to stand between me and the spectators. He rubs my shoulders. "Remember *Caddyshack*. Be the ball."

I finally hit it just right, and the ball goes into the cup. Relieved, I pick up my ball.

The next few courses are challenging.

I decide to "remember *Caddyshack*."

As he warms up for the swing, I ask, "So, what have you liked best about our London trip so far?"

He gives me an annoyed glance. "Shh . . . I need to concentrate."

Oh, he thinks I didn't do that on purpose. Poor baby. He raises the club back again and just as he swings, I ask, "Do you think our towels are fluffy enough? I think I like them fluffier."

He misses the shot. Rory shoots me a I-know-what-you're-up-to glance. "Two can play this game."

"La, la, la, la, la, not if I don't hear you."

I line up my shot, ignoring him. I just have to be better at ignoring him than he is at ignoring me. I'm prepared. I should not get flustered. I bring my putter back . . .

"My absolute favorite scene in *Aliens* was when . . ."

And he's got my concentration because I want to know what his favorite scene was.

I miss my shot.

I turn to him. "Is what?"

"When Ripley fights the alien queen. What was yours?" He smiles at me innocently, but not.

"When the annoying guy gets killed." I smile sweetly at him.

"I thought it would be when there were sparks between Ripley and Hicks." His hand grazes my elbow as he moves me slightly aside so he can take his next shot.

"Those are my second favorite scenes. Hicks is hot."

"Is he?"

Our gazes catch.

I hunch down to make the next complicated shot. Rory's eyes widen at the view. He misses the next shot. I smile wickedly.

We are tied. The last course is by the large windmill. The couple in front of us are still trying to get through it. She kisses her date when she wins. Zelda's right. Now I don't know what's real and what's not, and I don't have the option to just kiss Rory. I'm the idiot who said "no kissing."

Rory puts his arm around me. "This is perfect. Got me out of work mode."

Our score sheets are tied as we finish the course.

"We'll have to have a rematch," Rory says.

The hostess seats us at a table. Rory raises his glass to me. "Congrats again on the contest. I'm proud of you. I knew it was just a matter of persistence."

"It definitely allays some of my doubt. Especially after so many agent rejections." There's still a big leap from a publisher liking the first three chapters to agreeing to publish the whole book. Twice with *Midnight Masquerade*, agents requested the full manuscript but then rejected it.

"I don't understand the rejections," Rory says, shaking his head.

"Maybe it's just not what they're looking for. I don't fit the formula."

"You're better," he says.

I'm not sure if we are still talking about my manuscripts.

The waitress lights the candle in the center of the table. I catch him gazing at me, and he's smiling crookedly, as if besotted. I suddenly feel very warm.

"That reminds me." He digs through his coat pocket and fishes out a matchbox. "Saw this and saved one for you."

Matchboxes are useful for miniaturists. You can create a 1/144th-scale scene or use them as drawers in a 1/12th piece of furniture. And they're hard to come by now that nobody smokes.

"Thanks." I put it in my purse. "I'm impressed you remembered."

"How could I forget? I still have the matchbox scene you made for me."

I made Rory a little *Mad Men* 1/144th scene when he first got his job. I figured he could hide it but still appreciate it.

"It sits on my desk at work and gets a lot of compliments."

Rory suggests we order a dessert to celebrate. We order chocolate cake and vanilla ice cream to share. Our spoons clash while competing for bites.

"Last bite is yours, but only because we're celebrating your contest win," he says.

The contest win is for *Midnight Masquerade,* not *Fake Dating Folly,* but it's still a validation of my writing. I'm on the right path.

Chapter Twenty-Eight

IT'S BEEN A CRAZY three days. Rory has come home exhausted every night and climbed into bed, mumbling good night. We don't need the roller pillow. Meanwhile, I'm dragging because I'm having a hard time falling asleep next to him. I'm all on fire, and he's a log. So, it's pretty clear that we're just friends. And I do give myself a stern talking-to that being just friends is fine, but then I get sad and wallow in that for a while.

On the plus side, I've been rewriting non-stop, and my novel is getting better. Esther has been sending her revisions in fifty-page chunks, and I just sent a completely revised draft to her.

Today, Rory is showing the raw first edit of the commercial to the client. Then if Bernie and his team approve, they'll go into post-production, which Rory mumbled last night is the studio editing period. London is known for excellent editing and graphic design facilities. But if the client doesn't like it, then they'll have to shoot it again. If Bernie and the team do like it and they go out for drinks or dinner, I am on call. But that's not until later.

My friend Julia agreed to meet for lunch near her office, and she has comments on *Fake Dating Folly*. I sent it to her at the same time I sent it to Esther.

Julia arrives, and we hug hello. As we eat, she gives me her comments. They're similar to Esther's, so I feel like I'm on the right track. She flags two areas where I could deepen the conflict.

"That's so brilliant," I say.

We discuss her latest work-in-progress, throwing around ideas, and lunch is over way too soon. I return to the hotel room reenergized to implement Julia's suggestions. I do that, cackling.

And then I'm at the scene in my novel where my protagonist hides under the bed. I should see what that feels like so I can describe it realistically. I crawl under the bed, inching forward. I'm amazed that I fit. The carpet is rough against my clothes. And the dust bunnies are coming for me.

The door opens. Rory's shoes. Should I stay under here, hoping maybe he will go to the bathroom? Then I can crawl out before he sees me. Or should I just brazen it out?

"Hi." My voice sounds muffled under the bed. I'm not sure he heard me. "I'm under the bed."

He slips off his shoes by the door. His feet, in socks, are by the bed. Now his knees. Then his face.

He chuckles. "Is there something I should know? Was there an intruder?" His face is more relaxed than it has been the last few nights. The client must have liked the raw edit.

Using my elbows, I commando-crawl out from under the bed. "No, I'm writing a scene where she hides under a bed, and I thought I should experience it first so I can write about it. Looks like good news on your front."

"Bernie loved it." He has a huge smile. "So, we're having our wrap dinner tonight. I came home to take a shower, change, and pick you up."

"I'm going to need a shower, too. Dusty under there."

He asks me if I want to go first. I want to write my impressions down while they're fresh, so I say no.

He disappears into the bathroom. I jot down notes, but the sound of running water distracts me. And thoughts of Rory naked. Back to the bed. I mean under the bed. I mean hiding under the bed. I put my head in my hands.

The door opens. "Scene not going well?" He is in just a towel. It's probably not revenge for the other day, but I can't help admiring his muscular, well-defined chest. Butterflies start twirling in my stomach. I feel out of breath. I raise my eyes to his face. He works out a lot. I should work out more.

"I'm definitely done for the day." I take my shower and get dressed in a black cocktail dress and heels.

I'm excited for the celebration, but less excited to tangle with Myrtle again.

As I slip on my heels, he sits next to me on the bed. "Thanks again for coming and being so cool about my work schedule. How is your writing going?"

"It's good." I bump his shoulder with mine. "It's been an amazing writing retreat—good talks with Julia, an excursion to confirm setting details, and it's even included some of the best tropes."

"What tropes did this one include?"

Laugh lines crinkle around his deep blue-green eyes. His intense glance makes my stomach quiver in anticipation.

I say, "Apparently 'only one bed' is a subtrope of fake dating. When I met with Julia and I told her I was writing the fake dating trope, she said, 'You have to use the one bed. I love that trope.' I didn't even know it was a trope."

"And what usually happens?"

I lean closer to him. I put my finger to my mouth and say "Shh." I reach over and run my hand through his hair. I've been wanting to do that now for days. "She seduces him." *Did I just say that?*

He smiles. He raises an eyebrow. "Well, I'm quite looking forward to that, then." He sounds almost British.

My cheeks heat up. "So be forewarned. Mr. Pillow may need to sleep on the floor tonight." *Am I really going to try? Friday night?*

"I thought I'd have to duel him first," Rory says. His phone buzzes. The car is downstairs. On the way to the dinner, we discuss his work over the week, as I barely even got the highlights reel on those days before he collapsed into bed.

His face lights up when he talks. "It's been amazing. I don't know. I just feel like yes, this is what I'm supposed to be doing. The highs, the lows. I feel validated that I have chosen the right career. My parents give me a hard time, that it's all commercial. And it is, but it's also so much fun. It's such a high. When I saw my idea come alive, and it worked. My boss even called me from New York to say it was good. And then Bernie and his team liked it."

Rory puts his arm around me and pulls me closer to him. I relax against him. Maybe we *can* give off a couple vibe.

By the time we get back to our hotel room, Rory looks exhausted. I don't take out the blue negligee. Tomorrow is Friday, when I will tell him about my feelings for him, after we come home from our *Casablanca* Secret Cinema night, thanks to one of my London friends who has gotten us tickets. Secret Cinema is an immersive theatre experience where you feel like you are in the movie, interacting with the characters and becoming part of the story by going on secret missions and uncovering hidden secrets. That sounds right on point.

Chapter Twenty-Nine

IT IS FRIDAY—THE DAY I turn in my manuscript and tell Rory about my feelings.

I spent yesterday polishing this draft. There's just one issue. I call Esther.

After thanking her profusely, I ask, "What do you think about Rob?"

"I love him. If you know any guys like that, please send them my way. Why?"

"Well, he's made up, obviously." And he is. I even gave him divorced parents, which couldn't be further from Rory's familial life. "But I'm worried that people might think he's based on one of my real male friends. And I wouldn't want to be seen as baring his soul."

"It's not in his point of view. It's always told through Piper's point of view. But I don't think there's anything particularly soul-baring in there—not from his point of view, anyway. Piper, on the other hand, has quite a few revealing moments. I wouldn't worry. Good luck! I love this book. I'm sure Vera will love it."

We hang up, and I bite my nails. I don't think I'm revealing any of Rory's secrets. The male protagonist is a commitment-phobe because I needed to give the male partner some issues, but that's a common enough trope in romance books. I don't think Rory has commitment issues.

I thought about asking him to read it, but he's been working nonstop on this campaign. It's not like he had time. I return to proofreading my manuscript for the final time.

I press send. It's now in the hands of Strawbundle Publishing. I also send it to the developmental editor I hired to review it concurrently.

I order flowers for Esther because I am so grateful for all the help that she's been giving me. I can't believe how much of herself she's given to this manuscript. She even took a day off from work.

Me to Zelda: *I sent it.*

Zelda: *Woohoo! Congratulations! I'm so excited for you!*

Me: *Should I try to seduce him tonight?*

Zelda: *Yes, JUST DO IT.*

Me: *But plane trip back.*

Zelda: *Forced proximity will be good if it doesn't work. Have to get back to normal relationship.*

I frown. It will be a long plane ride back if we don't.

I should bask in this feeling of accomplishment and walk around London, but I take a nap instead.

At 5 p.m., Rory texts: *Have to meet you there. Still editing. Team wants to continue working.*

My heart falls. What if he can't make it? Getting this commercial right is critical for his career. Obviously, a Secret Cinema night can't compete with his career. Booking it on a work night was risky, but it was the only night available. These tickets aren't easy to procure.

Me: *No worries.*

A few hours remain before it starts.

I eat an early dinner by myself at a small, casual Italian restaurant a few blocks away and people-watch. It doesn't sound like it's a good idea to try to kiss him tonight, if he's all wrapped up in work. There will be opportunities when we get back, although he won't need a fake girlfriend once this is over. A chill runs through me.

The streets of London are buzzing with that Friday, end-of-the-week energy. People are spilling out of pubs, beers in hand, milling around tables set up outside under heaters. I change into my costume—a tailored 1940s suit bought long ago in a vintage thrift shop—that I hope channels the vibe of Ilsa, the love interest in *Casablanca*, and take the Tube there. I hope that Rory makes it.

We agreed to meet outside by the entrance, but already a big crowd has gathered. A person in a uniform hands me a plastic bag and tells me I have to put my phone away before I go inside. I nod.

My phone beeps.

Rory: *At the corner.*

A feeling of buzzing lightness sweeps through me. It's on.

"Hey, Ilsa." He hugs me. "This looks great. I'm impressed you were able to get tickets."

Julia knew someone who works for Secret Cinema and was able to procure tickets that they reserve for VIPs and the press.

"How was post-production?" I'm learning the advertising lingo.

"Going well. They're still there. I said I had tickets to Secret Cinema with you, and it's probably better if I let them do their thing anyway without me hanging over them."

We put our phones in the plastic bags and walk into the large warehouse. It's a maze of corridors. Costumes are available for rent in one area. I think my 1940s suit suffices for a costume, but Rory decides to dress up. We choose costumes for him to try on. Military uniforms, loose robes, fez hats, white and tan suits like Humphrey Bogart's are among the choices.

We enter a dressing room together, which is really just an area with small, square, curtained-off modules. I model a white hat like the one Ingrid Bergman wore. It looks good, but based on the brunch experience, a hat seems like a barrier, and I want to be approachable.

I sit on a small stool as Rory strips to his white shirt and boxers. He tries on the white suit first.

"What do you think?"

I nod. "Very handsome."

"So, we're done?"

"No. You should still try on the others just for the fun of it. I wish we could take pictures." The curtain wall billows as the person in the room next door bumps into it.

The French military uniform also looks dashing. I salute him. Then I hand him the loose robe, or djellaba. He takes off his shirt and puts on the robe and fez hat.

"Is it comfortable?" I ask.

"Yes. What do you think? Should I do this one instead?" He shakes his head. "I feel too naked and exposed."

"I like the Humphrey Bogart look better."

He switches out of the djellaba and into the white suit, storing his clothes in a provided locker. Then we go back out into the *Casablanca* world. Loudspeakers are blaring announcements.

We find the communications desk to ask for special missions. My assignment is to hand a note to a corrupt police chief at Rick's Café American. Rory takes one where he has to pass a note to a waitress wearing gold lipstick, but then he has to follow her and see who she gives it to and report back. They think she's an informer and may be a loose link in the resistance group.

We walk from the communications desk toward Rick's Café American.

"What's your plan? Buy a drink and give it to her when you pay?" I ask.

"But I have to follow her. Is that your strategy?" He quickens his pace as we approach Rick's Café American.

"No. I brought a handkerchief. I'll drop that with the note."

"What if the wrong guy picks it up?"

"Yes, I'll have to suss out the situation. Maybe I can just hand it to him. Or put it in his pocket."

Rory looks at me. "We should do this together. Tag team."

I'm definitely up for that.

We walk through the white door of Rick's Café American. Wow. It feels like we've stepped onto the movie set. There are arched, white ceilings, wicker tables, and fans whirring. "Ahmed" at the door allows us entry. A live jazz band is playing "It Had to Be You." A guy who looks similar to Sam is playing the piano. Everybody is in costume.

We share a look of "Yes, this is going to be fun."

The policeman in a white suit is surrounded by people at the bar, probably being deluged by people covertly handing him notes. He's not the only police officer, though. My mark is the one with the mustache.

"All right, here's the plan." I lean in to whisper to Rory. "I'm going to faint, and you're going to call for a police officer to help. If the mustached one comes, I'll give it to him. If the other one responds, you need to get on your knees next to me and get the note. Then give it to the other policeman in the diversion."

"Won't you hurt yourself when you faint?"

"I took this improv acting class—it was supposed to help me write comedy. And we learned this technique."

We saunter near the two policemen. I shriek and then crumple to the ground. Ouch. It hurts. I keep my eyes closed.

Rory calls out, "Help, police."

Unfortunately, several others respond as well. A crowd surrounds me.

Rory bends down next to me. "Are you okay? That looked painful."

I press the note into his hand. He disappears. I sit up.

"I'm with the show. Do you need to go to the nurse?" a very official-looking person asks, parting the crowd around me.

"No, no, I'm fine," I say. "I just . . ."

"It looks like you fainted," one passerby says. *Not helpful.* But I am pleased it looked realistic.

The official-looking person sits me on a chair. "I really think you should go to our nurse. Are you here with anyone?"

"Yes," I say, but I obviously can't tell them he's off delivering a note. "He just went to the bathroom."

Official guy repeats that I should go to the nurse. I whisper to him, "I was just acting. We're on a mission."

His face clears. He nods and disappears.

"I'll sit with you for a bit," says an unctuous man who looks a bit like Urgante. He tries to hold my hand. I pull it away.

"Are you looking for an exit visa? Because that can be arranged." The man leers at me. He moves his chair closer.

This feels way too realistic.

Rory shows up with a glass of water. "Penelope, what happened? I'm her boyfriend." Rory immediately pulls up a chair and tugs me close to him, away from Urgante. He looks really concerned and listens intently when Urgante tells him I fainted. He's better at acting than I would've guessed. *That's not exactly a good sign.*

"No exit visas?"

"We have exit visas," Rory says firmly. "Urgante" stands and fades back into the crowd.

Rory gives me a thumbs-up.

"How'd you give it to him?"

"I handed it to him when everybody was crowding around you. That was perfect. I can't believe it didn't hurt."

"It *did* hurt," I say. "I forgot we had padded floors in acting class."

"Where does it hurt?"

I shift in my wicker chair. "My butt. Don't touch it. Anyway, I'm kind of bummed I didn't get to give the policeman the note."

"You can give the waitress the note."

"Okay."

Major Strasser arrives with his soldiers and sits at a corner table. "Renault" moves to arrest Urgante. Urgante runs out the back door, just like in the movie. Shots are fired. People are screaming. We duck under the table, both on our knees. A smoky smell fills the air.

My face is very close to Rory's.

His glance holds mine. His hand strokes my face. I tilt my head to lean into his hand. His hand strokes my hair. My breath catches.

"Fancy meeting you here," I say.

"That's your tell." He is stroking my hair. I swallow.

"What?"

His face is so close to mine.

"You make a joke when you're nervous. Whenever there's a chance I might kiss you."

I nod. My glance doesn't leave his. My heart is thumping. He must be able to hear it.

I say, "Is there still a chance? I want to kiss you."

The kiss is tentative at first, as if we're both afraid. His hand moves up to cup my head, and the kiss deepens. I don't want it to stop. The background recedes, and it's just me and him, touching, tasting. My hand reaches up to caress his face, to tousle his hair. And then we shift. He hits his head on the top of the table.

The band leader says, "Sorry for the disturbance." The music starts up again. "Parlez-Moi D'Amour," sings a woman.

We stare at each other under the table. And he slants his head, indicating we should move out from under the table.

We climb out from under the table.

"I've wanted to kiss you for a long time," I say. I don't want him to feel any doubt.

He holds my face tenderly and kisses me again.

He says, "I've wanted to kiss you since college." We are both out of breath when we stop for air.

"College?" I ask, shocked.

"But I knew you didn't feel the same," he says.

I trace his jaw. "I was attracted to you. But you're right. I still needed time."

"Should we go look for the waitress?" he asks. We still have a mission to accomplish.

Holding hands, stopping every now and then to trade deep, heartfelt kisses, we wander around, looking for her. And the touches. We're acting as if they're inadvertent, but they're not. And we're both playing that game. My arm is around his waist, and my hand slips lower to appreciate the firmness of the curve of his butt. He runs his fingers up the inside of my arm. We wander down another alleyway. I trace his jaw with my finger. His hand grazes the underside of my breast when he puts his arm around me.

There she is, serving a bunch of tall bar tables. We grab one. The waitress is gorgeous, and when she comes over, she focuses all her attention on me. *Turns out I am the right person to give her the note.* I smile.

"What would you like?" she asks in a smoky voice.

"Whatever you recommend," I say. "And a seltzer for him." Rory has to work again tomorrow, which does give me some concern about my seduction plans.

Rory frowns. "I hope she doesn't get you something really wild."

She comes back with a strawberry margarita for me. It's yummy. I sip my straw with pursed lips and catch Rory's glance.

Roulette and other gambling tables have been set up in a corner. We finish our drinks and pay. I hand the note to our waitress with my credit card. She doesn't blink. She probably gets a note with every drink payment. As she turns to leave, she winks at me.

We're off to trail her. She has a quick conversation with the bartender. And then she skips out an entrance behind the bar. We run around to see where the back entrance of the bar might lead. It leads down a narrow alleyway that is filled with shops. Baskets hang from the ceiling while men in robes peddle wares. Stuffed parrots are sitting in bird cages. I don't see her. And she's tall, so she should be easy to spot.

"There she is," Rory says. We sneak closer and flatten against a wall. A faint buzzing like mosquitos makes me want to swat them away, but I know it's got to be a sound effect.

"Is she talking to anyone?" I can't see her. Just Rory's back.

"No, she's walking again."

We follow her, ducking behind a barrel when she looks back. A real donkey, laden with goods, being pulled by a man in a turban takes up most of the narrow passageway. She's leading us down different corridors, past Moroccan marketplaces. She stops. Rory hides behind some robes, pulling me behind him. The robes hang from the ceiling and on racks. We crouch lower and go deeper into the rows of robes in the store. Someone is approaching. It's her voice. "Did you see someone in here?" she asks.

"No," a German-accented voice replies.

"They're rounding up the usual suspects," she says. We tiptoe deeper into the store, behind racks of clothing, in case she decides to look for us.

Finally, silence. We stand. Rory pulls me close to him, and I caress his cheek. His lips lower to mine, his hands holding my face close to his. I close my eyes, losing myself in his kiss. His body is tight and solid against mine.

There's a shout from the front of the store, and we pull apart. I'm momentarily disoriented.

"We should go," he says.

We're trapped in a fabric maze. We push aside one robe and get blocked by another billowing piece of fabric wrapping itself around us.

"Should've worn that djellaba. Then I could have hidden inside it," I say.

"Had you suggested that, I would've definitely worn it."

"Hey, what are you doing in the robes?" someone asks.

"Go toward the voice," Rory says.

"Are you sure? He sounds angry."

We push robes out of our way following the voice.

A man in a djellaba greets us. "What are you doing? You want to buy?" He points at the robes.

"No," we say. "We were looking at them and then we got lost."

"You touch, you buy." *What is this, like fruit?*

"We don't really want to buy anything."

"I call the gendarmes." His voice rises. His face is turning purple. "You want to go to jail?"

No, I definitely don't want to spend my secret cinema night in a fake jail cell. That is definitely not part of the plan. The actors here take this very seriously.

"We'll buy one," I say. "We can use it for a Halloween costume." We buy a blue one for Rory and a white one with gold trim around the neck opening for me.

We look down the alleyway but don't see her. We report back to the communications desk that we lost her. We tell them that we heard her say that they were rounding up the usual suspects. The movie starts in an hour. Rory suggests we go dance at the Parisian Club. It turns out there's an entirely different set for the Paris café where Ilsa and Rick dated.

A Big Band is playing. We take a moment off to the side to remind ourselves of the steps. Rory takes me into his arms. It's Savoy swing dancing from the 1940s, which is very fast. Rory twirls me out, and then I do the fancy footwork, as does he. My butt doesn't hurt, luckily, as I wiggle it in time to the music. Baby got back. Zelda would be proud.

He pulls me in. We swing around, and I'm holding on to him as we go round and round. I laugh. It's so freeing.

We slow down from the spinning, and our glances meet. His gaze is intense, and he lowers his head. I tilt my head up. My arms move up from his waist to encircle his neck. I'm aware of only him, his lips, his hands holding me to him.

Someone jostles us on the dance floor, and we break apart.

The loudspeakers announce an air raid and direct us to move to a protected space. We join the crowds of people streaming toward the cinema area.

Six screens surround the seats. We find our seats. His arm is around me, tracing patterns, tantalizing tingles of sensation up and down my body. My mouth is dry. As the lights dim, he kisses me quickly again. I tighten my grip on his hand. Need to pinch myself. This is really happening. We watch *Casablanca*. On a stage in front, actors are acting out the scenes. It's perfect. Even if it is a love triangle and they don't end up together. *Don't be superstitious and worry that's some sign.*

Confetti showers us as we head toward the exit. Rory's arm is around me. His hand rubs my lower back—and lower.

"Does it still hurt?"

"No." That should have been clear after all the swing dancing.

"Good."

He gives me a "you're mine" look of longing. And I'm sure he sees the same message in my eyes.

Rory opens an app to hail a cab, but there are a million of us out here, and everyone is hailing cabs. The next ride is at least a thirty-minute wait.

We can't wait another thirty minutes. We take the Tube, packing onto the train with a lot of other revelers. Rory holds on to a strap with one hand, his arm encircling me, holding me closely against him. I rest my cheek on his chest, his heart beating against my ear. It feels more than right.

Chapter Thirty

WE ARRIVE BACK AT the hotel and run into Myrtle and Bernie. Unbelievably bad luck. They invite us for a drink.

"It's our last night, and you promised us a drink," Bernie says.

Rory looks at me apologetically and says, "Sure."

Is he having doubts? He was quiet on the subway ride home. *Get yourself together. This is his client, and he can't say no. Again.*

But I *really* don't want to talk to Myrtle and Bernie right now.

Rory whispers "sorry" in my ear and kisses my neck just under my ear. It tickles and makes me shiver. *We're still on.*

We sit down at the hotel bar, which is all gold and black with very dim lighting. Myrtle says they just came back from a dance performance. I take off my coat and hang it on the back of the chair. I let Rory take the lead in case he doesn't want to say he was out with me as opposed to working.

"We just came back from Secret Cinema *Casablanca,*" Rory says.

Myrtle leans forward. "What was that like?"

I describe it in detail. Rory puts his arm around me. His fingers are tracing patterns on my arm, leaving flickers of flame. But I am so wound up, I can't concentrate on the conversation. I put my hand on his knee and trace circles, and then I move slightly up his leg, feeling his tight muscle. He shifts in his chair. What is Myrtle saying? I remove my hand. She's talking about the dance performance. I nod. *Focus on her.* Rory's hand is going up and down my side tentatively, teasing, tantalizing, just brushing the underwire of my bra.

Bernie interrupts Myrtle to talk about the campaign. Rory removes his hand. If I were mean, I'd put my hand back on his thigh, but I'm not. I sip my drink. Rory responds, and they have some lengthy technical discussion about ROI and various advertising terms. I should have just made Rory talk about ROI out on Fire Island when I wanted to get over him.

Myrtle turns to me and says, "You really like to keep an eye on him, don't you?"

I sit back. "Well, he is easy on the eyes." I sound like some cowgirl.

Myrtle nods. "I have to watch my husband like a hawk."

I hope I don't have to watch Rory like a hawk. It seems her husband should be watching her, but the insides of relationships are mysterious and not for me to comment upon.

Myrtle continues, "Keep him on his toes."

Maybe her whole approach to Rory was to keep Bernie on his toes, but I don't think she should put Rory in that position.

Rory finishes his drink and says that we have to go. He has to get an early start tomorrow on the post-production. Bernie says they will come with us. We all crowd into the small elevator. It's packed.

It stops on every floor. I am pressed up against Rory. Second floor. Third floor. Rory's hands are on my waist. I can't wait.

Finally, the elevator door opens to our floor, and we say our goodbyes.

We race to the room. He closes the door behind him and kisses me hungrily. He tastes of chocolate and red wine. We are leaning against the door, pressed tightly together. His kiss is no longer tentative. It's sure. I kiss him back. With everything I have. *Everything I have never said.*

I throw my coat off to the side, not stopping the kiss, holding on to him with one hand.

Rory tosses his coat onto the chair, and we both scramble to remove our shoes. And then I am back in his arms, lost in his kiss.

We move backward toward the bed, until the backs of my knees hit the frame and we both fall down on the comforter, Mr. Pillow underneath me.

"I think we can get rid of this," he says, pushing the roller pillow to the floor.

"Yes."

Our glances meet, and he gives me that half-smile. There is no one for me but Rory. His face is so dear to me that I can see him even as I close my eyes. I run my hands through his hair, his lips firm against mine.

And then we're unbuttoning each other's clothes. Or trying.

"How many buttons does this jacket have?" he asks.

It's my 1940s jacket. Eight buttons. My 1940s blouse underneath, with eyelets, is even worse.

I pull his shirt over his head. *All mine.* I run my hands over his chest and the fine brown hair that tapers to his waist. *Smooth skin.* He takes a raspy breath. I look up.

"Are you going to give me a little help here?" he asks. He's unbuttoned my jacket. I shimmy out of my jacket.

"What is that?" He has just seen the eyelets. "How many buttons are there?" He counts. "So basically, you weren't planning to seduce me tonight?"

"I was planning to seduce you, but not in this. I brought lingerie. And condoms."

"More revealing than the red lingerie?" he asks.

"Was the red lingerie revealing?" I ask innocently.

He laughs. "I brought condoms, too. You know, thought this was the last chance." He stands to take off his pants, and it's just him in his black boxers.

"Eyes up here, Curls," he says.

I groan. "Must I?" Apparently, I am his type.

He lies down next to me, and I can feel the heat of his body. He smells of laundry.

He slowly and intently unbuttons the top button of my shirt. And another button. And another. Each touch of his hands against my skin is like a spark. His hand pushes my blouse off my shoulders, and he traces my collarbone. We gaze into each other's eyes, and it's just us, together. I brush back his hair tenderly and swallow.

His fingers trace the curve of my breast where the lace ends on my bra, leaving a fiery wake. I am transfixed by the sight of his hand touching my skin.

"The red lingerie was not revealing enough." He unbuttons another button. Our glances hold. Another button. His fingers brush my skin. Butterflies dance.

I touch my lips to his, running my fingers through his hair.

Rory unbuttons the last button, and I slip my blouse off. At least I'm wearing a black, lacy bra.

He looks at me like he can't get enough.

My breath catches.

He interlaces his fingers with mine. "I don't want to mess anything up."

"You can't." I want to say *I love you*. But I'm afraid. Maybe that will scare him off. I kiss him instead, wrapping my arms around him. We are skin to skin, softness against hard muscle, each exploring, discovering our unseen selves. I can't say *I love you* first. Even if we've known each other for years. Instead, I try to show him through touch, trying to give back to him what he gives to me.

CHAPTER THIRTY-ONE

RORY IS MOVING ABOUT in the bathroom. The bed still feels warm from his body, and I bury my nose in his pillow to breathe in his scent. But I'm almost relieved that he's not there to watch me wake up. It gives me time to center myself. Last night, I was so open and vulnerable, and I'm not sure if I can do that again in the daylight. Either of us. We can't walk around that emotionally bare.

He unlocks the door and smiles at me. His smile is open, unshadowed. I feel my mouth responding in kind. A big grin is bursting forth.

Mmm. Freshly showered Rory is wearing a crisply ironed shirt and underwear. I can't believe he has to go to work today.

He jumps back into the bed.

"I wish I didn't have to work."

He runs his hands through my curls, kissing me again. I pull him down, and he's lying on top of me, enveloping me. My body feels languid and warm. "I'd much rather spend the day here with you." He kisses the side of my neck—my weak spot.

I run my fingers through his hair. "Me, too."

We kiss again, firmly, yet also tentatively, as if confirming that last night's magic is still there. It is.

"Okay, must get up." He disentangles himself and stands. At a slight disadvantage.

I stretch, like a satiated cat. His gaze slowly slides over my body, as if tracing where his hands touched, fanning flames of longing. I swallow. He sort of limps over to a chair at a safe distance by the window and pulls on his pants.

I decide to go easy on him. He does have to go to work. "Should we discuss logistics?"

"Logistics for what?" He looks intrigued.

"Dinner tonight?"

He looks disappointed. "Oh." He says he booked us dinner at another rooftop restaurant bar.

"Okay, I'll think of some other logistics for us to practice tonight while I'm writing."

He raises an eyebrow. "I'll look forward to it."

And then he is off.

I want to shout it from the rooftops that *we are dating*, but everyone already thinks that. But this is nothing like fake dating. I can't wait to tell Zelda and my sister. But it's still the middle of the night in New York, and Zelda does not like having her sleep interrupted.

My reward is to visit the Kristin Baybars Dollhouse Store in London. It's like attending a dollhouse show: drawers and drawers of miniatures to ooh and aah over. I could spend hours there—and hundreds of dollars. So, my time limit is two hours. I'll do an Instagram and blog post of my purchases when I get back to the hotel room.

But first, I find a café for lunch. It's perfect, tucked down a side street. It sells tea, mugs, and teapots in the back and has lots of tables. Another woman is typing away on her laptop in the corner.

Last night was amazing. I've never felt that close to anyone before or so cared for. Just thinking about it, I can't wait for tonight.

At 1 p.m., 8 a.m. Zelda's time, I walk over to St. James Park to find a bench and text Zelda.

Me: *The walls of Jericho came down.*

Zelda calls me. "Yes! Did Rory make the first move?"

"Mutual," I say.

"That's even better," Zelda says. "How did it happen?"

I tell her about our first kiss under the table and leave the rest to her imagination.

"We didn't talk much, though," I say.

"Hell, no. That would've killed the mood," she says wryly. "Just enjoy it. You're in safe hands with Rory. Let the relationship take its course. You don't need to do a full-court press on what this means. You guys are best friends, so it already means more than if you were just casual acquaintances hooking up. He's not going to risk your friendship for a fling."

I nod. Last night didn't feel like a one-night fling, although it did have the electricity and energy of a "I need you naked in bed now" romance. I was wrong about Rory not feeling the ripping-off-clothes attraction. He does, just with consent.

"Yes, I know." I am going to try to give my all to this relationship—not to the extent of saying "I love you" immediately, of course, but communicating that in other ways? Yes.

CHAPTER THIRTY-TWO

"YOU NEED TO ORDER your own fries," I say to Rory. "I'm going to want to eat all of mine." We're eating dinner at a small restaurant off of Piccadilly.

"I only want a few."

"Once you have one, you're going to want more." I raise my glass of wine. "Here's to a successful ad."

"Here's to *Fake Dating Folly*." Rory clinks glasses with me and then studies me with those big, blue eyes of his that never fail to pull me in like the ocean. He reaches across the table to hold my hand.

"So, I'm really happy about last night," he says.

"Me, too."

"I hoped you'd feel that way," he says. "I should have acted earlier on my feelings. Or not backed off quite so much after talking to Callie. But I wanted to be sure."

"Same," I say. "And I need to give more credit to the magical than I have."

"Ah, that's quite a concession, coming from you."

I nod. The waitress sets down our food. We share bites of each other's dishes, although I only give Rory a few fries because he should've ordered his own.

"So, were you planning to seduce me?" I ask.

"I hoped that sharing a room might lead to more. It succeeded in one of the books you gave me."

I am stunned. "When did you realize you liked me as more than a friend?"

"I noticed you in college. But you didn't seem interested in anything more than being friends. And I accepted that. Or tried to accept that. Except it never worked out with anybody else. Plus, you were obsessed with Jamie." Rory teases my hand. "But then right after I broke up with Marie, we were out playing billiards with Audrey and Jake when you did a behind-the-back shot. Do you remember?"

"I remember the look you gave me." And that I made a joke to cover up my confused reaction.

Rory gives me that same look again—a look of "you're good and I want you." My insides melt.

I say, "It was a look like that. And then you missed the next two shots."

"It was a brilliant shot. And you were wearing a low-cut dress. But I couldn't see any signs that you liked me as more than a friend. And I didn't want to risk our friendship. Especially if you still liked Jamie." Rory says, "It took guts for you to tell Jamie you loved him."

"I think I was only able to do it, though, because I didn't love him as much as—" I pause. I can't say that yet. "I could take the rejection. He was a safe bet for me, safer emotionally."

"And I'm not?"

"I feel a lot more for you than I did for Jamie," I say, reaching out to hold his hand across the table.

Rory raises an eyebrow. "I don't feel safe?"

"I don't think you want to be the safe bet," I say. "Am I your safe bet?"

"Definitely not."

"Because your dad thinks I have commitment issues?" I might as well raise that if I'm on this new tack of being emotionally open.

"My dad . . ." He hesitates. "My dad thinks you're very much committed to me and our friendship." His tone is cautious.

"And that's a bad thing?"

"No, he doesn't think you have commitment issues. I'm the one with the commitment issues, per Callie." His voice is lighter. He's changing the topic, but I've pushed it far enough.

I ask, "So, when you first suggested fake dating, were you thinking of the possibility of something more?"

"No, it wasn't until we were out dancing again," he says. And the look he gives me ignites a shiver in my stomach. "Were you?"

"No, but I've always been attracted to you, and that brunch . . . it reignited those feelings for you."

"But you weren't over Jamie yet?"

"No," I say, "I wasn't. It wasn't until my sister's brunch that I realized I was well over him. And I was going to tell you I liked you after the art opening, but you said you weren't interested."

"That was a mistake. Callie just threw me. And I didn't want to lose our friendship."

"Yes, so then my plan was to have a disastrous weekend out in Fire Island and hope that would kill my feelings for you."

"Hah. I was thinking about trying to seduce you out there, but there were way too many pictures of Jamie."

I laugh.

We both finish our dinners.

He says, "It wasn't until I saw you both together again when he was launching your website and you treated him like a brother that I was sure you were over him. And then I came up with the London trip idea."

"Ah, quick thinking. And I thought London was my last chance to seduce you, too," I say. I'm tempted to tell him what Jamie said right before he arrived, but then he puts his hand on my knee under the table and I'm no longer thinking.

The waitress clears our plates and asks if we want dessert. We share an apple pie with whipped cream. I kiss off the whipped cream by his dimple. And then we rush back to bed.

CHAPTER THIRTY-THREE

AND NOW IT'S BACK to life in New York. I'm busy making the miniature art studio. Today I painted my $1/12^{th}$-scale art gallery box white and the "tin ceiling" copper. I've made the roof slant the final four inches with glass windows—like Rory's favorite Met gallery—and then the front wall has the typical big windows of Tribeca galleries. I create miniature gothic columns using a 3-D printing program. While the paint is drying, I make miniature roses.

The doorbell rings. It's the postman with a package. I run downstairs and come back up. It's little paintings from Rafael for the miniature art studio, which is the piece I'm donating for the charity auction. The five pieces of art are stunning. My art

llery will be just the setting for them. I carefully pack away

pieces, putting them in a safe place in my drawer.

n't looked at *Fake Dating Folly* again. I know I

just can't face it yet. I'm still finishing up my

y. I submit the first five pages of *Midnight*

lby's final homework exercise.

"How does she feel when she's grabbing

eel her nerves clenching, the drip of

emotions." I stare at the page. Should

ntemplate stealing something to get the

feeling—not that I would ever really steal anything. That makes me feel queasy. I lean into that emotion, putting it on the page. I should practice it. But the apartment I describe in *Midnight Masquerade* is Rory's apartment. I should practice stealing a painting from his bedroom to see how that feels. He gave me a spare set of keys for emergencies. And then I'll surprise him when he comes home tonight.

I pack my laptop and cleaning gloves in my backpack, grab my helmet, leave a note for Zelda, and go out into the night. As I bicycle down the bike path to Rory's apartment, a slight breeze brushes against my face. My bicycle light illuminates the path ahead under pockets of luminescence from the streetlamps.

I run a few red lights just to see if that produces any anxiety, but I only run them when it's completely safe, so it doesn't produce any fear.

I click the bike back into the Citi Bike lock. A man is walking a dog at one end of the block. Rory's apartment is dark from the street, so he doesn't appear to be home. Okay, I need to start pretending now. Slipping on the cleaning gloves (no fingerprints), I let myself in the front door, listening to see if any neighbors are coming down the stairs. No. I tiptoe up the stairs.

I unlock his door with my key and slip inside his shadowed apartment. I leave the lights off and tiptoe toward the back, through the hallway kitchen into the back bedroom where the picture hangs. I know Rory's apartment like my own. I take off my backpack and gently put it under his desk. The painting is above the bed. My feet bounce on the bed. Feeling along the wall, I gently unhook the painting. I lay the painting on the bed and clamber off. Already, more physical details are coming into play. I gingerly carry the painting across the room into the kitchen. The painting is heavier than I expected. I tighten my grip. I don't want to break the frame and then have to explain to Rory how I damaged one of his favorites. I should've picked a different one.

Creak. That's not from me. I stop short in the kitchen. My pulse races. That sound came from the living room. My breathing sounds really loud. I try to hold my breath so I can hear other noises. Another creak. It's coming from the living room, near the entrance. My heart is hammering. My hands are sweating. I peer around the kitchen wall. I can see the shape of a man. Rory.

"It's me," I say quickly.

He hits the light, and I blink my eyes to adjust.

"What the . . . ? I thought I was being robbed." He looks at the painting. "Are you robbing me?"

"Yes. I was practicing stealing your painting for my book."

"Man, I had no idea writing involved so much play-acting."

"I don't know if it's supposed to. It's just that Trilby said she wanted to feel the fear when she's stealing the painting. I always have such a hard time writing that, so I thought I should practice it. But it was perfect. I was terrified when I heard the floor creak by the door. I felt the clammy hands, all of it."

"Don't forget the ice chill down your back." He takes the painting from my hands and puts it gently on the floor. "Maybe next time you should warn me."

I hug him. "Yes, I should have warned you, but I didn't expect you home so early."

"It's not that early. It's 8 p.m.," he says. "Bernie and Myrtle invited us to a house party this weekend at their place in the Catskills. Are you free?"

"Yes, if I can bring some mini flower kits with me. Are you going to have to work?"

"Probably some, as we brainstorm our next campaign." He kisses me gently. "I missed you."

"I missed you, too." We move to the couch, and I sit on his lap. "And I'm desperate for a break. I've been bent over my desk all day, crafting. And I need some exercise."

"Do you? Any logistics you need to work out?"

I unbutton his shirt. "Just some pent-up desire."

"Anything for your art."

CHAPTER THIRTY-FOUR

THE WEATHER IS SUNNY and crisp, a perfect fall weekend. Or it would be—if we weren't spending it with Bernie and Myrtle. Myrtle is indeed leading a couples yoga session on Sunday morning. And apparently Rory's boss's wife is excited to do it as well, so his boss had decreed that Rory must be there.

We get out of the car, our boots crunching on the gravel and the leaves. The red, orange, yellow, and green foliage is striking, as if the trees are saying "look at me," like male birds mating. As Rory grabs our bags from the trunk, Myrtle emerges from the house.

"You're just in time," Myrtle says. "We're organizing a quick lunch and then a hike for the afternoon around two."

We air-kiss cheeks.

"Rory, I put you in a bedroom in the house, and Penelope, I put you in a bedroom in our guesthouse. I'm afraid we've run out of double beds." Myrtle smiles and then puts her arm through Rory's.

Our glances meet in surprise. So much for any hope of a romantic interlude in the midst of our weekend.

"I'll take you to your bedroom now," Myrtle says. "Bernie will be out in a minute to escort you to your room, Penelope.

There wasn't room in the main house; I put all of Bernie's business colleagues in there. I hope you don't mind."

"Not at all," I say with a straight face. "I can also just go there myself if you point me in the right direction."

"Why don't we go there first so I can drop off Penelope's bag?" Rory asks.

Myrtle makes a face of annoyance.

I say, "It's okay" as she says, "Fine."

Rory pulls away from Myrtle and picks up my bag. We walk on a gravel path around the house through the trees, down some stone steps, across a little, wooden bridge forking over a bubbling stream, and there, in the distance, is a small, stone cottage. It looks quite picturesque, even if remote from the big house.

"This was the original house, and then we built our own more modern and much larger house that you saw, but we decided to leave this one for guests," Myrtle says.

"It's charming," I say. I don't generally call things charming, but it is, and it seems to be the right thing to say as Myrtle smiles at me.

The key—and a spider—are under a flowerpot on the porch. She pushes open the heavy, wooden door and we enter the house. It's chilly, although it doesn't look quite as rustic when Myrtle turns the lights on.

"Are other people staying here as well?" Rory asks as he looks around.

"Yes, Anne and her boyfriend, Tom, Jack and his girlfriend, Nia, and Aaron and his boyfriend, Dan."

So, basically, we're the only couple that has been separated, and Rory is the only younger person staying at the big house. Somehow, I think the guesthouse is going to be the party house, provided we can warm this place up.

We follow Myrtle up the wooden stairs to my bedroom, which is the first on the left. It's clean, and the single bed looks comfortable. Rory sets down my bag and sits on the bed, bouncing slightly.

"No naughty thoughts," Myrtle says. Rory looks surprised, but winks at me. I feel myself blush.

"So, why don't you meet us back at the main house in about twenty minutes?" Myrtle asks, pointing at a map on the desk, showing us the walking route planned for the afternoon. "Dress in hiking clothes."

"I'm already dressed in hiking clothes." I point to my jeans and sturdy boots. Given that Myrtle sent out an itinerary for the weekend, which noted hiking for this afternoon, I'm not sure what she expected me to be dressed in.

"Oh, of course," she says, but looks annoyed that she won't have Rory to herself.

We trail Myrtle out of the cottage and back to the main house. Rory picks up his bag from the car trunk. The big house is heated and very modern. Myrtle shows us his room. It's a single bed as well.

"There's a connecting door to my study right here," Myrtle says.

Rory gives me a concerned look.

"Does it lock?" I ask.

"I lost the key," Myrtle says.

"We've slept together in a single bed before," I say to tease Myrtle.

Myrtle clears her throat. "Well, you definitely want to be well-rested for a weekend with your boss and your client."

"Yes, it's good that you separated us," I say to Myrtle.

She sniffs and excuses herself to see how the lunch is going.

"I think you're going to need to sleep with me in the single bed. Just for warmth alone," I say.

"I should get some sleep," Rory says.

"You'll sleep even better in the cold air," I say.

Rory gives me his skeptical look, and I feel a slight flutter in my stomach.

"Should we go to lunch? You can leave your coat and backpack here," he says.

Lunch is uneventful. And my disaster-prone fairy godmother doesn't strike on the hike, so I make it back in one piece. She must think her work is done. We meet the other couples banished to the cottage, and they're a fun bunch. As we all head off to the cottage after the hike, Rory and the three other business-important partners look jealous.

I'm about to head up to my room to make some mini flowers for a bit when I hear Tom give a shout of glee.

"They've got board games," Tom says.

"What's up with the lack of heat here? Is she trying to freeze us to death?" Nia asks. Nia and I search for the thermostat. Finding it, we adjust it five degrees higher.

We chat for a bit, then separate to get some work done and dress for dinner.

Dinner has a theme—the roaring twenties—so my hat makes another appearance. I could really get to like Myrtle.

After dinner, Bernie suggests that he, Rory, and Rory's boss continue their discussion about the next campaign with tea and coffee in the living room. The rest of us are excused.

I kiss Rory on the check. "See you in the morning. Sleep well."

Rory grumbles. "I sleep better with you next to me."

I wave goodbye and walk with the others to the cottage. We raid the supplies. We've been left tea, coffee, whole milk, and sugar. Breakfast is at the big house in the morning. Nia brings out two bottles of red wine, Tom produces several more, and I contribute a bag of peanut M&Ms and chocolate chip cookies, which I'm sorry to confess I brought as crafting fuel.

We play several games of Clue and one game of Scrabble, drinking the wine, and then Dan says, "We need to rescue Rory."

"No, I'm sure he's fine. Career goals and all that," I say.

"We just have to interrupt it, and then he can excuse himself to go to bed," Dan says. "But instead, sneak out over here."

"I can ask for an extra blanket," Nia says wryly. "Or I can ask for Tylenol."

"Or an ice pack after the hike," I say.

"I'll ask for an ice pack," Tom says.

"But won't that be bad for your career?" I ask.

"We're on a rescue mission," Jack says. "And anyway, Bernie is a good sort overall. Just once he's into an idea, he doesn't want to stop talking about it. And now he's got Rory off the clock so he's taking advantage of it. Sometimes, you have to remind him that we have lives. Not that Rory can do that when Bernie is the client."

"Okay, what props do we need?" Aaron asks. "You should bring the hat. We need to use that somehow."

I text Rory that we're coming to rescue him, but I don't get a response. He probably left his phone in his room.

We sneak up to the house.

"Shh," Aaron says as our shoes scrunch on the leaves and sticks. "We must be one with the trees and the air and the leaves."

The living room takes up one corner of the boxlike house. It has floor-to-ceiling windows, which gives you a feeling of being right there in nature. We can't hide there, so we slink around to the smaller windows on the other side. *Crunch, crunch.* The seven of us are all bent down below the two windows.

Tom peers into the living room first.

"Looks serious. We've got a tea platter out. Rory is in the middle of the couch between his boss and Myrtle. Bernie and Bob are on the other side."

Myrtle is next to Rory, serving tea. I probably should have stayed close to Rory, but he said I should go back. And she can't do anything in front of her husband and his business associates. And she seems to accept that we're in a relationship.

"Going in," Tom says. He disappears around to the front of the house. The rest of us remain crouched down by the two windows, our eyes just at windowsill level as we spy into the room.

Tom appears at the entrance to the living room, limping. He looks very earnest.

Myrtle gets up and disappears with Jack out of the room. Bernie's colleague excuses himself and leaves. Rory is talking intently with his boss and Bernie, his brow furrowed. This isn't going to work. He's so focused on this campaign. And I understand, I really do. And now he's looking off in the distance, like he does when he's mulling over an idea.

"At least he's facing the window," Aaron says. "And his boss is not."

"But he's not looking at the window," Nia says.

"Should we knock on the window and duck?" Aaron asks.

"Let's hold my hat up on a stick," I say, looking for a stick on the ground. "Maybe he'll see it as a cry for help."

"They'll both look over," Jack says. "Did you text him?"

"I don't think he has his phone."

"Okay, we need to slip him a note." Aaron rubs his hands together. "Anybody have paper?"

"Well, you're up then. We can't go in because we'll get dragged into this work discussion," Anne says.

I pull out my black notebook from my jacket pocket and write Rory a note that we're trying to rescue him, so he should excuse himself and come play Clue with us. But only if he wants to. I hand the note to Aaron.

"But what more can we ask for? Blankets?" I ask.

"I'll ask for more toilet paper," Aaron says.

We all crack up, laughing. Aaron disappears.

"Rory's looking over at the window. Quick, put the hat up!" Jack says.

I put the hat on a stick and wave it wildly while we all duck down. I peek over the windowsill. Rory's brow is furrowed, but I don't know if he can see us out in the dark. And hopefully, nobody in the room can hear us. We are making a fair amount of noise as we laugh and plot.

Aaron is now in the room. He's helped himself to a cookie from the platter. He hands Rory a napkin.

"Smooth," Dan says.

"Did he hand him the note with the napkin?"

"I think so," Dan says.

Myrtle arrives back, and Aaron turns to her. Myrtle looks surprised at his request. Understandably so, as the one bathroom I used had at least four rolls of toilet paper in the cabinet under the sink. He gives a thumbs-up as he leaves the room with her.

Tom slinks over. "What's happening now?"

"Aaron just asked for toilet paper so he could hand Rory a note to come out," I say.

Rory stands and walks over to the window. We all wave, with the hat on the stick bobbing up wildly with us. Rory grins and gives us a thumbs-up. He blows me a kiss.

"Aww," Dan says. "He's a keeper."

Rory is back talking to his boss. His boss nods, and Rory leaves the room.

And then Aaron and Rory appear at the corner. We all scoot back from the window. I run to join Rory and hug him. His embrace back is light, and I release him quickly.

"I'm touched that you all came out to rescue me," Rory says.

"Leave no man behind. We need to stick together against the powers that be," Aaron says.

We walk back to the cottage and all pile into the living room, but while the other couples are sitting next to each other on the couches, Rory and I are each on two straight-backed chairs we brought in from the dining room. Rory reaches out to hold my hand and smiles at me. I slide my chair closer to him.

We decide to play Mafia. I write out "villager" on six pieces of paper, "night watchman" on one piece of paper, and "murderer" on the last piece, and then crumple them up and place them in the hat. We each pick a piece of paper. I am a villager.

Aaron is the night watchman. He tells us to close our eyes.

"Okay, you can open your eyes. Nia, you've been murdered," Aaron says.

Now we have to guess which one of us is the murderer.

"I felt a swish of air near me," Tom says. "So, the murderer is definitely over here." Rory's chair is next to the couch where Tom is sitting.

Everyone except me decides it's Rory, based on Tom's swish theory.

"It's not me," Rory says.

"I didn't feel a swish of air near me," I say. I would have felt Rory move. I'm so attuned to his every shift.

"You're protecting him," Anne says.

Rory says he is not the murderer. We all close our eyes again. This time, Dan is murdered.

"Did you feel a swish of air this time?" Anne asks.

"Not as much," Tom says.

"It's Tom. He's trying to protect himself with this swish theory," I say. Rory puts his arm around the back of my chair, and I definitely feel that air gap between his arm and my back. I shift back slightly to rest against his arm.

They all decide it's me, again based on Tom's sensitivity to the air movement around him. I am not the murderer, so everyone has to shut their eyes again. This time, Anne is killed. Now it's just Tom and Jack, each saying it's the other. The ghost villagers are allowed to weigh in and we all pick Tom. It's not Tom, it's Jack.

"Why'd you kill me first?" Nia asks.

"Because you can tell when I'm lying," Jack says.

I don't know Rory well enough to tell when he's lying. Unless the person has a really easy tell, that seems to me to be the mark of a deeply connected relationship—when you know the other person that well. They probably don't need the elaborate sign language we cooked up when we were fake dating.

We play one more round. And I know when Rory says he's not the murderer that he's telling the truth. Rory catches me staring at him and smiles back. We do know each other so well. Does that mean he can tell I love him—or do I need to say it out loud?

It's now getting late, and we all have to be at Myrtle's couples' yoga session in the morning.

We follow the others up to the bedrooms on the second floor and say good night at our doors.

Rory and I look at each other ruefully in the room. I turn away from his glance to put my hat down on the dresser. The room feels even smaller than it did this morning when three of us were in it. Rory has rolled up his sleeves and his shirt is unbuttoned at the top, and he just looks so good.

He sits down on the bed and chuckles. "Myrtle. A single bed. What do you think is up with her?"

"I'm not sure, but I saw Bernie smile when you helped her over that log in the path on the hike," I say, shaking my head. "Maybe it creates more passion in their romance—like how women who read romances apparently have more sex."

"Do they?" Rory looks intrigued.

"So I've read."

"What about women who *write* romances?"

"Based on my years as a single woman writing romances, no," I say firmly.

"We should rectify that," he says. "And I can't let you sleep in this cold room alone."

CHAPTER THIRTY-FIVE

MYRTLE CLAPS EXCITEDLY AS we all enter her yoga space, which is in a beautifully converted barn. I can't help but notice it is warmer than our cottage.

"Partner yoga is all about creating a foundation for openness, confidence, and understanding with each other. Relationships can only grow if you are open and honest with each other and keep things lighthearted and fun," Myrtle says.

That's more profound advice than I expected from Myrtle.

"Okay, first we're going to do seated centering," Myrtle says. "Sit cross-legged, facing your partner, with your hands on each other's knees. Look into your partner's eyes. Truly see your partner. Take ten deep breaths in and out and allow for a deeper connection without words. We can get so busy in our daily lives that we forget the importance of truly seeing each other for who we are."

Bernie and Myrtle are focused on each other, cross-legged. Actually, they look really cute together.

Rory and I stare into each other's eyes. His eyes are deep blue, with green and almost gold around the pupils, his gaze a warm pool that's making me melt as if I stepped into a sauna to relax. I can feel his breath softly on my face as we each breathe in and out. It's intense looking into his eyes, baring.

"Now let's do the seated cat cow. Reach for each other's forearms, release your shoulders down and back. Release. Now inhale and lift your chest up to the ceiling," Myrtle says.

Rory reacts slower than me, which means I feel like I end up sticking my chest into his face. Not directly into his face, but close enough. He raises an eyebrow as he leans his head back. Maybe our arms are not supposed to bend.

"Now exhale, drawing your chin into your chest, rounding through your upper middle back, and spreading your shoulder blades wide apart."

I can feel the tightness of the muscles in my chest. It's too much to keep it all in.

"Let's do ten rounds of this movement. Use the support of your partner to find a sense of spaciousness in your chest and upper back."

Spaciousness is not what I'm finding. Rory pulls me closer with his elbows when we inhale again, lifting our chests up to the ceiling. I snicker and Myrtle looks over. We're inappropriate thirteen-year-olds. I school my face back into an expression of a woman in a mature relationship.

Rory smiles. I can feel him relaxing as I hold his forearms.

Myrtle then shows us how to do seated back pose where we lean against each other's backs and squat. I'm short compared to Rory, so we have a bit of a time getting the hang of it. The thigh burn is real. And it's weird to feel Rory's firm butt against mine, his back against mine. Metaphorically, though, Rory always has my back.

Next position up is a seated forward backbend, where we sit back-to-back and I lean back while he leans forward. I drape myself over Rory.

"Comfortable?" he asks.

"Very. You?"

"Waiting for my turn."

Yeah, stretching with Rory lying back on top of me is definitely pushing me farther than I want to go.

"Check in with your partner. Should they apply more pressure? Less pressure?" Myrtle asks. "Feel the physical connection."

Rory lightens the pressure before I can even ask.

Now Myrtle instructs one partner to do child's pose. I volunteer and curl over, grabbing Rory's ankles. He has to do downward dog, reaching to hold my hips. His hands feel warm against my back. We switch.

And then we're back to seated centering, staring at each other. I could get lost in Rory's eyes. Can he tell that my eyes say, "I am in love with you"?

Myrtle claps, and I jump.

"Namaste." Myrtle bows.

We all clap. It was so much better than I expected. I roll up my yoga mat. Rory rolls up his yoga mat next to me. A pit grows in my stomach. If it was just the two of us, I would have said "I love you." It has released too many feelings. I breathe deeply.

"Are you okay?" Rory whispers.

I dart a glance at him.

"Yes." I raise an eyebrow. "That was intense."

Rory gives me a more probing look. "It was."

The air pulses between us. Rory reaches out to take my rolled-up yoga mat and his hand brushes mine, a whisper of contact, which I feel everywhere. I look away at Myrtle in the front of the room.

"I should tell her she's converted me," I say.

"Yes," Rory says, but his brow is slightly furrowed.

I walk over to Myrtle with Rory following, carrying our yoga mats.

After a buffet brunch back at the house, we have corporate team-building exercises. The singles have already bonded pretty well from last night.

"I love these exercises," Dan says. "The company has a retreat every year."

"It works. I know Dan's colleagues pretty well as a result," Aaron says. "And you're much more fun than Callie."

I hadn't realized that Aaron and Dan knew Callie. I feel a stab of hurt because Callie was at the corporate retreat. I'm not the first girlfriend he's brought along. Maybe I'm just another girlfriend in a long line of girlfriends. He did really like Callie. Hopefully, that was his "sowing wild oats" phase.

He's my first serious boyfriend since college. Maybe he needs to worry that he's part of *my* "sowing wild oats" phase.

We're back in the converted and spacious loft-like barn. The first exercise is to keep balloons up in the air as a team.

"Watch out for any air swishes," Nia says. We all laugh.

We run around, keeping the balloons up in the air, joking around.

The next exercise is called Picture Story. It's Significant Others vs the Ad Team for the company, both internal and external, so Rory and I are on opposite teams. We each receive a card with a picture on it. The cards together will make up a story. We can't show the card to our teammates, but we have to describe the picture. Then we have to place the cards in a row to create the story in its correct order.

The ad team gets it first. We do a few more exercises, and then the weekend is over. We exchange numbers and all pile into our respective cars to drive home.

Rory's mom calls just as we are about to leave. He steps out of the car and walks over to the edge of the driveway for some privacy. I happily admire him from afar.

Then he returns to the car and slides back into his seat.

Rory says, "My mom is taking a spur-of-the-moment trip to Italy for a painting class, leaving October 31. I think you've inspired her."

"Wow, that's amazing," I say.

"I'm really proud of her for pursuing her dream."

"Where in Italy?" I ask.

“Florence.”

“That will be awesome,” I say. “That was so much fun. I wasn’t expecting it to be so lively and silly. I thought it was going to be formal and corporate.”

“Usually it is.” Rory laughs. “Your hat bobbing up and down.”

We both laugh and smile at each other.

"They want us to think of another romcom-inspired ad campaign," he says. "I wanted to do something ending with a rainy drive, giving that moody, but warm bubble feeling like we had on our drive to Fire Island. I was thinking maybe they first meet each other at a car wash. While he's in the line for the car wash, he sees her and he's intrigued. Then the car is in the car wash and the water is pouring down and he can't see anything. Then the window is clean and he's waiting at the stoplight as the car is dried. The light turns to green and he sees her glowing in the sunlight and there's that clarity that she's the one."

"I like that." We drive over a cute little bridge. A few mountains are off in the distance.

"In the next scene, they wash their own cars by hand, with some water play with the hoses, and then they go for a drive together in the rain ending up in front of a fire. They want to promote the car's safety features during the rainy drive."

I nod. "That sounds good."

"The water play isn't original, but Bernie loves the idea of wet models," he says. "I think I need a better meet-cute. It also could be raining and he could offer to share an umbrella, but that's also been done. And although I like the idea that he offers a garbage bag to make a raincoat, they're not going to want that imagery for their brand. Do you remember that time we all got stuck in that downpour in college and wore garbage bags to get back to the dorms?"

"That was so funny--and smart thinking on your part," I say, smiling at the memory. "You need to get a trash bag company as a client."

Rory laughs as he drives us down the winding road. We pass by farmhouses, cows, horses and small towns as we make our way to the highway.

"Why don't they meet at an amusement park? They can crash into each other at the bumper cars ride," I say.

"I like that," Rory says, glancing at me. "That's pretty brilliant." He reaches over to hold my hand, his other hand steering.

I smile. “I really liked everybody.”

“Me, too,” Rory says. “I feel like we should vacation with those guys.”

As if we are going to be a long-term couple. I smile, looking out the window at the passing greenery. I think we will be.

Chapter Thirty-Six

IT'S WEDNESDAY, AND I join Rory on his big, gray, overstuffed couch. We're watching *Casablanca* to plan his annual Halloween party this Saturday.

"That Secret Cinema gift." He kisses the top of my head. "It was—it just showed me how well you know me. It was so much fun."

"So much fun. I wish we had Secret Cinema in New York." I look down at my notes. "What about the map of Africa for the invite?"

He nods. "We need fez hats."

"On it." I google fez hats and find them discounted at an online party store. "I think five should be enough. For those who don't have costumes."

"But maybe we need some for the bartenders? Let me email Pat and see if he's up for creating his own costume or wants one."

"His rock star costume last year was great." I had also appreciated Rory's rock star costume last year, from afar. He'd worn a shirt open practically to the waist and tight pants.

"And then we need baskets for the chips and snacks," I say.

"Yes, do you think we can make a light that swings around? I have the seventies' disco ball from the rock star party."

"We need to add arches to the room so we give it more of the feel of Rick's Café American."

Rory adds that to the list. I work on the playlist, adding "La Marseillaise," "It Had to Be You," "Perfidia," and "As Time Goes By." We'll play those for the cocktail party and then move into the dance party later.

"My mom is extending her trip to stay for a month," Rory says.

Another one of his mom's paintings hangs on the wall behind the dining room table. It's an abstract portrait of their family set against a deep-blue background, evocative of the ocean, but you can still recognize Rory's wavy hair, his mom's arm around him, his dad's arm around her.

"Is your dad going as well?"

"No. She's going to be working. And he has several patients at a critical juncture right now. He said he might fly over to visit for a weekend when she's free. I don't think they've ever been separated this long before."

We watch the final scene where Renault and Rick walk off into the fog.

Rory brings out a pint of Ben & Jerry's New York Super Fudge Chunk. We take turns eating out of the carton but end up fighting over the white chocolate pieces. The party planning is interrupted as we wrestle—and more. He lets me have the last piece of white chocolate.

"How can we create those arches?" he asks.

"Sheets," I say. "We can use sheets; it will also give it an Arabian tent feel."

And then we create the guest list. We add Aaron and Dan, Jack and Nia, and Tom and Ann. Callie's on it. I can't object, but I can't help wishing that she wasn't.

"Do you want to invite Jamie?" he asks.

"It's not necessary."

"I think he's come in past years when he's been here. We should invite him. I'm not worried."

"And you shouldn't be." I lean back against the couch pillows and put my legs over his.

As I search my email for his address, I see an email from an agent—from the batch of queries sent out a month ago.

To: Penelope

From: Angela

Re: Midnight Masquerade

I really enjoyed your first ten pages. I'd like to request the full manuscript.

I received another request for a full manuscript! I shriek. And then Rory and I celebrate in a more physical manner.

Chapter Thirty-Seven

BENSON IS CHASING SQUIRRELS in Central Park when Rory calls to say he's at my apartment and he'll come join me. His voice sounds strained.

I've missed having Benson around. He's just staying for three days. Rory is sleeping over at my place, so I'm not abandoning Benson.

The afternoon sunlight hitting the tree illuminates its bright orange and yellow leaves.

Less than a block away, I see Rory, wearing a gray scarf. I call Benson back and gently tug on his leash. Rory's face looks pale and strained. He doesn't smile when he sees me. A sinking feeling fills my stomach. *Is he breaking up with me?*

Then he hugs me, clinging to me.

Whatever it is, it isn't us.

He starts walking south, down the path next to the roadway with runners, walkers, and bicyclists all getting in their end-of-day exercise. He doesn't look at me. "You know how my mom is taking that month-long retreat in Italy to do a painting course?"

"Yes," I say.

"She's not coming back at the end. She's rented a villa in Italy to continue painting for another month. She's hired a private tutor."

"That's good, isn't it? She's really going for it." Benson is tugging to sniff and pee on a pole. I stop so he can. Rory is a few steps ahead. The fallen orange, yellow, and brown leaves pepper the walk, adding splashes of color.

"She's leaving my dad." His voice is anguished. He turns back to face me.

He feels far away.

"What do you mean? Your parents are happily married," I say.

"That's what I thought. But my mom said she needs a break. That my dad needs to figure out his priorities. That he thinks he's there for her but it's all meaningless gestures." Rory sits on a bench. "I really thought that they had it figured out." He shakes his head. "Maybe you're right and love doesn't last forever."

I brush orange leaves off the green bench and sit next to him. "I don't think I said there was no such thing as everlasting love." Benson puts his head in my lap, and I pet him.

"You said you weren't looking for magical, that magical is dangerous."

"I was wrong. It's worth it. What we've got is magical." *Idiot. Don't tie this to us.* I hold his hand.

"And my parents thought what they had was magical. And my father . . . I mean . . . my father thought he *was* being there for my mom."

"Well, how did your mom say that he wasn't there for her? Can't he just change and do that?"

"It's not that easy."

"Isn't it?" I wouldn't give up my dreams for Rory, but I want to be there for him, too.

"I don't know. I'm just confused. And I feel silly for being confused because I'm a grown-up. It's not like I'm a kid whose parents are getting a divorce, but I don't understand."

"They're not getting a divorce."

"Yet."

"Maybe it's not your dad. Your mom just needs time alone to pursue her art career."

"It's not you, it's me." Rory smiles slightly. It's a sliver of a smile, but it's there.

"She'll probably come back all revived, and their relationship will have a new energy."

"I think it's deeper than that."

"It doesn't have to be. My mom always complained that the housework took up so much of her time; it was something as little as that that caused their fights. Making sure the house was stocked with food, cleaning up after everything, cooking. It all just takes time and it's constant. And it wasn't overtly appreciated by my dad."

The sun sets, and the lights in the lampposts come on.

"But couldn't she just say that, then—that she needs to focus completely on this but she is coming back?"

I give Rory a hug.

"Maybe she can't promise that. She may change as an artist. And if she wants your dad to change, maybe your dad needs that uncertainty as a catalyst." I shift on the bench. "My parents fought fiercely before they finally made it through—and then planned their trip to Peru to celebrate falling in love again. The fighting was terrible. I hated it. But maybe it was also good. It cleared the air, so to speak, like a thunderstorm. And they both said things they needed to say. And they came back together." I rub his back. "So, you're in the dark night of the soul part right now."

"This isn't a romantic comedy. This is my life—my parents' lives." He stands, hands jammed in his pockets.

"I know." I stand, too. He missed entirely what I just said about my parents. And the "my life" didn't include me.

Benson pulls to smell a light pole a few feet away. I go with him. He circles around it. Rory still isn't looking at me. He's looking off in the direction of The Majestic, its two towers outlined against the deepening dusk. Benson poops. I crouch down to pick it up with my plastic bag.

Rory looks back over at me. *Not ideal.* I stand, now holding a quite fragrant bag. I want to give Rory a hug, but first I jog over to throw the full bag out in a green receptacle a few feet away. He turns away again.

I come up behind him. I try again. "Of course, you're confused and hurt. They're still your parents, and they're a rock that you've relied on. They always seem so close, so in tune with one another. I'm sure they'll work this out. Or maybe it's not even the relationship. Maybe your mom wants to be independent of any constraints so she can create."

He turns back to me again. His eyes look desolate. I hug him. His arms enfold me back.

"But why? Is that a thing? Do you feel that way?"

"No, being with you energizes me. But there's a reason why many famous female artists never married or had children. Think Jane Austen—never married or had children, Virginia Woolf, Lee Krasner." Rory is looking more upset. My words are not helping. Now he's part of the problem, too. "I think she'll come back to your dad. Their bond is tangible. And she'll realize that once she's in Italy. She'll miss him, you'll see."

"I'm going to cancel my Halloween party."

"Really? Don't you think you should hold it? See your friends?"

"I'm not in the mood."

"Maybe push it back a week? It's good to be with your friends at times like these."

"I'll think about it. I'm sorry your parents fought so much."

"Yes. And the digs were nasty and personal. I was glad to go off to college to escape." But I should have gone back to see them before they left for Peru. My mom had wanted me to come back the weekend before they left—to spend some time with them. But I didn't want to spend time with them, not if they were going to be fighting. She promised me they weren't fighting anymore. But I didn't believe her. Not that I said that. But I think she suspected it. I said I was too busy. *And so, I missed my last opportunity to see them alive.* "Are they going to try therapy?"

Rory shrugs. "I don't know. That's kind of weird coming from you, given that you never went to therapy after your parents died."

I flinch. "I probably should've gone for therapy. It just wasn't very accepted in my family." Rory is like a wounded bear, striking out at me. I've seen that before—with my parents. I don't have a positive precedent for how to react. My parents just struck out at each other. Is it better to just ignore it? But he's hurting me. When it became really bad, that's when my mom asked for a divorce. So, it's not a positive sign. They did turn it around and decide to go together on the trip to Peru, but I was in college when they worked through it, so I didn't see how they did it. *It hurts to be vulnerable and to have someone know your secrets. And even more to twist them into a painful retort.*

I take a step back.

"I'm sorry," Rory says, and he hugs me. I hug him back. Benson puts his snout on Rory's shoe.

Chapter Thirty-Eight

RORY'S MOM LEFT FOR Italy last Saturday, a week ago, and he canceled his October 31 Halloween party. I can see he is still upset, but he doesn't want to talk about it, so I've given him space this week. He seems better because his Halloween party is back on—in its new guise of a *Casablanca* costume party next Saturday, November 14.

Callie invites us to some cocktail party, which could have clients for Rory. I tell Rory he should go without me because I'm in the middle of working on my miniature art gallery, which I have to deliver next week. I feel more sympathetic toward Callie now. I don't understand how she could have given Rory up, but I don't view her as a threat.

Rory says, "It could be material for your next book. It's at this rooftop loft space in Tribeca."

That does give me a moment's pause, mostly because the last rooftop vibe inspired my impassioned, failed declaration to Jamie, and I hope this setting doesn't similarly inspire Callie.

"Take pictures if it's really fabulous so I can use it as a setting. But I'll come to the next one. And you should have fun. I'm just going to be sitting here in my pajamas, working," I say.

The art gallery studio structure is done; I'm creating the food for the table now: fruit, cheese, and crackers. "Will you come back here afterward?"

"I don't know. It might go really late," he says. "I don't want to wake you guys."

"Hmm . . . I miss you. Should I come to your apartment and work there?"

"We can just hang out tomorrow."

I'm back in the Sunday brunch spot. Maybe I should go, but I still have a lot of work to do on this project.

I'm making tiny strawberries, and the red clay stains my fingers. I wash my hands and make a chicken stew for Zelda and me. Rory is having dinner with his dad before he goes to Callie's party. I hope that dinner goes well.

Rory sends me a picture of the space. It's a gorgeous, high-ceilinged room with white columns, similar to the Brooklyn art space, but then glass-wall windows on two sides with views of midnight Manhattan, apartment building lights twinkling in the dark like stars. An outdoor wraparound deck has firepits and heaters. It would be a good space for a wedding. I show Zelda as we eat dinner.

And then another picture, a selfie of Rory and Callie against the dark sky. Her head is close to his, and Rory is smiling—not a full smile, not the half smile, but the dimmed smile he's been making lately.

Zelda shakes her head.

"Why are you shaking your head?" Even though I know why.

"I don't trust Callie."

"But I trust Rory. And things are good. I got a bit worried when he freaked out about his parents, but, you know, we still can't get enough of each other."

"Okay, okay, I don't need to hear the details. I'm heading out."

I wave goodbye, and the door shuts behind Zelda.

Rory texts to ask if he can come over, and I text back yes, surprised. Twenty minutes later, and Rory is in our living room.

He slumps into the couch. "I wasn't feeling it. I met my dad for dinner and . . ."

"And?"

"I just don't want to hear all this stuff about my parents' marriage. I don't want to hear all the negative stories of she did this, he did that. I know that's really immature of me, but I don't want to look behind the curtain. They're each just presenting one side, and I don't want to take sides." Rory splays out his hands in a gesture of defeat.

I hug him. "I think that's normal. I didn't like it when my mom complained about my dad. I didn't want to take sides."

"I thought you'd agree with Callie. Callie said it was good for me to hear that marriage is not some crazy lovefest."

"Not through your parents' marriage. You need an example of hope."

"And it's not like I don't know marriage is difficult. My father's a marriage counselor. And his practice was in our brownstone basement. This one woman used to cry so loudly that I could hear it through the door, up the stairs, and into our living room. I've seen couples arrive separately, barely looking at each other. So, I know."

I rub his back. I don't know what to say to console him. His dad shouldn't be sharing all this with him.

"And my dad is even doubting his ability as a marriage counselor. How can he be failing at his own marriage and counsel others?"

"Maybe that will make him better, give him more insight into the process."

Rory runs his hand through his hair. "Maybe." His hand finds mine and holds it.

"He shouldn't be using you as a confidante. You're his son, and it puts you in the middle."

"I can't say that to him."

"No."

"He needs someone to talk to. I can't cut him off," he says.

"No," I say. Our living room, decorated in its bright colors, seems only to contrast with Rory's despair. "Is there anyone else he can talk to?"

"He doesn't want to share that they're having marriage problems."

"That makes sense. But maybe a professional?"

"He doesn't want to do it." Rory bites out those words. "Look, I think I might go home."

I feel a sudden coldness. "Why? You should sleep here. Stay."

"I think I just need to be alone. I'm not good company."

"Okay, but I'm here for you. I think it's good for you to stay and for you to talk about it." Which is admittedly ironic, coming from me, the master of bottling it all up.

"There's not much more for me to say. I don't know how to deal with this."

It's hard to see happy, romantic Rory look so defeated.

"But you are dealing with it. Talking about it is good. That's how I dealt with my parents' death. I talked about it a lot—until it became too much for me and others—and then I talked about it still with Zelda. And she just let me."

"Do you still talk about it?"

"Sometimes," I say, rubbing his back. "I recently talked about it with my sister. And I still get sad. But that's good. It's good to acknowledge those emotions. I'm sad that there are things about them that I will never know because I was eighteen when they died, and I didn't know to ask those questions."

"Maybe sometimes that's good. Maybe you don't always want those answers," Rory says. "My dad just told me how often they had sex. And I definitely didn't want to know that. And . . . it doesn't seem to have been the problem."

I lean my head against his shoulder. "True. But otherwise, they're a puzzle that you're still trying to piece together. And you find clues here and there. You can talk to their friends, but then it's filtered by that friend's perception and prejudice. And what they say is not always nice and not always true. I just found out that my father's friend was painted frequently by a famous female artist—because I liked her art and bought her art catalogue. I thought my father's friend had a slight acquaintance with this art crowd, not that he was an integral part of it. And although my father was definitely on the periphery, he was on the periphery of quite a famous art crowd. And I so wish I could talk to him about that. And maybe that's why he was so supportive of me when I was kid, writing my *Calico the Caterpillar* stories and getting rejections. And that makes me wish he was still here because sometimes I'd like that encouragement rather than the 'Shouldn't you be realistic? Haven't you tried enough now?' I get from Theresa."

"You and my mom should really talk—when she's back. Maybe she could even find someone from that crowd still alive whom you could talk to, even if you get a filtered version."

"I will."

Rory kisses me gently, and then passionately, as if seeking comfort. I hold him tightly, my hands rubbing his back to give comfort. *I am here for you.*

Chapter Thirty-Nine

TODAY, RORY SEEMS TO be back to his old self. Jake and Audrey are helping us set up for the *Casablanca* party. Jake's playlist creates a happy vibe.

The front hallway has a separate boombox with "La Marseillaise" on repeat. Old suitcases are stacked in the hallway, covered in travel stickers from all over Europe. Audrey and I hang signs that read "Exit visa this way," "Last plane to Lisbon," and "Vive la France." Dry ice in a cauldron adds a smoky feel and smell.

Rory and Jake are each on ladders, trying to hang the sheets from the ceiling. Jake asks Audrey to hand him a different tape. We can't find any tape that works to attach the sheets to the ceiling. We haven't yet resorted to hooks.

As I walk away to get baskets for the Moroccan ambiance, a sheet falls on me. "Boo," I say. So much for the tape.

Rory's laugh is deep. He helps me get out of the sheet. Hooks it is. We decide to tie a rope from a hook already in the wall to one in the ceiling on the other side.

We cut holes in the sheet and attach it almost like a curtain. It looks good. We hang a few more sheets in a similar fashion.

"Should we tell them about how we got caught in those robes in the Morocco set scene?" Rory asks me.

"I definitely want to hear that story." Jake pulls Audrey closer to him and kisses her.

Rory tells them. His arm encircles me, and I nestle into him. Rory is wearing his *Casablanca*-inspired robe, and I'm wearing mine. I put pin tucks in mine to shape it and give me a waist. At least it's easier to remove than my previous *Casablanca*-inspired costume.

One of Rory's friends, who works in set design, arrives—with a moving searchlight. It's expensive, so he's the only one who is allowed to touch it. He places it up high, attached to the wall, so that it is out of harm's way. He dims the lights. The searchlight sweeping over the room gives an eerie feeling.

Pat, Rory's usual Columbia University student bartender, enters, dressed in a French military uniform, and sets up the bar. As guests arrive, Rory is mingling and chatting. A sense of relief fills me. I'm hanging out with Zelda in the corner. Callie is dressed like the woman Rick rejected in *Casablanca*. This may be a good sign, but I think she just chose the skimpiest outfit in that movie. The shimmery halter top and white harem pants show off her completely flat stomach.

"Callie is glued to him. You've got to separate them," Zelda says.

"Callie has a boyfriend now, but he's divorced, so she wants to understand him better by hearing about what Rory's dad is going through."

"Rory told her about his dad?"

"I was surprised, too," I say.

"*You* need to be the person Rory confides in about his dad." Zelda's brow is furrowed.

"I try, but I sometimes say the wrong thing."

"Is there a wrong thing to say?" Zelda leans against the wall, sipping her *Casablanca* cocktail, Pat's special creation for the night. She mmms. Pat added a dash of cardamom spice, so it gives the flavor of Morocco.

"Yes." I nod decisively. "Because I've said it."

"That just means that Rory feels comfortable to express his frustration and hurt with you."

"I don't think that's it."

"I think a divorced guy would be a good prospect; they'd have learned from their mistakes and now be more aware of how to make a relationship work." Zelda frowns. "But I think she's still after Rory."

"Seems a little unlikely given that she's now dating someone." Then again, we fake dated to deter her, so all's fair in love and war. "Her boyfriend is coming tonight, so we'll meet him."

Jake puts on the dancing music. The second one is supposed to be "It Had to Be You," the song we kissed to. We're going to swing-dance to that, so I leave Zelda to find Rory. Rory has disappeared from the living room and the kitchen. Callie and Rory are sitting on the couch in his bedroom, and she looks like she's about to cry. Rory has his arm around her.

It will be callous of me to ask him to dance. But that's what we had planned. I want to stamp my foot, like a five-year-old who is not getting a dog for Christmas.

"Our song is next," I say, perching on the couch arm next to Rory.

Rory says, "Callie's boyfriend broke up with her."

"Oh," I say. "I'm sorry to hear that."

"I'll tell Jake to play it later." He texts Jake on his phone.

Callie rests her head on his shoulder.

I say, "Well, you're missing the party moping over this guy. You should get out there and enjoy it. Taylor Swift, shake it off, and all that."

"I'm not very good at 'shaking it off' and hiding my emotions," she says. There's an unspoken "unlike you."

I wince and look sharply at him. *Has he been talking about me to Callie?* Also, career-girl Callie is usually quite good at not showing vulnerability. Maybe she really likes this guy.

"You're certainly not begrudging me my time with Rory. I mean, I let him go on his monthly brunch dates with you when we were dating," she says.

I have to presume our brunches were not during parties they planned. And they involved no physical contact.

Rory looks apologetically at me.

"We'll be out soon," he says.

I nod and return to the party.

I look over to where Jake is fiddling with his iPhone. Jake looks up and gives a thumbs-up. Audrey comes and pulls me over to dance with her. "It's Raining Men" is playing instead. To take my own advice and shake it off, I dance.

Zelda joins us. "I thought you guys were swing-dancing to the second song."

"Callie's boyfriend broke up with her."

Zelda shakes her head.

"She was almost crying." I smile at Zelda to reassure her that I'm not worried. Zelda doesn't buy it.

"I'm going to do some reconnaissance," Zelda says.

Jamie comes over and asks if I want to dance. I hesitate. I do feel awkward that I am preventing Audrey and Jake from dancing together. I'd rather be dancing with Rory. And not dancing with Jamie when Rory is with Callie. The optics aren't good. But we are friends.

I dance two songs with Jamie, and then I excuse myself to find Rory, but Jamie says, "Can we talk for a minute?"

"Okay," I say, warily. He steers us to a corner near the windows. The light from the streetlight shines in, like a fake moon.

"My mom is going to sell the store."

I sit down in a nearby chair. "I was afraid of that."

He pulls up a chair. He leans toward me to be heard over the music. "It's just not doing well, and she has a really good offer from the guy next door."

"What about Kareem?"

"Kareem's been hired by a store focused on running. They were really impressed by your videos of him on Instagram, and they cold-called him. He's going to bring his running group down there. Maybe you can keep your walking group going. And the guy next door will hire Brian." Once I handed in my manuscript, I'd started a walking group, hoping that would help the store out. Five people joined, including Esther and a librarian. We mostly discuss books, so it's more like an unofficial book club. I doubt it has resulted in many sports items sales.

"At least they're taken care of. Is your mom really sad?"

"Yes," Jamie nods.

"Me, too." I feel bad. The store was Theresa's dream of self-sufficiency after her divorce from Jamie's dad. Her dream seemed more realistic than mine. It worked until now. I had hoped our efforts might save it.

Jamie pats my back awkwardly. "Where's Rory?" Jamie is probably afraid I'm going to cry.

Rory joins us at that moment.

"Our song is next. You guys look very cozy," Rory says.

Jamie stands quickly, knocking the chair over. "We're just friends. Penelope has made that clear."

Rory's brow furrows, as if confused.

"I was just telling her that my mom is closing her store," Jamie says.

"I'm sorry," Rory says.

Jamie nods and leaves us.

"You've made it clear that you're just friends?" Rory asks. "Was there an occasion recently that prompted that?"

"When Jamie came over to help me with my website, he said that he felt more for me." I still think that's a completely lame way to say it.

"So, I read the room wrong?" Rory asks. "Why didn't you say anything when I said that's when I knew you were over Jamie?"

"You read me correctly. I didn't feel anything toward him. I said I was happy with you."

"We weren't even dating at that point," Rory says.

"I was—" I say.

Rory's phone rings.

"It's my dad. He's upset about a call with my mom," Rory whispers. I nod.

"I can't hear you," Rory says to his dad. "Wait a minute. I'll go to the back." Rory disappears back into his bedroom.

The first lines of "It Had to Be You" fill the room. I step off to the side as couples dance close. Jake comes over and asks, "Where's Rory?"

"His dad called."

Jake nods. "Sorry about playing—"

I cut him off. "It's okay. Rory is just dealing with a lot right now."

Callie is dancing cheek-to-cheek with one of her business school friends. I start picking up stray cups and bringing them to the garbage under the sink.

I walk back toward the table of food on the side, now scavenged over, to see what else I can clean up. The picture of us in our *Casablanca* costumes is missing. The table has moved away from the wall. I lift up the tablecloth, and it's under the table. It must have fallen through the crack between the table and the wall. I hike up my robe, so I don't get any crap on it, and crawl under the table to get it. It's in the corner. The tablecloth falls back down, so I'm hidden. If I hear Zelda, I'm going to surprise her.

"I just don't understand what he sees in her." Callie's voice.

"I like Penelope." My heart stills. I don't recognize the male voice. *But thanks.* They must move away because I don't hear anything more. I'm clutching the picture of us. On all fours. I should just stay under the table for a while. I can't actually see the picture, but I know how happy we look in the fictional *Casablanca* world. I back out so that I can come out the other end of the table and slowly lift the tablecloth to make sure I don't startle anyone. Nobody there. I crawl out and stand, picking up the picture and taking it and some empty plates to the kitchen with me.

Standing alone in the empty kitchen, among piles of discarded plates, a row of finished wine bottles, and an overflowing garbage can, I watch the party out in the room. I rub my arms. My body feels heavy. It's not Rory's fault. I'm just disappointed. I should check on him.

I walk toward the bedroom. I hear Rory say, "Maybe you just need to give her time alone to think about things."

I stand at the doorway.

He's listening to his dad, his back to me. Then he says, "I'm sure she hasn't been dwelling on these things for the last twenty years. It's not all a mirage."

I walk into the room and touch his back.

He turns. "Penelope, I'm busy right now."

I step back. The turbulent feeling in my stomach swells.

I walk back into the living room. The party is winding down. Many people have left. Some people are looking for Rory to say goodbye. I tell them he's talking to his dad. I don't think he wants to be disturbed. Half-empty glasses are deposited haphazardly, chips are strewn on the floor, and one curtain is hanging crookedly from the ceiling.

Jake comes over. "Is Rory still talking to his dad?"

I nod.

Jake gives me a hug. "He's not thinking straight."

Zelda comes over. "I'm going to head home. Do you want to come with me?"

"I don't know." I feel like crying. I don't want to sob to Rory about not spending any time together at the party when he's dealing with his dad. That will probably look immature. My stomach feels queasy. But I also don't want to stay here in the front room by myself waiting for him. And I don't particularly even want to talk to Rory now. I'm upset. And I'm mad at him. It might be better if I cool down, if I look at this calmly after a full night of sleep.

"I should help clean up." I wave at the remains of the night.

Audrey joins us. "We'll stay and clean up."

I am drained. My disappointment is crashing down on me. I tear.

"Thanks, guys." My voice is a little wobbly. It's like Rory and I broke up publicly at this party, only I didn't get the memo.

I find my coat deep in Rory's closet and leave with Zelda. Jake turns off the music as we leave. The last of the partygoers follow us down the stairs.

Zelda hails us a cab. "I'm not taking the subway at this hour."

"Do you think it's over between me and Rory?" I lean against the cab's fake-leather seat, watching New York City whoosh by as the cab drives up 10th Avenue.

"No. He just got swept into Callie's drama. And then his dad's drama. And because you're not demanding like Callie, he probably thought you'd understand."

"Should I understand?" I ask.

"You should tell him how it made you feel," Zelda says.

It made me feel like I was being pushed out. This is why I'm afraid of love. It just ends up hurting you deep inside.

CHAPTER FORTY

I'M IN MY PAJAMAS, fluffing up my pillow, when my phone rings. Rory.

"You left," he says.

"I was tired. And I didn't want to be sitting out in the living room cleaning up the party after you barked at me to leave you alone."

"I'm sorry. I missed my whole party. I've never seen Callie fall apart like that. And then my dad."

"I know." I stare at my dollhouse at the foot of my bed--with its picture-perfect scenes. Even when I showed a mess, it didn't have the depth of this disaster.

"I wanted that party to be perfect for us," he says.

"I looked forward to it, too. I looked forward to our dance. It was like we were sharing the joy we found at the *Casablanca* Silent Cinema night with all our friends, and instead, you just threw that all over the minute Callie came calling." I'm angry.

"I didn't."

"You made me feel like the dumped girlfriend. I felt really sad." Expressing my emotions is good.

"I thought you were enjoying the party. I saw you dancing with Jamie. I came out."

“I danced two dances with Jamie," I say. "They weren’t even slow dances. And that’s not the point. You were occupied with other people for the *entire* party.” My bedroom is dark. Light from an exterior sconce on the outdoor deck of the building across the backyard filters through my shades, spotlighting Piper standing alone on the balcony. I can hear faint murmurs of a conversation from that deck outside.

“What am I supposed to do? I can’t tell my dad I’m having a party and he has to call back later.”

“But you can tell me repeatedly that you’re too busy to be with me during the party we are throwing together.”

“I’m sorry I yelled at you. He’d just yelled at me. And then I yelled at you.”

“Don’t take it out on me,” I say. “That’s not how it works.”

“How do you know how it works?”

I feel like I’ve been punched in the gut. My voice is quiet. “I know how it doesn’t work because I saw it with my parents.” I hang up.

Chapter Forty-One

I WAKE UP THE next morning, and I don't feel better. This is our first big fight. Ever. I'm not sure where we stand. I check my phone. An email from the agent who requested the full manuscript greets me:

> Dear Penelope,
>
> I'm afraid I have to decline. I have to fall in love with a project, and I didn't feel that level of emotion. It didn't live up to its promise for me.
>
> Best,
> Angela

I am completely deflated. I've poured so much of me into *Midnight Masquerade*. And yet it keeps getting rejected. And she didn't even throw me a bone of constructive criticism. Still, I also know from Trilby's notes that it could be better.

Strawbundle Publishing still has not contacted me, but Esther says that's a positive sign because it wasn't an immediate no.

I hope this isn't how Rory feels. I am a project. And maybe I'm not living up to the promise. Especially for Rory, with all his dreams of the magical. That was former Rory. Heartbroken Rory may have even less patience.

I probably shouldn't have left last night—and then hung up on him. I'll bike down to his apartment now, and we can have a talk and clear the air.

I leave my room. A note sits by a rose teacup on the table.

Penelope,

Thought some more about it. Callie wants him back.

Don't feed into her plans by letting her cause a fight between you.

Big hug,

Zelda

Biking, concentrating on the path ahead, watching out for traffic, helps to clear my mind. I text him that I am coming over and then let myself into his apartment. The dirty glasses and plates have been cleared, but the front room still looks like it's been through a party. The curtains billow, almost like wedding veils, as if the ghost of Miss Havisham haunts the room.

I walk to the bedroom, slowly opening the door. Rory is sleeping. I back out, closing the door softly, and retreat to the kitchen to turn on the electric tea kettle and add some water to the coffeepot for him. I take down the signs that dot the foyer.

Rory comes out. We stare at each other. A chasm widens between us.

"The coffee smells good." Rory slumps into a chair. "I'm sorry about last night. I wanted it to be perfect for us, and it all just fell apart. And I'm sorry I yelled at you when you came in when I was talking to my dad. This isn't me. I keep snapping at you, and I don't do that. And I shouldn't do that. I'm falling apart. I obviously can't handle my parents breaking up, even though I'm nearly thirty." He gives a sharp bark of laughter. He shakes his head. "Especially with both of them dumping all this stuff on me. All these slights and . . . anyway, I'm taking my pain out on you, and that's not right. And I think maybe I need a break from this relationship while I get my own head sorted out."

"You want to break up?" My skin shivers as if a cold draft suddenly hit it. I am cold and then hot. "Did your father recommend this?"

"I haven't told my father about us. I'm not adding to his issues."

"So, we're an issue? I don't see it. I can be there for you. We can face this together." I hate that I'm begging. "Don't do this, Rory. If you're not willing to fight for this relationship—"

"What am I fighting for? You've never even said you love me. You told Jamie you loved him."

"I thought I was in love with Jamie, but I was wrong. It doesn't compare."

"But you've never said *I love you* to me, like you said to Jamie."

I stare at him. I don't want to say it in the middle of a fight. I don't want to say it like this. We're so far apart in this room. It feels like the words are echoing in the gulf. A truck rumbles out in the street. The smell of cigarette smoke comes through the windows. Burning. My throat is dry. My eyes tear. "I'm not going to say it like this. I've shown that I love you in more ways than I've ever shown Jamie. And that's what counts—

more than the romantic gestures or statements. As your mother is saying."

He flinches. I've gone too far.

"I can't believe you didn't even tell me that Jamie came on to you," he says.

"It wasn't important."

"Not important? You've been in love with him forever, and now he's interested, and it's not important?"

"Jamie's not really in love with me. He said 'I feel more for you than I thought.' That's hardly a declaration of passionate love."

"Right." His eyes bore into me. "Hardly a declaration of passionate love, is it?"

He's using my words against me. I shrink back.

"I'm not in love with Jamie. I've realized I was clinging to the idea of Jamie and me because he was a connection to my parents. It's not like I think you're in love with Callie just because you spent half the party with her," I say.

"I'm not in love with Callie," he says. "You said it was okay that I spent time with Callie."

"That was okay. But last night was not okay. Don't you see that?"

"No. If Zelda was upset, I would understand if you spent the party consoling her. You just don't like Callie."

"I don't particularly like Callie." Our glances meet and hold. "Especially when she makes comments about my not sharing emotions. In front of you. And you say nothing."

"I didn't take that seriously. She was just lashing out."

I fold my arms.

"I didn't say anything to her about you not sharing emotions." His eyes are so blue, and he's staring at me like he's willing me to understand. "I didn't."

He continues, "I wouldn't betray you like that. But that's also why I didn't want to deny it and then give it credence to Callie when she's looking for weaknesses in our relationship."

I believe him.

He says, “And I’m not saying we’re breaking up. We’re just taking a break. I need to get my act together before we hurt each other more—before I hurt you more.”

I shake my head. “You shouldn’t need a break from me to get your act together. We can get through this together.” I feel nauseous and cold. I blink back tears, but I can feel one slipping down my cheek. “I’ll get my stuff.”

I can’t help but hope he’ll change his mind as I pass by him. But no. I go to my drawer in his room. I don’t even have a bag. I go back to the kitchen and grab some plastic bags from the dispenser under the kitchen counter. He is still sitting slumped on the couch. The mugs waiting for our coffee and tea are perched empty on the counter.

I grab my underwear, T-shirts, and jeans and stuff them into the cheap, plastic bag. The bag rips. I put the ripped bag into a second bag. Tears are running down my face. I grab a tissue and wipe them up. Rory comes into the room.

“You don’t have to take your clothes.”

“What do you mean?” *Is he changing his mind?*

“It’s just a break, not a breakup.”

“If you need to have a break from me in order to deal with this, it doesn’t bode well. I can’t . . . I can’t hurt like this.” I give up on packing the rest of my stuff, take my little, plastic bag, and brush past him. He can throw out my toothbrush and other bathroom stuff. He follows me to the door. I have to make an effort to move, as if I’ve lost all the energy that was sustaining me. Rory also looks gray. I take my coat off the hook and put it on; it feels so heavy. I snap on my helmet. If he lets me walk out the door, it’s over. My hand grips the cold, metal doorknob.

I pause. My back is to him. My other hand is clutching my plastic bag of belongings. My shoulders droop. *Please, don’t do this.* This is how it went wrong with my parents. He doesn’t say anything.

I straighten my shoulders. I pull open the door.

"You're overreacting. I just need some time alone. It's not a real breakup," he says.

I face him. "Maybe it's not a real relationship, either."

I jog down the stairs and out into the crisp, gray, November day. Tears are pouring down my cheeks, and my chest hurts. I take big gulps of air. A passerby looks at me, questioning. I turn my face away. I take out my phone to get my Citi Bike code, but I can't see the screen through the mist of my weeping. I walk, fleeing Rory's building, past the coffee shops and smoke stores, past the nail parlors, past restaurants, past couples in restaurants. And I let the tears fall, periodically wiping them away with my cold hand.

Chapter Forty-Two

I DON'T FEEL ANY better, even though it's day three after our breakup. I should revise the breakup scene aftermath in *Fake Dating Folly* while I feel like this. But I can't. I can't get out of bed. I should have known that Rory was my kryptonite. This is *so* much worse than Jamie. Realizing Jamie didn't love me wasn't the end. I didn't feel like I'd been run over by a truck.

Zelda looks in on me. "Do you want some breakfast?"

"I'll make it for myself." I don't want Zelda to worry or make me breakfast and then be late for work. Once the water is percolating in the electric kettle, I open a yogurt. Zelda looks relieved. I turn on my laptop on the dining room table.

"Okay, well, see you tonight." Zelda closes the door behind her.

The yogurt has no taste, but at least it's soothing. I look at my manuscript. Who am I kidding? I can't write. I just keep taking courses and it's not clicking. It's not good enough. And now I don't even have a job at the sports store as a backup possibility. At twenty-nine, I have only random work experiences, and I'm not on track for anything. The kettle bubbles, and the switch clicks down.

And I had given Rob divorced parents. I had based them on my parents, but now . . . I put my hands in my head and close my laptop. Goldie rubs against my legs. I lie down on the floor next to her and pet her. She puts her paw on my cheek as my eyes close. I'm so tired of being rejected and losing all the people whom I care about. If only my mom or dad were here to talk to about this. I pull a pillow off the couch and rest my head on it.

My phone rings.

"Get out of bed." It's Zelda.

"I'm not in bed."

"Oh, that's good," Zelda says, and then after a suspicious pause, asks, "Where are you?"

"I'm on the floor," I say.

"Go write what you're feeling," she says. "C'mon. It always helps you to write it out. And if you get your happily ever after, you won't remember this feeling."

"I can't. I'm too tired."

"Try later, then," Zelda says. "I'll come home by five, and we can go to your walking group. I'll join the running group. You've been after me to join the running group."

"I was going to cancel." My pillow is very fluffy and soft. The sky looks white outside the balcony sliding glass door. Not tempting at all.

"It'll be good for you to get outside and do some exercise."

Not really. But I do want Zelda to meet Kareem.

"Okay." I get up and go to snuggle in the very warm, cozy comforter on my bed.

But my thoughts swirl and won't let me rest. I shouldn't have opened myself up to this heartache. Better to be safe. I don't want to hurt like this again. And it's so hard when there's no guarantee. No guarantee that it will last forever. And if I put myself out there, open up emotionally, rejection hurts so much more. And I start to cry. I cry for Rory, but also for all my book rejections.

Because it's been a lot.

And each time, I've just said "okay" and moved on—not allowing myself to wallow.

Each time, I've sat back down at my keyboard, revised, or continued writing because I believe in my book. And myself.

I can take this. I am stronger than I think.

I get out of bed, sit at the dining room table, power up my laptop, and write my feelings down, putting it all into the *Fake Dating Folly* breakup scene. At least it's free therapy.

I pour my heartache out onto the page. And then I stop, drained. I reread it and cry. And then I send it as this week's chapter to my writing group. Now I'll just lie down for a bit.

"Maybe Rory does just need some time to deal with his parents' mess," Zelda says. We're walking at a fast pace to meet my walking group and Kareem's running group. "How long did he suggest for the break?"

"We never got that far because I said it was a breakup." So many couples are running in the park. There should be a singles-only section.

"Way to pour oil on the fire," Zelda says.

"His mother said she was going on a break, and his dad is freaking out, so I don't think I'm overreacting. A 'break' seems like a breakup to me." My heartrate is accelerating as we pick up the pace. Zelda is in much better shape than me. She likes to run to work off stress from her law firm job. "And shouldn't we be able to work this out together? Why is he pushing me away? We're not going to last as a relationship if we take breaks every time one of us goes through something difficult."

"Says the woman who never wants people to see her cry. Maybe he really is trying to protect your relationship if he realizes he's wrongly lashing out at you."

"I should have opened up to him more. Maybe I wasn't there for him enough." The dirt pathway under our sneakers gives slightly. We turn at the hot dog stand and pass by the Shakespeare in the Park theatre. The smell of pancakes from the vendor up ahead drifts down, reminding me of Rory and all our shared breakfasts. "But it really is his issues with his parents."

She nods. “Really, listening is the most important thing. That’s what I learned with you.”

I stop and hug her. “It’s true. I think his parents going on a break is giving him an identity crisis, like he doesn’t trust himself anymore.”

“Divorce can be like a death; it’s still a loss of that family unit. And particularly for Rory, who is so close to his family.”

We skirt around the field and walk up the pathway toward the road that runs through Central Park.

“I know,” I say. “And his dad shouldn’t be using him as a confidante.”

“Did you tell him that?”

“I did. It didn’t go over well.” The Metropolitan Museum of Art is now in view. I can even see the roof deck where we saw the sculptures. Now, none of my balls are still in the air—except for my one outstanding pitch to Strawbundle Publishing. The school rejected me, too. I don’t have enough teaching experience.

“It’s better not to have regrets,” she says. “Like when you liked Jamie and I told you to tell him. Even though it didn’t work out, you did your best. And you can’t have any regrets about that.”

Maybe just a few.

A disheveled-looking man sitting on a bench on the side of the walkway, with a backpack and a stuffed, blue, plastic shopping bag, a sleeping bag peeking out, yells, “Fear gets us nowhere.”

“On point.” Zelda gives him a thumbs-up.

We cross over a dirt pathway to our designated meeting spot. We moved it from the store to the park for convenience. A bunch of people are milling around a small, blue flag with

"Theresa's Sports Store" on it. I wish this had saved the store, but at least we're keeping the groups going until the bitter end.

"Who's holding that flag?" Zelda's voice is alert, intrigued.

"That's Kareem."

"You didn't tell me he was hot."

"I told you he was a great guy."

Zelda rolls her eyes. "Exactly. You didn't say 'he's a great guy and he's hot.'"

"So, you never actually watched my Instagram video?" I ask. "Because then you would've seen him. And I'm pretty sure I mentioned that his running group is about 75 percent female."

"I'm sorry. An Instagram video about shoe fittings sounded boring. And I figured the women joined to run. Not to run after Kareem."

We approach the group. I introduce Kareem to Zelda.

Zelda says, "Penelope speaks highly of you. I should've joined sooner."

Kareem smiles. "You definitely should have."

Sparks are flying. I back up before I get singed.

"Can I make up for lost time by buying you a drink sometime?" Zelda asks.

I shake my head. *Listen and learn.* How two polar opposites became best friends is one of the mysteries of the universe.

"I'd like that. What's your number?" And Kareem takes out his phone. They exchange numbers—just like that. Any guy who could catch Zelda would be so lucky. I leave them and join my walking group.

"So, how's the writing?" the librarian member of our group asks. She found us via my sneaker Instagram video. She said that the joy was so contagious, she came to the store to buy a pair of bouncy sneakers. And then she joined our group. And now she wants to host a book talk at the library with my book when it comes out. I'm finding my people.

"Still writing."

"That's what you gotta do. Persistence."

Esther and Maria come running up. Maria had said she might join, but I didn't think she meant it.

"I just finished your chapter," Esther says. "Wow, that was strong. So emotionally moving. That was a dark moment of the soul. But how are you going to get them back together?"

"It was strong," Maria says. "But Rob definitely has to say he's sorry. He's the one in the wrong. I don't even know if she should take him back. I mean, grow up."

"Even though she never said *I love you*?" I ask.

Maria pshaws. "He knows she loves him."

"What's the problem?" the librarian asks.

"He's a commitment-phobe who breaks up with her because it's going too fast, and she has abandonment issues, so she then feels abandoned and resolves that she's over him." I wrote the scene using my feelings from our breakup, but I still hope this doesn't sound like Rory and me. "I do agree that he has to say he's sorry. And show he's sorry. I can't wait to send you guys the next chapter—the grand gesture."

"I don't think the grand gesture works," Maria says.

"It totally works," I say. "If you show up and declare your love and risk embarrassment and public humiliation, that goes a long way."

"For that night, sure." Maria picks up the pace. "But you have to be willing to show up for the relationship *all* the time, not just that once."

I nod.

We walk up the curving hill near The Harlem Meer. I thought we were both showing up. But maybe I wasn't fully showing up. I was still holding back, afraid to get hurt. I hadn't told him that I loved him. *Don't cry.* Focus on the conversation. And keep up the pace.

Chapter Forty-Three

MY GLANCE FOCUSES ON my framed first rejection slip above my desk. My dad said I should be proud of that because at least I was out there trying. I had skin in the game. That little, typed, yellow slip for *Calico the Caterpillar* rebukes me. Eight years old and rejection didn't faze me, and now at twenty-nine, I was letting it define me. I was holding back with Rory.

I should have said "I love you" that night when he whispered, pained, that I had told Jamie I loved him. I shouldn't have let him think it was even comparable. I should have yelled at him, "I love you! When I told Jamie I loved him, I had no idea what love was, that love could be like this . . ." But even now, I can't think of the right words to describe what our relationship feels like for me, except that it feels so right—that I know that whatever happens, we'll be there for each other because we've already been holding each other up for years. He's my buoy, serving as my navigation mark and inspiring me to float up. I have to tell him that.

Now. It's been five days since we talked. I have to bike down to his office and say it in person.

My eyes feel drained, but still weepy. I clip on my bike helmet, pull on my coat, and run out the door, down the steps, and sprint to the Citi Bike rack.

One Citi Bike left, and a person with a bike helmet approaching from the other side. I all-out cannonball toward the bike. This one is mine.

We arrive about the same time—all right, he arrives a millisecond before me.

"I need the bike," I say, rushed. "I didn't tell this guy that I love him, and I hurt him, and I need to tell him right now because I don't want him thinking a moment longer that I don't love him, and I don't care if I have to tell him in front of his whole office. I just have to tell him."

The guy backs off.

"All yours," he says.

"Thanks." I sniff.

"Lucky guy." He smiles. "Go get him! Good luck!" And he gives me two thumbs-up.

And my eyes get all wet again. I love New York.

Round and round, the bike pedals bear me closer. I swoop around Columbus Circle and continue down Broadway to Fiftieth Street, feeling lighter already. The bike clicks into the nearest Citi Bike rack. And I walk up to the guard at the reception desk and ask to see Rory, handing over my ID. He calls his office.

The guard's brow creases, and he hands the phone to me.

It's Rory's assistant, Evan. "Penelope?"

"Yes, I came to see Rory."

"He took some time off." Evan's voice sounds puzzled. As it should. "He went on a fishing trip with his dad."

"Oh, thanks." I stare at the modern lobby. "For how long?"

Evan doesn't immediately answer. He's got to be wondering why I don't know. "A week."

"Thanks, Evan." I give the guard back the phone. That's not a good sign. That's a week of him being with his dad, who thinks I've got my own therapy-worthy issues.

I get back on my bike and cycle Uptown. The trees are bare now. The city looks gray, and people are bundled up against the cold. The tires feel deflated on this bike, or maybe it's just me. The Maine cabin has limited wireless reception, but I still try calling. His inbox is full. I want to say this in person, but as a lifelong New Yorker, I never learned to drive, so it's not like I can drive up to their cabin in Maine, not that I even know where it is.

I need a Plan B for Win Back Rory.

Chapter Forty-Four

THE PHONE RINGS. IT'S MaryAnn from *Mini Mania.* I shipped the art gallery to them earlier this week.

"The art gallery is fabulous! We love it, especially those paintings by Rafael. Do you think we can get him to attend the event?" MaryAnn asks. "And the food is so realistic."

"I think so. I will reach out to him."

"Let us know and we'll send him a formal invite. And include his name on the publicity. And we'd like to meet the man behind 'Rob.' We presume you are bringing him as your date to the 'Meet the Miniaturist' event," MaryAnn says.

"We're no longer dating."

"Again?"

Yes, I've been dumped again. "Obviously, that's not the storyline I'm running with on the blog. It's not biographical."

"Oh." MaryAnn seems flummoxed. "Maybe you have a friend you can bring as a substitute boyfriend?"

I'm not going to get into fake dating again. "No, I don't think so. I think it's just me."

"Well, I'll send over the brief speech we've prepared for you to say at the event and you can edit it as you see fit."

I email Rafael about the APT-TV event.

I want Rory to read *Fake Dating Folly*. I draft and redraft the email accompanying the manuscript. I write "I love you," then I delete it because I want to say that in person. And maybe it will sound flippant if I just write it in an email. Even if he says he's no longer interested. I sign it "Love, Penelope," then I delete that. "Hugs and kisses, Penelope" sounds like I am five years old. "All my love, Penelope"? I look back at my emails to him and they have no greetings or closures—they're just an ongoing conversation.

The door opens and it's Zelda, home from work. I sit on the couch as she hangs up her coat. I tell her about my attempt to tell Rory I love him.

I continue, "So, I'm worried. If he spends a week in the woods with his dad, who is devastated by the loss of his marriage, then I don't see Rory rushing back to me."

"Could go either way. I mean, I'd be rushing back to you after a week in the woods with my mom or dad. I love them dearly, but a week in the woods with no Internet, nothing but fishing for entertainment? No." She shakes her head. "And maybe that's just me. But he's a social guy. And it's November. It's cold out. And you guys have a good thing going."

"I'm going to email him *Fake Dating Folly*. I don't want him to think I've revealed too much about us, so I think he should read it." Now I'm worried I've shared too much emotion in it, like all my feelings for Rory. I don't want him to feel I've crossed a line, foregoing any chance of reconciliation. But I am not sure how I would change it if he does object.

"*Fake Dating Folly* reads like a love letter to him. And it's not like you're detailing your sex life."

But our emotional life definitely informs the subtext. "That's good, then." I tell her about the *Mini Mania* call.

"Well, they shouldn't think that it's based on your real life. Most of it isn't."

"She sounded disappointed," I say.

"She should imagine how disappointed you are, then," she says wryly.

I read her my draft email to Rory, which still sounds too formal:

> To: Rory
> From: Penelope
>
> I miss you. I hope that things are going better with your parents and they find a way to save what they created because the love and warmth of their relationship is real. I know that's the case because I see it in you and the way you treat me.
>
> I want to be there for you, so I don't want this to be a breakup. I freaked out because of my parents. But I know that's my problem, and I need to work through that. I hope you will give me another chance to show that I can.
>
> I hope we can meet soon to talk. Can we meet at The Barn on November 25 at 5? Evan thought you'd be back by then. Afterward, we can see the balloons being blown up.
>
> I revised *Fake Dating Folly* yet again. I've attached it for you to read. Let me know if it's too revealing.

Rory and I have a tradition of meeting to watch the balloons being blown up outside the Museum of Natural History on the night before the Thanksgiving Day Parade. We've been meeting since sophomore year of college. So, I figure that even if he wants to be just friends—I feel nauseous—we can go do that as friends. We can save that part of our relationship, even if I am not actually sure that I can go back to being just friends.

Zelda nods. "You should send it."

I click send.

CHAPTER FORTY-FIVE

I AM MAKING MINIS for my Etsy shop to give my miniatures business one last final push before I shut it down and look for a real job. Right now, I am making tulips. Flower books are open to the pictures of tulips on the table next to me.

My phone rings. Zelda and my sister keep calling me to check in on me. I think they've divided up a schedule.

"Hi, this is Vera. I'm calling about *Fake Dating Folly*."

It's the Strawbundle Publishing editor. I'm sitting in my pajamas, my eyes still tired from this morning's bout of crying. Time to pull myself together and shine.

"I really liked *Fake Dating Folly*."

I wait for the "but."

"I do have some edits," she says.

"Anything that makes it better. I've been revising it since I sent it to you. I can always see ways to improve it."

"Well, we'd like to publish *Fake Dating Folly*. I would like to work with you."

I cry. Again. "I'm sorry, I'm just so happy."

"It often happens. It's one of the best parts of the job. I'll send over my editorial letter and a contract, and you can let me know."

I hang up and sit there in shock. Good chills go through my body. I've done it. *Fake Dating Folly* is going to be published. Rory's mailbox is still full. I call Esther. And then Zelda. And then my sister. An unknown number calls when I'm in the middle of the call to my sister and I try to click over, but it doesn't work. I get off the phone with my sister and listen to the voicemail message.

"It's Rory."

I clutch the phone closer, my heartbeat accelerating as I listen to his garbled message.

"I miss you. A lot. I'm sorry . . . back on Wednesday and I'll see you at The Barn . . . my phone dropped in the lake, so I'm using my dad's . . . fishing boat disaster. But I . . . see you then."

I replay the message to see if I can understand any more. No.

I can't tell if we're back on or not from the message. I feel hot and cold. But he called, and at least we're meeting in person.

Chapter Forty-Six

DUSK IS SETTLING IN. I am early to meet Rory at The Barn, but I'm too nervous to wait any longer. The Citi Bike slides into its stall and clicks in. I wipe my hands on my jeans. Butterflies cavort in my stomach. Even though I think it will be good news, I am afraid. His message was so dry that I'm scared he may just want to remain friends.

I take off my helmet and fluff out my hair. I'm wearing just jeans and a sweater this time because it's just me.

I walk down the street toward The Barn, the store lights welcoming in the hazy, darkish-blue light. Michaels is still there, as well as the new beignet store, which provided the beignets for our sailboat ride. Some people are heading home already, bent over, bundled up against the wind that pushes me forward. A plastic bag blows along the sidewalk.

A small flag flutters from a lamppost as I approach The Barn. It's a piece of cloth tied with string onto the lamppost. Two hand-drawn stick figures are dancing on the cloth. They have fez hats.

Rory.

My heart feels like a balloon about to float up to the sky. I look around for Rory, but I don't see him. I want to take this home. The next parking signpost holds another cloth flag. And another. The second is a stick figure couple, backs to each other, sad faces. I run to the third. It's the stick figure couple kissing. I look up for Rory. He's coming out of The Barn. I run to him and hug him. He hugs me tightly back.

"I'm sorry." We both say it at the same time.

"Penelope, I'm so sorry. I was so wrong. I don't need a break from you. Maybe from my dad. But I need you. Not a break. I just got so thrown and confused."

"It's okay, Rory. I understand. And I shouldn't have gotten so upset. It's just that . . . you know, I freaked out and got scared. And I was afraid to be vulnerable, but I realized that I want to be honest with you and that I *can* be honest with you. I love you. I really do love you. And I thought I loved Jamie, but that was just me trying to reconnect with my parents, but this is —"

"I love you, too," he says against my mouth and kisses me, his arms holding me tight. "I think I'm good at forever if it's with you."

"Get a room," someone says off to the side as she passes us.

We pull away reluctantly, but Rory still has his arms around me.

"I'm not really hungry for food," I say.

"Me, neither. But I have presents for you." Rory lets go of me to swing his backpack around from his shoulder. He unzips it and pulls out two boxes. One is tiny, and one is a binder-size, rectangular box. I take the lid off the tiny one first. I unwrap the tissue paper. Inside are miniature roses and a little breakfast tray with waffles, strawberries, eggs, and bagels. I kiss Rory. The card says, "So Rob and Piper can enjoy the perfect breakfast in bed."

I open up the box. A rose petal flutters out. Rory has created a bound copy of my book, nestled in tissue paper and rose petals, like an Instagram post. The pink, yellow, and blue cover has two stick figures kissing.

"I presume you'll want to change the cover when it's published officially."

My eyes tear. "Oh, Rory." I kiss him again quickly.

"I loved it." Rory tenderly brushes away a tear from my cheek. "I've got to believe Strawbundle Publishing will want it."

"They do. They called. It's going to be published." I hop up and down. I still can't quite contain my joy at the news.

"Yes!" Rory swings me up and around. "Should we go back to my apartment? I'll light the fireplace."

I nod. "How are your parents doing?" I hold Rory's hand as we walk toward his brownstone building.

"Better. My dad told me I was an idiot to break up with you, that conflict can create growth in relationships, which is what he is learning, and that I needed to go win you back. He said conflict is couples trying to be both individuals and a couple, and it's healthy. Even if he hasn't always appreciated it in his own relationship."

I stop and look at him, "Oh, Rory."

"And I told him that he still has his relationship counseling skills and that this would make him a better counselor, but that he should focus on making the changes necessary to save his relationship with my mom. And that I wasn't his confidante, but his son, so we set some boundaries."

Rory unlocks the door to his apartment and switches on the light. He turns on his phone and presses an app. The opening notes of "It Had to Be You" fills the apartment.

"May I have this dance?" he asks.

"Yes," I say.

Rory takes me into his arms and says, "I'm looking forward to a life of magic *and* mundane with you."

I smile. "So, after this, can we get to the part where 'I'm on fire?'"

Rory laughs. "I thought you'd never ask."

Chapter Forty-Seven

EPILOGUE

IT'S THE NIGHT OF the APT-TV auction event, being held at the Central Park Zoo. I'm on the stage with Rafael, about to speak. Marilyn Hughes is introducing me. I stare out at the sea of faces, but so many of them are friends. All of my friends and family bought tables, and my paperbacks are on a display table next to the monkey island area, ready for me to sign later, so it feels like my book launch party.

I step up to the microphone. My hands shake as I unfold my paper speech. I have my speech memorized, but I still brought a paper copy just in case I blanked.

"I have always loved miniatures, since I was a child." I look at Rory. He's smiling at me, and I can feel his love enveloping me. "I delight in making these scenes of life in miniature. Miniatures allow me to play as an adult." A breeze blows through the opening in the tent wall near us, and an animal screeches. To the side of the stage is the sea lion pool. One of the sea lions flops up onto a rock and calls to a friend.

"At first, I only created these scenes of perfect mini lives—very neat apartments and happy couples. But then my miniature couple broke up, and that's when my miniature blog took off. Because life is messy, and there are ups and downs. Actually, the downs make us much stronger." Theresa nods;

she is sitting at the table Jamie bought. The "Meet the Miniaturists" TV show had been a huge success, and my miniatures business is booming. A bit too much. I couldn't keep up with demand. Theresa joined me in making miniatures to keep my Etsy store stocked.

I say, "And sharing those emotions can actually lead to real connections. So, as you can see, even in my mini art gallery, although the gallery itself is quite neat, if you look behind the curator's counter, it's quite a mess." I pause as the screen behind me shows a close-up of the miniature scene with sneakers under the curator's desk for changing into before she goes home, her workout bag, and lots of papers stacked all over her desk. "I am thrilled to introduce Rafael, who helped me realize how important it is to open up emotionally in our art."

I step aside. My legs are still trembling, but I did it. I made it through my speech. I barely hear Rafael's speech as I recover. Zelda gives me a thumbs-up. Audrey also smiles at me and nods her head. She insisted on buying her own table, so she's at another table with Jake, Eve, Pete, Tim, Colette, Winnie, and Jae. Our upstairs neighbors, Tessa and Miranda, also bought a table. Miranda invited her art dealer, who owns a gallery, so I'm hoping maybe she'll want my miniature art gallery. Even if nobody bids on my piece, at least I raised money for the charities via my friends' buying tables. Even Bernie and Myrtle bought a table and filled it with everyone from the Catskills house party.

And then Rafael is next to me, and Marilyn is introducing the auctioneer. The auctioneer is an older man with a bow tie. He reminds everyone again about how supporting the Fresh Air Fund and Boys & Girls will open up opportunities for children. And we're up.

Rafael holds my hand. It feels incredibly public. *What if nobody bids?*

"Opening the bidding at one thousand dollars," the auctioneer says. "Do I have one thousand dollars?"

Rory's hand shoots up in the air. My eyes tear. Even though I knew he would bid, I'm still relieved.

"The young man at table 32 has bid one thousand. Do I have eleven hundred?" the auctioneer asks.

Ciara raises her paddle. Rory's dad has his arm around his mom's shoulders. They are back together, after many good talks and counseling, and seated at our table.

Rory raises his paddle again.

"Twelve hundred," the auctioneer says. "Anyone else, thirteen hundred, we don't want that table to go home as enemies. Thirteen hundred, do I have thirteen hundred?"

My sister in the back raises her paddle proudly.

"We've got thirteen hundred to number 18 in the back. Fourteen hundred?"

A blond guy, whom I don't know and who is not seated at any of my friends' tables, raises his paddle. "Fifteen hundred," he shouts out.

A stranger wants it. I squeeze Rafael's hand.

"Fifteen hundred up front here. Do I have sixteen hundred?" the auctioneer asks.

Jamie raises his paddle. My eyebrows shoot up to my hairline. What is he doing? My friends don't have to bid anymore.

"Sixteen hundred to paddle number 7. Seventeen hundred?"

Miranda's art dealer raises her paddle. "Two thousand," she yells out. I bet she knows the value of Rafael's paintings. They could be worth that.

"Twenty-five hundred," the blond guy says in the front, raising his paddle again. An owl hoots in the night.

"Three thousand," Tessa calls out from her table. I know Tessa is a lawyer, but still. I feel so much love from all my friends. And I realize I have more than just Zelda and Rory and my sister supporting me.

"Thirty-five hundred? Do I have thirty-five hundred?" the auctioneer asks.

The blond guy raises his paddle.

"Thirty-six hundred?"

Tessa grins at me and raises her paddle. She hates losing.

"Thirty-eight hundred?" the auctioneer asks.

Miranda's art dealer raises her paddle.

"The bid is at thirty-eight hundred with the woman in the pink at table 9. Do we have four thousand? Anyone? Anyone? Or do I close this at thirty-eight hundred? Remember that not only are you getting some incredible works of art, but you're also providing after-school and summer camp opportunities for boys and girls from low-income families."

The blond guy raises his paddle.

"We have four thousand with the young man in the front. Thank you. Do we have forty-two hundred? Forty-two hundred? Anyone?"

No one raises their paddle.

"Going once, going twice, this is your chance to own this piece of art." The auctioneer pauses. I look across the room at all my friends who are smiling at me. "Sold to paddle number 14 for four thousand dollars here in the front." The auctioneer bangs down his gavel.

Rafael and I both jump up and down. I smile at the guy. We both say thank you and leave the stage as they call up the next miniature artist.

I don't even know how I make it to my table, but suddenly I am there, and Rory is hugging me. And I am hugging him back, holding on to him because I'm so happy, I might float off the ground. Rory kisses me.

"This is just the beginning," he says. "Wait until your book comes out next week."

I smile and say, "Yes, other authors have warned me about feeling naked and exposed once you have your book out in the world, so being up on that stage, hoping someone bids, was good practice for feeling naked."

"I thought we'd practiced being naked a lot lately," Rory says, his lips tilting upward as he pulls me closer. "We can warm up with some couples' yoga."

"Naked?" I ask.

"Your choice," he says, his hand stroking my arm. "Although, I haven't seen that red lingerie lately."

I kiss him, his lips firm against mine, and whisper, "I love you."

Chapter Forty-Eight

THANK YOU!

DEAR READER,

Thank you so much for reading *IS THIS FOR REAL?* I hope it left you with a warm, fuzzy feeling.

If you would like updates on new releases, behind-the-scenes news, and what's going on in my life, please subscribe to my mailing list at https://kathystrobos.com/sign-up/

Please leave a review if you enjoyed reading *IS THIS FOR REAL?*

Book reviews are critical to authors because they increase visibility. Booksellers want to sell books that other readers liked. A review doesn't have to be long; it can be a sentence or two.

Reviews on Goodreads and BookBub also help other readers discover books they might love.

Best,

Kathy

ABOUT THE AUTHOR

.

Author Photograph by Parinyarat Cutone.

Kathy Strobos is a writer living in New York City with her husband and two children, amid a growing collection of books, toys, and dollhouses. She grew up in New York City and graduated from Stuyvesant High School, Harvard-Radcliffe University *magna cum laude*, and Columbia Law School. She spent two semesters abroad at the Universiteit van Amsterdam. She previously worked as a lawyer. She left law to pursue her dream of writing fiction full time and getting in shape. She is still working on getting in shape.

Also by Kathy Strobos

PARTNER PURSUIT

ACKNOWLEDGEMENTS

I STARTED WRITING *Is This for Real?* when I was querying *Partner Pursuit.*

If you are interested in learning how to make miniatures, I recommend checking out YouTube videos, miniature-focused blogs, and joining the National Association of Miniature Enthusiasts.

Thank you again to the Romantic Novelists' Association (RNA) and the published author who read my very first (and very rough) draft of *Is This for Real?* in the New Writer's Scheme and gave me such constructive feedback. I did a significant rewrite based on that super helpful feedback.

My critique partners, Giulia Skye and Vicky Tiseros, continue to be invaluable. And again, with this novel, I was amazed at how they both pinpointed ways to improve it and increase the stakes. I truly value our friendship as well, and I feel privileged to be on this writer journey with them.

When I needed date ideas for Penelope and Rory in London, I did indeed consult my RNA friends like Giulia. I also called up my friend Richard Arnold, who lives in London. We met at the Universiteit van Amsterdam as exchange students many years ago, and we have stayed in touch. He was immediately game to discuss London date ideas, and he suggested the Secret Cinema night, which was brilliant.

And thank you to my friend Minke for helping me with the career details for advertising executives. Any inaccuracies are mine.

I also want to again thank authors Linnea Sinclair and Gay Walley, who taught me so much about writing and are gifted and giving teachers. If you want to be a writer, I highly recommend signing up for one of Linnea's courses, which you can find on her Facebook page.

Thank you to the judges of the Windy City RWA Four Seasons Contest. I submitted *ITFR* and it placed third in the Mainstream Fiction with Romantic Elements category. The feedback from the judges was so encouraging!

The RWA Contemporary Romance online group has a mentor/mentee program where a published author will review the first 50 pages of your manuscript. I was so lucky to be matched with Jeannie Watts. That was another amazing experience where Jeannie gave me so much valuable feedback.

I took a Women's Fiction Writers Association workshop, *Exploring the Emotional Frontier*, with Donald Maass. I highly recommend taking a class with him or reading his writing craft books. And if you like the scene where Penelope rents a Citi bike to go to Rory to tell him something (I am being purposefully vague to avoid spoilers), I submitted my first draft in that workshop. It was Donald Maass who suggested "the guy who surrenders the last Citi bike to her . . . could she plead with him in a way that tells him (and us) how much you lose if you don't get your butt on a bike and ride like your life depends on it . . ."

And it was in that class that I met fellow WFWA member Brooke Williams, and she suggested we exchange manuscripts as critique partners. I am so grateful to Brooke for her insightful feedback and detailed critique. She immeasurably improved *ITFR* with her questions and comments.

I also want to thank editor Emily Poole, of Midnight Owl Editors, for her story analysis and proofreading. I was so heartened because she grasped all the messages I was trying to convey and gave me hope that I was on the right track. She also manages to find the words I meant to write.

My thanks also to editor Julie Mianecki for her copy-editing and helpful feedback, which improved the pacing of *ITFR*.

And thank you to my copy editor and proofreader, Joyce Mochrie, owner of One Last Look. Her fastidious and diligent attention to detail caught my errors of grammar and punctuation, as well as my dropped or repeated words, and I'm very grateful that she was able to fit me in at the last moment.

As I write this, I'm in the middle of the launch of *Partner Pursuit,* and it's been such an amazing experience.

Thank you to all the readers who have posted reviews of Partner Pursuit. It is deeply moving to see my book be understood by other people. I am so touched by what readers are writing and so thrilled that readers love my book.

I want to thank Giulia Skye again for all her guidance and support. Thank you so much!

When I first pushed publish, and then posted the news to my Facebook group, I then sat there, worried that maybe I'd made a very public mistake. So, thank you to Amy who posted on Facebook that she was enjoying my book and calmed me down on my launch day.

I needed a professional photograph, so I asked a mom friend from my son's elementary school, who takes wonderful photographs of the kids on school trips, if she could take a picture of me. We did a photo session on an Upper West Side block of brownstones. So, a huge thank you to Parinyarat Cutone for my authentic author photo. The construction worker who stood there (for an hour!) while we took photographs, said at the end, "Are you done? Is it my turn now?" I should have taken a picture with him.

Thank you to Sharon for proofreading *Partner Pursuit* again for me—especially on such a short turnaround time. Especially with my current Korean drama obsession, I love that this gave you flashbacks to your days being the copyeditor on *The Korea Herald*.

So many moms (and dads) from my children's schools were supportive and enthusiastic. Thank you to Usha, Sejal, and Gina for believing in my book from the beginning. Our chats in the morning and afternoon at drop-off and pickup (and at the JCC) were such a highlight. Thank you to my book club group —Jen, Nupur, Yinka, Honey Sue, Megan, Nicole, Hannah, Kelly, Pri, Andrea, and Kathleen—for immediately buying my book as well.

Thank you to Juliette Kayyem for tweeting about it. A huge thanks also to my NYC Mini Club for buying my book too.

And thank you to all my friends who also bought *Partner Pursuit* as soon as they heard I had published it. I tear up when I think about it.

Thank you to Anna, Ellen, Judith, and Michelle of my critique group, Word-Slingers. Your support meant so much to me, especially because we've all been taking writing classes with Linnea Sinclair for some time now, trying to realize her high standards.

I felt like all the messages of *Partner Pursuit*—be true to yourself, women supporting women, hard work pays off, the importance of friendships, and follow your dream—were realized in its launch.

I want to thank my family for encouraging and supporting my dream of becoming a full-time author, specifically my husband, Claus, and my two children. A special thanks also to my mom, my brother, my sister-in-law, and my nieces.

One of the best parts about this new career is meeting other writers. Thank you again to Delphine (my partner in the querying trenches) and Evie Alexander for all the pep talks. I also love the camaraderie and supportive vibe of Anita Faulkner's Chicklit & Prosecco Facebook group and the RNA's RomCom Group. I'm always inspired by the critique group, Word-Slingers-Plotters-and Pantsers, who helped me with my blurb and my first chapter and is a great group for bouncing ideas around. My #TBR pile is enormous, but I love reading all your books and celebrating your publishing successes!

I also want to thank my Gotham screenwriting group and our teacher, Doug Katz. Our class met online once a week for the spring 2021, and I loved our discussions. Lisa, Amita, Iris, Susannah, Molly, and Kyle—I'm so happy we have kept in touch and become writer buddies.

And thanks to all my friends who read excerpts, brainstormed titles, commiserated about writing, suggested plot points, etc.: Michelle, Tammy, Becky, Sharon, Matthew, Charlita, Seetha, Ketsia, Koethi, Seendy, Crystal, Mary, Caroline, Jennifer, Jenny, Annette, Suzanne, Kim, Saika, Anne, Mark, Minke, Richard, Elliot, Nisha, Ruth, Mr. Tony, Jen, Nupur, Lin, Jessica, Dawn, Meredith, Elise, Juliette, Sherwin, Ayse, Michelle, Jen, Dolly, and all my other friends who cheered me on.

Thank you to my book cover designer, Lucy, of Cover Ever After. I love my covers!

Thank you also to my blog and newsletter subscribers and to my ARC reader team. I'm so happy to be on a team with you.

Finally, but not least, a huge thank you to you, my reader. It means the world to me that you've read my book. I hope you enjoyed spending time with my characters as much as I enjoyed writing about them and escaping to their world. That was the best thing about my release of *Partner Pursuit*—finding readers who loved my book.

Kathy Strobos

For Miranda's story, read on for the first chapter from *Caper Crush*:

KATHY STROBOS

Caper Crush

CHAPTER ONE

PUSHING UP MY FAKE glasses on my nose, I shuffle closer to the two other women to listen in on their conversation about the ultramarine abstract painting in front of them. I resist the urge to touch my straight, gray hair. I've learned that once I put on a wig, I shouldn't touch it.

This art gallery is a white-walled, square room in Tribeca, with paintings hung about a foot apart, about twenty colorful paintings in total. Between the cold air conditioning and the pops of color, I feel like I've stepped into the middle of a vanilla ice cream with rainbow sprinkles. Next to the entrance, the gallery owner is sitting behind a shiny, white, laminate counter, typing on her laptop. Two large paintings are spotlighted in the storefront windows. My ultramarine painting, unfortunately, didn't merit that prime real estate.

These two women are a mismatched pair. One looks like an Upper East Side matron, immaculate, brown hair, clearly professionally blow-dried that morning, armored in a crisp, two-piece skirt suit. The other woman has wild, gray hair and is wearing a long, flowing skirt, turquoise and gold bangles covering her wrists.

"Is this the one Jade recommended that we look at?" coiffed woman asks.

Bangles woman peers at the label. “I think so. She said to look at the works by the artist Miranda Langbroek.” She steps back, her multiple bracelets jangling as she puts her hands on her hips and stares at the painting.

“I don’t see what’s so special about it,” coiffed woman says. “Doesn’t it look like every other abstract painting out there?”

I cough. And that’s why people say no good ever comes of eavesdropping about oneself. I know I need to armor up, but I still take criticism about my work personally.

The two women look over at me in concern.

“Are you okay?” bangles woman asks.

“I’m fine. Got something lodged in my throat.” I clear my throat. “I think what makes this painting unique are the brushstrokes here building up the paint, almost like waves of color washing over you.”

“Oh, interesting,” bangles woman says. “I see that now.”

“Are you thinking of buying it?” coiffed woman asks me. Her perfume smells of honeysuckle.

That’s a tough question to answer. Some buyers like competition, and if another is interested, buy it immediately to scoop it up. But others back off. Plus, I don’t want to actually lie and say I’m going to buy it when I’m the artist trying to sell it. I never know if my disguise will actually work. But I really do need to sell this painting. My agent, Jade, will stop representing me if I don’t ‘take off’ soon. I didn’t sell anything at the last little show she got me into.

“No,” I say. “I love it, but I don’t have the budget to buy it.”

“Our dealer said we should get in now before this artist becomes popular after the Apex show,” coiffed woman says.

“But I don’t know,” says bangles woman, frowning.

This is torture. Why *did* I think covertly persuading art patrons to buy my work was a brilliant idea?

“You should only buy it if you love it,” I say. I don’t want my painting abandoned in a closet.

“I love the colors,” says a male voice to my left. “Do you know the price?”

A tall, lean guy with thick, ruffled, black hair glances over at me.

William Haruki Matsumura.

William is the nephew of my uncle Tony's partner, Takashi Matsumura. *What is he doing here?*

Our glances meet.

He's good-looking if you like the Secret Service type. I don't. I never know what he's thinking, which bothers me. He's quiet, so he could be full of deep thoughts. Or not.

I hope he doesn't recognize me. He'd probably give the game away if he did. But there's no way he could. I've aged my skin with shadows and highlights to look like a sixty-five-year-old woman, even adding a bump to my nose. Straight, silvery hair hides my wavy, red hair and I'm wearing glasses. It's not like we see each other that often that he'd recognize me in disguise.

Bangles woman looks at him, and her eyes widen in appreciation. She steps closer.

"Do you like it?" she asks suggestively, putting her hand on his arm.

He smiles, looking down at her hand, and says, "Yes, very much."

Ugh. I hope he's still talking about the painting. *Keep your attention on what's important here.*

"What do you like about the painting?" I ask.

"I feel like it shows movement through the painting, almost like the ripples of water," he says, gesturing across the painting.

That's exactly the effect I was going for.

"Exactly," I say, staring at him, surprised that he gets it. "And the cadmium yellow?"

"The yellow and orange give it warmth," he says.

"Yes," I say. "The lemon yellow and Naples yellow, uh, peach here are like a warm hug from a hot, sandy beach."

"It makes me feel happy when I look at it," he says. My chest feels all full. I tear up and look away at some black, red slashes and barbed wire painting next to mine. I shudder. It provides a good contrast. I smile at William.

"You should buy it then," I say. Put your money where your mouth is.

"Well, only if you don't want it," he says to the two other women. "Ladies first, of course."

"Maybe we should buy it," coiffed woman says.

"Only if you love it," I say.

William shakes his head at me.

"It makes me feel happy, too," she says.

"Oh, I'm definitely feeling happier now," bangles woman says, looking at William. "I love to meet other art collectors. Do you have an extensive art collection? Maybe you'd like to see mine."

Coiffed woman leaves and goes over to the gallery owner. She pulls out her credit card. I feel like I'm holding my breath as I watch her sign the iPad. The gallery owner comes over and puts a little green dot next to it.

The coveted green dot. I've sold a painting. I'm grinning, and I can feel the tension easing out of my shoulders. Now Jade will be more inclined to keep representing me, and this augurs well for the Apex show. My talent might finally get recognized and some bigger gallery names might pick up my artwork. And I can actually realize my dream of pursuing a career as an artist. No more smiling through gritted teeth at comments like, "I should also pick up a hobby like painting, like you."

I should make my escape before I get discovered as the artist. Artists have some license to be creative, but hiding my identity to eavesdrop on conversations about my painting and trying to persuade someone to buy it might fall under certifiably crazy.

"Congratulations," I say to them. "It was nice meeting you."

I turn and slowly walk out the front door of the gallery.

Once I'm out of the gallery, my pace quickens. Yes! Sold!

I walk the few blocks to Canal Street, passing by a restaurant and a shop that sells various smoking paraphernalia. A few guys are hanging outside, and a cloying clove smell fills the air. It's hotter today than it should be for a spring day.

I can't take off my wig because I've got nowhere to carry it safely. It needs to be put back on a mannequin head so that its shape isn't destroyed. Detangling wig hair is similar to combing through a child's knotted hair, only the grunts of pain would be coming from me as I chastise myself for not being more careful with the wig.

I cross over to the other side of the street where a mostly ochre-colored post office takes up the entire block, its black, terra cotta base covered in graffiti.

"Hey!"

I turn. It's William, jogging up.

"I thought that was you from the art gallery," he says.

William has never seemed to me to be the type who chats up strangers.

"Oh yes, nice to see you again," I say, but a bit distantly as I imagine an older woman would when approached by a stranger she briefly chatted to in a gallery.

"So, are you an artist or art patron?" he asks.

"I'm an artist," I say, sticking to the truth. "And you?"

"My uncle told me to check out the show," he says. "His partner's niece painted that painting *High Tide at 4:30* that those women bought."

He doesn't recognize me. This is brilliant.

"She's really talented. Do you know her?" I ask. "She must be amazing."

He glances at me and says wryly, "Yes, I know her."

"And is she amazing?"

"If you mean 'amazing' in the sense of bewildering or surprising or . . ."

I harrumph. "More like startlingly impressive. If you know her, you should buy up her artwork before the Apex show."

"Do you have any more paintings for sale?" he asks.

Just a wall full of unsold paintings.

"And why, Miranda, are you dressed as an older woman?" he asks.

I stop. Ugh. I can't believe he's been toying with me. He is so annoying.

He stops in front of me. He pushes his black hair out of his eyes and studies my face. He's probably trying to figure out what I changed.

Let him think that I knew he recognized me.

"To spy on people checking out my painting and persuade them to buy," I say. "Thanks for your help back there."

"Wouldn't people be thrilled to meet the artist?" he asks.

"Not if they don't like the painting."

"I thought you only wanted people who love your painting to buy it," William says. "You nearly lost that sale with that comment."

That's a good point.

"But I didn't," I say.

"You don't need to disguise yourself," he says.

A car missing a muffler roars by, and I turn to look at the four lanes of traffic maneuvering by on Canal Street. With no trees on this block, this corner has a very wide-open, exposed feel.

"How did you know it was me?" I ask.

"I don't know," he says. "I thought I recognized you from the back, even with the straight, gray hair, but then I had a moment of doubt when you turned around."

"Thank goodness for that," I say. "I thought I was really losing my disguise skills."

He scoffs. "Are you heading home?"

"Yes," I say. "I have to meet some movers. They're picking up my paintings for this Apex exhibit."

"I'm heading that way, too, to see Uncle Takashi," he says. My uncle Tony and his partner, Takashi, live around the block from me on Columbus Avenue on the Upper West Side.

We continue walking down Canal Street toward the subway. This side of the street with the post office is deserted. On the other side are shops more typical of Canal Street with suitcases and various other items hanging from the awning, and a long table with fake sunglasses and bags and NYC souvenirs set up on the sidewalk.

"Weren't you at the party last night?" I cover my mouth as soon as I finish asking the question. That's embarrassing that I didn't notice.

His warm, brown eyes glance at me, and he shrugs. I can't tell if the shrug means it doesn't matter because I wouldn't notice if you were there or not, or I expect that, or it's okay. A shrug can mean so many things.

"No, I just got back from Tokyo yesterday and I crashed," he says.

We wait at the corner for the light to change. Buds are starting to appear on the trees. I am so ready for spring—a new season, and a new start on my life as an artist. I feel like I'm bubbling over now that I sold a painting.

We cross the street and jog down the steps of the C subway station.

"What were you doing in Tokyo?" I ask as I slide my MetroCard through the turnstile.

"A friend's wedding," he says. "And seeing family."

We walk up the platform and stand by one of the wooden benches. The C train should arrive in two minutes.

I could make conversation, but I'm still annoyed that he pretended he didn't recognize me after catching up to me. We both look at the subway ad posters along the wall.

The subway pulls into the station. It is crowded, as usual, on a Saturday morning, with a mixture of tourists, families, and people with plans. We get in and stand, holding on to the aluminum bar. William lowers his backpack to rest it on the floor at his feet. I look to see if any of the subway posters announce the Apex show. It's my new favorite pastime. The train pulls quickly out of the station and swerves. I swing slightly, caught off guard. I grip the bar tighter.

The person seated in front of me looks up and rises. She says, “Here, you can have my seat.”

I had forgotten I look old.

“No, that’s okay,” I say. “I’m fine.”

“Are you sure?” she asks, looking concerned. “I’m getting off in a few stops.”

“No, it’s okay. It will be harder to talk then,” I say.

“Oh, of course, you want to talk to your son,” she says.

My son.

William snickers.

“Mom, you should take the seat,” he says.

I want to kill him.

“You’ve raised him well,” the seated woman says to me and stands.

William says, “Here, Mom, let me help you sit.” He takes my elbow as if I’m about to collapse. I sit. I can feel myself blushing, mortified.

The construction worker next to me says, “If you guys want to talk, I’ll get up, too.”

That’s so nice of him. My eyes tear a little at everyone being so considerate.

William says, “No, it’s okay. I can’t take your seat. We’ll have plenty of time to talk later.” And then he leans down and whispers loudly to the guy, “She’ll only nag me about whether I’m dating anyone.”

“I don’t nag,” I say stiffly, sitting upright and shooting a death glare at him.

The guy laughs.

William smiles sweetly at me and resumes studying the subway advertisements.

I say loudly, “I’ve found a nice girl for you to date.”

He looks down at me, one eyebrow raised.

“She is a very successful lawyer. She can’t cook, but she can support your derelict lifestyle.”

"Maybe you do want the seat," the guy next to me says to William.

"You shouldn't give up your seat. He's perfectly healthy to stand," I say.

"Not if I'm going to hear more about my 'derelict' lifestyle," William says simultaneously.

At 59th Street, passengers chaotically switch between the express train across the platform and our local train. William remains standing, even though the seat next to me opens up. A woman slides into that seat, guidebook in hand, and asks me if this stops at the Museum of Natural History. I confirm that it does.

When we get to the 72nd Street stop, William leans down as if to help me up. I swat his hand away.

"I can get up fine," I say grumpily.

He follows me out of the subway. Passing by the Yoko Ono "Sky" blue-and-white tile artwork, we push through the turnstiles.

"Are you okay with the stairs?" he asks.

I stop. I'm about to retort that of course I am, but then I smile. He looks back at me.

I reach up and pinch his cheek. "You're such a good boy. I think I will need to lean on you." And I proceed to heavily lean on him. I'm 5'8" and not stick-thin.

"You never do what I expect," he says. "Maybe I should just pick you up and carry you. That would be easier."

As he motions to do just that, I step away. "That's okay. I'll walk up by myself."

I hurry up the concrete stairs, William keeping pace behind me. We walk west down the wide expanse of 72nd Street, passing under the various apartment building awnings and skirting around the aluminum carts of the Fresh Direct and Amazon delivery personnel piled high with boxes.

"Was the party as dramatic as last year?" he asks.

I give him a confused look. "Uncle Tony's parties are always exciting." Uncle Tony is a costume designer, so his friends are all in theatre. He's the one who taught me how to create disguises. It's a useful skill to have, given that I'm the black sheep of a politically prominent New York family. Uncle Takashi is in IT security, which might sound boring, but actually, many of his colleagues are white-hat hackers and have an edgy, anti-authority vibe. "The karaoke machine came out."

"Last year, before Uncle Takashi's party, on the street outside, when you were yelling at your boyfriend about his cheating on you," he says.

I blush. I can't believe William saw me screaming like a fishwife.

I had caught my boyfriend-at-the-time and bandmate, Rex, kissing a fan right after our concert. I had said I never wanted to see him again and jumped in a cab to go to Uncle Tony's party. He'd followed me in the next cab. We'd met up again on the street outside Tony's apartment building. I had screamed at him that we were done. He'd insisted that she had kissed him first. "Oh well. I felt a lot better after getting it all out."

"You certainly didn't hold back," he says. We turn to walk up Columbus Avenue, pausing to let the couple ahead of us go first to pass the woman with the stroller and a coffee in hand, heading the other way. The street is crowded here with more people and less space as the restaurants have tables set out on the sidewalk, fenced off by plants or portable barriers.

"Well, I'm always good for a story," I say wryly. "I was wrong. The way he said it, I realized that the fan really had kissed him first. I apologized. Sorry to disappoint you, but it was all very civilized this year. Anyway, what would you do if you caught your girlfriend cheating?"

A shadow passes over his face. But then he stands straighter and says, "Do you really think someone would cheat on me?" And he gives me that patronizing, superior look that annoys me.

"If someone can cheat on me, they can cheat on you," I say. I may not be as objectively good-looking as William, but I do all right with those who like personality.

"But he didn't cheat on you," William says.

"Exactly. So, I guess we don't have to worry about that," I say as I realize what I said made little sense. "How was Tokyo? Did you get to see your grandmother? How is she doing? Did you bring back new types of candy? Uncle Takashi misses that. Did you get to see friends there?"

"Do you want me to answer or are you just asking questions?"

I laugh. "I want you to answer."

"I did see *Baa-Baa*. She's getting older, but she's still a strong character. I was able to see friends. That's why I stayed after the wedding—to catch up with friends." He swings his backpack forward. "And yes, I've brought gifts for Uncle Takashi. I wish I could've brought fruit back. That's what he misses the most. Nothing compares to Japanese peaches and strawberries."

We've reached Uncle Tony's apartment building entrance.

"Bye," I say. "I may see you later. I'm coming by to pick up my painting after the movers leave."

He does not look thrilled about the possibility of seeing me again. His facial expression is "resigned"—at best. He nods. I have a sneaking suspicion that he will definitely not be around when I come by later.

But then he smiles slightly and says, "Bye, Mom!"

I shake my head and walk quickly away. That's probably the most I've talked to William in years. I'd written him off after overhearing him discussing asset impairments accounting with his then-girlfriend at one of my uncle's parties two years ago. He's much more playful than I'd given him credit for.

Made in the USA
Columbia, SC
15 January 2022

54176487R00207